About the Authors

Olivia Miles lives in Chicago with her husband, young daughter, and two ridiculously pampered pups. Not a day goes by that Olivia doesn't feel grateful for being able to pursue her passion, and sometimes she does have to pinch herself when she remembers she's found her own Happily Ever After. Olivia loves hearing from readers. Visit her website, oliviamilesbooks.com

Bridget Anderson is a native of Louisville, Kentucky. She currently resides in North Metro Atlanta with her husband and their big dog she swears is part human. She writes provocative romance filled stories about smart women and the men they love and has published over nine novels and two novellas to date. Her romance suspense novel, *Rendezvous*, was adapted into a made-for-television movie. She is a member of Romance Writers of America, Georgia Romance Writers and The Authors Guild.

Joss Wood loves books, coffee and travelling – especially to the wild places of Southern Africa and, well, anywhere. She's a wife and a mum to two young adults. She's also a servant to two cats and a dog the size of a small cow. After a career in local economic development and business, Joss writes full-time from her home in KwaZulu-Natal, South Africa.

T0337547

Sugar & Spice

Sugar & Spice:

Home Sweet Home

OLIVIA MILES

BRIDGET ANDERSON

JOSS WOOD

MILLS & BOON

All rights reserved including the right of reproduction in whole or in part in any form. This edition is published by arrangement with Harlequin Enterprises ULC.

This is a work of fiction. Names, characters, places, locations and incidents are purely fictional and bear no relationship to any real life individuals, living or dead, or to any actual places, business establishments, locations, events or incidents. Any resemblance is entirely coincidental.

This book is sold subject to the condition that it shall not, by way of trade or otherwise, be lent, resold, hired out or otherwise circulated without the prior consent of the publisher in any form of binding or cover other than that in which it is published and without a similar condition including this condition being imposed on the subsequent purchaser.

® and ™ are trademarks owned and used by the trademark owner and/or its licensee. Trademarks marked with ® are registered with the United Kingdom Patent Office and/or the Office for Harmonisation in the Internal Market and in other countries.

First Published in Great Britain 2024
by Mills & Boon, an imprint of HarperCollins*Publishers* Ltd,
1 London Bridge Street, London, SE1 9GF

www.harpercollins.co.uk

HarperCollins*Publishers*
Macken House, 39/40 Mayor Street Upper,
Dublin 1, D01 C9W8, Ireland

Sugar & Spice: Home Sweet Home © 2024 Harlequin Enterprises ULC.

Recipe for Romance © 2014 Megan Leavell
The Sweetest Affair © 2019 Bridget Anderson
If You Can't Stand the Heat... © 2013 Joss Wood

ISBN: 978-0-263-32045-9

This book contains FSC™ certified paper and other controlled sources to ensure responsible forest management.

For more information visit: www.harpercollins.co.uk/green

Printed and Bound in the UK using 100% Renewable Electricity at CPI Group (UK) Ltd, Croydon, CR0 4YY

RECIPE FOR ROMANCE

OLIVIA MILES

For my family, for their love, support, and encouragement.

And for my editor, Susan Litman, for her invaluable feedback and guidance.

Chapter One

Reaching behind her waist to tie the strings of her crisp cotton apron in a jaunty bow, Emily Porter kept a firm eye on the clock, waiting with a quickening of her pulse until the long hand finally ticked to the twelve. She glanced to her friend and boss, Lucy Miller, who gave a nervous smile followed by a simple nod of her head. Eleven o'clock. This was it!

With a deep breath, Emily crossed the polished wood floors and turned the homemade sign on the door of the Sweetie Pie Bakery. They were officially open for business.

"I haven't been this nervous since my wedding day," Lucy exclaimed giddily, her voice high with sudden emotion.

"It'll be a huge success. I just know it," Emily said, grinning ear to ear. This was the most exciting day she'd had in a long time, and heck, it hadn't even started yet! Her stomach fluttered with anticipation as she glanced around the sun-filled bakery. The past few weeks had flown by in such a whirlwind of activity to get everything ready for the opening day that she hadn't stopped to stand back and take it all in. The walls were painted a creamy ivory, nearly the same shade as the sleek cabinets that lined the wall behind the gleaming glass display case now housing fifteen different kinds of pie, all baked fresh that morning, with more in stock in the kitchen. The counter was a warm rustic cherrywood, chosen to complement the spotless floor. Ten cozy tables dotted the room, all eagerly awaiting the guests who would soon be coming through the front door.

"I hope so." Lucy sighed, glancing out the wall of windows onto Main Street.

It was the first time Emily had seen her friend express any doubts since she'd first announced she was going through with the venture. She'd been working for Lucy for as long as she could remember at the diner across the street and never in all that time had she seen her boss so flustered.

"You've been in the restaurant business for almost twenty years," Emily replied, coming around the counter to get the coffee started.

"You calling me old?" Lucy winked. Then, on a sigh, she admitted, "You're right…" She began straightening chairs that were already straight. "I just don't want to let anyone down."

Emily poured another heaping spoonful of fresh coffee grounds into the filter. "You aren't going to let anyone down. Everyone in Maple Woods loves your diner and there's no reason why they won't love this place, too."

Lucy brushed an imaginary crumb from her pink and white pinstriped apron and squared her shoulders. "What would I do without you, Em?"

A ripple of guilt crept over Emily, but she pushed the feeling aside as quickly as it formed and distracted herself by setting the coffee to brew. She glanced around the bakery once more, wishing someone would just come in already! Deciding there was nothing left to do but wait until the first customer made their appearance, she announced, "I'll water the flower beds."

Lucy nodded her approval, her eyes never leaving the window.

"You know what they say about a watched pot…" Emily teased as she pushed through the front door with a wide grin, feeling the warmth of late morning sunshine on her arms and face.

Bright pink tulips lined the tall windows of the storefront, and Emily gave each one a healthy drink while gazing down Main Street, which was unusually quiet for this time of day. In an hour the lunch crowd would hit, and then…then Emily didn't know what to expect. She had visions of people pushing through a crammed door, eager to take a peek inside Maple Woods's newest establishment.

Still smiling at the thought, she whipped around to the sound of an engine revving in the near distance. A bright red sports car was sitting at the intersection of Main Street and Maple Avenue, the noise a dramatic contrast to the peaceful and simple life of Maple Woods.

Emily watched as the car took a sharp left when

the light turned, wincing as the vehicle rumbled offensively and took speed in her direction. She squinted into the sunlight as it quickly closed the distance, but as it zipped past her, her eyes shot open.

It couldn't be…not *him*. After all these years, there was no way. Why now?

Emily peered at the sidewalk as she tried to logically process what she had just seen. Her stomach tightened with each ragged breath. Scott Collins hadn't shown his face in this town in nearly twelve years. Would he really come back now, after all this time?

She pursed her lips. It had taken months of heartache and waiting to learn the answer to that question. It was about time she accepted it, too.

She swallowed the knot of disappointment that was quickly forming a lump in her throat, replacing her sudden shock. She hadn't thought of her high school sweetheart in years, and look at her: all it took was one drive-by, one trigger to open wounds she thought had finally healed. One double take to have her thinking of those blue eyes and that lopsided grin all over again.

She shook her head and pulled open the door to the bakery. The car had been too fast. Her mind had been playing tricks on her. Besides, Lucy would have surely announced if her own brother was paying a visit.

"I just got a call from George," Lucy announced breathlessly as soon as the door closed behind Emily. She finished untying the strings to her apron and hung it on a hook on the back of the kitchen door. "He needs me at the diner for a bit to help prep for the lunch crowd, seeing that we don't have any customers here yet." The last words of her statement were laced with disappointment.

Emily studied Lucy's face thoughtfully, wondering if she should even mention her possible sighting, but her friend's expression showed nothing that would indicate Scott's arrival any more than her words did.

"Hurry back if you can," Emily said as Lucy gathered her things to hurry to the diner that she owned with her husband. "I have a feeling that by tonight, we'll be so busy, we'll be wishing everyone would just go home." She paused to stare out the window, idly searching for the mysterious red car. Suspicion engulfed her all over again. No one in Maple Woods drove a car like that. She turned back to Lucy. "Were you expecting anyone special for today's grand opening?"

She knew from Lucy that her father wasn't well… but no. Scott hadn't so much as bothered to come back for a holiday in all these years. Surely he wasn't suddenly sweeping into town looking to make up for lost time. Unless…

"Just the usual group of friends and family showing their support." Lucy shrugged. She surveyed the empty room once more, her lips thinning. "I'm off, then. Call if you need me. I'll just be across the street."

"Will do," Emily said, sighing. *Silly girl,* she thought with a shake of her head. Of course it hadn't been Scott. He was gone, never coming back.

Besides, she was better off without him.

What the hell was he doing here?

Scott leaned on the hood of the red Porsche, his eyes narrowing as his gaze swept down Main Street

and over to the town square. The charming little gazebo bordered with hydrangea bushes. The bronze
statue of the town's founder standing tall and proud
under the umbrella of a magnolia tree. His stare lingered on Lucy's Place, his gut knotting at the familiar
sight. In all his life, he never expected to see that diner
again, or any place in Maple Woods, really. There
was no circumstance that could bring him back, he'd
thought, and yet here he was.

He shook his head in disgust, angry at himself for
giving in. He shouldn't have come back. He should
have stayed away. Twelve years was a long time. Longer than the innocence of some childhoods. Longer
than most marriages. But twelve years wasn't enough
time to put distance between him and Maple Woods.
Or the secret the town held. The one he had sworn he
would take to his grave.

Scott turned and regarded his rental car, grimacing
with regret. He'd rented the exact model he owned in
Seattle, out of habit, but with its flashy red paint and
six-figure price tag, that car didn't belong in Maple
Woods any more than he did. It would only garner
more unwanted attention and speculation, and God
knew this town was full of enough gossip. Sleepy little towns like this enjoyed a good scandal, or in his
case, a good secret. It kept things interesting, and gave
an otherwise dormant community something to talk
about other than marriages and births. Deaths.

Scott scowled as his stomach began to burn again.
It had been happening a lot lately—ever since Lucy
had called and begged him to come back to Maple
Woods, pleading with him to take over the rebuilding
of the town library, which her son had damaged in a

fire he had accidentally started. "Kids," Scott had told her over the phone, when she'd tearfully explained his nephew's involvement, but something about it touched a nerve, evoking memories that were better kept buried. Lucy wanted to set things right: Bobby was doing community service, he was working hard to get into a good college on a football scholarship, and the plans for the new library were moving along nicely…until their father got sick.

He didn't know why he gave in to her request in the end. Maybe it was because she'd let him stay away as long as she had, maybe it was because he respected her need to set things right for the wrongdoings of her son, or maybe it was because she didn't ask him directly to come back and be there for the family in their hour of need that he felt he couldn't say no to her. Whatever the reason, he was here.

You're gonna pay me back for this one, Lucy.

His breath hitched on a rueful laugh. Who was he kidding? He could never stay mad at her for long. How could he? With their seven-year age difference, they'd never had the kind of banter or rivalry one expects with siblings. Lucy had always doted on him, right up until the time she married George Miller and moved across town to start a family of her own.

She would probably be in the diner right now, filling coffee mugs with that no-nonsense grin and a twinkle in her eye. In a matter of minutes he could see her again. He had to admit the idea of it was appealing, despite the circumstances.

Scott pushed back from the car and straightened his shoulders. Hands thrust into his pockets, he began wandering down the sidewalk, taking his time in surveying the shops that lined the quaint street. He was struck with wonder as his eyes roamed over the storefronts. Absolutely nothing had changed. It was all the same. The pizza place. The flower shop. The bookstore. The fashions in the window of the clothing boutique sure had changed, though. He paused to study the dress on the mannequin with furrowed interest before his gaze slid to a wide-eyed face staring back at him through the glass. He flushed as the woman mouthed what he was nearly sure was "Oh, my *God,* it's Scott *Collins!*" and another slack-jawed face quickly appeared on the other side of the mannequin, eyes gleaming in the ray of sunlight that poured through the shop window.

Scott frowned before turning on his heel and quickening his pace toward the diner. He remembered those girls, all right. Women now. They were both in his math class senior year. They'd been some of the prettiest girls on the cheerleading squad. From the looks of it, they'd remembered him, too.

He'd put a hundred bucks on the notion that the women in the clothing shop were calling around to every one of their old classmates right this moment and grimaced to think of the reaction he was going to elicit when he pushed through the doors of Lucy's Place. After all, a man didn't disappear from this town for twelve years without prompting a reaction when he returned.

He didn't think he could stomach it, honestly.

Scott closed his eyes as his chest tightened. He could only hope that one person could be spared. If he was in and out of town quick enough, he might manage to avoid her altogether.

A chalkboard sign up ahead boasted the loopy script Grand Opening! and Scott grinned. Of course! Lucy's new bakery. She had mentioned on the phone that she was planning to launch this week but his mind had been so muddled with the thought of his return that he'd almost forgotten. He glanced to the diner across the street, noting the swarm of customers filling every table near the windows and exhaled in relief.

He couldn't face that diner—those curious faces and eager smiles—and now he wouldn't have to. He strode up to the bakery and registered the open sign. One glance through the windows revealed an empty establishment: a safe haven. With any luck he'd have a chance to catch his breath and reunite with his sister without forty sets of eyes memorizing the exchange, eager to report it verbatim at the dinner table later that evening.

He glanced back up the street to where the women from the clothing shop were now standing on the sidewalk, cell phones pressed against their ears, staring at him as if he was some carnival freak. He swallowed the acidic taste that filled his mouth.

It had been a bad idea to come back here. He had known it would be difficult to face his past but he hadn't realized how quickly the emotions he had tried to bury would bubble to the surface. Well, all the more reason to do his business and then get the hell out. And this time, he wouldn't be back. Under any circumstances.

The bells above the front door chimed, causing Emily to jump. The cookbook she'd been holding slid to the cool marble kitchen island with a thud. Their first official customer. Nearly an hour had passed since they'd opened, and she'd just managed to relax. Now butterflies danced through her stomach as Emily quickly smoothed her apron and made her way out of the kitchen and into the cheerful storefront.

"Welcome to Sweetie Pie! What can I—" She halted abruptly, her voice locking in her throat.

Scott Collins stood before the display case, casually eyeing the selection. His hands were pushed deep into the pockets of his chinos, accentuating his broad chest and well-toned arms. It had been twelve years since she'd seen him, standing in the glow of the summer sunset, waving to her from the base of her peeling front stoop, that lopsided grin tugging at her heart as she turned her back and retreated into the shadows of her old farmhouse—but she had been wrong in thinking she wouldn't recognize him now. He was just as handsome as he had ever been. Even more so, as luck would have it.

He lifted his sparkling blue eyes to her now, his lips already curling, causing her heart to flutter in a way she didn't think it could anymore. His ash-brown hair was cut in a more conservative style than she remembered, and he'd bulked up in all the right places, but one thing hadn't changed. He still had a smile that could stop traffic. And make her heart skip a beat.

Twelve years later and he still had this effect on her. *Damn him.*

But as his eyes met hers, his expression froze. That irresistible grin faltered.

"Emily." His voice was gruff.

"Scott." His name felt unnatural on her tongue. "What a surprise." *The understatement of a decade.*

"I didn't know you worked here," Scott said. "I mean…I didn't expect to see you. Lucy hadn't told me… This, well… It's nice to see you," he settled on.

Emily narrowed her gaze as he stumbled over his words, trying to draw some explanation from him, something that would clarify what had happened all those years ago. What had gone wrong? What had caused him to leave town without a word, without any hint or preparation, to break her heart and all his promises in one fell swoop?

Her heart squeezed as his turquoise gaze sliced right through her. "I didn't expect to see you around here again," she said. When he didn't respond, she added, "I just started working here, actually." She brushed aside the twinge of hurt that Lucy hadn't mentioned it to him. That she meant so little. That she was so forgotten. "Today's our grand opening, but I'm sure Lucy mentioned that to you."

"Is she here?" Scott looked hopefully around the empty room.

Emily shook her head. "She's at the diner, but she'll be back soon. Funny, she didn't tell me you'd be stopping by."

Scott grinned nervously. "She probably didn't want to jinx it. I don't exactly have the best track record for homecomings."

Emily's brows inadvertently pinched. She studied him for a long moment, gathering her thoughts, forcing a deep breath to temper her racing pulse.

"So, how've you been?" she asked, bracing herself for the answer. Lucy barely mentioned Scott, and no one else in town kept in touch with him. When Scott left home, he'd severed all ties. With his family, his friends. With her.

"Good enough," Scott said with a shrug. He dropped his gaze. He couldn't even look her in the eye.

Coward.

"Where are you living these days?" she tried again, disappointment tugging at her that two people who had once known every inch of each other, who finished each other's sentences, who shared the same dreams, could be reduced to this sort of awkward conversation. They were strangers now.

"Seattle," he replied, and Emily frowned. She knew he had gone to college in Chicago and had just assumed he'd stayed there. But all this time he had been living in Seattle, and for some reason that depressed the hell out of her.

She paused. "Married? Kids?" she asked, because there was no point in holding back. After all, she'd lost him a long time ago.

"Nope," he said, and in spite of herself, Emily felt her shoulders relax. "So you're still in town," he observed.

She gazed at him, disarmed by the incongruity between his sudden reappearance and the nonchalant way he strode into town. Nothing fazed the man—not then and, it would seem, not now. Silence stretched between them; the only sound audible was the pounding of her own heart and God did she hope he couldn't hear it, too.

"Yep." Emily she said tightly. "Never left." Twelve years after Scott had disappeared from Maple Woods, she was still right where he had left her. *Pathetic*.

Scott nodded again, dropping his gaze to the floor

as his face reddened, and she knew she had hit a nerve. Well, good! It was about time that Scott gave some sort of reaction for what he had done to her, even if it was a decade or so too late.

"I always wondered about that," he said, his voice so low she had to strain to hear. "I always wondered about you," he said, looking up to properly meet her eyes.

Emily's stomach rolled over, but she pushed back the temptation to dwell on his words, to extract more meaning from them than he'd probably intended. She straightened her spine.

"Well, you could have called. Or written." She cursed herself for allowing the hurt to creep into her voice. But damn it, she couldn't help it! His words were empty, falling flat and meaningless. She wondered briefly how many of the other things he had said to her were equally insincere. Most of them, she decided. As much as she hated to realize this, it was just the cold hard truth.

"I've never been good about keeping in touch. No matter how much I wanted to be," Scott said, frowning. His eyes locked with hers until her pulse skipped and she had to look away.

He wasn't here for her. He hadn't come back for her. That was all that mattered.

"I'm sure Lucy's eager to see you," she blurted. "Half the town is at the diner for lunch. I'm sure they'd be thrilled to see you walk in." Scott was the high school football star, after all, the kid from the good family with the good looks and "things going for him." He had always been loved around town. Especially by her.

"I had hoped to avoid the diner for a while," he admitted, offering her a rueful grin. "At least until everyone knows I'm back in town."

"People do love to talk around here," she mused as she set a stack of napkins next to the cash register.

Their gazes locked and she noted the warmth of his smoky blue eyes, and felt nearly sick with humiliation at the pity she saw float through them. She didn't want his sympathy, or anyone else's for that matter. She wanted to break free, to start over. To live a life where she could be so many more things than this town had allowed her to be.

"Too much," Scott said quickly, and Emily gave him a brief, tight smile. He knew the things people used to say about her family. It hung in the air, in the leaves of the maple trees that lined Main Street. It triggered family dinner conversations and prompted Sunday prayers. It was a name spoken in whisper, with lowered eyes and a shake of the head. *Those poor Porters.*

Emily shook herself from the darkening thoughts. "Well, I've just put on some fresh coffee and there's plenty of pie. Feel free to wait here, if you'd like."

He hesitated, shifting back on his heels. "Why not?" he suddenly said with a shrug. His eyes softened their hold on hers, causing her pulse to skip a beat.

"How about a slice of pie?" she asked nervously, squeezing her fists to keep her hands from shaking. "There's strawberry and cream, pecan, apple crumb— oh, we have a lovely cherry here," she offered before she could stop herself. She hadn't even remembered until now that it was his favorite.

"You know me well," he said with a sigh, sliding into a seat at the counter.

Emily offered him a small smile in return, then, her heart heavy, turned her back to him to plate the pie, paying careful attention in getting the first wedge just right. It was tricky, but she'd learned the knack through practice. Long before her father had died on a construction site when she was just a little girl, Sunday pie had been a ritual in her household, and she still took comfort in his memory every time she pulled one from the oven. No matter how rough the week had been, there was always some reassurance in the time-honored tradition. Pie could bring comfort in a world that could be cruel. It was something to be shared. It brought people together. In the most difficult of circumstances, she liked to think it helped keep them together, too.

"Here you go," she said to Scott now. "I made it this morning, so it's fresh."

"You always made the best pies, Emily Porter." He grinned, and his eyes shone bright on hers until he caught the heat in her expression and looked down at his plate.

She sucked in a breath. "So," she said briskly. "What brings you back to town?" It certainly wasn't her. He'd made a promise—dozens of beautiful, hope-filled promises—and broken each one right along with her heart.

"My dad asked me to help oversee the construction of the library." His jaw twitched and he scratched at a day's worth of stubble. "Well, Lucy asked, actually."

"Lucy mentioned once that you were in construction, just like you'd always planned." She frowned at the thought. Why couldn't he have stayed in Maple Woods and taken over Collins Construction, the family business? It was a fine company, well respected by the town. Her own father had proudly worked there.

Scott paused. "My father isn't up to the job at the moment."

Emily nodded. Scott and Lucy's parents had never been warm to her, but she'd decided a long time ago not to take it personally. Her father had worked for Mr. Collins for more than fifteen years before the accident on the job took his life when she was eight years old. It had been human error, the police had said, his own negligence in failing to put the emergency brakes on the excavator that rolled down the slope and killed him. Mr. Collins had been there that day. He'd dealt with the police, and as a courtesy to the family he had helped cover the funeral expenses, but he had been tense around her family in passing ever since.

"Sticking around for long?" She held her breath, waiting for an answer she knew deep down wouldn't make a lick of difference.

"Only as long as I have to."

Emily held his sharp gaze and then lowered her eyes with a slow nod of her head as her heart began to tug. He was still the same old Scott. The same charming guy with dreams beyond Maple Woods. And she was still the same old Emily, still living in the same small town, still waiting for life to really start.

Well, it was time to do something about that.

Of all the people he had hoped to avoid in this town, Emily was at the top of his list. So he supposed it made sense that she was the first person he ran into. The one girl who had crawled under his skin and remained there. No matter how much he wanted to resist her, to turn his back and leave, he just couldn't.

He rested an elbow on the counter, grateful for its barrier. If it wasn't there, keeping them apart, he wasn't quite sure he would have been able to refrain himself from greeting her with a hug, to feel the warmth of her body pressed against his, to hold her close and know that she was real and that she was okay. That no matter what had happened, what he had done, that she was all right.

It wasn't supposed to be this way with them. They'd had plans—plans he'd intended to stick to—until that horrible summer night, his last night in this town, when his entire world came crashing down around him and Emily was lost to him forever.

Swallowing hard, he allowed his gaze to roam over her as she repositioned the pie plate on its stand and swept some crumbs off the counter, her glossy chestnut waves cascading over her shoulders. He couldn't peel his eyes from her. His high school sweetheart— the girl who interrupted his dreams and haunted his waking hours was standing right in front of him, looking more beautiful than ever.

But time hadn't changed one thing. Emily was still off-limits.

"So what have you been up to all this time?" he asked, even though he didn't want to hear it confirmed. Emily had always had dreams. Dreams beyond this small town. Dreams that hadn't come true.

"Oh, not much," she said. "I worked at the diner before this, but you might have known that."

His stomach twisted at her words. Emily was the

smartest girl he'd known back in school. She should be running a restaurant of her own, not waiting tables. She should have gone to college, pursued her passions—opportunities she would have had if her father had lived. If his father hadn't deprived their family of insurance money that was rightfully owed to them as a result of the tragic accident. If Scott hadn't been on that construction site at all the day that Mr. Porter…

"No," he managed. "No, Lucy hadn't mentioned it."

Her eyes narrowed ever so slightly, before she pulled back and leaned against the far counter, crossing her arms over her chest. "Ah, well, I suppose you and Lucy have better things to talk about than some girl you used to know."

The hurt in her tone sliced through him, but the pain in her eyes was his true punishment. He'd earned it. He'd deserved it. He'd take it.

"You were more than some girl, Em."

She lifted her eyes to his, holding his stare for a beat, and then shrugged.

"Well." He sighed, "I should probably brace myself for the gossip mill." He gave a tight smile and set his fork on the edge of the empty plate. "If Lucy knew I was already in town and hadn't come to see her yet, she'd probably never forgive me."

"Probably for the best," Emily said softly. "It looks busy over there today. I won't be surprised if she's kept longer than she wants to be."

Scott stood and reached into his pocket for his wallet but Emily frowned and held up her hand. "No, please. It's on the house."

"Oh, come on," he said, frowning. *Take the money,*

Emily. Take what is owed you, what you should have had a long time ago. Take what my family stole from you. "It's your opening day. I want to help."

But Emily was adamant, shaking her head. "Lucy would never forgive me," she insisted, falling back on his own words, and he knew she had him there.

"I guess I'll get going then," he said, but he didn't move toward the door. For twelve years he had done nothing but imagine this moment, the things he would say to her if he ever saw her again. But he couldn't say them. And that was why he had never come back.

"Bye, Scott," she said coolly.

He gave a tight smile. "Bye, Em." He turned and walked to the door, pushed through it out into the warm glow of the morning sun and crossed the street, focused on the diner in front of him growing nearer with each step, his heart thudding in his chest.

He knew this feeling. It was the same one he'd had when he'd packed up his bags and gotten into his car that late-summer night twelve years ago after he'd overheard his parents talking about Richard Porter's death—after he'd found out what he had done, what they had covered up for nine years, only revealing the details once it was too late, once he was already in love with Emily, once he was eighteen and old enough to feel the toll of his actions, however unintentional. He'd sped out of town before he had a chance to look back, to think of what he was leaving behind, his heart breaking as he swore he would never love again.

He didn't deserve love.

And he certainly didn't deserve Emily.

There was no amount of time or distance that could put Emily Porter behind him. Oh, he'd tried all right.

He'd gone to the far end of the country, putting as many miles between him and Maple Woods as possible, only his dark, dirty secret to keep him company and serve as an aching memory of everyone he'd left behind. Of why he could never return.

He was the reason Emily had grown up without a father. He was the reason she'd been stuck in the mercy of this town and all its limitations, and that wasn't something he could ever forget. But it was something he would have to set right. Once and for all.

Chapter Two

The steady trill of the alarm clock pulled Emily from a deep slumber. She blindly slapped at it and rolled over in bed. The grand opening of Sweetie Pie had kept her at work longer than she'd expected, plus she'd stayed late to prep for today. Poor Lucy had been so busy bouncing from the diner to the bakery that she had barely stopped to take a breath. They hadn't even had a moment to discuss Scott's return.

Scott. At the memory of his startling arrival the day before, Emily's eyes popped open, and she sprang out of bed. She showered and dressed quickly, quietly, so as not to wake her sister Julia, who rarely emerged from her bed before eight. Tiptoeing through the living room, she paused at the stack of yesterday's mail piled neatly on the small table just beside the front door. She had been so preoccupied with seeing Scott again that she had failed to check the mailbox on her way home last night. It wasn't like her, and with a frown she realized the hold he still had over her nearly a dozen years later.

Recalling his words yesterday, she shook her head and silently scolded herself. She'd been a fool to pin any hopes on that man. There was nothing in Maple Woods for Scott—there never had been, it seemed— and he made it very clear that he wasn't planning on staying in town for long.

Well, neither am I.

Her heart began to thump as she picked up the stack of crisp envelopes and began thumbing through them. When she reached the end, she sighed—possibly in relief, possibly in disappointment. She wasn't sure which anymore. It had been three months since she'd sent her application to the cooking school in Boston, and as the weeks passed without a response, her anxiety grew stronger. So many hopes were hitched to this opportunity that a part of her was happy her fate wasn't yet sealed. It was good to have a dream, and this had been hers for as long as she could remember. She wasn't ready for it to be over just yet.

The bakery still wouldn't be open for another two hours, but the day was still young and there was plenty of work to do. Lucy was a pie-making expert—there was no denying her skill—but when she'd tasted a few of Emily's creations, she had decided to feature those each day, as well. Emily had free rein on what she could create.

Emily gave a sad smile whenever she thought of the irony of the situation—who would have known she'd get such an opportunity just when she might be able to finally break free of this town once and for all?

Determined to think about nothing but the second day at Sweetie Pie, she rolled up her sleeves and went into the kitchen. A couple hours of straight-up baking, fortified by strong coffee, were sure to banish the blues that had set in when Scott walked through that door yesterday.

"Oh, thank goodness you're up!" Julia gushed, bursting into the kitchen half an hour later, already dressed for her job at the yarn shop. Her cheeks were flushed and her green eyes flashed with excitement as she quickly pulled her hair into a ponytail.

"Good morning to you, too," Emily said mildly as she finished slicing pears into a bowl and showered them with sugar.

Julia's eyes danced. "You will *never* believe who is back in town!"

Emily smiled as she measured out a cup of flour, then diced a stick of cold butter and pulsed the mixture in the food processor with a teaspoon each of sugar and salt. This was a little game of theirs, and even at their age, it was endlessly amusing, adding a bit of suspense to an otherwise routine life. Julia would come home with a juicy bit of gossip, usually about who was dating whom, and question by question, Emily would narrow it down until the titillating conclusion was reached. Sadly, on this occasion, there was no buildup of clues; Emily already knew the answer.

"Scott Collins," she said and immediately wished she had just played along when she saw Julia's face fall with disappointment.

"You knew?" she cried. "And here I nearly shook you awake last night to tell you!"

"He came into the bakery yesterday," Emily said.

"Did you speak to him?" Julia's eyes were wide with interest. "What was he like?"

Emily heaved a sigh. "Not much different than I remembered," she admitted, catching the wistful edge to her tone.

"Still a hunk then, huh?" Julia dipped her finger into the sugar canister, and Emily rolled her eyes.

"Still a hunk, as you so delicately put it."

Julia regarded her for a long moment, a dreamy look creeping over her face, as if she were lost in time, clinging to a memory. "Sorry," she said, straightening herself. "I know it's a touchy subject."

"I was seventeen," Emily reminded her. "It didn't mean anything." *Clearly.*

"Well, it meant something to me." Julia lifted her chin, her eyes suddenly darkening at the memory. "I still haven't forgotten the way he took off without so much as a goodbye."

"Really?" Emily narrowed her gaze in mock confusion. "Because you seemed to have completely forgotten about that episode when you came bounding in here two minutes ago." She flashed her sister a rueful grin as she formed the dough into a disk and wrapped it in cellophane. She set it in the fridge to chill, swapping it for one that had cooled, and plucked her rolling pin from the drawer beneath the stove.

"Well, I admit, I did get a little swept up in the memory of how handsome he was," Julia explained, and Emily bit her lip to keep from laughing. "But the truth is that he treated you like a first-rate jerk, leaving you like that, without any explanation."

They were supposed to have gone to a movie the next night. Emily could still remember sitting on the steps of her front porch, waiting. She'd called his house, worried he might be sick or worse—that he'd had an accident. It was a fear of hers ever since she was little, since her father had died. Instead she was told in clipped tones by Scott's father that he was gone. He'd left town the night before, and they didn't know when he'd be back. *If* he'd be back. And he never did come back. Until now.

Emily shrugged off the twinge of hurt with a smile. "Please, Julia. That was ancient history. We were kids."

Julia watched her carefully. "If you say so."

"Are you accusing me of still pining after Scott Collins?"

Julia tipped her head. "I just thought that you would be interested to know he was back in town. That's all." She paused. "So...is he married?"

"No," Emily said, stirring more forcefully.

"And you know this—"

"Because he told me," Emily huffed, whipping around to face her sister. "Because I asked, okay. I... asked." It was a normal question, she told herself, but probably not when it was posed to the man whom she had once imagined an entire future with. His answer had filled her with a surge of hope that had no business being there.

A spark passed through Julia's bright green eyes. "Huh. Interesting."

"What's that supposed to mean?"

"Nothing." Julia shrugged. "Nothing at all." She smiled conspiratorially and then breezed out the door, as if there was nothing left of the subject to discuss.

Emily shook her head and chuckled softly. Leave it to her sister to get carried away with Scott's reemergence and the impact it might have on her. Of course she was interested to know that Scott was back. More interested than she should be. And that was just the problem.

Before she left the house, Emily took extra care in brushing her hair and selecting just the right shade of lipstick. It was silly, she knew, and she was probably jinxing herself with the effort, but if there was a chance of seeing Scott again today, she wanted to be ready.

Let him see what he's been missing.

"Well, don't you look pretty today!" Lucy proclaimed as Emily pushed through the back door of the bakery into the kitchen.

Emily shrugged off the compliment with a wry grin and tied an apron around her waist. "What's the plan for day two?"

Lucy regarded her suspiciously for a lingering moment and then, with a lift of her brow, changed the subject. Emily made a mental note to swipe off her lipstick the first chance she had. She felt suddenly self-conscious and foolish and overly aware of herself. She had never liked being the center of attention, and here she was, trying to be front and center in Scott's mind.

"Mayor Pearson agreed to the pie toss," Lucy said, and Emily smiled. Flyers and word of mouth went far in a small town such as this, but a little promotion helped with a new business, too. "I'm hoping it will pull in more customers today."

"I'm sure it will help get the word out." Emily thought of how the mayor prided himself on Maple Woods's sense of community. "People might love him, but I doubt few would resist the chance to see him covered in whipped cream."

"I'm hoping so." Lucy studied her inventory list. "A fresh shipment of apricots arrived this morning, so let's use those up where we can."

Emily carefully removed the three pies she had baked that morning from their boxes. "I made a pear-and-cherry tart this morning." She began plating it for display. "I'll start prepping a few apricot pies next. A lattice crust would be nice for those, don't you think?"

"What would I do without you?" Lucy said on a sigh of content.

Emily lowered her head, unable to answer the question knowing the information she was withholding, and pulled a canister of flour off the shelf, waiting for the wave of guilt to subside. She was getting ahead of herself, she finally reasoned. There was nothing to feel bad about yet. She might not even get into that school in Boston. There was no use getting worked up over something that might never even happen.

Feeling slightly better, she went about her task as Lucy brewed coffee, the pair working in companionable silence for a while until Emily finally dared to observe, "So…Scott's back in town."

Lucy whipped around. "Can you believe it?"

Emily opened her eyes wide. "Not really." She forced back the image of his handsome face by gathering ingredients from the refrigerator. "You must be really happy," she managed, hoping Lucy didn't detect the note of hurt that laced her words. She couldn't help it. She still wasn't over it. Twelve years later and that man still hadn't explained himself! Was he so beyond reproach?

She winced. He probably didn't think she cared anymore. After all, he obviously didn't.

Lucy huffed out a breath. "Yesterday was quite a day. The opening of this place, then seeing Scott again..." She paused. "I had to really work on him to come back here at all and a part of me still didn't think he really would—I guess I didn't dare to believe it until I finally saw him."

"It's been a long time." Emily nodded in understanding.

"Too long. When he first left town, I kept hoping he would be back one day. Then I guess I just learned to give up on that hope."

Emily looked down. *That made two of us.*

Her heart began to ache in that all too familiar way as she washed the apricots and set them to dry. It was the same feeling she got every time she thought of Scott over the years. Why did he have to come back? Why couldn't he have just stayed away forever? Surely at some point she would have forgotten the way his grin could make her heart skip a beat, or the way her hair rustled when he whispered in her ear. A dozen years might not have done the trick, but a dozen more might have...

She watched Lucy silently, wondering if she would say more, but Lucy just tied her apron strings, grabbed two pies, and tapped her hip against the swinging kitchen door. Emily sighed and got to work herself. She had always wondered why Scott had stayed away, but it wasn't her place to ask Lucy. Anyone who avoided Maple Woods for a dozen years had a reason. A big one.

Her heart dropped as she pulled out the cutting board. If Scott was that determined to put Maple Woods behind him, and get out of town no sooner than he had returned, it seemed like wishful thinking that he might ever be back again.

She began to measure out the sugar thoughtfully, reminding herself that she might not be in town much longer, either. Some things just weren't meant to be.

Scott locked the door to the apartment above the diner where Lucy was letting him stay and jogged down the stairs to Main Street. He eyed the bakery across the street and wavered slightly, wondering if he should give in to the temptation of what was tucked inside, his mind on anything but the pie.

Quickly, he looked away, assessing his options. He'd slept late, and by the time he'd dragged himself out of the comfortable solitude of his room, it was already nearing lunchtime. He was prolonging the inevitable trek to his father's office, but eventually he would have to head over—there was no getting around it.

Once he thought he would continue the legacy of Collins Construction, follow in the footsteps of his father and grandfather. Back then his plan was simple: he would marry Emily Porter, settle down in Maple Woods and earn an honest living at his family's company. But that was before he knew what his family had done to Emily's. Before he knew the part he had played in her father's death when he was just a kid, playing on the machinery, hanging out on his dad's job site, too oblivious to know the truth. Before he knew there was nothing honest about that company. Or his father. Or himself.

"Scott!" Lucy's familiar voice jarred him. He hated to think what her opinion must be of him now—she probably assumed he had gotten too successful for a small town like this, that he was better than it somehow, that he couldn't be bothered to make time for people who had meant so much to him in the past, including her. She couldn't be more wrong.

It was easier this way, he told himself, better that she wasn't in on the family secret. It was easier for everyone he cared about to be left out of his mess. Let them think he went off to college and never looked back, that he didn't think of Maple Woods every damn day of his life, that he didn't wonder how different things might have been. Let them think he was happy in Seattle, that city life fit him in a way Maple Woods never could. Let them all think what they wanted, so long as they didn't know the real reason he had left.

A man was dead because of him, and the surviving family had suffered as a result.

He forced a smile and crossed the street to stand next to his sister. "I was thinking about grabbing something to eat at the diner," he said as he approached the sidewalk.

"You're not sick of my cooking after dinner last night?"

Scott smiled at the recollection of sitting around Lucy's old farm table with her husband and son, talking and laughing long into the night like any other family would. A few times he'd caught himself thinking that maybe he could have a life like this, but that must have been the wine talking. There was no room for him in this place.

"I haven't had a meal like that in years." He grinned.

"Well, you can have another tonight, then. I'm going over to Mom and Dad's for dinner after work."

Scott's gut twisted as he held her eyes, carefully selecting his excuse. Lucy stood before him unwavering, her mouth a thin line. She knew what she was doing. And he didn't like it one bit.

"Lucy, don't do this to me." He sighed, running a hand through his hair in agitation. He broke her gaze and glanced down the street, desperate for an escape.

Her eyes were sharp when he turned his attention back to her. "Dad's dying, Scott," she said firmly, her gaze narrowing in disappointment. "The treatments aren't working. The cancer has spread."

"You know we don't get along," Scott insisted, but Lucy was shaking her head, clearly not buying it.

"Scott, I've put up with this nonsense for long enough," she said, her voice steely. "Whatever happened between you and our parents is old news. You were a teenager then, now you're a thirty-year-old man. Start acting like one," she snapped.

Scott took a step back, his eyes flashing with indignation. He forced himself to remember that Lucy didn't know the part his father had played in the events of the past. He'd kept in touch with her over the years, but he made sure to keep their conversations light, and mostly about her, George and Bobby. "You know I came back for you. You asked for my help in the re-building of the library, and I'm here. I'll see it through, but please don't ask anything more."

Lucy's eyes softened. "I know, and I'm so grateful, Scott. Honestly, I am." She lowered her eyes to the ground, her shoulders slumping. "I've lived with so much guilt knowing that Bobby accidentally caused that fire." She shook her head. "I just don't know what we would have done if Max Hamilton wasn't funding the project in exchange for some land George inherited. You can't imagine how that felt...the *relief.*"

No, Scott thought grimly. He couldn't say he did know how that would feel. There was no stranger to swoop into town and clear up his mess, the way Max had apparently helped so much since moving to Maple Woods after the holidays. Scott couldn't rebuild the past. He couldn't raise the dead. There was no righting his wrongs.

"It means everything to me that you're here to take over the job, Scott. Don't lose sight of that," she explained.

Scott eyed her warily. "I sense a 'but' coming on."

Lucy gave a sad smile. "Don't let this chance pass you by. It's been a long time. Let things go. Don't do something you'll regret forever." She held his gaze, and he almost felt his stance weaken, his resolve waver. Almost.

Scott shook his head adamantly, feeling the flush of heat spread up his neck. "I don't regret staying away, Lucy." And he didn't. His father might not have trouble looking people in the eye, knowing the part he played in one of the town's greatest tragedies, but Scott would rather give up everything he loved than build his life around a lie.

"Well, if you can't do it for yourself, then do it for

me!" she said, her eyes suddenly filling with tears as fury blazed bright.

Scott cursed inwardly, feeling the strain of her emotion, the weight of his burden. After a long pause, he said tightly, "No promises."

Lucy relaxed her stance. She nodded slowly, saying nothing more as she reached out to take his arm. It took everything in him not to break down then and there, to tell her everything. To shed the weight he had carried for so long. To divulge every last detail of what his parents told him that awful night—what their family had done to the Porters. *Those poor Porters.*

"Come into the bakery," she said to him. "We've got a special event as part of the opening week and I don't want you to miss it."

Scott hesitated. "You're not working at the diner this morning?"

"Not if I can help it." Lucy bent down to clip a sprig of blue hydrangea from a whiskey barrel planter. "I barely spent an hour at Sweetie Pie without being interrupted yesterday, they were so lost without me at the diner. I'm hoping things go a little smoother today."

Without another word, she pushed through the front door, frowning until Scott forced himself to follow. His pulse skipped when he saw Emily standing behind the counter, looking just as pretty as the day before. She met his gaze with a small smile and something deep within his gut stirred. He looked away, around the crowded room, noticing that nearly every table was filled. There was a cheerful buzz to the room, a soft tinkling of music in the background, and the sweet aroma of pie and coffee to make everyone, including him, feel at home.

Home. He hadn't thought of that word in a very long time. It was a vague idea of something he wasn't sure he had anymore. He hadn't dared to think of Maple Woods as home since he'd left, and his condo in Seattle was just a place to live.

"Emily!" Lucy called to Scott's horror. His breath locked in his tightened chest. "Mind getting Scott settled? I've got to check on that order of strawberries. We should have had them an hour ago."

Emily's face blanched and she darted her gaze from Lucy to Scott and back again. "Sure," she murmured as she finished plating a slice of pie for an impatient customer.

Scott turned to his sister. "I came in here to visit with you, Lucy," he said quietly.

"Emily will take good care of you. If you let her." Lucy winked.

"What's that supposed to mean?" he shot back.

"I'm just saying that Emily makes a damn good pie," she said airily. "Last I checked, that was the purest way to a man's heart."

Scott chuckled in spite of himself. "Lucy! Please!"

"What? I seem to remember you being awfully smitten with her at one point. I always thought you were going to marry her, in fact." She lifted an eyebrow and turned away from him with a coy shrug, shutting down the conversation.

Scott shook his head and reluctantly walked over to the display case, sparing an awkward smile for Emily. Guilt and shame haunted him, and he tried desperately to shrug off the unwanted feelings.

"Hi." Emily's soft voice dragged him from his darkening thoughts and he quickly recovered, perking up as he let his gaze roam over her pretty face. His stomach tightened as his attention lingered on the smoky gray eyes and that plump, upturned mouth stained a shade of red that excited him more than it should.

"Hey." He stared into his mug as she filled it to the rim. Just the way he liked it. His breath hitched as he caught sight of her feminine curves beneath the apron she wore, and he tried to recall what it had felt like to hold her waist and feel her body against his. The memory was so close, but just out of reach.

She held his gaze, not betraying any outward interest, and Scott felt a flicker of disappointment. She was being hospitable. Playing her role. Doing her job. He wanted to pull her into a back room, somewhere they could talk, and explain everything. He wanted to atone for the pain he had caused, to make it up to her—somehow. He searched her face, imagining her sweet expression crumbling before his eyes as he delivered the crushing news, and his gut twisted. He couldn't do it, he just couldn't, but to never tell her…

"So, I don't see you for twelve years and now it's twice in two days," she said, shaking her head on a sigh. "The pie must be even better than I thought."

Scott grimaced at the edge of hurt in her tone and took a quick sip of the steaming coffee. "Lucy invited me in," he began. "I don't want to upset you. I can leave if you want."

Fire sparked her eyes. "Leave?" She chuckled, a soft icy sound that pulled at his chest. She really did hate him, and who could blame her? "Leaving seems to be something you've had practice with," she said evenly.

Scott drew a ragged breath and ran a hand over his face, every inch of his heart aching to set her straight, to tell her the truth. It wasn't supposed to be this way.

"Believe it or not I had my reasons." He cleared his throat and finished the rest of his coffee. His body temperature was starting to rise. He needed to get out of here. Even his father's office would be better than this place. Anything was better than seeing that hurt expression in Emily's eyes.

Emily leaned a hip against the counter and folded her arms. "I'm all ears."

The knot in his gut tightened. Not now. Not like this. Not ever. Emily could never know what he had done, the part he had played in her misfortune. The losses she had suffered at his hand. "It was a long time ago, Em," he finally said.

After a beat, she gave him a withering smile and slapped a hand over his empty mug, pulling it toward her. "You're right," she said, before turning her back on him. "And I stopped holding my breath before you'd even crossed the state line."

He scowled. "You don't mean that."

"Is it really so hard to believe?" She snatched a rag from under the counter and began scrubbing furiously at the polished wood counter. "We were kids, Scott. It was a fling, it was fun, and then it was over."

"Emily." She couldn't mean those harsh words. She couldn't. They'd been in love. "It wasn't a fling."

She stopped scrubbing, but her hand remained clenched on the rag. "Maybe it wasn't. But it was just as meaningless in the end."

She turned on her heel and walked away before he could open his mouth to reply. From the entrance to the kitchen, Scott saw Lucy smiling at him, her eyes full of hope. He wrapped a hand around his neck and rubbed at the tense and aching muscles.

If Lucy thought she was playing matchmaker here, she was doing a very bad job of it.

The nerve of that man!

Emily's blood pounded in her ears as she assisted the next customer on autopilot. From the corner of her eye she could see Scott, sitting at the counter, fingers tented before him, his mouth a thin, grim line.

What was he still doing here? Why wouldn't he just leave?

She lifted her chin and turned away from him once more, denying the temptation to steal another glance. So he knew he had hurt her, knew how badly he had broken her heart. And now—now!—he wanted to spare her? As if he assumed she was still holding on, still licking her wounds from a dozen years ago.

She gritted her teeth. He knew her better than she wished he did in that moment.

She turned her head slightly, waiting to take another quick peek, her pulse quickening as she did so. Yep, still there all right. Well, no bother. He was here for Lucy, after all. And the freaking pie. Honestly!

He looked up, catching her stare. Flustered, Emily spilled the coffee she had been pouring all over the counter. She hissed out a curse and grabbed a rag, hiding her burning face behind the curtain of hair spilling from her ponytail as she wiped up her mess, trying to ignore the tremble in her hand.

Damn you, Scott Collins! After everything he had done to her—the way he had treated her—she was still irresistibly, hopelessly, foolishly attracted to this man.

A commotion was starting near the door and Emily looked up to see Jack Logan and Cole Davis hollering to Scott, both men grinning ear to ear as they strode past the counter and greeted the town's prodigal son with slaps on the back and high fives. Emily bit back a scowl. The kid who put Maple Woods on the map with that tie breaking touchdown senior year had graced them with his presence. A photograph of Scott's victorious win still hung in the principal's office.

She listened passively as the men caught up, making promises to meet up for beers one night, to talk about the good ol' times. Her heart fell, wondering why the same hadn't been offered to her. Hadn't she been just as much of a mark on that time in his life as his teammates? Hadn't she been more?

"Emily, we have a problem," Lucy announced, coming out of the kitchen flushed and breathless.

Emily studied her in alarm. "What is it?" she asked, realizing that Scott had stopped talking with Jack and Cole long enough to eavesdrop.

"It's the mayor. He has a last-minute meeting. He isn't going to make it." She gestured around the packed room of customers, all waiting for a chance to partake in the pie toss. "I hate to let them down. Our first week in business!"

Emily opened her mouth to put her boss at ease when Scott cut in. "What's the problem, Lucy?" he asked.

Emily trained her eye on Lucy, refusing to feed into his concern. So he felt like being nice now. Felt like playing hero. Where was this chivalry twelve years ago? Where was his sense of responsibility then?

"It's the pie toss," Lucy explained. "We seem to be missing our target."

"Let Scott do it!" Jack suggested, and Cole laughed heartily, slapping Scott soundly on the back.

The men grabbed his shoulders, cajoled him until his face was red and his smile was broad enough to reveal that elusive dimple she had almost managed to forget. He held up his hands in mock defeat. "Okay, okay," he said, grinning. "But only as a favor for my sister."

A cheer went up in the room at this and Lucy beamed, leading the group through the front door to where a chair had been set up on the sidewalk for all of Maple Woods to see. If this didn't pique interest and generate business, Emily wasn't sure what would. Already a few curious customers from Lucy's Place had emerged from the open door, lifting their chins to take in the show across the street.

"Don't go too easy on the whipped cream," Jack advised her, and she slid him a smile. Oh, she didn't intend to. "Hey," he said, tipping his head. "Didn't you and Scott used to date?"

Emily felt her cheeks warm, but before she had a chance to shut down the question, Jack turned to Scott, who was settling himself into the folding chair. "It's a real reunion over here, today. You and Emily used to date, didn't you?"

Emily filled another pie plate, holding her breath. Seconds seemed to pass as she waited for Scott's answer, her heart racing with expectation.

"Yeah, we used to hang out," he finally said.

Her hands went still. They used to *hang out?* Three years of her life, all those days spent laughing and talking, curling into each other's arms, dreaming of a future. They were just hanging out!

Tears prickled the backs of her eyes, whether from fury or sadness, she wasn't even sure anymore. She thought it had hurt when he disappeared without a trace twelve years ago, but hearing him dismiss their relationship all over again only broke her heart for the second time.

She set the pie plate down and turned to him, resting her hands on her hips. Watching him sit there with that expectant grin on his face that used to be reserved just for her, practically basking in the attention of half the town who had gathered to see Scott Collins—back at long last!—she felt her heart begin to rip all over again.

"Who's up first?" Lucy called out, and a shuffling and nervous laughter fell over the crowd.

"Why don't I kick this off?" Emily heard herself say.

Scott swiveled to her. Dread clouded his eyes, but there was no denying the amused twitch in that cocky grin.

Setting her jaw, Emily swiftly picked up a pie plate and walked to the line Lucy had drawn out in white chalk. Without waiting for a signal, she hurled the plate in Scott's direction. Whipped cream splattered at his feet.

A rumble went up in the crowd, but Emily barely noticed it. Her chest heaved with each breath as she stared at him, remembering the way his mouth used to curve when he saw her across the room, the way his brow would lift ever so slightly, the way he would quietly come up to her and place one hand on her hip. Lifting her chin, Emily marched back into the bakery, ignoring the way the crowd hushed and then slowly started to whisper with speculation. She walked around the counter, grabbed Scott's beloved cherry pie from its stand, and beelined back to the door. An audible gasp released from the crowd as she stepped onto the sidewalk, but they were of no concern to her at the moment. There was only one person on her mind, and he had it coming. This was well overdue.

"Emily—" Scott's old buddy Jack started, but she nailed him with a hard look and he clamped his mouth.

She positioned herself before she lost her nerve, but the adrenaline pumping in her veins showed no signs of slowing. She locked eyes with her target, noticing the way his brow had furrowed to a point. He let out a nervous chuckle. *This is for stealing my heart, Scott.* She pulled her arm back, fixing her eye on that lopsided grin that quickly vanished as she released the aluminum pan, sending it flying in his direction. *And that's for breaking it.*

She knew even before it hit him square in the face that her aim was perfect. And he knew it, too—she saw his expression dissolve into one of frozen shock just before the pie slammed into him, dead center, knocking him slightly to the left. Bright red filling oozed from the sides of the flimsy pan as it slowly slid down his nose. Scott swiped at the cherries and bits of crust that clung to his face, his eyes wide and confused, and for a moment, Emily almost felt sorry for what she had done. But then she remembered. He was no friend of hers. And she had nothing to apologize for. That was his department.

The crowd was laughing now, but Emily wasn't amused. Blindly muttering something to Lucy about going back inside to man the counter, she wove through the throng of onlookers, ducked into the empty storefront, and pushed past the swinging door to the kitchen. And only then, only when she was sure no one would ever see or ever know, did she allow herself to cry over Scott Collins.

Chapter Three

Scott pulled his car to a stop and shut off the ignition, sighing as he leaned back against the smooth leather headrest. The evening sunlight reflected off the windows of his parents' house, making it impossible to see inside. He felt an odd sensation of disbelief that he had once lived here at all, much less that he had spent the first eighteen years of his life knowing every inch of the house by heart, thinking of it as home. Still one of the prettiest houses in all of Maple Woods, time was obviously posing a challenge for its upkeep: white paint peeled from various corners of the siding; grass was sprouting up through a few cracks in the brick path leading up to the center door; the yard needed weeding and the bushes needed to be pruned.

Lucy's car was parked at the top of the driveway, and Scott couldn't fight the twinge of resentment he felt toward her. She had won—dragged him here against his will. She didn't understand the circumstances that had kept him away, but why the heck couldn't she just respect his wishes? Wasn't he doing enough for her already?

Scott gritted his teeth. *It's now or never.* He pulled on the latch and thrust the car door open, closing it behind him with quiet force. Shoving his hands into his pockets, he strode up the cracking path to the faded green door, wondering if he should knock or just try the handle. Hesitating, he knocked twice, peering through the slender window that framed the door for any sign of activity inside. Seconds later, an older woman with gray hair and a plump middle entered the front hall. When she saw him through the glass, she stopped walking and her hand flew to her heart.

His mother.

Instinctively, he pulled back from the window. He ran his fingers coarsely through his hair. The last time he had seen her she was an attractive woman in her late forties. Now she was sixty. Rationally he knew it had been a long time. He just hadn't realized the toll the years had taken on her.

The door flung open and his mother's bright blue eyes locked with his. Blinking back tears, she leaned forward and grabbed him, squeezing him tight to a body that still felt familiar.

As soon as he could, he pulled back, standing uncomfortably in the door frame, allowing her gaze to roam over him with nostalgic appraisal, as though she had just stumbled upon a once-cherished childhood toy in the attic. He hated this. He *hated* this. He had thought he had cut off his feelings a long time ago—that he would be strong enough to deal with this reunion if it ever came—but the ache in his chest proved otherwise.

"It's so good to see you," his mother said breathlessly, and Scott managed a weak smile.

"The house looks nice," he offered, stepping into the hall. He glanced around. Everything was exactly the same. Every painting hung on its same hook, every chair sat planted in the same position. Yet somehow, it was all different.

"Ah well, I've been meaning to get someone out here to take care of the yard now that..." she trailed off and inhaled sharply, closing the door behind him and then smoothing her hands over her skirt.

Scott balled his hands at his sides. "Is Lucy in the kitchen?" he asked, following the smell that was wafting from the back of the house.

Lucy was standing at the big island in the middle of the room, tossing a salad. Her eyes were unnaturally bright when she smiled. When she said hello, her voice was a notch higher than usual. It was then that he realized she was nervous. Well, she was the one insisting on this awkward arrangement. He wasn't sure why she thought it would be easy. For any of them.

"I see you're all cleaned up," she observed.

Scott shrugged. He had hoped to avoid thinking of Emily for just one night, but that was impossible. Being here in this house only stirred his emotions to the surface. "Keep tossing pies at me and I'll never get into the office to get the library project under way," he warned.

"Don't worry," Lucy replied. "That's it for the promotional stunts. But between you and me, I think you were a bigger hit than the mayor would have been."

"Glad I could help." He glanced around the room. "Where are George and Bobby?"

"George's at the diner. Bobby's studying for a test tomorrow."

Scott nodded. Topic closed, the room fell silent again. He released a heavy sigh. "Where's..."

"Dad?" Lucy lifted an eyebrow. Tight-lipped, she returned her attention to the salad. "He's upstairs."

His mother appeared in the arched doorway that led to the dining room. "He's so pleased to know you're here," she added.

That makes one of us.

Scott rolled his shoulders, pushing back the resentment. He was angry at his parents—angry to the bone—but damn it if a part of him didn't ache when he thought of them. It was easier, with time and distance, to just focus on the bad—on the event that had severed his ties with them for good. But all it took was one hint of his mother's smile, the lull of her voice, to make him wish with all his might that things could have been different, that he could have just loved his parents and let them love him. That he didn't have to look at them and be reminded of everything that had been lost instead.

He set his jaw and turned to the window, looking out over the backyard that stretched to the wood. Tulips had sprung up around the edges of the house providing a cheerful contrast to the situation within.

"Your father won't be able to come down for dinner," his mother was saying as she pulled three place mats from the basket on the baker's rack. "We'll take some soup up to him after he rests."

They wandered silently into the dining room, his mother taking her usual place at the head of the table closest to the kitchen, he and Lucy sliding into their childhood seats on autopilot. Scott unfolded the thick cloth napkin and placed it in his lap. "Looks delicious, Lucy," he said as she handed him a plate with a large steaming square of lasagna.

"Lucy's been keeping us well fed," his mother said through a tight smile. "More food than one person can eat, really," she continued, her voice growing sad. "Have you been over to the office yet?" his mother continued.

It both amazed and saddened Scott that his relationship with his mother had come to this: polite, stilted conversation. As though there was never a bond between them—not a shared love, not a shared life, not a shared secret.

He took a bite of the lasagna. "Not yet." He forced his tone not to turn bitter when he said, "Given Dad's commitment to the company, I think it's safe to assume everything is in place for the library project and I can just take over where he left off." A heavy silence fell over the room.

Lucy bit on her lip and then asked tentatively, "Why don't you go upstairs and see him after we're finished with dinner?"

His stomach twisted, but he nodded. Wordlessly, he finished his meal, slowly pushed back his chair and followed his mother up the stairs, his pulse taking speed with each step. He kept his gaze low, noticing how the floorboards creaked under the weight of each step. Lucy stayed downstairs, under the guise of cleaning up the kitchen, but he knew better. She was down there wringing her hands, saying a hundred desperate prayers that progress would be made, and that all would be forgotten.

Oh, Lucy.

"He might be sleeping," his mother whispered as they approached the master bedroom. She stopped, her hand clutching the brass knob. "Let me just go in and tell him you're here."

Scott stepped back and his mother slipped through the door, leaving it open an inch. Through the crack he could hear her soothing voice telling his father that "Scottie" was home and wanted to see him. If his father said anything in return, it wasn't audible from this distance.

His mother tipped her head around the door frame and nodded. With one last sharp breath, Scott entered the room, his blood stilling at what he saw. His father, once a strapping, robust man with a handsome face and personality that could intimidate even the strongest of men on a construction crew, had withered into a frail wisp of his former self. His skin, once bronzed from days spent on job sites, was now an alarming shade of grayish-white. Propped up on two pillows, his eyes were hollow and dark.

Scott crossed the room, his body numb.

"Dad."

"I knew you would come home." His father's voice strained with effort, but it was still deep, still authoritative. "I knew someday you would put this business with the Porters behind you and finally come home."

Scott's pulse hammered. "I haven't put this business with the Porters behind me and I never will," he said evenly.

"Scott!" his mother cried out, but he couldn't stop now if he wanted to. Even now, after all this time, the man still refused to acknowledge what he had done. The part he had played.

"A man died," Scott insisted, silently pleading with his father to set things right once and for all. "A man with two daughters and a wife. And I was the one who took him from them," Scott said quietly, feeling the anger uncoil in his stomach as the words spilled out. "You knew I was responsible for the accident that day and you kept that information from everyone. From the police. From Lucy. Even from me."

"You were nine years old, Scott. We were just trying to protect you—"

"No." Scott shook his head forcefully, trying to drive out the words, the excuses. "I should go, Dad." *Before I say anything I'll regret.* "You need your rest."

Scott paused with his hand on the door, and then slipped into the hall. His mother grabbed him by the elbow.

"Thank you for seeing him, Scott. It means so much to us."

Scott's eyes flashed on his mother. "Why can't he just admit it, Mom? Why can't you? You denied the Porter family insurance money that was owed them."

She visibly paled and looked away. "It was an *accident,* Scott."

"Maybe so, but it didn't have to happen. I had no business being on the machinery that day. A nine-year-old kid shouldn't be on a job site." He shook his head. "If I had never overhead you talking about it all those years later, would you ever have told me that I was the one responsible for the accident?"

His mother hesitated. "Probably not. You were already upset by the commotion that day. And what were we supposed to tell you? You were nine, Scott. We didn't want you or your sister to have to live with this. Lucy still doesn't know," she added.

"I'm aware of that," Scott said, "and I don't intend to burden her with this.

"Then you can understand how we felt. We were trying to protect you."

"By blaming the victim?" Scott cried.

"We never could have recovered from a lawsuit. Richard Porter was gone. There was nothing we could do to bring him back."

"Then you admit it. You chose to protect yourself financially."

"We chose to protect the company financially," his mother corrected him. "Nearly a third of the men in this town were employed by Collins Construction. They had wives and children—families of their own, depending on that paycheck. Would it have been better to make them all suffer?"

"So it was fair for Emily's family to suffer? They had nothing. Nothing!"

It was a no-win situation, he knew that now. A man was dead, his family impoverished and the only way they would have been reimbursed was for others to suffer at their expense. The only way everyone could have been spared was if Scott had never been on that machine that day. If his father hadn't let him tag along to work.

"We covered the funeral expenses," his mother offered, and Scott clenched a fist, willing himself not to lose his temper.

"It doesn't change the fact that we are all living this lie! The police took Dad's statement for the events of that day. Collins Construction had just finished building that addition on the Maple Woods police station—at cost. He knew they wouldn't pursue a criminal investigation when everyone was pointing the finger at Mr. Porter's negligence, and so it all just went away. And Emily and her family were not only denied the money they were rightfully owed for their father's wrongful death, but worse—" his throat locked up when he thought of it "—is that you allowed them to think their father's carelessness led to his death."

"It wasn't easy for us, either. We thought you would never have to know your part in this. And then all those years later you had to go and start dating Emily Porter. Of all people! Believe me when I say we *never* intended you to know the truth, especially when we saw how much you cared for her."

Scott lowered his voice. "You *knew* how much she meant to me, and you never even welcomed her into our home."

"You didn't honestly think we were going to be able to invite that girl into our lives, feeling the reminder every day of what we did."

Scott narrowed his eyes. "And here I thought you walked away with a clear conscience."

His mother stared at him levelly. "My conscience will never be free."

"Well, that makes two of us," Scott retorted. He ran a hand through his hair. "I have to go," he said, taking a step back, and then another. This was a useless, maddening effort.

"What are you doing?" Lucy cried in alarm, her face pale, her expression stricken as he bolted down the stairs.

"I shouldn't have come here!" he said, bursting past her toward the front door. "Now do you see?"

"What is *wrong* with you?" Lucy hissed. "Our father is dying. Do you hear me? *Dying.* Why can't you get over yourself for once and be the bigger person?"

Scott whipped around and met his sister's desperate gaze. "Lucy, when it comes to our parents, I do not want to hear another word about my relationship with them. Not. One. Word."

"You're a jerk," Lucy snapped.

Scott hesitated. "I'm worse than that."

"What's that supposed to mean?"

Scott shook his head. "You have no idea."

Lucy's voice softened. "Try me."

"Forget it," he said, striding for the door. He placed his hand on the knob and twisted it, hesitating. Turning to face Lucy again, his gut tightened at the sight of her anguished face. "I'm sorry you got dragged into all of this, Lucy," he said, closing the door behind him.

The spring air was cool and fresh on his lungs, and crickets chirped in the distance. He ran his hands down his face, staring at his ludicrous rental car, so sleek and bold and out of place. The image of his father lying in that bed was too clear to banish, but the words were what haunted him the most. What had he been expecting? He grimaced to think a part of him had wanted the same thing as Lucy. Closure. Peace. Some glimmer of relief to this endless, lifelong misery that hung over their family like a plague. And now he knew, perhaps he always had though, and that's why he had stayed away. It just was what it was.

"I just don't know what came over me," Emily repeated, closing her eyes to the memory of her outburst that afternoon.

"Well, I do!" Julia declared. "The man had it coming, Emily."

"But, Julia, I work there. That's my boss's brother!"

Julia waved her hand through the air. "Please. Lucy knows you and Scott have a history. Besides, she was the one who commissioned him for the contest."

Emily considered her sister's reasoning. "Maybe you're right," she said quietly.

"Maybe? Emily, Scott Collins is a *jerk,*" Julia said firmly. "I'm so sick of hearing everyone in town go on and on about his return. If it were up to me, he'd never have come back. Seriously, I mean who does he think he is, huh? He might have been Mr. Popularity back in high school, but he's thirty years old now and he needs to get over himself. But one day he'll see that he can't just tromp around on his high horse, zipping through town in his fancy car, flashing that smile and expecting every woman in the street to just *swoon.* Oh, what I wouldn't like to do to him…just kick that butt right to the curb, right out of Maple Woods, back to wherever the heck it is he's been hiding all this time…"

Emily heaved a sigh and glanced at her sister, whose eyes had narrowed to green slits, her pink lips pinched in fury as she detailed the revenge she'd like to take on Scott Collins, and burst out laughing. It was the first good laugh Emily had enjoyed all day, and she needed it more than she'd realized. "Are you finished?" she asked, when she'd settled down.

"It's not funny!" Julia exclaimed, shaking her head in disgust. She leaned over and took a long sip of wine from her glass and then set it back down on the coffee table with a scowl. She reached for her knitting needles and motioned to Emily to flick on the television. The sisters had just finished eating dinner and were getting ready to catch up on the soap opera that they recorded each afternoon and watched together each night. It was a cozy ritual, and one that Emily cherished, even if she sometimes did worry that she and Julia were destined to become two spinsters, living in a four-room apartment above the town diner for the rest of their lives.

Emily's stomach tightened. There was still a chance that she would get into that school in Boston. Today's mail had brought no news with it, but eventually an answer would arrive. The anticipation of opening the mailbox each day was starting to become almost too much. For so long she had dreamed of the opportunity to leave Maple Woods, to go out into the world and begin her own life, to put everything she hated about this town behind her. She longed to start fresh. She was a person in her own right, and the longer she still lived with the weight of her family's past, the more she resented the town that had defined her by it.

She had applied to the school with big dreams and a flutter of hope that caused her heart to soar. Now that the thought of leaving Maple Woods and everyone in it was becoming a possibility, she began to wonder if she could really go through with it.

She glanced at Julia, then swept her gaze over the

small room that housed a hand-me-down couch and coffee table, and an old television propped on some milk crates. *Be real.* If this was all Maple Woods could offer her, then she had no other choice. If she got accepted to the school in Boston, she was going.

"I guess Scott had it coming." Emily sighed as she settled back against a couch cushion and tucked her feet under her. It felt so good to sit down. Between the anxiety of waiting for the mail each day, the stress of seeing Scott and the long hours at the bakery, she felt as if she could shut her eyes and fall asleep right then and there. And it was only eight o'clock!

"Oh, he had it coming," Julia insisted, wide-eyed, and Emily bit back a smile at the indignation in her voice. She was a girl of principles, and Emily loved her for it. It was something she was going to miss if she left—she really needed to stop thinking that way.

"Still, I guess we can't exactly call him a jerk for not being interested in me," Emily summarized.

"Oh, yes we can!" Julia slammed a bamboo knitting needle down on the coffee table and reached for her wineglass again. "You dated for three years and he up and disappears. Just…vanishes. Then he saunters back into town without so much as an explanation?" She shook her head. "I'm sorry, Emily, but you're too forgiving. I saw how crushed you were when he left, even though you tried to hide it from me."

Emily eyed her sister coolly, taking a sip of wine from her own glass. Julia didn't remember their father's funeral as well as she did—she was only six at the time, while Emily was already eight. Emily had cried herself to sleep for at least a year after that day, and she knew that no other heartache could ever be as painful as losing her dad. When Scott had left, it didn't seem right to cry for him—he had chosen to leave her after all, he wasn't taken from her. He wasn't worth her tears, she'd told herself firmly, but then today, after all this time, she finally released the pain she'd been holding inside.

"You're right," she suddenly said, flashing Julia a conspiratorial grin. Her sister's eyes gleamed in return. "He is a jerk."

"Thatta girl." Julia winked and, satisfied, snuggled back on the couch with her sister as the opening credits to the soap opera started. They watched in silence, fast-forwarding through the commercials, occasionally gasping at some dramatic turn in events. They had grown up with these characters—had watched them every day after school together while they did housework and got dinner ready. Some people thought growing up in Maple Woods was boring. Small-town life. No excitement or fun. The Porter girls had enough uncertainty in their young lives to make up for the shortcomings the town experienced in general. This television show, while silly, was one constant they had over time.

"My prediction for tomorrow?" Julia reached for the remote and turned off the television. "Brad's not the father."

Emily's mouth curled into a smile. "Ooooh. I like that!" The sisters giggled.

They began gathering up their dinner plates and glasses, both groaning as they sauntered into the kitchen and noticed the pile of dishes from what had seemed like such a basic pasta recipe, and begrudgingly started rinsing the pots when the sound of heavy footsteps on the other side of the door caused them each to freeze midtask.

Emily's heart began to pound, even though she rationally knew she was being ridiculous. This was Maple Woods. There was no crime here. The last instance of a burglary had been at the penny candy shop on Oak and Birch, when little Molly Roberts plucked a lollipop from the counter and ran off to the park.

Standing at the sink, Emily glanced sidelong at her sister and met her fearful gaze. "Did Lucy mention that someone was staying in the spare room down the hall?" Julia whispered.

Emily shook her head and peered into the soapy water and tried to remember if Lucy had ever hinted at such a thing. Surely she would have mentioned something like this, even if it was just to ask Emily to give a friendly wave to the newcomer. Maple Woods was small, and in the six months since Julia and Emily had moved into the apartment above the diner that Lucy and George had lived in for the first five years of their marriage, no one else had come through the second floor of the building. There was only one other apartment and it was just a room really that Lucy kept on hand for guests.

Guests. The air tightened in Emily's lungs. Without another glance at her sister, Emily wiped her hands dry on a dishtowel and tossed it on the counter. *Of course.*

Straightening her spine, she lifted her chin, marched the eight feet to the front door of the apartment and flung it open.

Scott's face blanched and his wide blue eyes shifted from her to the door at the end of the hall and back again. "Emily. What are you doing here?"

"I live here," she said calmly, even though her pulse was doing jumping jacks.

He combed a hand through his hair and chuckled. "George and Lucy's old apartment... I'm staying in the spare room at the end of the hall."

"I figured as much. It was either that or a break-in."

His frown deepened. "Oh. Sorry about that. I... Well, I should let you get back to your evening. You're probably busy."

Emily opened her mouth to respond but Julia's voice purred smoothly from behind her. "Oh, but quite the contrary."

Emily whipped around and flashed a warning look at her sister, who pretended not to catch it.

"It isn't often we're graced with the talk of the town." Julia smiled sweetly, and Emily closed her eyes, bracing herself. "Please, Scott. Come in. We have a lot of catching up to do and I was just about to put the water on for tea."

Scott cupped his tea and saucer in his lap and glanced up at Julia. She'd grown up from a freckle-faced, scrawny little teenager into a striking beauty with creamy skin and distinct coloring. Deep auburn hair and green cat eyes stared back at him.

"So, Scott," she said, setting down her mismatched cup to pick up her knitting. "I heard Emily really let you have it today."

She arched an eyebrow as her lips curled mischievously, and it was then that he realized she was talking about the pie toss. He chuckled, feeling some of the nervous energy roll off him. "Ah well, it was all in good fun. It washed off."

Julia's eyes were sharp. "Not quite the same as a dagger to the heart, I suppose."

"Julia!" Emily snapped, but Julia just pinched her lips and casually returned to her knitting.

"You'll have to forgive my sister," Emily said, reddening.

Scott shrugged. "I probably deserved that one."

"My goodness!" Julia snorted. "Is that actual remorse I detect?"

"Julia!" Emily said sharply. "Don't you have to finish knitting those cashmere socks for the window display at the shop?"

Julia let out a sigh. "I know when to take a hint." She stood, gathering her yarn in her hands. "Besides, you two have unfinished business to discuss."

She held Scott's gaze as she retreated from the room, and he made a mental note to steer clear of her until she'd calmed down.

He waited until he heard the door click shut, but as he looked down the hall to make sure, he noticed the brass handle silently turn, and the door to Julia's room remained open exactly an inch after that.

"Sorry about that," Emily said as he settled back against his chair. She rubbed her forehead, something he remembered she did when she was feeling stressed.

"She's protective of you," he said affably. "I think it's sweet."

Emily dropped her hand, spearing him with a sharp look. "I can fight my own battles."

She sat less than three feet from him, but the distance felt much greater as she stared at him flatly, her eyes sad and tired, her face pale. She looked weary and exhausted and Scott had never felt like a bigger jerk in all his life. He had intruded on her home, interrupted her evening and now he was sitting in the heated silence of her living room like an unwanted piece of furniture.

He glanced around the small room, sweeping his view into the adjoining kitchen. A small hallway led to two rooms that scarcely qualified as bedrooms and a shared bathroom. He hadn't been in this place in years—not since Lucy and George moved in when they were first married at barely the age of twenty. It seemed bigger then. Special and grown-up.

"So how long have you lived here?" he asked, hoping to lighten the mood.

Emily heaved a sigh. "Julia and I moved in about six months ago when our mother sold the house and moved down to Florida to be with our aunt. It's small, but it's convenient."

He stole another glance at the living room. It was cramped but cozy, but not cozy enough to make him wish this on her. If she'd been able to go to college, instead of sticking around to support her mother, she would have had more options. Instead… He set his cup on the coffee table.

"I should probably get going," he said, pulling himself to his feet. "Please thank your sister for the tea."

"Are you kidding me?" Emily's tone shattered the silent chill of the room. "That's all you have to say?"

No, it wasn't all he had to say. He had a lot more to say. A hell of a lot more. Things he'd been aching to say for years. Things he'd kept bottled up. Things he'd tried to bury.

Scott drew a ragged breath. "It's late," he settled on. He would make things right with Emily, but what that entailed he wasn't yet sure. All he knew was that tonight the best thing he could do was to walk out the door and leave her alone. "I should go."

"This seems to be the way you operate." She crossed her arms over her chest. Against the well-worn floorboards, her bare foot tapped expectantly. Unable to resist, Scott let his gaze trace the curve of her calf to her toes. He swallowed hard and forced himself to look back to her face as heat rushed to his groin.

"What's that supposed to mean?"

Emily's shadowed gaze remained cool and steady until she abruptly shifted her eyes to the clock on top of a nearby bookshelf. She shook her head and, standing, muttered, "Forget it."

"No, I can't forget it," Scott said. "I've never forgotten it. Any of it. Emily, I can explain—" He stopped himself. He could explain, of course he could, but explaining why he had so abruptly broken up with her would entail telling her about the horrible, tragic, irreversible thing he had done.

She chewed at her bottom lip, sizing him up, deciding perhaps if she wanted to hear what he had to say, or if she'd rather let it go.

"Forget it," she said again, this time through a sigh of disgust that punched him straight in the gut. "Actions speak louder than words. You didn't even say goodbye, Scott." Her voice croaked and she looked away, blinking quickly.

He could still remember the way she looked, the last night they were together. It was one of those hot, sticky days in August. The kind of days that never seemed to end, and he never wanted them to—not when he was with Emily. They'd spent the day wandering through town, resting in the cool shade of the trees in the park, taking heat in each other's embrace and not even caring, so eager were they for the other's touch. Her long brown hair was damp at the forehead, pulled up in a ponytail, and he remembered the way he traced his fingers down the length of her neck, how her cheeks flushed from more than just the summer sun. He'd spent many days like this with her, but for some reason, on that day, he'd lingered at the edge of her porch, watching as she smiled to him from the top of the stairs, waiting until she was safely inside, and even then, wishing he could still cling to the sight of her for just a few more moments.

He'd clung to the image for years. The perky ponytail, the bright pink cheeks that made her gray eyes shine, and most of all, that smile. It was the smile of innocence, the smile of a girl who loved him completely, who trusted in him to never let her down. And he never wanted to.

"It was too hard to say goodbye," he said gruffly.

"Too *hard?*" Emily's eyes were steely and sharp, darkening to midnight as they locked his. "What was hard, Scott, was waking up one morning and discovering you were gone. And then waking up every morning after that wondering if it might be the day I heard from you again. And then realizing every night that I probably never would. That was hard."

Scott held her steady gaze, wanting more than anything to close the distance between their bodies, between the twelve years of disappointment he had caused her and the years of pain he had brought into her life. He wanted to take her into his arms and kiss the frown off her sweet mouth, to feel the curve of her waist under his hands, to make up for every tear he had ever caused her to shed.

He nodded, edging toward the door. She was right. Actions did speak louder than words. The way she saw it, he had led her on, made promises he had never intended to keep, and then never spoken to her again. She had no idea how far beyond that betrayal his actions had extended.

"Just tell me this much," she said. "Do you ever wonder how things might have been? If you'd stayed in town?"

He looked her square in the eye, grateful for a chance to be brutally honest. "Every day," he replied. Every damn day.

She nodded, but said nothing more.

"Have a good night, Emily," he said with a nod, his tone more clipped than he had intended. It was the only way to keep the conversation from continuing down a path that would only lead to more heartache. He needed to let her go. For the night. Maybe for good.

"See you."

See you. See you, she had called that evening, throwing him a casual smile, holding up a slender hand in a careless wave before turning her back and disappearing into the shadows of that old, run-down farmhouse she lived in with her mother and sister. Those were the last words she had ever said to him. If he'd known it then, he would have pressed for more, for an "I love you," a last kiss—something. But somehow, somewhere deep in his mind, in a nugget of hope that had no right to fight for life, he always found optimism in those two simple words: *See you.* It wasn't a goodbye. It wasn't the end. It was the promise of another encounter and perhaps, he'd sometimes dare to imagine, another chance.

He watched her for a long moment, his gaze lingering on the gentle flare of her hips, the way her long chestnut hair brushed against her shoulders. He hesitated, going so far as to even open his mouth— *Just tell her, tell her it was an accident, tell her how you feel!*—before he pulled his eyes from her for the night, knowing the image of her would stay with him until morning.

Her father was gone; her life had taken a new path in his absence. Nothing he could say to her now could make up for that. Nothing at all.

Emily was sitting on the couch reading a well-thumbed paperback, when her sister came out of her room. From her vantage point in the living room, she could see Julia's wide-eyed sweep of the small apartment. She tucked her head around the door frame and whispered, "Is he gone?"

Emily bit back a sigh. As if she didn't know. "You shouldn't have invited him inside," she scolded.

Julia's eyes flung open. "Are you kidding me? I told you, the two of you have unfinished business to address." She flopped onto a chair and tucked her feet under her, settling in for a long chat. "So tell me, what did he have to say for himself?"

Julia was watching her expectantly and Emily reluctantly dog-eared the page in her novel and set it in her lap. "Nothing. He said he had to go home."

Julia pinched her lips. "Figures."

"You didn't exactly help matters, Julia."

"Me?" Julia frowned. "You might be two years

older than me, but I am still your sister. You're all I've got. So if I want to say something to Scott, I will."

Emily closed her eyes, even though a part of her was touched by Julia's loyalty. It was a trait in her sister she had always admired—the ability to speak her mind and stand by her opinions, regardless of the consequence. Growing up, Emily had been the responsible one. The one who put dinner on the table when their mother worked late; the one who made sure Julia completed her homework each night. Julia was the tough one, though. The one who fought for what she believed in, who didn't take life passively. And Emily…well, Emily supposed she was always just grateful when something eventually worked out.

"I still can't believe you slammed that pie in his face," Julia said. "It's a start, at least."

Emily glanced toward the front door, thinking of Scott alone in that small room, and her heartstrings began to pull. She banished the thought, thinking instead of the man high-fiving Jack and Cole at the bakery, the man who was celebrated just for strutting back into town. The man who didn't have to take responsibility for the pain he left in his wake.

A giggle began to erupt in her as she replayed the memory of the afternoon. The astonishment in his eyes when she actually hit her target with that pie.

"What's so funny?" Julia asked, but a smile was already playing at her lips.

They laughed together, reliving the hilarious memory. Oh, the look on his face! She didn't know what had come over her to do such a thing, but oh, it had been worth it. Really, truly worth it.

"You're going to be laughing about this for a while,"

Julia said, shaking her head with a mischievous smile. She picked up her knitting needles and resumed where she had left off earlier. "Well, half the town will be talking about it by noon tomorrow."

"Julia..."

Julia flashed her a glance, her expression the picture of mock innocence. "What?"

Emily dipped her chin. "Don't go spreading gossip."

"Me? I'm insulted you would even suggest such a thing. I mean, I can't exactly help it if I have a knitting circle tomorrow morning, or if the expected topic of conversation will be the return of Scott Collins..."

Emily picked up her book and stood, stretching until her back arched. With a tired sigh, she regarded her sister and shook her head. "You missed your calling, my dear. You should have taken to the stage. You're all about drama. Especially when it's not your own."

She walked over to her sister, planted a kiss on her the top of her auburn hair and then padded off down the hall to her bedroom, unable to stop thinking of the fact that Scott Collins—the one man other than her father she had loved with all her heart her entire life— was somewhere on this floor, only a matter of twenty feet away from where she now sat, on the edge of her bed, staring out the window onto the quiet streets of Maple Woods.

She wondered if he was awake, or if the strange events of the night had exhausted him. She wondered if he was still thinking of her, of their conversation.

She wondered if in the past twelve years he had been gone, he had ever really thought of her at all. Or if that was just another one of his lies.

Chapter Four

It had rained overnight, a soft and pleasant tapping of drops against the windows accompanied by random bursts of lightning that lit the dark sky. The spring storm started at about midnight and went on until just past three, and Scott knew this because he was awake the entire time. Thinking about Emily.

He couldn't resist the relief he felt to know that Mrs. Porter had moved out of town, and that he wouldn't have to face her, too. She'd always been a kind woman, pleasant despite her circumstances, with a dullness in her soft gray eyes—the light having been replaced by sadness. For all the time that he and Emily had dated, her mother had always been off at one odd job or another, coming home harried and tired, but always with a smile on her face at the sight of her daughters. Mrs. Porter had always been kind to him, even as a child.

He remembered the time when he was riding his bike down Willow Road and hit a rock, she had run outside to help him, inviting him to come sit on her front porch while she cleaned and bandaged his scraped knees, offering him a glass of cool, sweet lemonade with a reassuring smile. "I don't have any sons," he remembered her saying with a wistful grin, "but I imagine you get into your share of trouble around here."

More trouble than she knew.

The memory of that hot summer afternoon made him feel queasy and restless, and he fitfully tossed and turned as the small room above the diner—just a mere twenty feet from Emily and Julia's apartment—illuminated with lightning, until the storm passed over and he finally fell into a disoriented sleep filled with nightmares, waking drenched in sweat only a few hours later.

The morning glow filtering through his window came as a welcome relief and by seven he was dressed and eager to escape the confines of his small room. He drove past the job site, surveying the damage to the historic town library. It was an accident, he knew: a stupid, careless incident that had resulted in serious structural damage of an entire wing of the building. He didn't blame Bobby. He hadn't done it on purpose. But could the same be said for Emily? Would she blame him?

Scott narrowed his eyes as he inspected the wreckage. Some accidents were pardonable. Others were permanent. They could never be put right.

He picked up a chunk of cement and tossed it back to the ground with a sigh. The crew couldn't start until they had plans in place, and with his father's condition

Scott knew it was up to him to lead the project or find a suitable replacement. He should go into the office and get started on this immediately, but he couldn't bring himself to do it. Not yet.

He shuddered when he thought back on those summers of his youth spent tagging along as his dad went about his work. He supposed it was ironic that he still pursued a career in the construction business, but maybe starting his own Pacific Northwest-based company was his way of taking back control of the events that had gone so awry in his past. Or maybe there were just some things in life you couldn't escape, no matter how hard you tried. The day Emily's father died was a fog—a disjointed stream of memories. But the one thing he could never forget were the shouts. The panicked, horrifying shouts. He'd just had no idea at the time that he was the one who had set it all into motion.

Scott straightened his back and marched to the car. His father had no problems covering up the truth, denying it. Well, not him. So many times over the years Scott had thought of picking up the phone and telling Emily the truth, but then he wondered if he would only hurt her more by setting himself free.

Scott drove into town and killed the engine at a spot in front of the diner. He needed a clear head before heading over to the office, and a Reuben sandwich with hot coffee would do just the trick.

"Scott!" The sound of his sister's voice across the room as he walked through the door pulled him out of his dark mood and Scott grinned back at her, moving eagerly through the crowded tables to grab the last stool at the counter. It seemed the room went quiet as he wove his path, but he refused to give in to it.

"What can I get for you?" Lucy asked with a smile. There was something in the crinkle of her eyes, an apology perhaps, an understanding. He closed his eyes briefly, showing his gratitude.

"A Reuben with extra fries," he said with a grin.

Lucy scribbled out a ticket and clipped it in line with the others. "Scott, this is Holly Tate. She runs The White Barn Inn down at the edge of town. Holly, this is the kid brother I've told you so much about."

"So you're the one who stuck a snake under Lucy's pillow?" Holly's lips curled into a sly grin, and Scott chuckled.

"The one and only." He extended his hand. "It's nice to meet you, Holly. I hope you won't judge me too harshly based on my mischievous past. I was only four when I captured that snake out at Willow Pond."

"Are you kidding? I love that story." Holly's laughter was soft and pleasant, and the warmth in her eyes helped his shoulders to relax. "I'm an only child myself. I would have killed for an annoying little brother."

"Hey, I'm the only one who's allowed to call my brother annoying," Lucy protested. She slid him a knowing glance as she filled his mug with coffee from a glass pot. "You were pretty annoying, but you turned out just fine."

Scott set his jaw and forced his attention back to Holly. "I don't think I remember you growing up in Maple Woods."

Holly shook her head. "I only spent the summers here so you might not have seen me. My grandmother lived here in the old white house I turned into the inn—"

"I know the one." Scott smiled at a fond memory of the stately old mansion and the kind woman who lived there. Studying Holly more closely, he had a vague recollection of a cute little granddaughter a couple years younger than himself.

Holly paused, her gaze becoming wistful. "I always loved Maple Woods. Once I inherited the house and moved back, I knew could never leave it."

Scott gave a noncommittal grunt. "It is a charming town," he managed. From the corner of his eye he could see Lucy watching him carefully. He fought to ignore her.

"My fiancé mentioned you were here to oversee the rebuilding of the library," Holly continued.

Scott nodded. The anonymous donor. According to Lucy, Max Hamilton had come into town with the intention to buy out the parcel of land housing the inn and turn it into a shopping mall. George's family owned the land, but had been leasing it to Holly's family for years. The opportunity to sell would allow them to pay to have the library rebuilt, but when Max fell in love with Holly and decided to stay in town and keep the inn running, Lucy was spared having to make the difficult decision of taking her friend's home out from under her in order to right her son's wrongs.

Scott swiveled in his seat to reach for his coffee, allowing the heat to coat his throat before he answered. "With our father unwell, Lucy asked me to take over the reins for a bit. I'm just in town to make sure all the projects on the books continue to run smoothly until a replacement can be found."

"I heard about your father," Holly said softly, darting her gaze to Lucy. "I'm sorry."

Scott shrugged but his stomach tightened. "Ah, well…" He lowered his eyes to his mug to avoid looking in Lucy's direction.

"So you're not going to oversee the library project, then?" Holly pressed. Her brow knit together. "I thought Max said you were."

Scott cursed to himself for being so careless with his words. He sensed her concern and he understood it—her fiancé was financing the project in exchange for George's land; they wanted to make sure the project would be built to their satisfaction. He knew he should just tell her the truth—that he would find a replacement, a project manager for the job, and that it wouldn't be him overseeing a minute of that project or any project having to do with his father's company—but for some reason, he couldn't. Not in front of Lucy. He couldn't let her down just yet. "I still have to get over to the office and sort through some things. We want to make sure the most qualified person oversees that job."

He scrolled through some work emails on his phone while Lucy began chatting with Holly about her various guests at the inn, and when his food arrived, he was grateful to have something positive to focus on. Within a few minutes, Holly left and Scott felt the heat of Lucy's gaze on him. There was a change in her expression, one he was familiar with; she had something on her mind. He took another bite of his sandwich, trying to avoid her stare.

Please don't talk about Dad. Not now. He knew he should offer her comfort, lessen the burden of the pain for her, share in the fear, but he didn't trust himself to speak. He'd been doing his damned best not to think about his parents since last night. He'd gone there for Lucy but he couldn't go back. He wouldn't.

"I'm sorry for the things I said last night," Lucy said.

Scott relaxed. "I know what you were trying to do. I'm just sorry you were disappointed with the outcome."

Lucy nodded, her lips thin. It was clear she had a lot more to say on the matter, but was refraining. "I could use a favor from you, if you don't mind picking up a hammer."

Well, this was a pleasant surprise. "You name it!" Scott said, smiling.

"The last of the cabinet doors for Sweetie Pie just arrived this morning. George is too busy to get to it this week, so I hoped you might be up for the job."

Scott stifled a frown. The prospect of yet another painful encounter with Emily didn't appeal to him. "Today?" he asked, his tone conveying his sudden shift in enthusiasm.

Lucy shrugged. "Or tomorrow." Her voice was pleasant and light but it was clear she wasn't going to let it drop.

"Isn't there someone else you could ask?" He asked before he could stop himself. Lucy's face had already folded in confusion and before she could say anything he blurted, "Don't worry. Of course I'll do it. In fact, I'll do it today, as soon as I'm done here."

Lucy regarded him, unconvinced. "If you're sure…"

Scott forced a grin. "You can always count on me, Lucy, and you know that. Now, where's the toolbox?"

He tried to tell himself it was a simple favor, and the least he could do for her after his outburst last night. After all, she didn't realize what she was asking of him. She didn't know what had happened to make him leave town and stay away—why he and their parents had severed all communication when he left. She wouldn't understand why Emily Porter was the last person in Maple Woods he had any desire to spend time with, much as he wished the circumstances were different.

Emily saw Scott coming across the street and felt the air lock in her chest. She quickly ran into the kitchen and fumbled in her handbag for a tube of lipstick, using the side of the toaster for a make-shift mirror. Frivolous nonsense! But she couldn't help herself—the image of that sheepish grin and apologetic shadow in his deep blue eyes made her hands shake, and she hastily swiped at her mouth to repair the damage. If only he wasn't so damn cute!

The chime of the bells above the door kick-started her pulse, despite her effort to remain calm. With one last deep breath, she squared her shoulders and sailed into the storefront before her nerves paralyzed her completely. If the way they'd left things last night was any indicator, today's forecast had awkward written all over it.

Scott stood behind the glass display case, idly pe-rusing the pies. Smiling for courage, Emily said with forced cheer, "Back for more already?" *Maybe he's here to apologize,* she thought. To finish the conver-sation they'd started last night. Something told her she wasn't going to like what he had to say to her, though, and if he was going to let her down gently for something that had happened half a lifetime ago, then she'd rather be spared the further humiliation.

"My mouth says yes, but my stomach says no." He rubbed his rock-hard abdomen.

Even through his lightweight polo, Emily could make out the chiseled contours of his corded muscles. Heat pooled in her belly as she traced her eyes up the hard plane of his chest to the broad shoulders that filled his shirt, causing the material to go taut in all the right places.

"Actually, I'm at your service for once. Lucy asked me to install a couple of cabinet doors."

Well, that was interesting. Emily studied him through narrowed eyes.

She glanced around the shop to make sure no one needed her attention, but it was nearing two o'clock and there wouldn't be another surge of traffic until after dinner. "Sure, right this way."

Scott crossed behind the counter and she led him into the kitchen, a blush heating her cheeks at the awareness of his eyes on her. Her stomach tightened as she worried she might have somehow gotten some flour on the seat of her skirt when she'd leaned on the counter earlier. An uncomfortable silence hung heavy in her footsteps and she racked her brain for something to say to lighten the mood, or at least an excuse to get him to walk in front of her.

Finally, they were in the kitchen and she heard him place a toolbox down on the marble-topped island with a heavy thud before she came to a halt. Without daring to look at him, she stopped where a large flat box was propped against the wall.

"It arrived this morning. Back order," she explained, stealing a quick glance and then immediately looking away. She motioned to the empty space above the range. "Just up there, if you don't mind."

She caught another glimpse of his well-muscled form as he bent down to pop the box, her heart tightening with longing, recalling the way they used to be. The way he'd hold her hand when they walked home from school, the way he'd shout out to her when she sat in the stands, watching his football games, and the way she swelled with pride that he was hers and that he cared that she was there to cheer him on.

Yes, he'd *cared*. Once. She could still feel the sweetness of his first kiss that cool fall day of her freshman year—the gentle, almost hesitant way he had grazed her lips behind the old maple tree in the park next to their school. The way over time his body had become one with hers. She knew every contour, every slope—he was a constant in her life she had come to rely on, when she hadn't dared to take anything as a given since her father died. And then…poof! Gone.

She forced back the aching sensation in her chest. Did he have any idea how much he'd let her down? Did he even care?

From the looks of it, he didn't.

Without a word, Scott stepped closer and Emily felt her body warm on reflex. The musk of his aftershave caused her thoughts to revert to something primal and instinctive, stirring a part of her than had been dormant for too long. She shifted her eyes to her left, and dropped an arm as Scott reached up to take a measurement. He was absorbed in the task, his brow furrowing in concentration as he studied the small numbers.

Emily dared to regard him a little more closely, noticing the fine lines around his deep set eyes, the way his strong, chiseled jaw was laced with the faintest bit of stubble, the way his biceps flexed as he pulled the measuring tape taut.

She pulled her gaze away. She was only indulging in a fantasy by standing here, only wishing for things that could never be. Somehow she had thought when she was nearing thirty she would be more reasonable when it came to matters of the heart, that she would know how to reserve her feelings for a man who could return them, not run from them.

Leave it to Scott Collins to have her feeling like a teenager all over again.

"I'll get out of your way and let you work," she said, unfolding herself from his proximity.

She barely made it to the kitchen island when she heard his husky voice behind her. "Wait."

Her pulse lurched as she turned to face him. Was he going to explain? Finish the conversation they had started last night?

He stood where she had left him, arms at his sides, staring at her with an intensity that closed the gap between their bodies. She swallowed hard, her eyes locked with his. Did he regret the way things had left off last night? Or was he going to tell her he never loved her at all—that he was wrong to have ever let her believe otherwise? She didn't think she could bear it—in fact, she knew she couldn't—and suddenly she felt choked for air, dizzy with anticipation. She wanted to run out into the storefront, escape the magnificence of his raw, masculine energy and his heated gaze. She wanted to get on with life. Forget him. The way she should have forgotten him a long, long time ago.

"Mind passing me the flathead?"

Her eyes widened. After a pause, she clarified through a choked breath, "The flathead?"

His mouth twitched into a smirk. "The screwdriver."

Oh. So he just needed her help. She bit back a twinge of disappointment and the weight of it rested firmly in her gut. After a pause, she studied the contents of the toolbox impassively, aware of his watchful gaze as she searched for the specific tool. Finally, she plucked it from the box and handed it to him. "Here you go," she said in what she hoped was a breezy tone. The heat of the kitchen was beginning to feel stifling, and the penetrating gaze of Scott's misty blue eyes left her rattled and confused.

"This isn't the flathead," he said, flashing a set of straight, even teeth.

Her stomach tightened. "Oh." She paused and studied it in his hands. "It's not?"

"Nope." He strode by her and plunked it back in the box, swiftly retrieving another red-handled tool. "See the flat edge to the tip?" he asked, running his finger over the metal. "That's how it earned its name."

"Oh," Emily managed weakly. She shifted the weight on her feet, eager to get away from him, from those hooded blue eyes with their bright green flecks around the center. From the way they gleamed at her with a certain level of mischief that could only be born from intimacy.

Scott tipped his head toward the cabinet. "Do you have a few minutes to give me a hand?"

Emily glanced desperately through the kitchen doorway and into the empty bakery. There was no excuse she could give. "Sure," she said on a heavy sigh.

Scott pulled a chair over to the counter and stepped up, and Emily bit down on her lower lip as she gazed up at his form, mentally chastising herself for the ridiculous notions that began to spring to mind, unfiltered in their unabashed desire. She raked her eyes up the length of his legs, nearly groaning as she absorbed the curve of his hard thighs. She looked sharply away. She really needed to get out more. Or stop watching those damn soap operas!

Clenching her teeth, she handed him the screwdriver and watched him set the hinge. Something in his competent attitude elicited a swell of attraction deep within her, and she imagined what it must feel like to have a man in the home—a strong, capable, take-charge man. A man who could fix what was broken, and set things right. She was being silly and naive, she supposed, idealizing the missing piece in her life.

Her dad had died when she was only eight, but she still had the dollhouse he made for her for that last birthday he was with them, and she often admired the handiwork—the pride he took in the task. After he died, her mother had never remarried or even dated. She didn't have time, Emily reflected, thinking back on the two jobs her mother maintained to pay the bills. It was a fearful time, Emily recalled, and although her mother hid her grief and money concerns as best she could, Emily was old enough to be aware of their situation, and perceptive enough to know that she was helpless to make it much better.

Emily handed Scott the level he asked for and smiled sadly. If her dad were still alive, he would have probably built this whole kitchen himself. But then, if her dad were still alive a lot of things would have been different.

Scott opened and closed the cabinet door and smiled proudly at Emily, who stood below and granted him a small applause. "How about that?" he bantered, unable to resist flashing a grin at the beautiful woman whose company he just couldn't seem to get enough of, even if he was desperate to avoid her.

"Perfect," she said, sliding the chair back into place after he stepped down. "Lucy will be pleased. I know she's really glad you're back in town."

Scott loaded up the toolbox and closed it tight. Turning to face her, his eyes locked with hers and a shadow fell over her soft gray irises. *Just tell her. Tell her now. It's just you and her. Get it over with.* He cleared his throat. "Emily, I wanted to say—"

"If it's about last night, Scott, please…let's forget it." A flush had crept up her cheeks and she traced a path on the tile floor with the toe of her shoe.

"But that's just the thing, Emily. I can't forget it." *Any of it.* "Did you mean it when you said you moved on after I left?"

She looked up at him. "Would it matter if I had?"

He raised his eyebrows. "I suppose it wouldn't. If it made you happy."

Emily snorted. "Since when do you care if I'm happy, Scott?"

"Since always," he said firmly, searching her face. "You know how much I cared about you."

She held his stare, her lips growing thin. "No, I don't know that. I thought you did once, but then—"

"I'm sorry the way things ended between us, Emily. Please believe me when I say it because it's the truth."

"That's not exactly the way I remember things, Scott. The way I remember it, nothing ever ended with us, you just disappeared."

His jaw flinched. "I had my reasons," he said.

"Enlighten me." She tipped her head, locking her gaze on him.

He inhaled deeply, holding her stare, willing himself to let it out, to spill the truth. The horrible, awful truth. The minute hand ticked its way around the clock behind her. With a sigh of defeat he broke her gaze and shook his head. "Does it matter why? Can't it be enough that I'm sorry?"

She sighed, her eyes silently roaming his face. "You're really sorry? You really mean that?"

"More than you know," he insisted.

Emily paused with a hand on the counter. Finally she softly said, "You could have contacted me at some point. You could have told me what went wrong, why you left."

"It had nothing to do with you, Emily," he lied. He couldn't hurt her anymore. It was the last thing he wanted. He rubbed his forehead, his mind whirling with memories of that awful night when his parents told him the role he had played in her father's death so many years earlier, the night he realized that his entire life up until that point was an illusion, that he wasn't the person this town thought he was, that he could never be the man they wanted him to be. "It was this town, my parents. These…expectations!"

"I never expected anything from you, Scott," she said, searching his eyes. "All I ever expected from you was what you promised me."

He grimaced at her words. "I wanted to fulfill those promises, Emily. I just…" He shook his head. "I was too young to know how to handle it."

The expression in her eyes went flat. "It wasn't the time for us, I guess."

"I guess not," he managed.

Silence fell over the kitchen. In the distance, he could hear the old church bell toll the hour. He remembered how much Emily loved that sound. She used to tell him it gave her a feeling of hope, a feeling of anticipation that something wonderful was happening. He'd told her she was being romantic, caught up in fantasies about wedding days and white dresses, but inwardly he was charmed by the simple pleasures she found in life.

"What are you smiling about?" she asked now.

"Do you remember the time you told your mother we were going to be studying all day in the library for a big test and we drove to New York instead? Made it less than two hours, too."

"You always drove too fast." Emily laughed. "That was the worst lie I ever told and I still feel bad about it."

Scott felt his gut stir. Determined to cling to something good, he pressed, "I remember you came with me to the top of the Empire State Building, even though you were always afraid of heights."

"I still am." Emily's lips twisted into a smile. "I knew how much you wanted to go up, though. And I didn't want to miss a moment of the day with you."

"After that, you insisted I keep your feet on the ground." He grinned as the details of that day came clearer. He hadn't thought of it in a long time. "I took you to Central Park."

"You set up that picnic for us, even though it was freezing outside. My hands were shaking so hard, I spilled my coffee all over the blanket." She smiled.

"Hey, I thought I was being romantic!" he said, but he was laughing now, too. He would do it all differently if he took Emily back to the city again. He'd do a lot of things differently.

She tipped her head. "You were romantic," she said lightly, but a shadow crossed over her face. "You were…very sweet."

His chest tightened. "We had a lot of good times together, Em."

She smiled sadly. "We did."

Scott took a step back. He didn't trust himself around her. Her full, pink lips were slightly parted, and an irrational and all-consuming urge to step forward and claim her mouth with his erupted in him. But as always, his desire for her was drowned with guilt.

In a perfect world he and Emily might have had something, but he had learned a long time ago that the world was cruel and she of all people probably shared the thought.

"Emily—" he started, and then stopped. Without thinking, without processing his actions, he had reached over and placed his hand on hers, as naturally as he had a thousand times before. She stiffened under his touch, her gaze widening as she glanced down to his hand, and he knew he should release it. He should let her go the way he intended to all those years ago. But he couldn't, damn it. He couldn't.

He wrapped his fingers around hers, watching the soft rise and fall of her shoulders, the way her lashes fluttered. Her hand felt small in his, exactly as it always had, and he realized in that moment that no matter what had changed, some things still hadn't. She was still the girl he'd always loved.

"I should probably get going," he said, releasing her and backing away. He smiled as she lifted her gaze to his. "It's been nice talking to you, though, Emily. Really nice."

There was a lingering sadness in her eyes. "You too, Scott."

He hesitated, wishing he could reach out and take her hand again, pull her close and kiss her lips and feel her body close to his.

He turned on his heel, inhaling sharply. No good would come of that. No good at all. He had caused Emily enough grief to last a lifetime; he didn't need to think about breaking her heart again while he was at it.

Chapter Five

Emily heard the tread of Scott's footsteps on the stairs at about half past six. She'd been waiting for his arrival with bated breath since her shift ended at four, and now she tilted her head and strained her ear as she mentally followed his path. His stride remained even as he approached her door and passed it.

She checked her watch. It was Wednesday, which meant Julia would be indisposed at the yarn shop with the weekly open project knitting group. Emily usually looked forward to Wednesday nights—it was a chance to see her friends Holly Tate and Abby Webster from The White Barn Inn, as well as a few of the other women from town—but tonight she had more important things on her mind than finishing the merino wool cowl she wouldn't wear until October or catching up on the latest gossip in town or over at Holly's inn.

She popped into the bathroom and regarded herself in the mirror. Carefully, she applied an extra touch of blush to her cheeks and took a brush to her long, thick hair. Better. She inhaled deeply, checked her reflection from a few more angles, flicked off the light as she tiptoed into the kitchen, and then stopped. Why was she was sneaking around her own apartment like a cat burglar?

She shook her head at her folly. The truth was that since learning Scott was staying only one door down the hall, her heart had been permanently filled with anticipation. For what, she chastised herself, the odd chance he came knocking at three in the morning to profess his undying love?

Life just didn't work that way. Much as she wished it did.

Still, she wasn't ready to give up on him just yet. She knew he had been as surprised as she was when he'd taken her hand today. She'd seen that glimmer of shock—and heat—pass through his eyes. But he hadn't snatched his hand back, hadn't made up an excuse at all. Instead, he'd let it stay there, the weight of it on hers reminding her of the closeness they had once shared, making her long for him in places deep inside herself, places she had forgotten even existed.

She shivered now, recalling his touch. No, she couldn't give up just yet. Something about the softness in his voice when he apologized gave her reason to hesitate. He'd sounded so sincere. Maybe there was more reason to his departure than he'd let on. If so, she was determined to get to the bottom of it.

Emily picked up the fresh cherry pie that was cooling on the counter and bent down to inhale its sweet aroma. Perfect. Listening for any further sounds of life in the building, Emily carefully unlatched the door and padded quietly down to the end of the hall. Her knuckles felt tentative against the smooth grain of Scott's door, and she chewed her lip, wondering if she should try again—more assertively this time—when the door swung open and Scott's inquisitive gaze met her eyes.

Well, you've done it now, Em. Keep going, girl. You can't exactly turn and run...

She tipped her head and curved her lips into a smile, willing her voice not to quiver. "Thought I'd thank you for helping with the cabinet today," she said, extending hands that were holding the pie swaddled in a crisp cotton tea cloth. It had seemed like such a good idea two hours ago, and now watching Scott's sea-blue gaze roam from her face to the oozing pie in her hands, she began to waver. "It's cherry," she added, even though that much was glaringly oblivious.

Scott's lips twitched into a grin. "Should I grab a towel? Start running the shower?"

She laughed—louder than she had planned as the nerves found release. "Don't worry. I think my pie tossing days are behind me."

"I have to admit you have a better arm than I remembered." He flashed a megawatt smile and pulled the door wide. "Want to come in?"

Emily feigned hesitation and then said with a forced shrug, "Um...sure. Why not?"

She stepped over the threshold and swept her eyes over the room, from the perfectly made bed to the small kitchenette to the en suite bathroom to the open suitcase, still packed and ready. He certainly hadn't made himself at home, she observed.

Her heart sank. He really wasn't planning on sticking around for long.

"I had been thinking of stopping by your place later, actually," he said, watching her carefully, and her heart skipped a beat.

"Oh?"

He cast her a crooked grin. The sudden boyish quality to his expression took her back twelve years, to the time and place when he'd captured her heart. She could still feel the lurch of her pulse when he took her in his arms... If she closed her eyes she could still smell the damp heat of his skin, the musk of his hair. The way his soft lips had—

"I wasn't sure it was such a good idea, though," he continued. A shadow crept over his rugged features.

"Couldn't bear to face the wrath of Julia?" Emily lifted a brow as she met his gaze and they both slipped into easier smiles. "She was a little hard on you last night," she admitted.

Scott shrugged. "She had her reasons." His jaw set. "I had it coming anyway."

He caught her eye and her breath hitched. She swallowed hard, forcing herself to remember the way they had left things this afternoon, the memories they shared and treasured. "Some things are best forgotten," she said lightly, wondering if she was convincing him of this any better than herself.

She stared at the still-packed suitcase, open on the top of the dresser. Memories or no memories, she and Scott weren't meant to be. Not then. Not now. Not ever. Why couldn't she just accept it once and for all?

"First love isn't easily forgotten," Scott replied, his voice so low she barely heard him. She glanced up to him, noticing the way he stared pensively out the window. He turned to her suddenly, his smile sad, his eyes still distant and focused on something beyond this room. "I know I never forgot you, Emily."

Scott led Emily to the drop-leaf table near the window, sliding over two chairs, then handed her a plate. It was either that or the bed, and something told him that inviting Emily to sit there was more than his self-control could handle right now. As it was, he barely trusted himself to be alone in this small room with her at all. There was too much bubbling below the surface, screaming for release. He was torn between blurting out the dark, hidden secrets or reaching across the table and pulling her into his arms. He wanted to taste her lips, explore her mouth and feel the swell of her breasts against his chest. He wanted to run his fingers through her hair and trace the length of her neck with his kisses until she shivered under his touch.

He gritted his teeth. Obviously, none of those were options at the moment.

"You're very talented, you know," he said as he sank his fork into the pie. "Have you ever thought about pursuing your culinary skills?"

Emily's brow seemed to furrow slightly at the question, but she recovered quickly. "Well, I work at Sweetie Pie," she pointed out.

Scott nodded. "True. I guess I just meant something of your own. With your talent...well, there must be something you could do with it."

As he met her bewildered expression, his heart tensed with regret. Damn, he couldn't do anything right with Emily!

"Well, I didn't have the means to go to college, and my mother needed my help here," Emily said, and Scott felt the evidence of his shame heat his neck. "But then, you knew that."

"I didn't mean to upset you," he protested, his eyes searching the small oak table for retribution. "I honestly meant it as a compliment."

Emily offered him a slow grin. Scott shifted uncomfortably on the stiff wooden chair to ward off his growing attraction.

"Don't worry," she said easily. She lifted her chin and chewed thoughtfully. "If I didn't know better, I might think I make you nervous."

A scoff released from his lips, but he didn't bother to deny it. He'd done enough lying for one lifetime. "Would that be so hard to believe?"

"As a matter of fact, it would."

"Well, you do make me a little nervous," he admitted with a wink.

Emily guffawed, but her eyes shone with interest. "Since when?"

Scott shrugged. "Since always. You were…special." He held her eyes from the hood of his brow. "I guess that's why you meant so much to me."

Her mouth thinned. "Not enough," she said matter-of-factly, glancing down at her plate.

It was the moment he had waited for, alone with her, calm, simple. He wanted to tell her the truth and shield her from it all at once. "I know you still don't believe me," he said, swallowing hard. "I did love you, Emily."

Her brow furrowed. "You sure had a weird way of showing it," she said, but he could hear the pain scratch through her voice. He could take the confusion away in one simple sentence. Give her the reason she craved for why he'd left so suddenly. But doing so…

He couldn't do it. He'd lost her once. If she knew, she'd be gone forever. He didn't think he could face that. Not yet.

"Young and dumb." He forced a casual tone, smiling tightly. He held her eyes with his, watching the light flicker through her wide black pupils. "Guess some things aren't meant to be."

"Guess not."

Silence stretched in the room, and Scott forked off a piece of the crumbling crust. When he'd cleaned his plate, he cut another thick slice, noticing Emily's watchful eye across the table. "Sorry, couldn't resist," he said with a grin.

She smiled. "Enjoy. The leftovers are yours. If there are any," she added, and then started giggling into her napkin.

Scott chuckled and broke through the lattice crust with his fork. "I don't know how you keep your figure working in that place," he said, dragging his eyes over her slim shoulders and taught waist.

"If you're trying to butter me up, you don't have to go that far," she said, but a flush had crept over her soft porcelain cheeks.

Scott leaned across the table. "It's Julia I really need to worry about kissing up to now, isn't it?"

Emily gave him a sly grin. "I think she's had her say and now she'll let it drop."

Scott watched her, unconvinced. "I'm not so sure." Emily's sister had always been a spitfire, even when she was younger. He could still remember the time he'd had to bribe Julia to keep quiet with a bag of candy after she'd spotted him through parted curtains giving Emily a good-night kiss on the front porch. Looking back, he almost chuckled aloud. Emily's mother wouldn't have minded. It was his parents who had never supported the relationship.

Emily waved her hand through the air. "Oh, don't worry about Julia. She might never admit it, but deep down I think she's tickled pink you're staying down the hall. It's the most exciting thing that's happened to her outside of *Passion's Crest.*"

Scott sputtered and coughed into his hand. *"Passion's Crest?"* he repeated.

A pink blush stained Emily's cheeks. "It's a soap opera. Julia's, um, rather caught up with it."

Scott's lips twitched with amusement. "I see."

"So, don't let her scare you off," she added hurriedly. "She can take a bit of drama."

Scott considered the meaning behind her words. She didn't want him to stay away, he realized. He sat back in his chair, watching her pick at the crumbs on her plate with the tip of her fork. "I'd really like to move forward, Emily," he said. "I never felt right about the way things ended. I...I want to make things right for you while I'm here in town." He forced a grin, wondering if his tone betrayed his inner concern. "Think you can forgive me?"

Emily's eyes roamed his face quietly. "You seem to feel really guilty," she pondered aloud.

"More than you know." He swallowed the last of the pie, tasting nothing.

Interest flickered in her gaze. After a pause, she tipped her head and smiled pleasantly. "I can see that cherry pie is still your favorite," she commented, motioning to his empty plate.

"And on that note, I think I'll take seconds." As he cut into the pie once more, he stopped himself, and slid her a glance. "I mean...thirds," he said, grinning.

"Comfort food," her voice came softly.

"When I was younger, my family and I always looked forward to a homemade pie. It seemed to always make things just a little brighter."

His stomach burned and he attempted to numb the pain with a hearty bite. If he kept going like this, he'd lose the physique he'd achieved by spending an hour in the gym each morning. Right now, he honestly didn't care.

"You remember how tight money was for my family after my father died." She paused, and drew a deep breath. "My mom was working two or three jobs at times and couldn't always make it home for dinner, but Sunday she was always at home, and we looked forward to that night all week, because that's when she made pie."

It was a sweet story, nearly pleasant enough to make him forget the horrible part he had played in her young life. It gave him some hope to learn that there were glimmers of happiness in her childhood after all. "She baked every Sunday?"

"Every Sunday." She smiled at the memory. Catching his stare, she smiled and shrugged. "Guess I associate pies with a feeling of comfort and safety. Sounds silly, I know."

Scott swallowed hard, his gaze lingering on the fullness of her mouth, the slender frame of her shoulders as she hunched over her plate. "I don't think it's silly at all."

He cleared his throat. "My family could have learned a lot from yours. My dad was always at work and when we did eat together, there was no real laughter, no warmth."

"Guess I should be happy you never brought me over for dinner, then," Emily said, but through her smile Scott could sense the twinge of hurt and confusion.

He pressed his lips together, thinking of how cold his father had always been to Emily, how his mother would casually change the subject when Scott mentioned her. He'd asked to bring Emily to dinner once in the entire three years they dated, and his father had made it clear that she wasn't welcome. At the time, he'd attributed it to snobbery on his parents' part. Collins was a big name in town, an established name, and Emily was one of…*Those poor Porters.*

"My family wasn't like yours, Em. You know that. You all had something. Love, joy. You knew each other."

Emily tipped her head. "You didn't know your parents?"

"Not one bit."

Emily studied him thoughtfully. "I remember the time your father saw us walking down Main Street, holding hands." She shook her head at the memory. "I swear, he turned white as a ghost."

Scott scowled. "He barely said hello to us. Typical."

"Well, Lucy's been like the big sister I never had." She gave him a wan smile.

Scott nodded. "Lucy's great. But my parents… It was a reflection of them, not you, Emily."

A shadow darkened her gray eyes. "I've been meaning to tell you that I was sorry to hear about your father's condition."

Scott stiffened, sobered by the shift in topic. "Thanks."

"If you ever wanted to talk about it, I'm around." She hesitated. "I…I understand." Her eyes pleaded with his in a knowing connection.

"I appreciate that," he said tightly. He hated that everyone in town knew why he was back. His father was dying; he couldn't deny it any more than he could hide from it. It was a fact, and in a small town like Maple Woods, the truth had a way of seeping out and spreading like thick molasses. He grimaced to think of the secret he had only managed to harbor by leaving town all those years ago.

Nausea rose in his stomach as he sat in Emily's presence. Even after everything he had done to her, she was still standing here, offering to be his friend. And he needed a friend, damn it. He needed a friend now more than ever.

The problem was that he wanted a hell of a lot more than friendship from Emily. He wanted everything he knew she could have given him if things had been different. But relationships couldn't be founded on lies, and in twelve years he still hadn't found a way to explain himself to her.

"It's hard to lose a father," she commented, her eyes once again warming with understanding and all at once Scott knew this was a bad idea. He shouldn't be near her.

Shame bit at him, and he didn't trust himself to speak. If he did, he might tell her everything just to set himself free of the weight that he had carried with him for so long. Every word he spoke to her felt like a lie, but the truth was too unbearable to say aloud.

His hand inched across the table. Searching her soft gaze, he saw a kindness there that tugged at his chest. She was compassionate, sweet, but everyone had their limits.

She was watching him closely, her expression so pure, her eyes so trusting and sure, that he had to snatch his hand back before he did something he would later regret.

Finishing her last bite of crust, Emily's lips twisted with mischief as she eyed the pie. "Since you've had thirds, I suppose I may as well have seconds...."

"You don't want me eating alone." Scott smiled.

"No, that would be rude...."

"And it would give you a reason to stay and chat a little longer—"

A shadow crossed over Emily's face but when her lips curled into a slow smile, his heart soared. "I'd like that. I'd like that very much, actually."

Not tonight, he decided as he placed another slice of pie on her plate. Tonight wasn't the night to make up for the sins of his past. Tonight he was simply going to enjoy the present.

Julia was already home by the time Emily turned the key in the door, and she forced a sober expression as she stepped into the kitchen, where her sister was preparing a pot of tea.

"Want a cup?" Julia asked, barely sparing her a glance.

"I'd love one." Emily slipped off her sandals while Julia stacked the teapot, two mugs and a plate of cookies on an old wooden tray and then followed her into the living room.

"You're getting home late tonight," Julia observed, carefully setting the tray on the coffee table—it rattled precariously from the weight and Emily reached out a hand to steady it. "Thanks." Her sister settled back into the sofa and pulled a chenille throw on top of her pajama-clad legs. While the day had been warm with sunshine, a cool spring breeze filtered in through the cracked window. "If Lucy keeps working you this hard, you're going to need to plan for early retirement."

Emily smiled benignly and reached for the remote control. "I wonder what drama unfolded today," she mused aloud, her tone ominous but laced with mock excitement. It didn't feel good to skirt Julia's comments. Her sister thought she was being worked to the bone, when really she had been enjoying a pleasant evening with Scott. There was plenty she would love to share, and she was sure that Julia would be thrilled to glean further insight into the elusive Scott Collins, but for some reason, she wasn't ready for the spell to be broken just yet. It would seem like a betrayal in a way, to sit here talking about Scott when he was only twenty feet down the hall from where she sat. Besides, something about keeping the details of her visit with him to herself made it feel more special. Once she opened up to Julia, there was no telling what type of speculation and doubts her sister would inadvertently stir up. Not that there was anything to speculate about.

Emily pinched her lips and glanced sidelong at her sister. Beside her, Julia was happily munching on a cookie, her eyes wide as the opening credits of *Passion's Crest* rolled. It was then that Emily realized she hadn't even checked the mail yet today, and that for some reason she didn't really want to. For today at least, she had everything she wanted right here in Maple Woods: a job she loved, her sister and the man she had loved for as long as she could remember.

As she stirred two lumps of sugar into her tea and cupped it in her hands, her stomach began to stir uneasily. She tried to force her concentration on the television and the gripping ups and downs of her favorite characters, but it was no use.

"Emily? Emily?" Startled, Emily turned to see Julia motioning to the remote next to Emily. "Are you going to fast forward through the commercials or make me sit here stuffing my face while I wait for the next scene?" She held up a cookie to drive her complaint home.

Emily chuckled, picked up the remote and did as she was told.

"I thought I smelled a pie when I walked in here tonight," Julia said casually a few seconds later, her eyes shining. Emily looked away as her sister continued, "Since you weren't at the bakery when I passed by, I thought maybe you had made some dessert for us tonight." She held her gaze steady, her expression blank. "Guess I wasn't the lucky recipient."

A heavy pause fell over the room and Emily bit back a wave of frustration laced with amusement. Pursing her lips, she paused the screen just after the last commercial of the set and placed the remote control on the coffee table so she could give Julia her full attention. "If you knew I wasn't at the bakery tonight, why did you make that comment when I came in the door?"

Julia shrugged and her lips curled with mischief. "It seemed easier than asking what the view is like from Scott's window."

Emily's eyes flung open. After the shock had left her, she tossed her head back in laughter. "I can't get anything past you," she said ruefully, wagging a playful finger at her sister's triumphant expression. "How'd you guess?"

"*Guess?* I heard." Julia arched a brow. "The walls here are very thin, you know," she said pointedly.

Discomfort tightened Emily's chest at the thought of Scott still so close by. Lowering her voice and hoping Julia would follow her lead, she confessed, "Fine. I stopped by Scott's room this evening."

Julia's grin lingered. "How'd that go?"

Emily shrugged. "Fine, I guess."

"Doesn't sound just fine to me."

Emily sighed. She leaned back against the couch and blew on the steam rising up from her mug. "The truth is that it doesn't matter how things went, Julia. The guy's only passing through town. He's made it very clear he doesn't want to stay any longer than he has to."

"Unless he can be convinced otherwise."

"Please," she said, but despite her protestation, Emily couldn't help but feel her hope becoming somewhat restored by Julia's words. She pushed the thought aside immediately and locked her sister's eyes. "This isn't like our soap opera, Julia. This is Maple Woods, not *Passion's Crest.* I'm not Marlene and Scott isn't Rafe Turner. I can't stir up some drama and twist things around to keep him here. Real life doesn't work that way."

Julia just tipped her head mildly, and said, "If that's how you want it to be."

"What's that supposed to mean?" Emily shot back.

"Seems to me that you sat back and let Scott walk away from you all those years ago. And now you're about to do it all over again."

Emily's temper flared. "That's not fair."

"Isn't it? What Scott did to you was wrong, there's no doubt about it, but I don't remember you asking for his whereabouts, demanding an explanation or trying to understand why things didn't work out. Seems to me you made it pretty easy for him then, and you're making it just as easy now."

Emily's chest was heavy with the pounding of her heart and she set the cup of steaming tea down before her shaking hands caused it to spill. She turned to glare at her sister. "What do you suggest then, Julia? Last I checked, you were up in arms about the way Scott treated me, and you made sure he knew it last night, too. Why the sudden change of heart?"

"Scott's no angel, but you like him and you always have. You've never been good at opening your heart since Daddy died. Then when Scott let you down…"

"This isn't about Dad," Emily said sharply.

Julia stared at her, unconvinced. "I just think that if you want something enough, you have to go after it. Take the risk."

Unbelievable. "And going over there tonight wasn't a risk?" The pitch in her voice caused Emily to wince.

Julia paused. "I just don't want to see you spend the next twelve years the way you've spent the last, that's all."

Oh, believe me, Emily thought with newfound resolve, *I don't plan to.*

She stood and handed the remote control to Julia, ignoring her younger sister's pleas to sit back down. "But we still don't know if Brad's the father!" she protested.

Lifting her chin, Emily excused herself to bed, denying the little part of her that really did want to know who had fathered Fleur's baby—Brad, or his evil twin brother, Chad? The suspense was killing her, but she thickened her determination. It could wait.

As she passed by the stack of mail Julia must have brought in with her, she glanced through the contents halfheartedly—nope, nothing for her except bills—and then wandered back to her bedroom. The week had caught up with her, but it would not keep her awake. No, tonight she would dream, but not of girlish hopes or unfilled dreams. Tonight she would dream of the future. The one she could control and make her own. Even if Scott would never be a part of it.

Chapter Six

Julia's words still haunted Emily the next morning as she walked down Main Street, holding an umbrella over her head as shelter from the morning drizzle. Leave it to her sister to voice every sinking sensation she had tried desperately to ignore for so many years of her life. Sometimes it was easier to put your head in the sand and keep going than to the face the truth. Even about yourself.

The soft glow illuminating from the Sweetie Pie Bakery was warm and inviting on this dreary day, and despite her equally drab mood, Emily felt herself perk up as she opened the door and stepped inside. The sweet scents of butter and sugar teased her as she shook out her umbrella. "Hello!" she called out.

"In the kitchen!" cried back Lucy's familiar voice.

Emily propped her umbrella in the stand near the

door and wiped her feet on the mat before heading back to the kitchen. Lucy's face was flushed, her eyes bright, and Emily immediately noted it wasn't from the heat of the oven.

"Is everything okay?" she asked gently, tilting her head in concern.

Lucy blinked a few times and managed a watery smile. "Sorry about this. It's just..." She inhaled sharply, unable to finish her sentence.

Slowly, Emily retrieved her apron from the hook on the door, taking time in tying it around her waist. Lucy and Scott had always had a complicated relationship with their parents from what Emily knew, but that didn't mean they didn't love them. Mr. and Mrs. Collins rarely ever came into the diner or town, but the few times they did, Emily couldn't help but notice the way Lucy fluttered around nervously, clearly hoping to meet her parents' approval. She wanted them to be proud of her, even if she hadn't chosen the path they had wanted for her.

"I stopped by my parents' house last night to drop off a casserole," Lucy explained, her back to Emily as she carefully set a pie on a cake pedestal. "My dad looked even worse than the night before."

"I'm so sorry to hear that." Despite the hard edge to Mr. Collins and the standoffish, cold nature of his wife, Emily couldn't wish any sorrow onto her friend. Or Scott.

"I'm afraid there might not be much time," Lucy continued, and Emily frowned. "All the better that Scott came back when he did, though I'm not sure what good it's done." She hesitated, rubbing her brow. "At least I can know I tried."

Emily nodded slowly, working up the courage to ask the burning question she had harbored for so long. It was one of Maple Woods's greatest mysteries. "Why do you think he stayed away so long?"

Lucy shrugged heavily and shook her head. "Oh, who knows really." She sighed, whisking some chocolate mousse. "I was out of the house and married with a kid when Scottie left. All I know is that he and my parents got in some huge fight that summer after he graduated from high school. I thought going off to college would help him calm down, let things blow over on both sides, but the distance only seemed to become permanent then. And he never came back."

Emily narrowed her eyes in concentration as she added some heavy cream to a stainless steel bowl and whisked in a few teaspoons of confectioners' sugar. She tried to connect the events, but to her frustration, she couldn't make sense of them.

As the cream began to hold peaks, she mused, "Did your parents ever tell you what the disagreement was about?" Deep down she'd always assumed it was about her. Though Scott had never said it, she'd known his parents hadn't approved of their relationship. They'd wanted him to go to college and take over the family company. Not marry a girl whose father had used to work for them.

"No, never." Lucy stopped stirring as a shadow crept over her face. "It was strange, actually. I tried to talk to them about it at first, but the more I pressed, the more firm they grew in their insistence that I stay out of it. I was so stunned by the intensity of their reaction that I never directly approached Scott about it, either."

"And he never opened up?"

Lucy shook her head. "Nope. I always gently encouraged him to come home—God knows how much I missed him and wanted him back. Each time he turned down the suggestion, I knew that was my answer. He wasn't ready. He hadn't gotten over whatever had happened between him and our parents."

"Do you think he has now?"

Lucy's brow pinched and she huffed, "No. I don't. I had to practically beg him to come back to town and when he came to the house the other night, it was very clear he wasn't ready to forgive them. A dying man, can you imagine?" Her eyes flashed on Emily's, and Emily, startled, stopped whisking the cream. This was very odd, indeed.

"What did he say?" she murmured, trying to imagine the scene.

Lucy threw up her hands and a dollop of chocolate mousse splattered against a wall. "I couldn't hear. It was muffled through the door and the next thing I knew Scott came flying down the stairs, telling me that I never should have made him come back, that it had just made everything worse." She sighed, and Emily noticed her hand was trembling as she reached for a dishrag. "Maybe he was right."

"He loves you," Emily said, and Lucy granted her a brave smile.

"In his own way," Lucy said with a bob of her head.

"How were your parents afterward?" Emily asked carefully, sensing Lucy was on the verge of tears.

Lucy considered the question. "I don't think they were surprised," she said simply. She turned to the oven and bent down to check on the status of a meringue.

A tight knot formed in Emily's stomach and she set her whisk down on the counter, staring into the thick peaks of whipped cream. If Scott couldn't even handle being in town after all this time, what made her think he would even consider staying in Maple Woods a day longer than he had to?

All the more reason to get out of town herself, she decided, her mouth thinning to a grim line as she began crushing chocolate cookies for the crust with the back of a rolling pin. Today's special was Chocolate Truffle and so help her, she would pound her emotions out on the cookie crust if it took all day.

The phone trilled and Lucy walked over to the counter to answer it. Emily bit back the wave of disappointment that their conversation had been interrupted. All for the better, she knew deep down. The more she thought about Scott, talked about Scott, schemed about Scott, dreamed about Scott, spent time with Scott…well, the bigger this rut would get. It was time to start living her own life and stop worrying about what Scott did with his. He had chosen his own path for reasons she might never understand but would simply have to accept.

From behind the wall, Lucy murmured a few words and then set down the receiver. "They're short staffed at the diner," she explained. And then, before Emily could comment, her expression collapsed. "I don't think I can handle going over there today," she admitted, her eyes pleading.

Emily searched her friend's face in bewilderment. "Of course not," she said, realizing that Lucy's Place required too much energy and pep when you were feeling as low as Lucy was this morning. She set down her rolling pin. "Why don't I cover the diner today and you can stay put? It's quieter here, and baking is therapeutic."

Lucy managed a smile and placed a hand on Emily's arm in affection. "Thank you." The intensity of her tone struck Emily and she frowned as she wordlessly untied her apron and placed it back on the hook. The diner was one of Lucy's favorite places to be—she usually loved chatting with the regulars that stopped in. If the thought of going there was this unbearable, then things with Mr. Collins must be very bad indeed.

How, then, could Scott still be so hardened to it all?

It was nearly eleven o'clock by the time Scott looked up from the pile of papers he'd been studying all morning. The large, polished mahogany desk in his father's office was strewn with blueprints and spreadsheets. Scott had been staring at them for hours, and he still didn't feel any closer to knowing how best to handle the information in front of him.

Collins Construction had been around for generations, serving as one of the largest businesses in Maple Woods, and it had always been a sound and financially secure company—his father had made sure of that, Scott thought bitterly. Judging from the books, business was now at a standstill, and the company had downsized in the past twelve years, resulting in two sets of layoffs already. Scott knew that the local economy hadn't been strong, and of course there was only so much building a town like Maple Woods required, but the surrounding towns that had once called on Collins Construction to bid seemed to be opting for larger, more modern companies, and the only project even scheduled was the rebuilding of the town library.

Scott reached into his pocket and pulled out a tube of antacids. Popping one into his mouth, he couldn't help but reflect on the irony of the situation before him. This was exactly the situation his father had wanted to avoid—financial ruin of his beloved company. Everything he had done—or failed to do—had been in a vain effort to avoid this exact scenario.

What a waste.

As darkening thoughts encroached, Scott rolled up the blueprints and tucked some papers into a file folder, opting to take the back door to his car to avoid any potential exchange with the staff. The last thing he needed was someone inquiring about the health of his father, or wanting to engage in a conversation about how it felt to be back in town after all this time. It felt lousy. And confusing as hell. But try telling them that.

He grinned wryly as he imagined the shock of his father's white-haired assistant if he gave her such a retort, and with a newfound smile on his face, he slipped into the red convertible and revved the engine. The familiar sound eased his mind, reminding him of the life he had waiting for him back in Seattle.

Even if it was a lonely life.

The drive to town was short—less than eight minutes—and he forced his attention on the road as he drove down Main Street, doing his best to ignore the ogling from the townsfolk strolling past. Let them think what they would. They'd probably already come up with some tantalizing speculation for what had kept him away and what had brought him back. He smiled grimly. Their wildest imaginations would never beat reality.

Or so he hoped.

After parking the car in a spot behind the diner, he pulled open the door of the establishment and glanced around. In a brief phone call with Max Hamilton that morning, they'd agreed to meet at noon, but he hadn't thought to ask for a description. He'd assumed he'd notice an unfamiliar face, but his recollection of the locals had faded. He struggled to remember names, and a dozen years had turned old neighbors into strangers. He swept his eyes to the back of the room, interest causing his pulse to take speed as he spotted Emily cheerfully chatting with a customer. The man was laughing at something she was saying, and he reached out and patted her hand in a friendly way. Too friendly, Scott thought, frowning.

"Emily. Hi." His abrupt tone forced her attention from the other man and Emily's sharp gaze darted to his, brightening as he closed the distance between them. He broke her stare to size up the man who was casually sitting on the barstool as if he owned the place. The man's familiarity with Lucy's diner and with Emily unnerved him, and he clenched his teeth at the sudden disadvantage.

Regret, he realized, owning the emotion. But then, neither his sister nor Emily were his to be so possessive over. He'd given up that right twelve years ago.

"I don't think we've met." He stared grim-faced at the man beside him, disturbed by the easy grin his opponent wore.

"Max Hamilton," the man said, extending a hand.

His shoulders relaxed. "Scott Collins," he said. He gave a firm shake. "Good to meet you."

"Emily and I were just talking about the Spring Fling this Saturday," Max explained. "Apparently they need a few volunteers for the pie-eating contest."

"You up for the challenge?" Emily asked from across the counter. She shared a grin with Max, clearly a good friend, and then drifted her gaze suggestively to Scott.

"I think I've had enough of pie contests for one week," he bantered, and Emily's cheeks grew pink.

"Ah, yes," Max chuckled. "I heard you stood in for the mayor this week. Made you a bit of a town hero, from what I gathered."

Some town hero all right. Even after his disappearing act, somehow he was still the football champ in the eyes of the locals. Still the kid who had put Maple Woods on the map.

If they only knew.

"Needless to say, I think I'll stick to watching from the sidelines from now on." He grinned, and catching Emily's eyes, gave her a wink.

Emily's face flushed. She turned to Max, refusing to meet Scott's eye again. "Well, Max, it looks like it's all you, then."

"What can I say? I think I'm as in love with Lucy's pies as I am with my own fiancée," Max joked. Then turning to Scott he explained, "It was actually right at this very counter that I first realized I was in love with Holly."

"Let me guess," Emily said, "you were eating a slice of pie while you were at it?"

Max lifted his hands helplessly. "I was smitten."

"You know, I probably made that pie," Emily said. "Lucy and I always share the task."

"Well, then I'll give a toast to you at our wedding," Max said gallantly. Elbowing Scott he said in a loud whisper, "Clearly, the woman knows her way to a man's heart."

That she does, Scott thought as his chest tightened. He shifted his gaze to Emily, whose face showed no sign of losing its pink glow anytime soon. He smiled to himself, looking down at his feet to spare her further attention. She hadn't outgrown it, in all these years. He used to love to tease her in school until she blushed, until he knew he'd gotten to her.

"Or at least the way to his stomach." Emily refilled Max's coffee and poured a fresh mug for him.

"Is Lucy at the bakery?" Scott asked, glancing around the crowded diner for his sister.

Emily's face took on a worried expression. "She felt like avoiding the hustle and bustle, and they were short-staffed here today."

Scott felt his brow furrow with concern, and he peered out the far window, hoping for a glimpse of his sister in the storefront across the road, wishing he could make things better. She was probably upset about their father, and why shouldn't she be? She didn't know who he was, not like Scott did.

Scott swallowed a swig of coffee. He was the last person to be comforting Lucy.

Lifting his chin, Max said, "Ready to talk about the project?"

"I'll let you two chat," Emily said, already backing away to take an order from a couple at the other side of the counter.

"I'll see you at the Spring Fling," Max said to her before her attention had fully faded. He turned to Scott and suggested, "You'll be there, too, right? We can all grab a drink or something."

Scott felt Emily's wide eyes lock with his. A shadow passed over her pale gray irises and a question sparked in her large pupils. Despite himself, he said, "That sounds great!"

Because it did. It sounded really, really great.

Emily watched from the corner of her eye as Scott and Max settled into a corner booth, a stack of rolled blueprints and paperwork spread between them. Her mind on anything but the job, she stopped herself just seconds before she overflowed Mr. Hawkins's coffee cup. His eyes narrowed with judgment when they met hers and she bit back an exasperated sigh. Mr. Hawkins was a regular at Lucy's Place. The diner wouldn't be the same without his familiar presence, but seriously, how much coffee could one old man consume?

"Can I get you anything to go with that, Mr. Hawkins?" She forced a pleasant smile and held his dark gaze patiently.

"Just another bowl of creamers," he grumbled.

Emily pinched her lips and nodded before sliding a fresh bowl of creamers to the side of his coffee mug. "Anything else?"

Mr. Hawkins held her gaze with challenge, and she straightened her spine. They both knew he didn't plan to order anything—he never did—but she couldn't help herself. Once or twice a week, she liked to encourage him to eat something, if not for Lucy and

George, then for himself. He was painfully thin and she knew that since his wife had died, all hope of a hot meal had probably disappeared with her. She smiled, relaxing her shoulders, and made a mental note to bring a pie over to him one day. He'd enjoy it. Even if he'd never admit it.

The sandwiches Max and Scott had ordered were up, and she slid them off the hot plate and balanced them on her palm and forearm, grabbing a fresh pot of coffee with her free hand. It still amazed her that she could do this—ten years ago when she started working at Lucy's Place she often came home in tears. Lucy and George had been patient with her, despite the chaos she caused. "Waitressing is underrated!" Lucy would quip with an encouraging smile, and sure enough, Emily had gotten the knack after awhile. Now and then, Lucy still broke out into random laughter when she recalled Emily sitting on the floor, broken plates surrounding her, covered in three customers' orders and a butter knife stuck in her hair.

The two men were deep in conversation, hunched over the table, and oblivious to her presence as she rounded the counter and strode to their table. "Here you go," she said cheerfully, her heart flip-flopping as she caught Scott's eye. He smiled and looked down quickly, causing her chest to swell with sudden hope.

Nervous. He said she made him nervous.

Scott cleared some papers away to make room for the plates, and she set them down, squaring her shoulders as she stood again. "Can I get you anything else?" she asked, eyeing their mugs. Max's mug was still full and as she began to walk away, Scott tipped his own mug back, devouring the dregs.

"A refill would be great."

Well, that was interesting. She paused and tightened her grip on the handle of the coffeepot, planning her next move. It was ridiculous to think this way, truly masochistic. The man had shattered her heart and fled town. He was just being friendly. Or thirsty. There was nothing to read into. The facts were what they were and the fact was that Scott Collins wasn't going to be a regular in this place. No matter how badly she wished he would be. They were just two people who used to know each other. Two people who shared a moment in time. A moment that was long over.

"Are you going to be around the building later tonight?" he asked.

Her pulse stilled and she forced a breath before she replied evenly, "Probably…" She noted Max's amused grin from the corner of her eye and gritted her teeth. Must be easy for him to find this funny now that he was living in domestic bliss with Holly. How soon he had forgotten what it was like to be single. "Guess it depends on what time I get out of here tonight," she said briskly, forcing all her attention on Scott as she did her best to ignore the sparkle in Max's electric blue eyes.

Why? she wanted to ask. *Why does it matter if I will be home tonight? Why do you want to know?*

"Why?" she blurted, unable to stop herself.

Scott's expression froze. She waited, heart pounding, for his answer. "Just wondered," he said, breaking her stare, and Emily bit back a fresh wave of fury. Great, so she looks eager and he's just wondering!

"Well, enjoy your meal," she said and turned her back to refill Mr. Hawkins's coffee cup before he could start complaining.

Scott bit into his sandwich and chewed thoughtfully, trying his best to concentrate on the project details in front of him and not on the sight of Emily's slim hips as they swayed ever so alluringly away from the table. He rubbed his jaw, agitated. He was getting too used to her presence. And no good could come from that. For either of them.

"You know Emily well?"

Scott met Max's inquisitive gaze and shrugged. "We grew up together more or less. We went to school together. She was a year behind me."

"High school sweethearts?"

Scott narrowed his eyes but detected no menace in Max's expression. He was a decent guy. A guy's guy. Someone he'd probably be good friends with outside this town. They were roughly the same age, and both had a straightforward head for business. And a weakness for the women of Maple Woods, it would seem.

Scott shook his head. "Nothing serious," he lied.

Max nodded thoughtfully but something told Scott he wasn't buying it. Was it that obvious? He set down his sandwich and focused on the blueprints. Emily's presence was a distraction he couldn't afford right now, or ever. Max had commissioned Collins Construction to rebuild the library—a project that was budgeted for enough money for Scott to sit up and take seriously.

A real estate tycoon by profession, it was evident that Max knew the ins and outs of a project this size.

From the small bit of research Scott had done on Hamilton Properties, Max had more than ten years of experience with retail and commercial development projects of a much larger scale than the Maple Woods Library.

"So I have to ask," Scott said. "Why invest in the rebuilding of the library? It doesn't seem to fit with the rest of your portfolio."

"Interesting question." Max chewed his club sandwich and sprinkled his fries with salt from the shaker. "I guess you could say my priorities have changed since I moved to Maple Woods. I came here to build a shopping mall, and ended up deciding I couldn't ruin the integrity of the town."

Integrity. A bitter taste filled Scott's mouth and he coated it with a mouthful of fries when what he really wanted was a cooling slice of that lemon meringue that was perched on the counter over near Emily...Emily. He broke his stare, catching Max watching him, and took a swig of his coffee.

"I'm told you're aware of my sister's involvement in this," he said, lowering his tone. "My nephew is a good kid."

"I agree, and Lucy and George are like family," Max added. Lightening the mood, he grinned. "It's nice that we can partner up and make things right for this project."

"About that—"

Across from him, Max's brow pinched. "Something wrong?"

"I have my own construction business back in Seattle, and as you can imagine, they can't operate without me for the duration this project will take."

Max frowned. "What do you propose?"

"I'm sure you're aware that my father is in poor health." He gauged Max's simple nod by way of response. "He's not expected to recover."

"I heard. I'm sorry." Max didn't feign surprise or overt emotion and Scott felt his shoulders ease, grateful to be able to keep the conversation focused.

"Yes, well…" He cleared his throat and shuffled through the papers until he found a printout of the plan he had compiled that morning in preparation for this meeting. He handed it to Max, who studied it carefully. "I've decided to take Collins Construction on as a subsidiary of my own company. This will allow me to hire the appropriate crew and overseers for the project."

It would also allow him, he knew, to take responsibility for what had happened to Richard Porter—to own the mistakes his father had tried to bury, to repair what could be fixed, even though the broken life the Porters had lived at his hand could never be glued back together.

"So you'll essentially manage it from Seattle?"

"Yes."

Max rubbed his chin thoughtfully, finally tilting his head in acceptance. "As long as the job gets done, I can't argue. You know what you're doing, and I trust you to handle the project as you see fit. I guess my one question for you is this…Why the hell do you want to get out of this town so badly?

"That obvious, huh?"

Max rose his eyebrows in response at the same time that Emily reappeared at their table to refill their water.

There was one reason Scott was desperate to get out of town. It wasn't his father. It wasn't even the business. Or the memories. The reason was the person standing less than two feet away from him. The person that was strangely starting to look like every reason to stay, rather than to go.

Twelve years ago he knew he would rather never see Emily again than lie to the girl he loved. And twelve years later, it was still the truth. He loved her, damn it. No amount of time was going to change that, and no amount of wishing was going to undo the reason they could never be together.

Chapter Seven

The caw of the crows through the half-open window next to her bed woke Emily as the first crack of sunlight peeked over the treetops in the distance. She rolled over and glanced at the clock on her bedside table. Then, with a groan, she flipped back over, snuggling deeper under the duvet, squeezing her eyes shut. She wished she could stay in bed all day, but it wasn't possible. Even though Sweetie Pie didn't open for another four hours, she knew she had to go in early to get a jump start on the baking.

They'd kept her at the diner until closing last night, which had its perks, really. After Scott's strange mood yesterday, she wasn't sure what was running through that handsome mind. She could spend the rest of her life wondering why Scott had treated her as he had, she could force it out of him, or she could see it for what it had been. Two young kids. Ancient history. Who was she to punish him for the sins of his past?

All the same, having a valid reason to avoid coming home last night had put her at ease just as the thought of another confusing conversation made her gut tighten. She didn't need to be falling for him all over again, and the more time she spent with him, the more she increased the odds of that happening. When she'd counted her tips last night, she'd known the extra shift was worth the effort double-fold. Her plan was to pay the rent for this place for six months out, just to give Julia a cushion and ease the blow of her departure. If she even ended up getting accepted to that cooking school, that is. Yesterday's mail had once again brought nothing but a stack of bills and catalogs for clothes neither she nor her sister could afford.

A knock on the door caught her attention and she turned to see Julia standing in the open doorway, looking hesitant. "I thought I saw you moving around. I didn't wake you, did I?"

"No," Emily said, her voice tight. It was the first exchange the sisters had shared since their argument the other night. She thought she was over it, but now she realized Julia's words still stung a bit. "I was going to make blueberry pancakes," Julia offered, her expression hopeful enough to make Emily soften her stance. "You interested?"

Emily glanced at the clock. "Sure, so long as it's quick. I need to be at Sweetie Pie's soon to get a start on today's menu."

Relief swept Julia's face as she bounded away, and the sound of pans clanking in the kitchen quickly followed. With a long, tired sigh, Emily pushed back the blankets and sat up, rolling her feet onto the old oak floors. Outside her window, the sun had fully risen, and the rain from the past two days seemed to have dried. It would be nice if this weather held up for the Spring Fling, she thought, and then noticed the hope she still felt over the possibility of seeing Scott there.

She frowned as she tied her lightweight robe around her waist, remembering some of the sweet things he had said to her back in high school, in those magical days and nights when they were finally free of everyone's prying eyes. She grit her teeth, banishing the memories. She wasn't a teenager anymore. Those words didn't matter now.

"Thanks for making breakfast," Emily said as she wandered into the kitchen and poured herself a mug of coffee from the freshly brewed pot. "This is a nice surprise."

"Figured it was the least I could do for upsetting you." Julia whirled around and met her gaze, her green eyes murky with concern. "I feel really bad."

"Let's forget about it," Emily said as she stirred a teaspoon of sugar into her coffee. She tapped the spoon against the rim of her mug and set it down. "Besides, you made some good points."

She took in a breath, wondering if now was the time to come clean about applying to the culinary school in Boston. After the speech Julia had given her the other night, she was starting to think her concern that Julia would feel let down or betrayed was all in her own head. All this time Julia thought Emily was fine with things as they were—that she didn't long for more out of her own life—and nothing could have been further from the truth. Emily *did* want more. A lot more. The problem was that none of it was really in her control. The school could reject her just as easily as Scott had—the two things she wanted most. She couldn't have both. She might not even get one.

She stopped herself right there. What was she thinking? She and Scott were just exes now. There was nothing more to it than that.

Then why, she wondered, as she slid into her usual chair at the small kitchen table, did it feel like there might still be something between the two of them?

"I made some good points? Really?" Julia brightened as she turned back to the stove and plated the slightly burned pancakes. "Oops. The edges are a little black." Her face darkened with guilt and Emily bit the inside of her check. "Guess you should never turn your back on pancakes."

"They cook pretty quickly," Emily agreed and then shrugged, "Come on. I'm sure they're delicious. A little syrup will cover up any of the crunchy bits."

They sat in companionable silence, eating their breakfast and leafing through the catalogs that had gathered on the kitchen table. Several times Emily opened her mouth to tell Julia about the application she had sent in, but each time she thought she could mention it, her heart would pound so loudly she had to stop herself. Up until now, the application was her own special secret. If she didn't get in, it would be her own quiet loss. If she did…well, wouldn't that be the more appropriate time to share the news? When there was actually news to share at all?

"Spring Fling's tomorrow," Julia mused.

Emily's pulse skipped a beat. "That's right," she

said, forcing a casual tone. Feigning disinterest, she flicked a page in the catalog.

"I wonder if Scott's going," Julia continued.

Refusing to feed into her sister's overt insinuations, Emily took a large bite of the nearly inedible pancakes and leaned in closer to the catalog. It was useless. The page blurred and all she could see was Scott's face. That boyish grin that tugged one side of his mouth, the sheepish way he'd glance at the ground and back up at her. Her heart started to flutter.

"With everyone in town attending, I wasn't sure what his plans would include," Julia was saying. "But when I talked to him last night, he told me he was thinking about going."

Emily snapped her eyes to Julia's grinning face. Her mind whirled as her breath went still. Julia's bright green eyes sparked and she hid her growing smile behind the rim of her mug.

"You talked to Scott last night?" Emily clarified.

"Uh-huh." Julia smiled and casually cut into her pancakes. "Oh," she said, bringing her fingers to her lips. "These are delicious if I do say so myself."

"Julia." Emily stared at her sister, imagining a hundred different turns a conversation between her sister and Scott could have taken. "When did you talk to him?"

Julia regarded her quizzically. "I told you. Last night."

Growing impatient, Emily forced a deep breath. Her sister was having quite a bit of fun with this, but Emily didn't find it amusing in the least. In fact, she downright cared. Too much.

"Yes, but when last night? Did you run into him somewhere?"

"He stopped by here." Julia lifted an eyebrow. "He was looking for you."

Emily felt herself pale. So he had been serious when he'd asked her if she'd be around last night. But why?

"He wanted to return the pie plate," Julia continued, motioning to the cleaned and empty pie plate sitting on the counter.

Well, that about summed it up.

Emily shrank back in her seat, and stared listlessly at her plate of burned pancakes. She knew she had no right to feel as disappointed as she did, but nevertheless her heart felt heavy. She was getting hopeful, setting herself up for a fall, wishing for something that wasn't there, for someone who was long gone, just passing through. For someone who wasn't hers to miss anymore.

"He asked about you," Julia added, and Emily felt her pulse skip.

"Really?" She cut into her pancakes, attempting to cover her rising hope with the taste of charred batter.

"He seemed genuinely let down that you weren't here."

Emily sat back in her chair and gave her sister a level stare. "Maybe he was afraid you'd give him the third degree again."

Julia laughed and waved her hand through the air. "Oh, please. He knows my bark is worse than my bite. I always used to tease him when he'd come over."

Emily smiled at the memory. There seemed to be no greater amusement to the young Julia than spying on her sister and Scott, building up their romance to be so much more than it was in the end.

"So what happened then?" she dared to ask.

Julia shrugged. "I invited him in. He hesitated at first, but he couldn't think of an excuse quick enough for me, so I gave him a beer and we talked."

Emily dropped her chin and stared at her sister. "Beer? Since when do we have beer?"

"Since I bought some yesterday on my way home from work. You know, just in case we had any male suitors…"

Emily held up her hands. "Okay, then what happened?"

Julia took a sip of her coffee and pinched her lips. "My, my, aren't we suddenly curious? And here I thought you were no longer interested in the comings and goings of Scott Collins?"

"Are you going to tell me how the conversation went?" Emily's voice felt shrill, even to her own ears.

"Maybe you should ask him yourself," Julia said with a sly smile, and Emily let out a shaky sigh.

"Fine," she said briskly, pushing back her chair to stand. "I will."

Julia's smile widened. "I thought you'd say that."

Emily paused from picking up the dishes. "Thought or hoped?"

Julia seemed to consider this for a moment. "Both, I think. Yes, both." She shrugged. "Just in case you see him today, why don't you borrow my black cotton sundress?"

Emily hesitated. "Thanks. I will. But not because I want to impress him or anything," she added in a rush.

"Sure."

"I mean it, Julia. Scott and I are just exes. Now he's in town, and we're behaving like civil adults. There's nothing more to it than that."

"Is that what you really want?" Julia gave her a hard stare and crossed one long leg over the other.

Emily released a long sigh and set the dishes in the sink. She turned the tap on high. "It doesn't matter what I think. Scott has his own ideas."

"Oh, that he does," Julia said.

Emily whipped around to face her sister. "What's that supposed to mean?"

"Emily, I saw the way he looked at you the other night. He still cares about you."

Emily hesitated. "You're not making any sense," she muttered.

"I know I gave him a hard time the other night, but I wanted to see his reaction. I wanted to see if he felt bad for what he did to you all those years ago."

"And what did you deduce?" As much as Emily was trying to tell herself not to care, she couldn't help it. She had so many unanswered questions, and if Julia could give insight into the situation, then she wanted to hear it.

"He still cares about you, Emily. I thought maybe he'd be a jerk about it, brush it off, but he didn't," she said. "You saw for yourself. He looked like he felt genuinely…guilty."

Emily hesitated. "Maybe," she shrugged, turning back to the sink.

"So has he told you why he left like that, then?"

Emily tossed her hands up in the air, spraying soapy water onto the counter. "It doesn't matter now, Julia.

That was half a lifetime ago. It's over. He's moved on. It doesn't change anything."

"Sure it can," Julia said easily. "I see two people who might still have feelings for each other who aren't being honest about where things broke down." Julia set a hand on Emily's arm. "You'll always wonder, Emily. You might have been too hurt back then to ask, but now is your chance to find out. Once you know, then you can move forward."

Emily tried to ignore the implication that she hadn't gotten over Scott yet. She let out an exasperated sigh. "I told you! He's not even staying for long. He might not even be back."

Julia just shrugged. "All the more reason to ask then. It's now or never."

"Why are you pushing this, Julia?"

"I just see two people who meant a lot to each other who have a lot of things left to say," Julia said. "I say it like I see it, Em. What can I say? I'm a hopeless romantic."

Emily blinked, wondering if she should take her sister's opinion to heart or not. Julia had a way of getting ahead of herself, letting imagination take control, but she wouldn't be so careless when it came to Emily's well-being. If Julia thought that Scott still cared about her, then maybe her sister was onto something.

But no… Emily frowned, thinking of the things Lucy had told her yesterday, the way Scott was so eager to get out of their parents' house. Out of town. His bags were still packed and waiting. He'd rented a car.

Disappointment tugged at her again. Scott had cared for her once, and maybe a part of him still had some lingering fondness for the time they'd shared. But there was no room for her in his life. There hadn't been for the past twelve years and there wouldn't be for the next.

Hopeless romantic. Emily shook her head. That's exactly what Julia was. But when it came to herself and Scott only one word in that phrase applied: *hopeless*.

Scott leaned back against the old bench swing on his sister's front porch and gazed over the hedge onto Main Street, for once looking to the center of town and all its buzz as an escape. Anything felt more desirable than sitting here, having a heart-to-heart with his sister.

Lucy pushed open the screen door and handed him a glass of iced coffee, taking a long sip from her own as she joined him on the swing. It creaked under the weight of their two bodies and began to sway slowly, naturally. They sat there quietly, as though no time had lapsed and they had never been apart. Scott glanced up at the back of the diner at the corner of the narrow side street the Miller cottage was nestled on.

He studied the second story of the building, trying to remember the exact layout of Lucy's old apartment—well, Emily's apartment now. If the bedrooms were across from the living room then, yep, the windows all the way to the left corner were the bedroom windows.

Realizing he was staring like some Peeping Tom into the bedroom windows of the Porter sisters, he jerked away his gaze, his pulse kicking up a notch as the fire escape door flew open and Emily appeared on the metal landing.

Beside him, Lucy chuckled and called out, "Emily?" Under her breath she muttered, "What is that girl up to?"

Having reached the ground, Emily swiveled toward the house, alarm transforming her features when she registered her audience. "Oh. Hi." Her normally pleasant smile was replaced with something tight and stilted.

Scott raised a hand by way of hello, matching his sister's effort.

"You off to the bakery?" Lucy inquired.

Emily hesitated. Frowning, she looked around helplessly, as if searching for someone else to come along and answer the question for her. Scott watched her heave a sigh and then take a few long strides toward the cottage.

"I was going to get an early start on the baking," she explained as she reached the bottom of the porch steps. She glanced at him and then quickly away.

"That a new dress?" Lucy asked.

Emily glanced down at herself and gave a modest shrug. "I borrowed it from my sister." She cast another brief look in his direction and then looked down at her black cotton sundress.

"I think it's cute," Scott said before he could stop himself. The heat from his sister's sidelong glance was enough to melt the ice in his glass, and he felt a rush of warmth creep its way up his neck.

After a deliberate pause that Scott would later pay her back for, Lucy said, "I agree, Em."

"Oh, well…" Her eyes darted to his and she quickly

looked down and dragged her foot through a patch of dirt.

The silence felt like an eternity and when Scott turned from Emily's reddening cheeks to focus on the ice cubes in his glass, he could almost hear them crackling.

"Well, I should go," Emily said at last, and Scott felt a twinge of disappointment.

His gaze lingered on her as she walked back toward the diner, her shoulders squared and proud, before she strangely seemed to break into a sprint as soon as she rounded the corner.

"I wonder what that girl is up to," Lucy mused. "She seemed to be almost running from something, taking the back stairs and all."

Scott had the unsettling suspicion that she had been running from him. Not that he could fault her.

"If I didn't know better, I'd say Emily seemed a little flustered around you." Lucy took a slow sip of her drink, staring casually ahead into the distance. "If I didn't know better, that is."

"Please. Emily and I are ancient history."

"If you say so," Lucy said archly.

Scott snorted. He couldn't deny the disappointment—or relief—he'd felt last night when he'd finally just marched over to the door down the hall and knocked on it, ready to come clean, ready to set things right, only to learn that Emily wasn't even home. The thought of hurting her again killed him—but the thought of leaving this town without telling her everything was worse.

She deserved the truth.

"I say so," he said, but his heart said something altogether different. "We were just kids when we dated. That rarely amounts to anything."

"George and I were just kids when we got married, and look at us now," Lucy pointed out.

Scott bristled. "That's…different."

"Maybe so. And I can't say it's always been easy. Financially, that is."

Scott dragged a hand down his face. He didn't like to think of his sister worrying about money when he had so much. But she was a proud woman, a hardworking woman. An honest woman. "Sometimes I think about how different life would have been if I'd stayed," he said, catching himself only after he'd spoken.

Beside him, he heard his sister sigh. "Oh, well. Maybe it's for the best, really. Look at how far you've come."

He turned to her, his temper stirring when he thought of his father and the lingering consequences of the choice he had made all those years ago. He took a long sip of his iced coffee, waiting for it to cool him, slow his racing pulse.

"Mom and Dad never wanted me to stick around. They told me if I married Emily, I could forget being a part of the family business. They ever tell you that?" He glanced at his sister sidelong, noting the dismay in her expression, and the lack of surprise.

"They never agreed with the choice I made to marry young, and you know that. They wanted something else for you. Something more. You'd been accepted to a great college. They didn't want you to squander opportunities. They thought they were doing what was best for you."

She really didn't get it. It was better that way, he

told himself firmly, before he steered the conversation in a direction it never needed to go. "Well, funny that now I'm suddenly needed so badly at the family company," he said bitterly.

"You're older now, Scott. It's different." She paused. "So there's really nothing left between you and Emily?"

Scott stared into his glass. "Nope."

"You two do look good together," Lucy mused.

"Lucy." His tone was firm. She couldn't drag him down this path. He wouldn't let her. He had to be strong and fight these feelings. "Stop. You know I'm not in town for long."

"I know." She sighed. "I was just hoping you would change your mind. I guess I thought maybe you might find a reason to stay."

"And you thought that reason might be Emily?" How little she knew. A moment of weakness caused him to wonder if he should set her straight. But he couldn't, not yet. First he needed to tell Emily, and find a way to set things right as best he could. He needed to take responsibility for his actions.

And he needed to see if somehow, someway, he could make her believe in him again.

Emily sighed as she hung her apron on the hook and smoothed the black dress Julia had lent her. Another long, busy day at the bakery had kept her distracted, but now, as the last customer settled their bill, all those uncertainties came swimming back to the forefront. She couldn't shake the image of Scott sitting on Lucy's porch this morning—she'd purposefully gone out of her way to avoid him by taking the back stairs, but the spark of excitement she felt when she saw him was undeniable.

It was the fatigue talking, she told herself. There was so much going on all at once with Scott being back, the bakery opening, and of course, the possibility that she might be accepted to culinary school. All at once life had gone from being painfully routine to bewilderingly unpredictable.

The first week at the bakery had been a success, but not without a lot of hard work and effort. Emily glanced at Lucy, who was looking over the books, tallying up the profits, and felt a twinge of dread. She'd applied to that school in Boston back when she was working at the diner, pouring coffee and shuffling orders to and from the kitchen. Now she felt queasy when she thought of the opportunity she was giving up—of how much she was needed here, and how much Lucy depended on her.

"We had a good week, Em," Lucy said, still focused on the spreadsheets in front of her. "Why don't you get out of here early? I'll finish off the rest of the pies for tomorrow's festival."

Emily frowned. "You sure?" The Spring Fling was already tomorrow, and they still had two dozen mini-pies to bake for the pie-eating contest.

"Go home," Lucy said. "That's an order from your boss."

Emily smiled tiredly. "Thanks, Lucy. See you tomorrow, then?"

"Sure, we can all go together," Lucy suggested, looking up from her paperwork. "Scott's coming, too."

Emily paused. "That sounds like fun," she managed. Too much fun. If she knew what was good for her, she would stay away from Scott and focus on the future, not the past.

With a wave, she pushed out into the late afternoon sunshine, walking quickly in an effort to pound out any fleeting hopes that had no place in her current life. She halted when she saw Scott walking casually down the street, and then slowly resumed her path.

No place at all, she reminded herself. Scott had taken those hopes with her when he left town, and he'd take them with him again if she let him.

Emily turned her key in the side door that led to the staircase and the rooms above the diner, but it was no use. Scott was coming closer now, he'd seen her, and when she dared to steal a look in his direction, he held up a hand. Her pulse skipped a beat as his bright blue eyes shone in the sunlight.

"How was work today?" he asked, coming to stand next to her. As his eyes roamed over her face, she held her breath, thinking of what Julia had suggested that morning.

"Busy," she said. "But I suppose that's a good thing." She fumbled with her key, but her hands were beginning to tremble.

"You've been putting in long hours," he commented. "I stopped by to see you last night, but your sister said you were still working."

See her? So it hadn't just been to return the pie plate.

"Yes, Julia mentioned that." She bit her lip. "I… hope she didn't give you a hard time."

Scott smiled affably. "Nah. We had a nice conversation, actually."

"Oh?" Emily's mind began to whirl with possibilities.

"Yeah, we reminisced a bit. She caught me up on some of the happenings around town." He shrugged. "She really looks up to you."

Emily frowned. "Oh?".

Scott's grin widened. "She couldn't sing your praises enough."

Oh, Julia. Emily felt her cheeks flush and she forced the key abruptly, fearing for a moment she had snapped it in half, and then let herself into the darkened vestibule. A stack of letters sat at her feet, having fallen out of the open mailbox. She bent down to retrieve the pile, aware of Scott's presence behind her as she did so. Straightening her spine, she kept her back to him for the length of a good hard breath before she whirled again to face him. Her heart dropped with longing as her gaze met his handsome features.

Damn it, was there ever going to be a day where the sight of that chiseled jaw and those twinkling eyes didn't leave her physically aching? His presence was so all-consuming, that when she was alone with him like this, she forgot to breathe. Attraction this deep was dangerous. And rare. No wonder she had never been able to shake the image of him. No wonder, despite how deeply he had hurt her, she still dared to dream of him.

"You coming in?" Her voice was choked and breathless.

He held up a stack of blueprints and a binder nearly four inches thick with papers. "I'm heading over to the office, actually. It's easier when most of the people there have already left for the day."

Emily nodded. She understood how it felt to live in a town where you were the object of speculation and gossip.

"How are the plans for the library coming along?" She had been wondering how his meeting with Max had gone at the diner the day before. From what she could tell, the men hit it off well. She wasn't surprised though. The two had a lot in common. They were both successful, they were both charming and they both seemed to hold a sadness in their eyes at times despite their heart-melting grins.

"I think we'll start construction in about six weeks," Scott said, revealing nothing as Emily locked his gaze, searching for more insight. She couldn't deny the flutter of hope that filled her chest: Did he plan to stay until then? A lot could happen in six weeks.

She waited for him to elaborate, but when he did not, she volunteered, "I'm sure the town will be thrilled. It was the children's wing that was damaged, right?" She motioned to the blueprints, curiosity getting the better of her. "Can I see?"

Scott raised his eyebrows in surprise but he looked pleased as he set down his binder and unraveled the blueprints, awkwardly spreading them against the inside of the door as he crossed into the vestibule. As he spread the blueprints out wide, she oohed and ahhed over the truly beautiful design, but her gaze lingered firmly on Scott's biceps, which flexed as he adjusted the large scroll. His golf shirt stretched under the width of his broad shoulders. She traced the contours of his back with her eyes, imaging her fingers skimming all the way down to his waist. And beyond.

"I can't take credit for the design," Scott said,

shrugging as he began rolling the print. "My dad brainstormed that part with an architect."

"Well, he did a great job. He should be proud."

Scott's smile fell. Instantly, Emily regretted saying anything, but Scott had opened the door to the conversation. What was it between Scott and his father? It went beyond him not wanting to discuss his father's declining health. Noticing the way Scott's jaw twitched and his mouth took the form of a thin, grim line, Emily pondered what could keep someone this angry at their own parent for this long. Especially under the current circumstances.

"I hope Lucy likes it," Scott said and then quickly added, "I know she was really upset about Bobby's part in it."

Emily smiled kindly. "It was an accident. At least no one was hurt."

Scott nodded and seemed to swallow hard, taking pause at her words. Emily glanced down at the mail in her hands, realizing she had overstepped, and her breath caught when she noticed the return address on the top envelope. The culinary school in Boston.

"I should probably get to the office," Scott said, and Emily couldn't help but detect a thread of disappointment in his tone.

She nodded, unable to bring herself to speak. She clenched the envelopes in her hands until she felt them become slick with the sweat from her palms, but Scott made no movement toward the door.

"What did you want to talk about?" Emily asked suddenly, pulling herself from the thoughts whirling through her head as she stared at the letter. "Last night, when you stopped by."

Scott's gaze pierced through hers, until her heart started to race from more than the possibility of her fate tucked inside the sealed envelope.

After a beat he said, "Nothing that can't wait."

Emily frowned. "I have time."

"I wanted to thank you for the pie again." He grinned.

The pie plate. Emily internally scowled. Julia had obviously built the visit up to be more than it was. Much more.

Scott held up his blueprints, flashing her a grin. "I should really get going."

Emily tried to hide her disappointment.

"See you later, then."

She watched him take the three steps down to the sidewalk, lifting her hand as he turned back to wave his blueprints at her, and then she leaned back against the wall, closing her eyes, listening to the pounding of her heart.

Glancing down at the letter in her hands she held it up to the light, pursing her lips when she was unable to make out any of the words written inside. Her entire future was in this envelope, all her hopes for something more in life.

Without stopping to think about what she was doing, she ripped open the envelope as quickly as she could, not bothering to care about the rough jagged edge she had forced with her fingertip. She pulled the letter from the sleeve, her chest heaving with emotion, her hands shaking as her eyes skimmed the page so quickly, she only made out random phrases rather than the collective point.

By the time she reached the bottom she burst out

laughing. A change in the fall schedule. They had sent her a letter about a modification in the course catalogue! Depleted of energy, she sat down on the bottom step and waited for her breathing to return to normal as she folded the letter back into the badly torn envelope and tucked it into her handbag.

She was spared the demand of being forced into a decision. Only a matter of months ago when she had sent in her application, she had thought this was all she wanted. The chance to hone her skills, pursue her passion. The chance to start over and be herself and define herself by her future, not her past. Suddenly, she wasn't sure that was even what she wanted.

The only man she had ever loved was back in town. For how long, she didn't know. A part of her wanted to run from him, run from the town that had caused her such pain, that reminded her of her loss everywhere she turned. It was exactly what her sister had accused her of doing—avoiding more heartache.

A few months ago she had thought sending in her application was taking a risk. That starting life over in a new town with new people was the biggest leap of faith she could ever make, that it would take courage she didn't even know she had. But now…now she wondered if sticking around and dealing with the life she had been given was the biggest risk of all.

Chapter Eight

Scott glanced down at the date on his email and blinked. Nearly a week had passed since he'd first driven into town, and against his reservations, he was beginning to think he might miss the place when he was gone. His gut twisted when he thought of the day when he would get in his rental car and drive away, this time knowing he would never be welcome to return.

Closure, they said, did wonderful things for the healing process. Well, he was banking on it. In Seattle he lived an anonymous life, free of the burden of his past. His friends there knew nothing of him other than what he chose to reveal. The brief relationships he'd had over the years never amounted to more than casual flings—the common complaint among the women he'd dated was that he had too many walls up, that they never felt they knew the real him. Scott had let them go, knowing they were right, hoping that eventually he would meet someone he could trust enough to be himself with, trust enough to take down the mask and expose the man beneath.

He just never expected that person would be Emily. After all these years, she was still the only one who could reach him.

Scott ran his hand over the stubble on his jaw and released a long sigh as he tore his thoughts from Emily and tried to focus on the chain of emails that had collected in his in-box over the past few days. Two major projects were scheduled to break ground next month, and he probably had another week—two at best— before they'd need him back in the office. He supposed in a pinch he could fly in for a few days and then come back, but that was dangerous thinking. The sooner he severed himself from Maple Woods, and everyone in it, the better. The longer he was in town, the easier it was to think of what might have been. He clicked on the next email, pushing away the thought that refused to budge.

His stomach began to burn and he peeled another antacid free of its wrapper and set the roll back on the table. From the window in his room above the diner, his eyes rested on the festivities below, where a large tent was being set up in the middle of the town square. It was one of the few days of the year that Lucy's Place closed down, and Scott could sense how much Lucy was looking forward to eating food she hadn't cooked. He chewed on the chalky coating in his mouth. Chances were high that Emily felt the same way.

Scott leaned forward in his chair and forced his eyes to the computer screen, where he worked without stopping for the next few hours. After a quick shower and shave, he stepped out into the hall, careful to keep an ear out for Emily, but the building was silent. He pushed through the back door and jogged down the fire escape. Lucy and George were already on their porch when he strolled past the overgrown hydrangea bushes blooming with blue, purple and pink flowers.

"Bobby's coming along later. With friends," Lucy informed him after he'd greeted his brother-in-law, standing to smooth the skirt of her sundress.

"Shall we, then?" Scott gestured down the quiet street toward the center of town.

"Not yet," Lucy interrupted. "I asked Emily to join us."

Scott's eyebrows shot up as he met and locked his sister's eyes. He clenched and unclenched his fists as he waited for his temper to subside. "I thought you weren't going to play matchmaker anymore."

Lucy laughed easily and waved her hand through the air. "Settle down, Scott. I've given up any hopes of that. You're safe."

"Then—"

Lucy narrowed her gaze. "This has nothing to do with you, Scott," she said sharply. "Emily is my co-worker and a very good friend of mine."

"I'm sorry," he huffed in response. He stared down the road, wondering what Emily thought about all this. It hadn't slipped his mind that Max Hamilton had suggested they all meet up for a drink at the event and that Emily had looked like a deer in the headlights.

"What ever happened between you and Emily?"

Scott whirled to face Lucy, his chest pounding. "What do you mean?" he asked, but the hardened edge in his tone only confirmed his guilt.

"You used to like her when you were kids and now…" Her eyes searched him, crinkling in confusion, her mouth a thin line of displeasure. She shook her head. "It's too bad. She's a really nice girl."

"I know that," Scott bit back.

"Then why do you get so shifty every time her name is mentioned? If you're worried about sending her the wrong message, I can assure you, you don't need to worry."

"What's that supposed to mean?"

Lucy tipped her head, a sadness taking over her features. "Emily keeps to herself. She doesn't date much, and she's the last person I know who would assume someone was interested in her romantically. Especially you."

"Why would you say that?"

Lucy gave him a knowing look. "You broke her heart." Scott began to protest but Lucy raised her hand to stop him. "You were eighteen then. It's forgivable. But you're a grown man, Scott. What's your excuse now?"

Scott stood at the base of the porch, his eyes shifting from Lucy to George and back again. *What's your excuse now?* He squared his jaw and thrust a fist into his pocket, his mind whirling somewhere between rage and hurt so deep he thought he might just shout out loud—scream out the truth of his actions, of his reasons behind breaking up with Emily. It was an excuse all right, and a damned good one. It would be sure to get his sister off his back about his interactions with Emily. But it might also kick her out of his life for good.

Suddenly brightening, Lucy waved over Scott's shoulder and shoved past him without another word, calling, "There you are!"

Scott turned to follow Lucy's gaze, his chest tightening as he saw Emily strolling up the sidewalk in a navy blue sundress and lavender cardigan, her chestnut hair flowing softly around her shoulders. Her smile was bright and unsuspecting, and Scott felt the knot in his stomach loosen, offering a smile in return as she met his gaze.

"Hi," he said, and then cleared his throat as his voice caught.

"Hey." Her voice was pleasant and sweet, the simple word so melodic that he longed for her to say something more.

"Ready to go?" Lucy asked, ignoring Scott altogether.

Emily stopped walking as they bridged the gap, and Scott soon found himself at her side, grateful for her nervous chatter that overshadowed the heavy, heated silence emanating from Lucy. When they arrived at the town square, Lucy muttered a quiet excuse and walked away with George in tow.

Scott turned to face Emily head on, finding her gray eyes bright, her full pink lips curving at the corners. "Alone again," he said with a slow smile he couldn't fight.

"That's becoming a theme with us." She held his gaze, perhaps in challenge, perhaps in curiosity.

Scott felt his pulse take speed. "Is that a good thing or not?" *Tell me, Emily, because I don't know anymore.*

His world seemed so clear when he was away from her, so black-and-white, so factual. He was responsible for her father's death. His father had covered the entire thing up. He would have to tell her. She would hate him. How could she not?

But when he was with her like this... Scott inhaled deeply. Everything was different when he was alone with Emily. The situation was as gray as the irises of her large searching eyes. All reason and strength left him, and all he wanted to do was grab her by the shoulders and press her close, to feel the smooth curves of her body against his, to beg her for forgiveness or maybe to never tell her at all, but instead to just go on like this...forever.

"Well," Emily said shyly. She lowered her eyes, causing Scott's gut to pull taught. Looking up, she said softly, "I was sort of thinking it was a good thing."

"I was hoping you would say that," he murmured, the release of the words sending a rush of air to his chest. Just admitting that one small truth lessened the burden that had weighed on him for so many years.

It was just like that age-old saying—*the truth shall set you free.* In this case, however, he couldn't help but wonder once again if the truth would do more harm than good.

Emily forced herself to remain as outwardly calm as possible, even though her heart was racing. Scott sat next to her on the grass under the shade of a large maple, resting his elbows on his knees. Sitting close to him like this, sipping at her ice-cold lemonade, Emily couldn't help but feel a twinge of sadness. It was just so perfect. So achingly, terrifyingly perfect.

She slid a glance at Scott, letting her eyes roam greedily over the broad width of his back, the wide, chiseled shoulders and the confident grace of his profile as he looked out onto the square, taking in the scene. She wondered what he was thinking, if being here made him want to stay. She sighed, fearing that it might make him just want to leave all the more.

Emily quickly looked around the square, hoping to spot a few friendly faces in the crowd. She spotted an older couple she recognized as regular guests of Holly's at The White Barn Inn and waved. With a sharp turn, the woman—Evelyn Adler—peered at her, her expression transforming into something altogether more interested when she noticed Scott.

"Well, hello there, young lady," Evelyn said to Emily as she approached, but her eyes rested firmly on Scott. The woman pinched her lips like a little bird while her deep blue eyes glimmered with awareness. "And *hello,*" she cooed to Scott, widening her gaze hopefully while her husband stood dutifully at her side. She patted her graying hair girlishly.

"Hello," Scott said pleasantly, though Emily detected an undertone of curiosity.

"I don't think we've had the pleasure of meeting," Evelyn purred, the intensity of her gaze sharpening like a hawk about to swoop in on its prey.

"I don't think so, either," Scott said, standing to extend his hand. At the gesture, Evelyn stepped back in shock, unabashedly raking her eyes over the length of his body as her lips curled into a hundred-watt smile. "Scott Collins. I just came back to town, so you must have moved here while I was away."

Emily was standing by now, brushing a bit of grass

and dirt off the skirt of her dress, and she noticed Max and Holly watching the exchange in the distance. Holly was shaking her head in dismay while Max laughed heartily. She waved them over as Evelyn continued, "Oh, we don't live here. We just visit every few months. Have you been to The White Barn Inn? It's *bliss*ful!"

"Well, thank you for the compliment!" Holly said as she joined the group. She slipped a wink to Emily and Emily nudged Max in the ribs. Scott's gaze passed over the three of them, clearly realizing that he was at a disadvantage when it came to the persistent Evelyn Adler.

"It's good to see you here, Emily," Evelyn said pointedly, making an obvious show of shifting her eyes to Scott and leaving them there. "It seems that Maple Woods is just bursting with lovebirds this year!"

Emily felt her face blanch. She could feel the steady shaking of Max's laughing torso beside her and she watched as Holly gave him a warning glance, fire in her eyes.

"We're old friends, Mrs. Adler," Emily said as her cheeks began to burn.

"Pity," Evelyn huffed, folding her arms across her fragile chest. She glared at Emily, as if this were somehow her fault. "A handsome man like this? In my day, men and women weren't just friends. But then, in my day, a woman didn't strut around town in pants, either." She clucked her tongue as her gaze lingered on Scott, and Emily could hear Max chuckling.

"Come on, Mrs. Adler," Holly said, taking the older woman by the elbow and giving Emily a knowing glance. "I've entered my raspberry preserves in a contest and the judging is about to start."

"Exciting times," Max said with mock enthusiasm, and Holly swatted him playfully. Undeterred, he shot a grin at Scott and said, "You gotta admit, this town's got a hell of a lot more going for it than we city guys are used to."

"Young man!" Evelyn's sharp cry punctured the din of nearby conversations. "Did you just *curse?*"

Affronted, Max took a step back and then pressed his lips together, laughter shining in his eyes. "Guilty as charged, Evelyn," he admitted, holding up two palms as he pleaded his innocence.

"Well…" Evelyn bristled, her brightly painted lips twisting coyly. "I could never stay mad at a young man as handsome as you."

With a chuckle, Max led the group away and Emily laughed to herself as Holly turned back and shook her head. "Sorry about that," she said to Scott, whose eyes were searching hers for some sort of explanation. "I didn't mean to throw you to the wolves."

"Who *is* that woman?"

"Evelyn Adler." Emily sighed, falling naturally into step beside him as they weaved their way through the stalls selling everything from local artwork to children's clothes. Julia was even selling a bunch of knitted goods she'd created on her downtime at the shop. "She's a regular at The White Barn Inn. She's a little eccentric, but we love her dearly."

They settled into a spot near the gazebo. Scott grew silent and rested his forearms on his knees. "So, old friends, huh?" He glanced at her sidelong, and Emily felt her stomach drop.

Her gaze fell to the grass, and she plucked a few dandelions before tossing them to the side. "Seemed like the easiest thing to say." She stole a glance in his direction, her breath catching at the intensity in his eyes.

"You were a hell of a lot more than just a friend to me," he said, and Emily looked away, frowning.

What was done was done. When her father died, she had learned to savor the moment, to not take the present for granted. Sometimes it was easy to lose sight of that, especially more recently when she was too busy getting lost in the future and all of its conflicting possibilities.

She straightened her shoulders. There would be no thinking about the future today. Today was all anyone really had.

A little shiver down her spine told her that today she had everything she had ever wanted, anyway.

"Tell me they won't do the Chicken Dance," Scott said with a grin as he watched the couples spin on the dance floor.

"Maybe the Hokey Pokey," Emily replied with a wink that sent a surge of heat straight to his groin. He tempered his desire with a sip of his beer. The sun had faded nearly an hour ago, and the band had picked up on its cue. Evelyn Adler was front and center on the dance floor, dragging her poor husband along for the ride. Max Hamilton lifted his hand in a wave and then twirled Holly until she threw her head back, laughing. Emily rubbed her arms as a cool breeze cut through the trees, rustling the leaves. It was all the ammunition he needed.

"Want to dance?" Scott asked with a slow smile, tipping his head in the direction of the dance floor, where half of the townspeople were bouncing around the band's whims.

Emily hesitated just long enough for him to wonder if he had stirred up an old wound and then turned to him with a smile that took his breath away.

"I'd love to," she said, hopping out of her folding chair. With one hand on the small of her back he guided her onto the makeshift dance floor and then curled his arm around her waist, his free hand taking hold of hers as they fell in step with the beat.

She kept her gaze lowered aside from a few telling glances from the hood of her lashes, her lips curling into a smile that pulled his heart so tight, he thought the ache would cut off his air. The music was too loud to make conversation possible, but Scott didn't mind. Without words, he could focus on her presence, on the way her smooth, soft palm felt so small in his own, and the way his arm rested so perfectly on the curve of her hip. He grazed the soft cotton of her dress with his fingertips, remembering how her bare body felt in his arms.

As the dance continued, he gradually pulled her closer, and she didn't resist, instead curling herself naturally into his chest, her chin hovering above his shoulder. He craned his neck and closed his eyes, drinking in the smell of her hair, feeling the pounding of her heart through his chest, wondering what it would be like to hold her like this forever.

If he tried hard enough he could almost be that kid again. The kid who had no awareness of what he had once done. The kid who was just crazy in love with Emily Porter.

Emily pulled back as the song ended, but he kept a hand on her hip, unable to let her go just yet. The strings of light cast a glow on her face, catching the glint in her eyes. Something deep within him began to stir.

"Want to take a walk?" he suggested, noticing that the band members were stepping aside from their instruments for a water break.

Emily nodded and they walked into the shadows of the trees, the buzz of the party behind them soon fading. The night was clear and quiet once they were well beyond the square, and the sound of crickets could be heard at random.

"I love that sound," Scott murmured.

"What sound?"

He stopped and leaned back against a fence post. "The sound of town, I guess. It's soothing."

Emily glanced around with a shrug. "I guess I don't even notice anymore."

"It's funny, you know? I've been gone for so long, I didn't think I would remember any of this, but being here…it's like no time has passed at all."

"I was thinking the same thing," Emily said with a small smile.

"I'm really sorry about how things left off with us, Emily," he said, his voice husky. *Just say it, just say it.* "I never meant to hurt you. Believe me when I say that I only ever wanted you to be happy. I still do."

Emily held his gaze, searching his eyes with hers as if trying to confirm the validity of his words. Eventually, she nodded. "I am happy," she said, and Scott felt a jolt. He hadn't seen that coming.

"Really?" he asked. He had to know.

"Everyone has sad times, Scott. You know that. But that doesn't mean I haven't been happy. I mean, look around…I get paid to do what I love. I have a great boss. I live with my sister, and even though she can be a handful, she's still my best friend. There are a lot of reasons to be happy."

"And now?"

"Am I happy right now? In this moment?" A smile played at her mouth. "I'm very happy."

He had taken so much from her, stolen her innocence with the blink of his eye. Yet here she was, standing before him with eyes soft and longing, lips parted and waiting. He could reach out and touch her; he could try to fill the part of her heart he had left empty. Her father was gone, and nothing could bring him back, but there was another wrong that Scott could set right. He had a chance, right now, here in this moment, to take back that day all those years ago and make her see how badly he had wanted her then. How much he still did.

He took a step forward, watching as Emily's eyes widened ever so slightly as he lowered his mouth to hers. His lips grazed hers softly, a caress so light it sent a shiver down the length of his spine, until her mouth parted to his, hesitantly at first as their tongues began their dance. He tightened his hold on her waist, pulling her body close to his chest until heat flared deep within him. Her hips pushed against his groin until his need grew with each lace of their tongues, and he claimed her mouth with determined energy, needing to be as close to her as she would allow him.

She sighed into his mouth as his kisses became urgent, but instead of pulling back as he feared, she dug her hands deep into his biceps and then up and around his shoulders, raking her fingers through his hair as their mouths persisted hungrily and their bodies fused. He could feel the swell of her breasts against his chest, and as desire drove him forward, he traced a hand around the curve of her hip, snaking his way up her stomach until he cupped her breast in his palm, feeling her chest rise and fall under his hand as her breathing became ragged.

Breaking the kiss, he locked eyes with her for the briefest of seconds before clutching her so close he felt he could break her, and she sighed into his ear as her hair cascaded down her back, glistening in the moonlight. He ran a hand through her chestnut locks, a memory seizing his chest as he rested his head on hers.

If they could just stay like this. If it could only be so easy.

Chapter Nine

"Well, there you are," Julia said as Emily shuffled into the kitchen, yawning. Leaning a hip against the butcher block, she added, "I was beginning to wonder if you made it home last night."

Emily glanced sleepily at the freshly brewed coffee and smiled. "Sorry I lost track of you at the festival," she said, filling her favorite mug. "Did you manage to sell a lot of your knitting samples?"

"Oh, the stand did fine enough, but when I couldn't find you anywhere, I got a little worried."

"Sorry, I should have called you." Emily sat down at the table and wrapped her fingers around her mug. She eyed the clock, making sure she didn't lose track of time.

Julia finished spreading some of Holly's raspberry preserves on her toast with quick, determined strokes.

She pursed her lips into a coy smile. "So I take it you and Scott had a nice time—"

"Oh, don't you start!" Emily cried, rolling her eyes. Across from her, Julia looked mesmerized, but for once she held her tongue. "Before you say anything, you should know that there's nothing going on between Scott and me. We've decided that we're just... old friends."

Just old friends who had kissed.

Julia held her gaze, her expression impassive, her head tipped. Finally she shrugged and bit into the corner of a triangle of toast. "If you say so."

Emily narrowed her eyes in suspicion. It wasn't like her sister to let things drop so easily. "Well, I do say so," she said with a huff. She blew at the steam curling up from her mug and took a tentative sip, her pulse twitching at the memory of last night.

She set the mug on the table. It was different now, she reassured herself. Scott was a grown man. He wasn't going to behave like a teenager and leave her hanging without so much as an acknowledgment.

"Well, I guess if you're just friends then you won't care that he stopped by here again, looking for you this morning," Julia said mildly.

"What? When?"

With a glimmer in her eyes, Julia pushed aside her plate of toast and met Emily halfway over the table. "About half an hour ago. I told him you were sleeping."

"What did he say?"

"He said he'd look for you later."

"He told you that?" Emily gasped.

Julia looked insulted. "Would I ever lie to you,

Em?" She sat back in her chair and played with the handle of her coffee mug.

"No, of course you wouldn't lie to me." Emily glanced at the clock once more. Realizing it was nearly time to leave for work, she gulped the rest of her coffee, hoping the heavy dose of caffeine might help clear all the conflicting emotions muddling her head.

She washed her mug in the sink and then turned to face Julia, who had already recovered and was grinning suggestively. With a knowing chuckle, Emily shook her head and patted her sister on the shoulder as she walked out into the hall, craning for the slightest sound behind Scott's door. With only a twinge of disappointment, she deduced he had left for the day, probably hard at work already. Last night he'd told her the library project was moving ahead and a crew was already on-site to clear out the rubble. What that meant for the two of them, she didn't know—she hissed in a breath, catching herself. *The two of them.* Was it really possible?

Emily pressed her lips together and hurried to the stairs, dropping her to hand to the rail as she quickened her step. She stopped at the landing when she spotted Scott standing in the vestibule at the base. The faintest furrow gathered between his brows when he looked up at her.

She paused at his hesitation and then offered a tentative smile. "Hi," she said.

"Hey," he said, shoving his hands into his pockets as she slowly took the remaining stairs. His low voice sent a shiver down her spine. She waited to see if he would reach out to her, touch her, give her a sign that last night hadn't been a fleeting occasion. A mistake.

But all he did was stand there.

"Julia mentioned that you stopped by this morning," she managed.

"You off to work?" he asked, and Emily frowned.

"Yep." Her tone was clipped but she didn't care. Something between them had shifted since last night. The spark that seemed to have been reignited in the past week was suddenly snuffed out.

She drew a breath and turned to the mailboxes. Yesterday's mail still filled their box, forgotten in the midst of everything else. Emily paused, realizing how consumed with Scott she had allowed herself to become, and then pulled the stack free from the slot, her heart lurching when she saw the thick, solid envelope with the telltale return address. She held it in her hands, blinking in disbelief, as her breath wedged in her throat.

Scott inhaled. "Free for dinner tonight?"

Emily turned her attention back to him, trying not to think of the letter in her hands, the decision she would soon be forced to make. "Sure."

"I have to go through some paperwork over at the office, but how about I swing by your place around… seven?"

Her mind immediately went to Julia, who would surely be home and who would undoubtedly get carried away with the idea of a date—Emily stopped herself. A date? Was this what it was?

"Seven will be perfect," she managed, her voice latching in her throat.

"Good, good." He nodded his head, holding her gaze, and she clung to his stare, unable to peel her eyes from him just yet. "There's something I need to tell you."

Her breath snared in her tightening chest, wondering just what he had to say, and wishing she didn't have to wait until this evening to find out.

Julia's words rushed back to her, speaking the unspoken thoughts she had harbored all those years. Maybe, just maybe, she had let him get away once. But not again. Not this time.

Before she could process what she was doing she took a step forward and carefully, slowly, clasped her lips to his. He remained still at first, but he didn't resist her, and she tried again, parting her lips to his, sighing as his tongue skimmed against her bottom lip. She felt his hand brush against her hip as the other slid behind her back and then she was against him, the hard, solid plane of his chest, her mouth clamped on his, their tongues lacing more quickly, hungry in their need. He tasted like coffee and mint toothpaste, and his hair smelled like soap. She grazed a hand down his chest, feeling the hard ripples under her fingertips and then she spread her palms to his arms. The dusting of hair against his smooth, warm skin prickled her desire on contact, and she rubbed her hands over the hard curves of his biceps.

She combed her fingers through the thick hair at the base of his neck, moaning into his mouth as he searched her with greater need, her body melting into his, and she felt in that moment that she could become his, that a part of her had always been right here in his arms, holding on to this feeling. All she needed was him—him and the sensations he aroused in her. Nothing else would matter. Not the pain he had caused her, not the loss she had endured, not her lonely childhood. Nothing. She didn't need anything other than him. This.

Slowly, Scott pulled back, ending the kiss. "I'll see you tonight, then," he said, and Emily could only nod, frowning at the change in his expression. His smile seemed too tight. His eyes looked flat.

She waved as he slipped out onto the sidewalk and she watched his back retreat until there was nothing left to see but the slew of familiar faces passing down Main Street. He felt like a ghost again—like a person she had once held and whose memory she still clung to, but a person who had slipped away from her a long time ago.

Emily shook her head, trying to clear away the cobwebs. The envelope in her hands felt heavy—like a burden rather than the relief she had expected it to be. She stuffed it into her bag unopened and then ran as fast as she could to Sweetie Pie, and despite knowing Lucy was waiting for her, she felt more alone than ever.

She was pinning her hopes on dreams, and she had a bad feeling they were all about to come crashing down.

Scott hated being at the offices of Collins Construction. Everything about it, from the beige Berber carpeting to the awards and plaques lining the walls, made his insides churn. The office felt like a sham—a cover for a well-preserved scandal. One of their own had died, but the company had continued, and these four walls and everything they contained felt hypocritical. Callous. Cold.

He had once again slipped in through the back door, even though the offices were closed on the weekend. The files he needed were in his father's cabinets, and he flicked through the folders, pausing to study their contents. Scott pulled up the details of the library project, adding a few ideas here and there as he cross-referenced the blueprint spread before him. It was a shame, he knew, that such a large part of the old library had been damaged, but the reconstruction would turn the entire building into a monument, a pillar of the town. The architect had been clever with his details, ensuring the new wing would maintain the authenticity of the quaint New England town and the existing structure that hadn't been damaged, while inside, the most modern amenities would guarantee it could last long into the future. It was an important building, a community center in many ways, and despite the wall he had put up around this town, Scott couldn't help but feel a little proud to be a part of this project. It felt good to be able to do something positive for the town. For Lucy.

Scott stood up and paced the room, looking at it with fresh eyes. As a child, he used to think his father's office was enormous, but now it felt cramped and dim. The furniture he once thought so stately just looked old and worn. The room had always been like this, he supposed, but back then he just wasn't disillusioned to it yet.

On a console table near the window, Scott noticed a picture of himself wearing a hard hat and holding his father's hand. He turned it face down on the table with a scowl.

It was really time to get out of here.

Gathering a stack of files together, he grabbed his keys to leave when his sister's voice cut through the silence. "Scott!" It was a panicked cry. A cry he had heard once before, a long time ago. A cry of fear before the commotion dimmed his clarity, big men came running, shouting and his dad was grabbing him by the back of the shirt, pushing him faster than his legs could carry him until the car door slammed shut, locking him safely inside. "Scott! Scott!" His blood went still.

"Scott!" Lucy's voice sounded strangled, frozen in fear. Before he could react, she burst into the room. Her face was tearstained. Scott noticed the red rim of her eyes, the clutch of wet tissue in her hand.

"Thank God I found you," she gushed.

"What is it?" His tone was brusque, hardened in a way he hadn't intended. He was bracing himself for the worst. The anticipation was nearly choking him.

"It's Dad," Lucy whispered as her words caught in her throat. "He's been taken to the hospital in an ambulance. We have to go. Now."

He nodded abruptly. "I'll drive."

His focus remained on the back door at the end of the hall as he wove his way to it and pushed it forcefully, until it ricocheted off the back of the building. Lucy was crying harder now, explaining what had happened, if only to walk herself through it.

"I guess he passed out and hit his head on the corner of that desk near the window. I was just out there this morning, too, and he almost seemed a little better. I dared to hope…" Lucy sniffed. She hesitated before adding, "He was asking about you."

Scott ground his teeth. "That's nice," he said flatly.

"He's so proud of you, Scott," Lucy said hopefully, and Scott felt his anger begin to stir.

"Please don't, Lucy."

"Why? Why shouldn't I say something?" She almost shouted. Scott gripped the steering wheel, his mind whirling as he made a quick right at the intersection. "Why should I always have to pretend that none of this has anything to do with me? That it's only between you and them and that somehow I am just unaffected?"

"Because this *isn't* about you, Lucy," Scott said, determined to keep a clear head.

"Yes, it is! Of course it is!" Lucy insisted. "You're my brother! They're my parents! You disappeared for twelve years—twelve *years*—and now you finally come back just in time to watch Dad die! Do you know what this feels like to me? Do you, Scott? Do you even care?"

Scott kept his eyes on the road. "Of course I care."

"Then why did you have to come back and ruin everything?"

"I came back because you asked me to."

"But why couldn't you have just let things go? Why did you have to come over to the house and make everyone upset?"

Scott forced a breath, willing himself to remain calm. "I told you I shouldn't have come. You didn't listen to me."

"But—"

"But nothing, Lucy." He could no longer keep the frustration from his tone. "I didn't come over to make everyone upset. I can promise you that."

"All I wanted, all I *hoped,* was to have my family together again. I never knew what happened or why there was a rift, but I thought maybe someday... someday..." She trailed off, crying.

"Don't you think I wanted the same thing?" he asked.

"But you made it worse!" she accused.

"Maybe. Maybe so." He sighed. He certainly hadn't made it better. Scott drove on, his heart aching as her weeping filled the car. "I'm sorry you were dragged into this, Lucy."

"They wanted you to come back, you know," she hissed, fury flickering in her watery gaze. "It was you who stayed away, Scott! You tore this family apart!"

Scott fought back the mounting emotion that seized his chest. He exhaled slowly, willing himself to stay calm. "I don't expect you to understand."

"I just don't understand why you can't be the bigger person here, Scott."

"You're right, you don't understand," Scott repeated.

"Try me."

Scott slammed on the brakes at the red light and turned to lock her heated stare. He took a few breaths, and then steadied himself. "Now isn't the time," he said. "Our father is in the hospital, he's terminally ill, and I want your last image of him to be the good one you've always had. So don't make me turn you against him."

Lucy blinked. She held his gaze until the light turned green and then deflated back into her seat, crying until Scott thought he couldn't take another second of it. Had he not been punished enough? Had he not atoned for his sins? Had he not spent twelve years hating himself, wishing he could undo the irrevocable damage? Of all the pain he had endured, this was by far the worst. He could bear the self-loathing and the sleepless nights, but listening to the hopeless cries of someone he loved and knowing there was nothing he could do to ease her pain was unbearable.

His mind immediately trailed to Emily.

As the theme song of *Passion's Crest* gained momentum and Fleur studied the results of the paternity test with shaking hands, the television screen faded to black. Julia leaned back against a sofa cushion and sighed. "Fridays are such a good cliffhanger," she mused, smiling wistfully. "It was killing me to wait this long to catch up, but what choice did I have with how busy you've been lately. Out and about. Working. Dating…"

"Hmm," Emily said distractedly. She had long since stopped watching the clock, but her heart still seemed to register each passing minute with a sharp pang. Nine-thirty. The only relief she could garner was knowing that Julia wasn't aware of the silent humiliation she was suffering all through the episode of *Passion's Crest*.

It wasn't like her to keep secrets from Julia. After all, she wasn't just her sister—she was her best friend, too. Sitting catty-corner from her now, Emily felt a wave of sadness wash over her. She wanted to just blurt out all the emotions she was keeping bottled up inside her, but for some reason she just couldn't.

Scott had stood her up. Tears stung her eyes and she held them back, feeling more angry than sad. She blinked furiously, pressing her lips tightly together.

She had only herself to be upset with now. She had dared to open her heart, and once again, he had let her down.

It was her own doing for pinning so much hope on one man. A man who had made her no promises. A man who had made it very clear that he wasn't looking for anything permanent. A man who had once told her he loved her and then disappeared.

But then, Scott's actions were never consistent with his words.

"Is everything okay?"

Emily glanced at her sister and forced a tight smile. "I'm just tired is all."

"Well, get some rest." Julia sighed, flicking off the television. "I think I'll take a shower and turn in early myself. It's been a busy weekend."

Emily walked into her room and closed the door behind her. Her heart felt heavy, like deadweight within her chest. Pulling open the top drawer of her nightstand, she fished out the letter from the culinary school, not stopping to pause as she ran her finger through the small opening and tugged free the folded piece of paper enclosed. She read the letter impassively at first, but as the meaning of the words took hold and she processed their implications, she felt her pulse begin to race.

They'd accepted her.

A tapping at the front door caused her to jump guiltily, and she quickly stuffed the letter back into the envelope and into her drawer. Opening her bedroom door, she held her breath, listening for the sound she had just heard. There it was again—she hadn't imagined it.

Emily walked through the kitchen and opened the door, gasping when she saw Scott standing in the hall. His usually broad shoulders were slumped, his ash-brown hair tousled, and his eyes... Something was wrong.

"Scott," she breathed as anger left her body. "Is everything okay?"

He shook his head. "My father's in the hospital."

"Oh, no. Is he going to be all right?"

Scott rubbed a hand over his face. His eyes were tired, and the frown seemed cemented into his squared jaw. "He's in intensive care. Lucy's there, with my mother. It's just..." He trailed off, shaking his head. "I should have called."

Emily stepped into the hall, dismissing his concerns with a wave of her hand. "No, no. I'm just sorry to hear about your dad. How are you holding up?"

He managed a hint of a smile. "Not great."

She tipped her head. "Can I do anything for you?"

He locked her gaze. "Some company would be nice."

She smiled and followed him down the hall to his room, waiting as he unlocked the door and flicked on the bedside light. The bed was made—poorly—and she recognized the stacks of paperwork and blueprints spread out on the little table where they had eaten their pie just a few nights ago.

The suitcases were still open, still prepped and ready to go.

She sat down on the bed, telling herself not to think about that now.

Scott sat next to her, close enough for their legs to touch, and stared pensively out the window. "Growing up, I always thought my father was this unbreakable force. It's not easy to see him like this."

"I can't imagine it would be. It's good you were able to come home and see him again."

"My father and I haven't spoken in twelve years," Scott said, his eyes still fixed in the distance. Emily could see his jaw twitching in his profile. "Lucy's mad at me. She thinks I should be the bigger person."

"She's just in pain," Emily said. "She just wants her family to get along, for all of you to be happy."

Scott's brow furrowed. "My father and I...I can't be sure we'll be able to make peace before it's too late."

Emily closed her eyes as her chest tightened. "You know the day my father died, he asked me to give him a kiss before he left for work, and I refused because I was angry at him for not letting me eat a piece of candy for breakfast."

Scott pulled a face. "You were just a kid. You can't take that seriously."

Emily felt the same pang of remorse she felt every time she thought of that morning. "It was all I could think about for months. For a while I wondered if I would have felt better if the last thing I said to him was 'I love you' instead of..." Tears prickled her eyes and she stopped talking.

"Do you think it would have been easier?"

"No." Emily stared at her lap. "I think we all do things we aren't proud of in life at some point or another. I can't go back and change the exchange I had with my dad that morning, but I can change the way I think about him. He wouldn't want me to live with that guilt. He'd want me to focus on everything else we shared. He'd want me to live my life to the fullest."

He'd want her to go that culinary school. She could almost see his face now when she told him the news. That broad, ear to ear grin. The pride flashing in his eyes. "That's my girl!" he'd say.

Her heart swelled until she thought it might burst. God, she missed him.

"There are a lot of things I've done that I'm not proud of, Emily."

She turned to meet Scott's heated gaze, sensing the shift in conversation. None of it mattered now. If tonight had reminded them of anything, it was that life was too short to be spent dwelling on the past.

"I know," she said, sliding her hand onto his lap to hold his hand. She squeezed his fingers as her eyes searched his face. "It's okay," she murmured softly, leaning in to graze his lips.

His tongue laced with hers, exploring her mouth with growing hunger, and she gasped at the strength of his desire as his mouth claimed hers with more greed, his hand quickly breaking her grip to slide to her waist. He pulled her close, gasping as their tongues continued their dance, and she wrapped her arms around his shoulders, pulling him close. She wanted to comfort him, but she needed to be comforted, too. She didn't know why, but somehow being touched and needed by the one person who had hurt her so much was all she needed to feel that life could go on, and that no pain lasted forever.

Gently, he pushed her back onto the bed, and she inhaled as the weight of his body pressed against hers. She ran her fingers down the length of his chest until she found his waistband and then she tugged his shirt free, tracing her fingertips ever so lightly up the smooth width of his back. His kisses became frantic, incessant in their desire, and she dragged her fingers harder down his back, clinging to him as warmth pooled in her belly.

Tearing his mouth from hers, Scott grazed his lips down her neck in tiny kisses that sent a shiver down her spine. She quivered at the lightness of his touch, the intimacy of this moment, and when her body shook he pulled her closer.

Emily gazed into his deep blue eyes, feeling more connection to him in this moment than anyone else. She held her breath as he slowly unbuttoned her blouse, and her back arched as he loosened her lace bra and met her breast with his mouth. She stifled a cry as his tongue flicked the soft flesh which budded under his touch. The feeling of his mouth on her skin and his hands on her flesh made her long for his touch all the more. She pulled his shirt over his head and then rested back against the bed, taking his bare chest in her arms, caressing his cool skin until it warmed beneath her palms.

His hands circled her abdomen and then unbuttoned her jeans. She shimmied out, freeing herself of the material that served as a barrier between their two bodies, and anticipation built as he discarded his own pants. His fingertips skimmed the line of her panties as she leaned into him, molding her flesh to his, aching to become one. She gasped as he slowly, carefully, pulled the thin material free, sliding it down her thighs with one hand as his mouth once again met hers.

Pulling himself free, he discarded his boxers and sheathed himself with a condom from his wallet. Just like high school, Emily thought with a nervous giggle. Only there wasn't anything like high school about this.

She opened her legs to him as he hovered above her, caressing the hard plane of his chest with her fingers. He locked her eyes before closing them on a kiss, stifling her moan as he entered her. She held him close, raking her hands through his hair, clutching the length of his back as he pushed deeper, the weight of his body on hers making it impossible to know where her body ended and his began. She inhaled his scent and the heat from his body, and she held him as his body shook on release.

They lay in each other's arms until their breathing had steadied, their bodies cooled. "Stay the night with me," Scott murmured, his eyelids heavy with fatigue. "Stay every night with me."

Shock slammed into her. "What?" she whispered. She waited as her pulse hammered. His eyes were closed and his chest rose and fell evenly.

She watched him sleep long into the night, finally closing her own eyes just as the first hint of morning filled the room. For so many years she had lived in a dream world, imaging what-ifs, imagining something different, better. Even sleep couldn't spare her now. Reality had come knocking, and now she had to decide what to do about it.

Chapter Ten

Emily tiptoed down the hall when dawn broke. As much as she would have loved to have remained tangled in the sheets, feeling the heavy rise and fall of Scott's chest against her back, she had to get ready for work, and she preferred to slip back into the apartment unnoticed. She enjoyed living with her sister, but there were some times when she longed for a little more privacy, and today was one of those times. She supposed if she ended up in Boston, she wouldn't have to worry anymore about Julia commenting on her whereabouts.

Her hand froze on the doorknob of her apartment as realization took hold. The letter from the culinary school. Was she even still considering it after last night? And Lucy—how could she leave Lucy in such a lurch when her father was in the hospital? As it was, Lucy was already scrambling to run both Sweetie Pie and the diner, even with George's help. How many times a day did Lucy express her appreciation, or mutter how she would be lost without Emily?

A queasiness coated Emily's stomach as she turned the handle. The apartment was thankfully still, and seeing that it was only six, Emily could only assume that Julia was still asleep. She hedged toward her bedroom, eager to seek haven behind the door, when Julia's bedroom door flung open. Startled, Emily jumped.

"My God, Julia!" she gasped, placing her hand on her heart to steady her racing pulse. "You surprised me!"

A devilish light sparked Julia's green eyes. "Well, well, well. What do we have here?" she asked, folding her arms across her chest as she leaned against the doorjamb.

Emily flashed her a warning look. "Not now, Julia." She opened the door to her own room and crossed to her closet, selecting a black skirt and top for work. "I'm running late as it is. I have to get six pies in the oven before we open at eleven."

"That's fine. I'll just talk with you while you're getting ready." Julia stood in the doorway of Emily's room now, blocking her escape.

"Please, Julia." She sighed. "Not now."

Julia narrowed her gaze but her lips twitched with a smile. "You were with Scott Collins last night, weren't you?"

"What? Why would you say such a thing?" Emily asked, but she knew it was pointless. She fumbled through her drawers mindlessly, hoping to avoid eye contact.

"Well, Sherlock, let's see... You're wearing the same clothes as last night and your bed hasn't been slept in." She tsked. "If that doesn't add up to a little hanky-panky down the hall with the mysterious blast from the past, I don't know what does."

"You really need to stop watching *Passion's Crest*," Emily countered.

"No more than you do," Julia said lightly. Then, collapsing onto the bed, she gushed, "Oh, please tell me. Please!"

Emily stared levelly at her sister, her impatience melting into something softer. With a slow smile, she tipped her head in the direction of the hall. "I have to take a shower. Get the coffee started and I'll meet you in five minutes."

Julia squealed and shot out of the bedroom, leaving Emily standing alone in her room. She grimaced at her reflection in the mirror, wondering what Julia's reaction would be to everything. As much as she dreaded coming clean with her sister, a larger part of her would be relieved. The verdict was in, and it was time to tell Julia about the culinary school.

She showered and dressed quickly, wandering into the kitchen to pour herself a fresh cup of coffee. There were grounds at the bottom of her mug and the brew was too strong. Emily added an extra teaspoon of sugar to hide the bitter taste. Julia was dancing around excitedly, practically rubbing her hands together in anticipation, and Emily experienced a flicker of hesitation. This wasn't going to be as tantalizing as Julia expected.

"Let's sit down," she said, taking her usual chair. When Julia had settled herself she began, "Mr. Collins is in the hospital. He's been getting weaker and he fell and hit his head quite badly."

Julia's face fell. "Mr. Collins was never very nice, but it's still very sad all the same. I feel sorry for Scott." She cupped a hand to her mouth as her eyes widened. "And poor Lucy!"

"I know." Emily rubbed her forehead. "I feel horrible for her, too. Which is why I'm so conflicted."

Confusion knit Julia's brow. "Conflicted? About what?"

"This." Emily slid the acceptance letter across the table to Julia, watching as her sister silently read the single sheet of paper, her expression hovering somewhere between bewilderment and disbelief.

"I don't understand," Julia finally said, looking up. "You applied to this culinary school in Boston?" Emily nodded. "But why didn't you tell me?"

Emily winced at the twinge of hurt in her sister's voice and shrugged. "There didn't seem to be much point if I didn't get accepted. I guess I was afraid of jinxing it."

Julia stared at her, her mouth a thin line, her eyes sharp. She wasn't buying it. "You were afraid I would be upset, weren't you?"

Emily tipped her head. "I didn't know what I wanted to do, Julia. I don't want to leave you when Mom just moved away, too. But—"

"But you want something else," Julia said. "Something more."

Emily nodded. "I guess so."

Julia's mouth tipped into a slow, awestruck smile. "I

can't believe I accused you of not trying to make more for yourself. Why didn't you tell me, then?"

"I told you, I don't know what I'm going to do."

Julia frowned. "You're going to attend this school, that's what you're going to do."

Emily laughed softly, feeling as though she could weep in relief. "It's not as simple as that, though. Not anymore, at least," she added.

"Oh?" Julia said archly. "This wouldn't have something to do with Scott, would it?"

"I don't know what's happening with him," Emily admitted, feeling lighter than she had in days now that she could open up to someone about her innermost fears and feelings. "I think he really cares about me, but then I can't help thinking it will all go wrong."

"Does he know about the school?"

"No." Emily leaned across the table. "How can I tell him? Lucy is his sister—she'll be crushed about this, Julia. Crushed!" Her heart began to throb as she imagined Lucy's reaction. She hated the thought of upsetting her friend right now. And Scott…could she really walk away from him now, just when she'd finally found him again? "I'm not going," she said firmly. The finality in her tone brought her comfort—an end to her anxiety over the consequences of her decision— and she said it again, with more conviction this time. "I'm not going."

Julia held her gaze, unblinking. Her eyes were unreadable, her expression flat, but Emily thought she saw something there. Something that looked an awful lot like disappointment. "All your life you've sacrificed for me… Don't think I haven't noticed."

Emily felt her shoulders slump. "It wasn't a sacrifice, Julia. We're family. That's just what you do. You support each other."

"Exactly," Julia said. "And that's why I'm supporting you now. I'll be fine, Emily! And I want this for you. You obviously want it, too, or you wouldn't have applied in the first place."

Emily hesitated. "I was never sure I would really go."

"This is your chance to make something of yourself, to give yourself a whole new set of opportunities!" Julia insisted. "It wasn't a possibility for you before, but it can be now. Why wouldn't you seize this chance? Are you scared?"

Emily scoffed. "No, I'm not scared." But maybe she was. Maybe the thought of leaving her comfortable life behind was starting to feel unsettling and strange. Or maybe she was afraid of turning her back on the man she had always loved, of doing to him what he had done to her.

"Well, for what it's worth, I think you should go." Julia stood up from the table. Emily tucked the letter back into its envelope as her sister poured a mug of coffee for herself. "I think Dad would have thought the same thing," she added softly. "He wanted the best for us, and it would have saddened him to know he couldn't give it to us. This would be your way of showing him we pulled through. That we didn't miss out on things we could have had. Don't you see, Emily? You can still have the life you always wanted. You created it for yourself."

Emily smiled grimly. Leave it to her sister to always voice her own innermost sentiments. Especially the ones she was trying so hard to overlook.

* * *

It was already past eight when Scott opened his eyes to find Emily gone from his bed. For a moment the room felt still, his mind quiet. Then, like a tidal wave, it all came crashing down on him. He closed his eyes, wondering how he would get through the next twelve years as he had somehow endured the last. It was no life to live.

Deep down he had never expected to make amends with his parents, but it wasn't because he didn't want to. Somewhere within him was a need to find peace, to put the past behind them, to move on. He just wasn't sure they could find a way before it was too late.

His father had had more than twenty years to make things right for the Porter family. To take responsibility for the part his company—his son—had played in a man's death. But instead he had done nothing, kept quiet, and Scott had followed suit. At first he had done so out of horror, and fear. Of the worry of losing the only girl he'd ever loved if he told her the truth. In the years since, he had questioned his decision not to run and tell Emily everything that day. If he had told her, explained to her the part he had played in it all, would she have still loved him? Or was it better for everyone that he had left town without another word, disappeared without a trace?

Scott heaved a sigh and pushed the covers back off the bed, forcing a piece of paper onto the floor. His pulse skipped as he picked it up and read it. A note. From Emily.

His pulse quickened as he remembered the way her body had writhed beneath his. He could still feel the desire in her touch if he closed his eyes. It was a memory he would have to savor because it would never happen again. The one woman he could love forever was the one person who would soon hate him for life.

He had to tell her. Today.

For the second day in a row, Emily sold the last slice of pie an hour before closing. The demand the bakery was stirring only furthered her resolve that she should stay where she was needed. If things kept up at this pace, they'd have to double their supply. They might even need to hire a third person to cover the counter while Lucy and Emily tended to the baking.

But then, if they brought on a new person, maybe Emily wouldn't feel so bad about leaving. Lucy hadn't been to work that day, and she would probably be out for another few days more. In the brief phone call they'd had, Lucy had said her father would be in the hospital for the week at least, but that he was fortunately being moved out of the intensive care unit later that night. Now wasn't the time to make any decisions that could further distress her friend. Julia could say what she would, but Emily needed time to think about what she really wanted. What really mattered.

Still, the thought of not going to the school made her heart sink. She had only visited once as part of the admissions process, but she could still recall the way she felt when she was there. She had never felt so excited about the future—at least not since she was seventeen, dreaming about a life with Scott.

One by one, she flicked off the lights of the bakery and turned the sign on the door. The evening air was cool and refreshing, stirring up memories of long walks along the lake at the edge of town, the anticipation she would feel of long summer days and Scott's bronzed skin beside her on the rocky beach.

He was sitting on the steps leading up to the second floor apartments when Emily stepped into the vestibule. Judging from his presence, he hadn't spent the day at the hospital as Lucy had chosen to do.

"How are you doing?" Emily asked as she approached.

He gave a tight smile in return. "Feel like going for a walk?"

Emily nodded. "Sure," she said softly, waiting as he pulled himself up to standing and led her back out the door. Why couldn't she have cleaned up a bit more at the bakery? She probably had flour in her hair. She slid him a glance and realized with a pang that he probably hadn't noticed. Not necessarily a good thing, actually.

"Did you talk to my sister today?"

Emily nodded. "She told me your father was being moved into a private room. That's good news."

Scott glanced at her through hooded eyes. "It is. That was a close call last night."

They walked east on Birch Street, past the white picket fences that lined the road. A dusting of cherry blossoms showered the pavement as they approached some of her favorite houses in Maple Woods—white colonials with black shutters dating back to the eighteenth century. She knew every owner of every house, and she had been in many of them. They were good people—kind people. People she couldn't imagine leaving behind.

"There's something I should tell you, Scott." Her voice strained against the tightening in her chest.

He turned to her, his brow knitting. "What is it?"

"Do you remember the other night when you asked me if I ever considered doing something with my baking skills?" Scott nodded and she drew a sharp breath. "I wasn't completely honest with you. The truth is that I actually applied to a culinary school in Boston. I got the acceptance letter yesterday."

She lifted her eyes to his, watching as his expression brightened. "That's wonderful!" he exclaimed. His smile was broad and for a moment she felt herself get swept up in his excitement.

"But it's in Boston," she added, sobering.

He shrugged. "So?"

Emily stiffened. "So that's two hours from here."

"But it's what you always wanted, Emily. It's what I always wanted for you. To be able to live your dreams, to—"

"But we had dreams together then, Scott!"

His smile faded to a grim line. "Don't make this about me, Emily," he said.

Her heart plummeted into her stomach. So there it was. What a fool she had been.

"I wasn't planning on it," she said flatly, shifting her focus to the road. She knew he hadn't promised her anything. He had made it clear since his first day back that his visit was temporary. He had a whole life in Seattle, after all. Had she really expected him to just give it all up?

She supposed she had.

"I haven't made a decision yet so I'd appreciate if you didn't say anything to your sister. I should be the one," she said coolly. Her heart began to race with determination. She would go to that school. There was no reason not to anymore. To think she had almost given up the opportunity for Scott. She had thrown enough years away on him.

When they reached the park on Orchard Lane, Scott came to a stop. "Can we sit over there?" he asked, pointing to a wooden bench under a crab apple tree.

Heart sinking, Emily walked over to the bench. "Are you regretting last night?" she blurted before he'd even had a chance to sit down.

"What?" His brow furrowed as he ran a hand through his hair. "No, no." He sat down heavily beside her, rubbing his hand over his jaw. She could hear the soft scratching of his skin over the faint call of blue jays. "Quite the opposite," he said, his voice low and soft, and Emily felt her insides flutter.

Stay with me tonight. Stay with me forever.

Well, she had intended to do just that. Now it seemed he couldn't get rid of her fast enough. "So you don't regret it?" She frowned. "I'm sorry, Scott. I don't understand."

"Of course I don't regret it. Last night was... amazing." He huffed out a breath. "But that's just the problem, Emily," he continued.

Emily's heart sank. "What do you mean?" she asked quietly.

Scott turned to her, suddenly looking like he had aged ten years overnight. "Emily, I need to tell you something." His voice was low, barely audible, and her breath locked in her chest.

"You're scaring me."

His stare penetrated hers, reaching the depth of her heart, pulling her toward him like a magnet. She couldn't have torn her gaze from his if she wanted to.

"You always wondered why I broke things off with us."

She nodded, unable to speak from the lump in her throat.

He drew a deep breath and closed his eyes before slowly lifting his gaze to hers once more. "There was a reason."

"Okay," Emily said, encouraging him through the pause. What was done was done. She had decided to forget their past and to focus instead on their future. Their present. They were adults now, and they had something—something real—she was sure of it! In the brief amount of time since Scott had returned to town, they had formed a connection, and after last night, they had formed a bond. It couldn't be broken. Not like this. Not so quickly. Nothing he could say about that night twelve years ago could undo what they had now.

"Did anyone ever tell you the cause of your father's death?"

Emily felt like her gut was being squeezed through a vice. "What does that have to do with anything?" she replied, hearing the hysterical pitch in her voice. She didn't want to talk about her father's death or imagine the brutal way in which he had died. She'd tried to push those images from her mind a long time ago—how dare he try and bring such pain to the surface? "Why are you bringing this up? Are you trying to upset me?"

"He died on one of my father's job sites," Scott said softly.

"I know that. Of course I know that!" Emily said

sharply. She stared at him angrily. "What are you trying to tell me, Scott?"

Scott pulled his hand free of hers and raked his fingers through his hair. "They said it was human error, that he didn't pull the brakes on the machinery before stepping down into the ditch."

Well, thanks for reminding me. "Please stop," she said over her pounding heart. She could hear the blood rushing in her ears. Her legs were shaking and she pushed on her knees with both hands to still them. "I don't want to talk about this."

"It was human error, Emily, but it wasn't his."

Emily felt the blood drain from her face, and the world went quiet. She could hear nothing—not the birds in the trees, not the wind through the leaves, not the beating of her own heart.

"It was me, Emily," Scott said.

She sat paralyzed, unable to move or even blink. Scott's clenched jaw pulsed; his profile was hard and unyielding, betraying no emotion. The bastard couldn't even look her in the eye.

"I don't understand," she said calmly, her stone-cold voice unfamiliar to her own ears, as if the sound was coming from someone else, somewhere far away. It echoed from a hollow place.

Scott turned to face her, his expression full of anguish. His bright blue eyes were full of regret, full of pain. Fear knotted in her stomach as she searched his face for understanding.

"It was me, Emily! I was the one! I was on that job site that morning, climbing on machinery no kid that age should be allowed near."

She was frozen to the bench. "But the police—"

"The police were wrong, Emily! They didn't have all the facts. My dad set the stage, he got me out of there. It was easy for them to just assume what he told them was correct. There was no evidence to the contrary."

"I don't understand." Her voice was shrill. She reflexively pulled back on the bench, desperate to distance herself from him. From his words. "I don't understand."

"It was me, Emily! Me! I got in the way. I was climbing on the machine. I left it in gear before I climbed off, and…it rolled. It was an accident, but—" His voice broke on the last word. "I wasn't even aware of what I did, Emily. I was a stupid little kid. But… I'm to blame for your father's death."

He had feared this moment for twelve long years. He had rehearsed his words, anticipated her reaction and played out every possible scenario until he was in a cold sweat. He hadn't planned on this. He couldn't have.

Emily sat on the bench, unmoving. Her creamy skin had paled to a ghostly white. She wasn't crying or screaming or shouting that she hated him. She was just sitting there. Shaking.

Words he could deal with, but silence was something he was unprepared for. He watched her guardedly, waiting for her to speak, to do something. He ran his hands down his face; his head was pounding. What did she want from him? What did she want him to do? He would do anything in that moment if he knew it would make her feel better. He would get up and leave. He would take her into his arms.

He reached out a hand but she pushed it away before it could reach her. Her eyes were narrowed and sharp. "Don't touch me."

"Okay," he said. He heaved a breath and tented his fingers on his lap.

"How long have you known?" she asked. Her voice was barely above a whisper. Her eyes were focused somewhere in the distance and he followed her gaze to a little bird pecking at a bruised and fallen apple.

"Since the night I left town." He paused. "I was always fooling around on equipment, running around my father's job sites. I never knew until my parents told me, until I heard them talking—I never knew the part I had played."

"You were there that day."

He nodded. "Yes."

"And you don't remember?"

"All I remember is playing on the machines, hopping off. Then suddenly there was all this shouting, and next thing I knew my dad was grabbing me, telling me to get away." He drew a sharp breath. "My last night in town, I overheard my parents arguing about it. When I confronted them, they told me. For nine years they'd kept me from knowing it had been my doing."

"And you kept it from me for another twelve," she murmured. "Is that why you left Maple Woods?"

Scott nodded as shame weighed heavily in his heart. "Yes." He regarded her carefully before adding, "I didn't want to hurt you any more than I already had. I thought it was better that way."

"And now?" She turned a sharp gaze on him. Accusation flashed in her gray eyes.

He hadn't been expecting that one. He searched for

the right words, anything that might ease her pain. "I'm older now. I've had time to think. I couldn't live with myself anymore."

"Do you feel better now?"

Her words were a punch to the gut. "No."

She held his eyes miserably, her expression withering as a tear released. She brushed it away quickly with a sniff, turning her attention back to the little bird. "Who else knows?"

"No one," Scott began and then halted. "Except my parents. That's why I stopped speaking to them. When they told me what had happened, what they had kept from me—" he glanced at her "—and you…I couldn't forgive them."

Emily jaw flinched but her profile held unwavering stoicism. "Not Lucy?"

"Not Lucy." He drew a breath and reached into his pocket and handed her the folded check.

"What's this?" Emily asked, taking it.

"It's what your family should have had a long time ago," Scott said quietly, watching as Emily unfolded the check and stared at the number.

Wordlessly, she handed it back to him. "I don't want this."

He scanned her face, frowning. "Emily, take it. It's what your family deserved. It would have made your lives easier. Better."

"Better. You think my life is better now, knowing this, knowing you kept this from me? What was this week all about, Scott? A way to ease your guilt? A way to make up for breaking my heart? A way to make up for—" Her voice cracked and she shook her head, lowering her eyes. Sitting at the end of the bench, she might as well have been sitting across the park or across the town. Across the country. He had never felt more helpless or more incapable of reaching out and just touching her.

"You have no idea how much I care about you, Emily," he said with quiet force.

She shook her head furiously, releasing a bitter laugh. "Yeah, right."

"Emily." He was pleading now, and he didn't care. "I mean it. Just tell me what you want me to do. Is there anything I can do?"

She nailed him with a look of scorn. Her tears had dried, her eyes reflecting something far worse than sadness. "Anything you can do?"

Her tone cut him deep. "It was a stupid question."

She scowled. "You never should have come back."

He swallowed hard. So there it was. Worst-case scenario. She hated him. Had he really ever expected anything different? His chest felt like lead as he nodded slowly, resigning himself to the consequences of his actions. "I'll go. I'll go tonight."

"I think that's a good idea," she said, her tone turning his breath to ice. She stood and walked calmly away without so much as a look back. His eyes never left her until she was completely out of sight. It was the last time he would ever see her and he had to hold on to her right up until the very last second.

Chapter Eleven

It was time to leave Maple Woods. For good this time. There were just a few more things to take care of and he could catch the red-eye to Seattle.

The sadness in Emily's eyes was a memory he would have to live with forever, but he told himself it was better than leaving again without telling her. A niggling of doubt began to creep through his mind, causing his gut to stir uneasily. He had done the right thing, even if it had opened old wounds—hadn't he? Emily deserved the truth. Mr. Porter deserved to have his family know that his death had not been a result of his own careless error.

Scott walked slowly through town, past Sweetie Pie and Lucy's Place, past the town square where a few nights ago he and Emily had danced together. His mind filled with an image of Emily framed by the glow of the lights hanging from the trees, stepping toward him under the umbrella of the leaves, her lips curving into a smile as he took her in his arms and twirled her to the beat of the music.

He'd never forget that smile.

The lights were on in Lucy's house, and he climbed the stairs to her front porch slowly, prolonging the moment when he would say goodbye to her again, when her opinion of him would change forever. If he didn't say something to her, Emily surely would.

Before he could turn and run from his problems again, he forced himself to knock loudly on the door. He peered through the long window frame until his sister appeared. She hesitated when she saw him, drawing a breath before she approached the door.

"Good of you to come," she said, struggling to meet his gaze.

Scott frowned. "How are you?"

Lucy looked around the room, seeming to try to hide from his question. "Not good, Scott."

Of course she wasn't good. He didn't even know why he'd asked. "I'm sorry, Lucy. If there's anything I can do—"

She snapped her eyes to his. "Are you going to stop by the hospital again? Dad's awake, and I'm sure he'd appreciate a visit from his only son."

From the briskness in her tone and the defensive lift of her chin, he suspected she already knew the answer. "I'm heading out of town tonight, actually."

A bitter burst of laughter escaped from her lips. "Of course you are."

Scott ignored his sister's biting tone and crossed into the living room. "We need to talk," he said firmly.

His blood felt thick and cold. There was no going back now.

Lucy hesitated, sensing the change in his mood. "What's going on?" she asked, her brow furrowing. She looked tired and worn-down. Her hair was pulled back in a loose knot and her face was pale and wan.

It killed him to do this to her but she had to know. Now. Before he left for good.

He motioned to the sofa near the window. "Can we sit down?"

Lucy bristled. "I have a lot to do before I get back to the hospital, Scott. Can this wait until after visiting hours, or will you already be halfway to Seattle by then?"

"This can't wait." He grimaced at the sharp edge to his voice, watching as his sister's eyes darkened. Her brow furrowed as she took a seat at the edge of the sofa. She looked impatient and restless, and more than a little curious.

Scott averted his gaze from the handful of framed photos Lucy kept on the mantle, unable to look at the face of the man who had determined his path and who had selfishly put their family above all others. Too restless to sit, he gripped the back of a wing chair as his gut tensed with emotion. There was no time for sentimentalities now. It would only make this more difficult than it already was.

"Scott?" He looked down to meet her stricken face. "What is going on, Scott?"

Dragging this out wasn't an option. "Do you really want to know the truth? Why I left all those years ago? Why I couldn't forgive Dad?"

Lucy looked on the verge of tears. "Of course I do,"

she said. "But—maybe I should let it go. What's done is done. It's too late."

"It's not too late," Scott said sharply. He heaved a sigh, steadying himself. "It's not too late," he repeated more calmly. "We have to make things right when we still have the chance. And that's what I've decided to do."

"What are you trying to say?"

"It shouldn't have gone on for so long." He swallowed. "The night I left home, I discovered something that I couldn't live with."

Lucy's frown deepened. She nodded. "Go on."

"Everyone always said that Mr. Porter died by his own carelessness. That he forgot to pull the emergency brake on the excavator, that human error caused it to roll over him."

Lucy stared at him in confusion. "Richard Porter? Emily's father?" Lucy's brow rose. "Scott, why are you even bringing this up?"

He held up a hand. "Mr. Porter's death was an accident. But I was the one who caused it."

Lucy stared at him in disbelief. Scott held his breath against the silence of the room. "I don't know what you're talking about," she said calmly.

Scott sighed, burdened by the need to repeat himself, to confirm the horrible circumstances. "I was on the job site that day," he explained. "Just like I always was in my spare time as a kid. And I was the last person on the machine before it rolled down into the ditch."

Lucy was staring at him with an intensity he had never seen before. She didn't blink. "You remember this?"

"No!" He combed his hair off his forehead, stared into his hands. "I was nine years old. That day was a blur to me. I just remember climbing on the equipment, running around in the dirt, and then the screams. The frantic way Dad grabbed me and thrust me into your car, hissing at us to go straight home and to never say a word if questioned."

Lucy nodded. "Right. I remember that, too."

"But I heard Mom and Dad talking the night I left town. They were talking about it, Lucy. They were talking about that day, and what happened. They kept it a secret from me for nine years. That's why they never liked Emily. That's why…why I couldn't be with her after I found out."

She leaned forward. Her eyes looked wild, her face was a chalky-white. "They said *you* caused the accident?"

Scott nodded. "Yes!"

Lucy stared at him wordlessly, and then finally relaxed against the couch. Her mouth was parted, but no sound came out, until finally she said, "I'm sorry, Scott. But that's not what happened that day at all. I was there. I was dropping off sandwiches for Dad's lunch when it all happened. I'd just finished putting them in the trailer when the shouts rang out and Dad started yelling for me to get back in the car and go, to take you home. I was there, Scott. And in the chaos of everything, no one bothered to ask me what I saw."

The timer to the oven buzzed. Right on time, Emily thought with a small smile. The test of a true baker was being able to know when a pie was done by the smell, and by the scent of cinnamon and apples wafting through the kitchen, instinct told Emily this was going to be one good deep-dish pie. Almost good enough to fill that hole in her heart.

She placed the dish on the cooling rack and closed the oven door with her hip. With hands already coated in flour, she rolled fresh dough into a large circle and then carefully positioned it in a glass pie plate. The comfort of the routine distracted her, and she felt her shoulders relax as she filled the shell with the fruit mixture from her large ceramic bowl. She took care in spreading the filling evenly with the back of her wooden spoon. A sprinkling of brown sugar would add a nice flavor under the second crust, she decided on a whim.

Crimping the edges together, she took small pleasure in the well-honed skill, remembering the way her mother had first taught her to squeeze the crusts between her thumb and forefinger. It was comforting and peaceful to work with her hands—a constructive way to work through the grief.

She carefully set the pie in the oven and turned the timer. The kitchen was a mess and she huffed in dismay as she tossed a dish towel over her shoulder. There was only one issue she took with baking: cleaning up afterward.

Still, cleaning was better than wallowing in pity and eating her way through half a gallon of fudge ripple ice cream. The past week had been a whirlwind of emotions, and it would take some time to get back on track. If she could focus on the normal routine of her day, then she should be okay. Someday.

In a way, she should probably be relieved. After all, for years she had held on to the pain Scott had caused her when he dumped her without a word. Now she could at least scratch that ridiculous sentiment off her list. To think she had been so shattered over something so…trivial! In light of the damage Scott had really caused her, it seemed almost laughable that she should have ever been so upset over a teenage romance that never led to anything more. There was no room for pining now. Last night had been an illusion. An experience built on hopes and dreams. And lies.

For twelve years he had hidden this secret from her—from everyone!—all this time knowing that her father hadn't died by his own careless error, the way everyone in town believed.

It was wrong, and so very unfair that this was all they remembered him by. And it wasn't even true! Deep down she had never believed it—her father was good at his job, he took pride in it, but she knew her mother lost sleep about it, and she could still remember her mutterings at the funeral. He had worked too hard. He was tired. Worn-out. Maybe…

The thought of her mother that day haunted her almost as much as the memory of her father's grin, the way he would swoop her and Julia into his arms each night when he came home, as if they were weightless. He'd lift them up and somehow, with his support, it was as if they could fly.

And now she alone knew the truth. She would have to tell her mother, and Julia. She would have to bear that responsibility, brace herself for their reaction.

Emily bit her lip as she scraped the pie filling from the wooden spoons. She would not think of the pain in Scott's eyes. She would not think of the remorse in his tone. The anguish—*no*.

Tears prickled her eyes. She quickly blinked them away as she heard a key turn in the lock and her sister appeared.

"Hey there!" Julia smiled brightly and plopped her bag down on the table with a heavy thud. She glanced around the dirty-dish-strewn kitchen, eyes gleaming as she spotted the pie. "Oh, yum! Or…" A wave of disappointment crossed her face. "For Sweetie Pie?"

"For you," Emily said impulsively. She could always make another tonight. God knew she wouldn't be finding sleep, and keeping busy was better than dwelling on her own misery.

Julia's face brightened. "Really?" she said, already grabbing a plate from the cabinet. "Should I get one for you?"

Emily shook her head. "I get enough at work," she fibbed. She pressed her hand to her stomach. It had churned itself raw. She wasn't sure she would ever have an appetite again. With a tight smile she cautioned, "You might want to let it cool a bit first."

"Oh, pshaw." Julia sliced a large wedge and eagerly cracked the crust with her fork. "Delicious," she said when she had swallowed the first bite. "You really do have a gift, Em. I'm not just saying it to be nice, either. You know I'm honest to a fault."

"Thanks." Emily turned her back and lifted the faucet handle to soak the dirty mixing bowls.

Julia leaned a hip against the counter. "So have you given any more thought to that school?"

Her chest felt heavy. She had given quite a bit of thought to it, but her emotions weren't to be trusted just now. Her judgment felt clouded. "I'm still thinking about it," she said evenly.

"Did you talk to Scott about it?"

Emily closed her eyes. "Julia." She sighed.

"Well, don't let him be the deciding factor, Emily," Julia said. "Promise me that much at least. If there's something between you, he can wait. There are some things in life you have to do for yourself, Emily. Not for me. Not for Mom. Not for Scott."

Emily turned around to face her sister and wiped her hands on a nearby dish towel. She felt weary, but she knew if she went to bed and closed her eyes she would just be haunted by demons she didn't want to face. "What about Lucy? She's depending on me."

"You've done nothing but take care of us since Daddy died," Julia said. "Don't you think it's time for you to do something for yourself? I know how much you care about Lucy—she's a great friend to all of us—but she can take care of herself. She would want this for you, Emily. She sees your talent! Don't hold yourself back. It's too big of an opportunity."

Emily held her sister's gaze. She couldn't hold back the truth any longer. As tempting as it was to shelter Julia as much as she had tried to all her life, keeping this information from her sister would make her just as guilty as Scott.

"Julia." She stopped. "Can we talk for a minute?"

Julia frowned and then took another bite of pie. "We are talking."

Emily hesitated. "It's about something else. Something...serious."

Julia set her fork down, her expression sobering. Immediately Emily wished she could have kept her mouth shut. In a matter of seconds she was going to shatter her sister's world, tear open wounds that had never properly healed and now never could.

"What is it?"

Emily tipped her chin in the direction of the cramped living room and they silently settled into their usual spots. Unable to make eye contact, Emily stared into her lap. "It's about Dad. It's about what happened to him."

She waited for Julia to say something, but for once, her sister was speechless. There was no turning back.

"The accident wasn't Dad's fault," she said.

"Then whose was it?" Julia demanded quickly.

Emily pressed her lips together. "It was Scott's fault."

The room went still. Emily wasn't even sure she could feel her own pulse. She waited for Julia to speak, to say something, but she couldn't be sure her sister was breathing, either.

"Scott?" Julia finally said. "But how—"

"He told me. Today." Emily gave her sister a level stare. Julia's eyes were so wide, Emily could make out the whites around her green irises, which had darkened to mud. "He was nine years old and he was the last one on the…" She couldn't bring herself to say the word. "He didn't know it was his fault. And when he found out, nine years later, he left town."

"He didn't know until then? No one told him?"

Emily shook her head. "He didn't realize what he had done, that he was to blame. His parents covered it up. As a result, we didn't get a dime of insurance money."

"Oh, my God," Julia groaned. "I didn't even think

of that part. Not that money could have brought Daddy back."

"No." Emily's voice was clipped. Anger was setting in. "No, but it would have made Mom's life a heck of a lot easier."

Julia nodded. Her expression was pained as she stared to the far wall. The temperature had dropped with the setting sun and an evening breeze flew in the half-open windows. Emily shivered.

"Poor Scott," Julia said, and Emily felt her jaw drop.

"What?"

"Poor Scott," Julia said, searching her face. "He loved you so much, Emily. And then he found out what his parents did—"

"What *he* did," Emily reminded her. Her chest was heaving with emotion. What the hell was Julia thinking?

"But he didn't know. It was his father's fault for allowing a kid on a construction site!" Julia leaned forward. "My God, Emily. What was he supposed to do? Run and tell you then and there? He was torn between you and his parents! And finding out what he had done—" She broke off, shaking her head. "It must have torn him apart! It must have driven him nearly *mad!*"

"You're getting carried away with that ridiculous soap opera again, Julia!" Emily snapped. She silently vowed to stop watching *Passion's Crest* for good.

"No," Julia said. Her tone was firm enough to make Emily sit up a little straighter. "No, Emily, this is reality. Real life. Yours, mine. Scott's. Think of what he's carried with him all these years."

"He should have told me," Emily insisted.

"And what would you have said if he had? Huh?" Julia cocked her head. "If he had told you twelve years ago what he had done, how would you have reacted?"

Emily frowned. She shook her head, searching for an answer. It didn't matter. It didn't matter what she would have said. "I don't know," she said.

"It took a lot of courage for him to tell you, Emily. He ran away because he loved you, because he didn't want to hurt you. And he told you the truth now, after all these years, because he still loves you. And because he knows you deserved to hear it."

A painful knot had wedged itself in her throat, but Emily willed herself not to cry. What did it matter if Scott loved her then or loved her now? It didn't change anything. Not a damn thing. But for some reason, it did matter. It mattered an awful lot.

Scott stared at his sister in disbelief. "I don't understand. Mom and Dad said that it was me—my fault."

Lucy shook her head forcefully. "No. No, I was there. I remember, because I was worried you were going to slip climbing off that machine. It was parked right at the edge of that ditch, and it made me nervous."

"Rightfully so," Scott said grimly.

"You started walking around, picking up nails. You were always collecting little things like that."

Scott rested his elbows on his knees, leaning forward. "But what happened then?"

"Right after you hopped off the machine, Richard Porter climbed back on. He moved the machine an inch, then cursed, like he'd forgotten something. It was the curse that caught my attention." She frowned deeply, as if reliving the moment all over again. "And then he jumped down into the ditch, and the next thing I knew…"

"The excavator rolled," Scott finished for her.

Lucy closed her eyes. "Yes," she said softly.

Scott dragged a hand down his face. "So it really was Mr. Porter's fault?"

"But Dad thought it was you?" She sighed. "It all happened so fast. You must have been the last one he saw on the machine before it happened. And he just assumed." Urgency flared in Lucy's eyes. "You have to speak with Emily."

Scott's pulse was racing. He pressed his lips together, fighting that war of emotions that waged within him. "It's too late," he huffed. She wouldn't want to hear it. She had told him to leave town. To never come back. "What am I supposed to do, just go knock on her door?"

Lucy widened her gaze, driving home the obvious. "Yes. That's exactly what you should do."

"And tell her it was her father's error all along? That's going to go down nicely." He pounded a fist against his thigh. He didn't know which outcome was worse. "Lucy, maybe it really was my fault—"

She looked at him with pity. "No, Scott. I saw. I remember it clear as day. Who would be able to forget something so awful? You hopped off and Mr. Porter climbed on. He moved the machine. He was the last one operating it. It…it was just a tragic accident."

Scott released a long sigh, dragging his eyes over to the photos that lined the mantle in silver frames. His eye caught one of their trips to Martha's Vineyard when he was about eight. It was a black-and-white photo, glossy enough to have been torn from a magazine. Happy enough, too. His hair was lighter then and his teeth were crooked. Lucy stood beside him with a mouthful of braces, sporting a hairstyle that was popular back then but which probably made her cringe now. His parents stood behind them, tanned and young.

It was before the accident. Before their lives were shattered forever. After that day, his father became distant and removed, and his mother had a tired look about her. Nothing was ever the same again.

Scott shifted his gaze back to his sister. "She'll still think I lied to her, Lucy. It doesn't change anything."

"Yes, it does," Lucy urged. She reached over and set a hand on his wrist. Her eyes were pleading, but he didn't want to believe her. He didn't want to hope. "Go to her, Scott. For me."

He managed a tight smile. "I'm always doing favors for you."

"Good, because I have one more." She paused. "Find forgiveness in your heart for Dad, Scott. He thought he was protecting you. He made a bad decision—a bunch of bad decisions, honestly—but it wasn't black-and-white. He thought he was taking the path that would cause the least amount of damage. For you. For us. For all the other people that depended on their jobs with the company. It doesn't make it right, but he was trying to survive a horrible situation. Please try to understand that."

Scott gritted his teeth. "I'm not there yet, Lucy."

"I'm just saying that I understand the lengths people will take to protect their loved ones," Lucy said and they both knew she was referring to Bobby's involvement in the destruction of the town library. "That's all Dad was trying to do. In his heart, he thought he was protecting you."

Scott nodded slowly. "I'll stop by the hospital tonight. But first...I have to see Emily."

He tried to dismiss the uncertainty that filled him as he hugged his sister goodbye and walked through the door, a much freer man than when he had entered. There was a chance that Emily wouldn't care what he had to say. The truth was one thing. Trust was another.

He strode around the corner, toward the doorway to the apartments above the diner. The key felt heavy in his hand. This was his last chance. His last chance to win back the woman who had somehow found the way to his heart, and who would forever hold a place in it.

Emily had just taken another pie out of the oven when she heard the knock. She froze, bent over at the waist, oven mitt gripping the side of the scalding pie plate, her breath locked tight in her chest.

It was him. She knew it was him. The only other person it could be was Lucy, and Lucy would have called first.

But what more could he possibly want from her now? Hadn't he said enough for one day?

Maybe if she was quiet enough he would think she wasn't home and go away. Maybe he would turn and walk back down the stairs and climb into that flashy red sports car and speed out of town. Out of her life the way he had twelve years ago. She'd never see him again and eventually...well, eventually she would forget him.

So why did her heart feel so heavy at the thought?

Slowly, she stood, listening over the sound of her own shallow breaths. He was still there. Even through the door she could sense his presence. He knocked again. Louder this time. Why was he so determined? Why couldn't he just let her go?

Emily set the pie on the stovetop with a thud and untied her apron strings. Inhaling deeply for courage, she walked to the door and opened it. Scott stared back at her. And damn if she didn't want to just fall into his arms right then and there, go back to that magical place they had been in only the night before. *Stay with me forever,* he'd said.

She bit back on her teeth. He had known then. Known when he'd spoken those words. Known that he was lying to her.

"You're still here."

Scott blinked. "I'm heading out of town tonight, just as you asked."

Emily hoped the disappointment wasn't evident on her face. She tucked the emotion back into place. She was holding on to an illusion, a hope for what could have been. Not what was.

"But I need to talk to you before I go." His tone was urgent and quick.

"I think you've said about enough for one day, Scott."

"Emily, please. I wouldn't be here if it wasn't important."

Down the hall, Emily could make out the sound of Julia's door opening, and she stepped out into the hall, closing the apartment door behind her. "I don't know why I'm agreeing to this," she said, folding her arms tightly across her chest.

"I know why you're agreeing to it," he said, and her eyes widened in surprise. "Because you love me, Emily. And I love you. I always have. I—" His voice broke off. "I always will."

Her heart skipped a beat. She didn't need to hear this. She didn't want to hear this. It was hard enough already. Scott's admittance had seared open wounds much deeper than his betrayal, of the loss of her first love. Over and over she played out the circumstances of her father's death; the horrible, pitying look people would give her mother, Julia, her. "You certainly have a strange way of showing it," she said tightly.

Scott huffed out a breath. He took a step closer to her. She took a step back.

"Please—"

"Don't deny what we've shared these past few days. All these years later, there's still something between us."

Emily struggled to meet his eyes. "Maybe so, but it's not enough."

"Yes, it is. For me, at least. You're the one, Emily. I let circumstances tear us apart once before, and I'll be damned if I let it happen again."

She looked at him sharply. "What do you mean?"

"Emily, twelve years ago I was scared. I was shocked. And I was…I was horrified, Emily. For a dozen years I have done nothing but think of you. The guilt has nearly destroyed me."

She snorted. Raking her eyes down his fine physique, she quipped, "Could have fooled me." But even as she spoke, she felt ashamed of herself, uncertain. Julia's words came rushing back to her, and she thought of that eighteen-year-old boy who had made her a picnic in Central Park and who held her books every day after school. The boy whose blue eyes sparked with each grin, and the way that grin never faded when he was with her. And she thought of how it must have felt to have learned that he had hurt the person he loved so much.

Because he really had loved her. Once.

"I just had a long talk with Lucy," Scott said. His eyes were locked on hers, their intensity so penetrating she wanted to look away, but she couldn't. "Emily. Emily, it wasn't me. I wasn't responsible."

She felt the blood drain from her face. "Excuse me?"

"Lucy was there that day, and no one knew she'd seen what happened, no one ever questioned her. It was— Emily, I'm sorry. She confirmed the story. The events that were officially reported were the true events."

She blinked. "You mean the false report your father gave?"

"No." Scott dragged out a breath. "My father was trying to protect me, yes. But Lucy saw the entire thing. And my father ordered her to drive me home, so no one knew I was there. Or her. She couldn't give a statement. She couldn't report what she'd witnessed."

Understanding took hold as she held his gaze, saw the sadness in his eyes, the pain this was causing him.

"It was human error," she said softly. "My father's error."

Scott took a step toward her. "I'm sorry, Emily. Lucy's downstairs, if you want to talk to her."

Emily pulled away. She frowned at the floor, trying to process this turn of events. "No. No, if Lucy said that is what she saw, then I believe her." She met his eyes. "Lucy would never lie to me."

"I'm sorry I hurt you. Then. Now. It was the one thing I wanted to avoid. I only ever wanted to protect you. If I thought it would have been better to take the blame myself, I would have left tonight."

"Why didn't you?"

"Because I love you, Emily. I always have. I always will. I couldn't leave town again without making sure that this time I took the risk and told you the truth."

Emily bit on her lip, considered his words. When she looked up at him, she saw a shadow of the man she saw that first day he had strolled into the Sweetie Pie Bakery. Gone was the confident prodigal son who had swept into town. In his place was the man who had been burdened with this secret for twelve years. Even now, even when he had been vindicated, he was still turning to her to set him free.

"I'm not leaving tonight, Emily." He took another step toward her, and this time she didn't recoil. "I'm not going to lose you twice in one lifetime."

Her heart skipped a beat. "You really mean that? You're staying in Maple Woods?"

He nodded. "But I want you to go to that school. I want you to live the life you always wanted."

She tipped her head as a slow smile crept over her mouth. "This is the life I always wanted, Scott. You and me. Just the way it should have always been."

"But you had so many dreams. I thought I stole them from you once. I won't be the one to take an opportunity from you now."

Emily nodded slowly. "I won't give up that dream. I do want to go to school, but there are closer options. Before I wanted to run away from Maple Woods and start over. Now, I'm right where I want to be."

He grinned ruefully. "I know the feeling."

She nodded. "We share a lot, Scott."

"Too much to get past?" He cocked a brow.

She beamed. "Enough to build on."

Epilogue

Emily's eyes widened as she watched Scott attempt to lift the pie crust off the marble work top. The edges were jagged and there was a definite hole in the center, and she could tell from where she stood at the end of the kitchen island that the dough was much too thick and should have been rolled longer.

Scott's forehead was creased in concentration as he arranged the crust over the filling, attempting to stretch it to reach the edges of the plate and inadvertently causing another tear, which he simply pinched back together with his thumb and forefinger.

Emily laughed; she couldn't help it.

"You're laughing now," Scott said, glancing in her direction, "but trust me, by the end of the night you'll be saying this is the best pie you've ever eaten."

She arched a brow. "Oh, will I?"

"Wait and see," he teased, sliding the pie plate off the counter and putting it into the hot oven. "You might be the one in culinary school, but this is one recipe you're never going to forget."

"Oh, I have no doubt about that," Emily said.

Emily shook her head as Scott stood before the oven, staring through the glass, waiting for the pie to bake. "You're going to be waiting for a pretty long time," she said, setting her hands on her hips.

"What can I say?" he asked, turning around with a suggestive grin. "The best things in life are worth waiting for."

She kissed him softly on the mouth, beaming at the compliment, and then commented, "When you said you wanted me to teach you how to make a pie, I didn't realize I was dealing with such a confident pupil."

"You've been working hard lately," Scott said, taking the rag from her hand. He wiped the flour off the counter and took the mixing bowl and wooden spoon to the sink. "Between working here and driving over to Hartford for your classes three times a week, I figured it would be nice for someone else to do the cooking for a change."

She tried to hide the skepticism in her expression. From the corner of her eye she could the see the pie filling already oozing through the lumpy crust, hissing as it hit the hot oven rack. She bit back a sigh. She'd have to clean the oven before they left tonight; Lucy wouldn't appreciate walking into Sweetie Pie in the morning and finding one of her ovens covered with the sticky remnants of Scott's baking efforts.

"I do have a bit of homework for tomorrow," Emily admitted.

Scott grinned. "Perfect. You do that while I clean up this mess. Trust me, Em. You're in for the surprise of your life."

Emily laughed softly as she glanced at the oven again. Oh, she didn't have any doubt about that.

An hour later, the buzzer went off and Emily looked up from her notebook just as Scott was pulling his pie from the oven. If he noticed the way the berry filling had exploded onto the top crust, staining it red, he didn't seem to mind any more than he did about the strange way the crust hung over one edge of the plate and didn't quite reach the other.

"What do you think?" he asked, flashing her a smile that lit his eyes.

"It's the most beautiful pie I've ever seen," Emily had to say, because in many ways it was. He'd made it with his own two hands, just for her. It didn't get more perfect than that. "Maybe we should let it cool first," she suggested, but Scott just waved away her concern.

"Stay here," he instructed as he slipped through the kitchen door.

A moment later he returned, looking considerably less confident than he had only minutes earlier. His blue eyes were a notch brighter, but they studied her with newfound interest, as if gauging her every reaction. She made a mental note to eat every last bite of the pie, no matter what it tasted like. She had experience, after all, from when Julia decided to contribute to meals.

She crossed the room and took Scott's hand, noticing the way he gripped hers ever so slightly tighter than usual. He moved slowly, too, as if savoring the moment, and finally pushed open the door with his free hand.

Emily gasped. Somehow, in the time they had been in the kitchen, Sweetie Pie had been transformed. Hundreds of translucent pink balloons hung from the ceiling, and the entire room glowed from the flickering votive candles lined along the glass display case. A path of pink rose petals led to the only table remaining, with Scott's pie resting proudly in the center.

She walked slowly, taking it all in, sliding a shy smile to Scott, who was watching her carefully, eager for her approval. "Lucy helped," he whispered. "Do you like it?"

"Like it? This is…" She trailed off, turning to take in the entire room, and then looked up to meet Scott's nervous grin. He was staring at her with an intensity she hadn't seen before.

Her stomach dropped as she realized what was happening. What this all meant. What he had been up to.

"Emily." Scott's voice was low and deep, but never more certain. He reached down and took her other hand in his, throwing her that lopsided grin that made her heart turn over.

"Oh, my God." Her pulse was racing, and she could feel the tears welling in her eyes.

She watched in slow motion as he dropped to one knee and looked up at her, his smile never faltering, his hands warm and strong as they clung to hers. They'd found each other in this room, after twelve long years, and soon she would have the certainty of knowing they would never be apart again. She stared into the eyes of the boy who had held umbrellas over her head on those rainy walks home from school, who had met her with an eager smile on those lazy summer evenings when she could spend hours lying in the cool grass, listening to the smooth sound of his voice, and she saw the man she was going to spend the rest of her life with. And she knew then and there that he was right: that the recipe he had cooked up for her tonight was the best one she could have ever imagined. Lumpy pie and all.

* * * * *

THE SWEETEST AFFAIR

BRIDGET ANDERSON

To Shirley Harrison, who's always there to help me out
of a tough spot.

Chapter 1

Tracee Coleman closed the barn door to the Coleman House's U-pick store. The Coleman House estate was part bed-and-breakfast and part organic farm. Tracee worked part-time in the kitchen with her aunt Rita, cooking breakfast and pastries for the guests and family members who worked there.

"Well, that's it. Another successful season comes to a close. And not one cookie or pastry left." Tracee walked over to the empty bin that had earlier held bags of pastries. Her heart swelled with pride thinking about how well her sweets had been received at the bed-and-breakfast over the years. She hoped that same success would follow her into her own shop.

Tracee's best friend and soon-to-be business partner, Mae Watts, helped her gather empty bins and stack them up against the wall. "Girl, this is just the beginning of great things to come. When are you going to tell Rollin you're leaving?" Mae asked.

Tracee shrugged. "I've been juggling both jobs pretty well so far. Besides, they know I'm trying to open my own store. That's not something I can keep from my family."

"Yeah, I guess not. Why would you even want to? If it wasn't for Rollin, you probably wouldn't be where you are. Girl, you've got the best family."

Tracee finished stacking all the bins on their shelf against the wall, thinking about how she'd gone from baking cakes and pies for the bed-and-breakfast to taking orders from customers all over town. If Rollin hadn't let her use the bed-and-breakfast kitchen on numerous occasions, Tracee's Cake World would still be a pipe dream.

"Ladies, thank you for everything."

Tracee turned around as her cousin Rollin and his wife, Tayler, walked into the barn. They were the cutest and most generous couple she'd ever met. When they hired her and her sister, Kyla, two years ago, she'd had no idea the experience would be such a rewarding one. At the time, she was only looking for a part-time job. Instead, she found her future.

"No need to thank us," Tracee said as she came around to meet them at the front of the store by the registers. "We're just tidying up so we can get out of here. My shift is up."

"He means thank you for hanging around while we helped settle up the church folk. They cleaned us out today. We don't have a lot of produce left to donate to the shelter this evening."

Mae walked over to join them. "Yeah, those ladies purchased everything that wasn't nailed down. You have such a supportive church community."

Mae lived over in Garrard County and attended a Presbyterian church in her neighborhood. However, she'd attended Shiloh Baptist with Tracee on enough occasions to know half the congregation. And it was those networking skills that Tracee counted on to help them in the future.

"Oh, Tracee, I almost forgot." Tayler pulled a piece of paper from her pocket and handed it to Tracee. "Mrs. Bond gave this to me for Kyla. She heard about the money Kyla's collecting to help with her African project. She doesn't get online, so she wrote a check made out to the nonprofit. Can you pass this on to Kyla?"

Tracee took the check and read the amount— twenty-five dollars. "That is so sweet of her. Didn't they just have some major work done on their house?"

Tayler nodded. "They did, but everyone's so proud of the work Kyla's doing they want to be a part of it." Tayler reached out and fluffed her hands through Tracee's hair. "Look at you, looking all like Tracee Ellis Ross on television with this big hair today."

Tracee shook her head, happy that her curls were popping today. "I know, huh." She folded the check and put it in her pocket. She was proud of her little sister, too. Kyla was a PhD candidate who'd started a small, local nonprofit program teaching people where their food came from. Now, with the help of her fiancé, she was expanding to several small communities in Africa, which was where she'd been for the last few weeks.

Mae cleared her throat. "You ready to go?"

Tracee shook the thoughts from her head. "Sure, let me run up to the house and get my purse. I'll meet you in the car."

"What are you guys up to tonight?" Tayler asked.

"First I'm taking Tracee to pick her car up from the shop, then we're going to stop and get Gavin and Donna a baby shower gift. What is this, Tracee? Baby number three?" Mae asked.

Tracee stopped at the door and turned around. "Oh, I almost forgot about that. That's right, I need a gift before Saturday."

"That little family of Gavin's is growing," Tayler stated.

"It sure is. I'll be right back." Tracee opened the door and hurried toward the house. Mae wasn't aware of what she'd just done, but by bringing up Gavin's coming baby, she'd only added to the feeling of failure that Tracee was battling. She wanted a family of her own one day.

She walked through the back door of the bed-and-breakfast so as not to disturb the guests enjoying the front porch. On this last day of September, they were at capacity. Once in the back office, she pulled her purse from a drawer before going to find her aunt Rita and cousin Corra in the kitchen discussing the evening's dinner preparations.

"You gone, baby?" her aunt Rita asked.

"Yes, ma'am. Mae's taking me to pick up my car."

Tracee's cell phone rang, and she excused herself and stepped away.

"Hello?"

"Hey, Tracee, this is Melanie—we spoke a few weeks ago regarding cakes for my upcoming wedding."

Tracee almost dropped the phone. Of course she remembered Melanie Jefferson. Her family owned the largest winery in the area, and she'd snagged herself one of the richest guys in the state. "Hi, Melanie. Yes, I remember our conversation. I baked a cake for your social club, I believe?" Tracee knew that was right, but she didn't want Melanie to know how excited she was to get this call.

"That's correct. Well, I've narrowed my search, and if you can fit us into your schedule, we'd love to sample your cakes."

Tracee thrust her fist into the air and waved it around. It took everything in her not to jump around and scream at the top of her lungs. "Of course I have room in my schedule for you and your fiancé, Melanie. How soon are we talking?"

"I was thinking about a week from now. My fiancé, Harry, is in France right now, but he'll be back on Sunday. How about Tuesday afternoon?"

"Sure, one moment, let me check my calendar." Tracee put her cell phone on mute and ran her hand through her hair, pulling it back as she caught her breath. Her excited fidgeting captured the attention of Corra and her aunt, who stared at her with raised brows. All she could do was smile as she checked a nonexistent calendar.

"Melanie, Tuesday at noon is perfect. I usually meet clients at the Rival Hotel, if that works for you guys?"

"That's perfect—they're in the middle of town."

"Great, now let's talk a little about what you have in mind." Tracee hurried around the kitchen looking for a piece of paper. As if she knew just what her cousin was doing, Corra opened a drawer and produced a notepad and a pen. Tracee took it, mouthed *thank you* and eased into a kitchen chair. While Melanie described what type of cake she had in mind, Tracee scribbled everything down. They spent the next few minutes discussing Tracee's specialties before she gave Melanie her Pinterest URL, where she could see more samples of her designs.

The ladies in the kitchen continued going over dinner plans until Tracee hung up. The minute she did, they stopped everything.

"Was that really Melanie Jefferson?" Corra asked.

Tracee smiled and set her phone down. "It most certainly was."

"I heard she was getting married. Did she ask you to do the cake?" Aunt Rita asked.

"She wants to have an official tasting—can you believe it? She might hire me to do her wedding cake."

"Tracee, that's wonderful!" Aunt Rita added. "You know that is going to be a huge wedding. And a huge opportunity for you."

Tracee stood up. "I know. I have to make sure we get this wedding. I did a cake for her aunt's social club a few months back, and everybody practically drooled over the cake."

"That's because your cakes are to die for. You see how fast they leave our shelves. I have all the faith in the world you'll get this order," Corra said.

Tracee sighed. "I know Melanie likes my cakes. We'll just have to hope her fiancé does, too. I've scheduled the cake tasting for Tuesday."

"Do you want to have it here?" Corra asked, excitement dancing in her eyes.

"No, I can't. I've infringed on you guys too much with my side business. I'm going to use the Rival Hotel. They have several small meeting rooms that I've used when I didn't want to meet clients at my apartment. I don't think I want to invite Melanie and her fiancé to my apartment—he'll wonder what type of ghetto cake lady she hired."

Corra walked over and opened the pantry. "Girl, there's nothing ghetto about you or your business. You and Mae are so professional in your approach. Why do you think so many people want to patronize you? And your Pinterest page, oh my God! That page makes my mouth water every time I check it out."

Tracee took the sheet of paper from the notepad and put it in her purse before returning the pad and pen to the drawer. "That's Mae's excellent photography skills. She's working on a website now."

"You guys are going to be such a huge success. Just wait until Melanie's wedding details hit the papers and the internet. Your phone is going to start blowing up. I hope you're ready for what's about to happen to you."

Tracee thought about all the success happening around her—she was beyond ready. "I've been waiting for a break like this ever since I moved to Danville. I didn't know the idea of opening my own place was even remotely possible, but with a little help, I may be able to pull it off. And Ms. Melanie offers the type of visibility I need."

"Go get what's yours, girl. We're going to have to start purchasing our treats from you from now on."

Tracee laughed. "Don't worry, you're not losing me just yet. I'm not going anywhere until we're able to open the doors on our own place."

Aunt Rita crossed her arms over her chest. "Well, I've been around you Colemans long enough to know that when you go after something you want, you get it. Melanie won't be able to say no."

Tracee hugged her aunt and cousin before running out to the car to share the news with Mae.

Laurent Martin pulled his Mercedes up to the valet station at Brandywine in Woodland Hills, California, got out and then tossed his keys to the young man with the restaurant's logo embossed on his black shirt. He was having lunch with his father, and Thomas Martin didn't like to be kept waiting. Time Is Money and Money Is Time was his father's motto. *If something is taking up too much of your time, it's eating into your bottom line. Get rid of it.* That was another of Thomas's sayings.

Inside the restaurant, Laurent spotted his father right away. Standing at six feet five inches, an inch taller than Laurent, his father had a way of commanding the room, even if he was sitting down. Thomas Martin had taught his boys to work hard for everything they had. Just because the family owned a chain of luxury hotels didn't mean they were guaranteed a piece of the business unless they earned it. And all three Martin boys worked their tails off.

Laurent briefly stopped at the hostess station, where he was pointed in his father's direction. He glanced down at his new Tom Ford suit, hoping it would meet his father's approval. Appearance was everything in the world of luxury, according to his father.

"Laurent, you're right on time." Thomas Martin looked up as Laurent reached the table.

Laurent glanced as his watch before pulling out the seat across from his father. Fifteen minutes early was on time, on time was late. He'd arrived fifteen minutes early.

Thomas smiled as Laurent took a seat. "So, how has your day been?"

A waiter hurried over to take Laurent's drink order. He thanked him. "So far so good. No fires to put out—yet anyway."

"That's good." Thomas took a sip of red wine, his preferred drink at lunch, then he set his glass down. "Well, now that the summer's over, it's time to prepare for the upcoming holiday season. Do you have any new developments you want to run by me?"

Laurent gave his father a questioning gaze. This wasn't the kind of conversation they usually had in public. The waiter came by, and Laurent glanced at the menu before ordering his favorite onion soup and petite filet mignon. "No new developments. Why? Are Marquis or Aubrey working on something new?" His oldest brother, Marquis, always had something in play, but Aubrey spent most of his time maintaining what they had.

"As a matter of fact, yes. Marquis is working on a renovation project for the Grand Cayman location. I initially thought he was only trying to get a vacation out of the deal, but if he can make some improvements at the same time, I'm not going to sweat him over it."

"That sounds like a sweet plan," Laurent added.

"If he finishes before the holiday rush, it will be. If not, and he causes us any cancellations, I might have to move him back to cover the US locations. You know how he can talk his way into just about anything."

Laurent laughed at the reference to Marquis. His father was correct—Marquis could talk his way into a royal wedding if he had to. In fact, he was so good he'd talked their father into letting him run all the Caribbean hotels by himself. Aubrey was just as persuasive and had talked himself into the European market. Trips to France and Italy were on his calendar frequently.

While his father continued to discuss a little family business, Laurent sat wondering what they were really here to discuss. Thomas Martin wasn't in the habit of calling a lunch meeting just to catch up. His father wanted something from him.

After their meal was served, and his father went

through another drink, he finally got around to the reason for the lunch.

"I don't think I ever told you how impressed I was with the way you handled that harassment situation at Abelle Toronto last month."

Laurent nodded. "Thank you."

"You're living up to your title as family troubleshooter. Whatever the situation, turn it over to Laurent—he can handle anything. I appreciate you, son. I can't be everywhere."

"It's not a problem. It's what I do best," Laurent said.

"Which brings me to another challenge for you."

Here it comes. Laurent lowered his fork and took a drink of water to clear his palate. He sat back and waited for his father to dump some project on him that neither of his brothers wanted.

"You're also an excellent negotiator. I've watched you over the years. And you're who I need to help close the deal on a small-town hotel chain I've been trying to purchase."

Laurent was surprised. Thomas Martin was a master negotiator. All of their hotels were in prime locations due to his father's stellar skills. Why would he need him to step in? "I don't understand. This is something you've been working on?"

Thomas nodded. "I have. From a distance, with very little luck."

Laurent squinted as he tried to read the truth from his father's eyes. "What's the real story?" he asked.

His father shrugged. "No story. Just a stubborn old man who can't see a good deal when it looks him right in the face. I need you to help him see the benefits of selling to us. Tonight I'll email you all the details. You should be able to wrap things within the next week or two."

Laurent shook his head. "I'm leaving for the Caribbean tomorrow for the next two weeks. I take vacations, too, you know."

"Laurent, this deal can't wait for you to come back from vacation. This is a simple acquisition that we should have closed already. Your gift of persuasion is required on this one. I need you to leave by this weekend at the latest."

Oh, no, you don't! "You want to hijack my vacation and send me off to some godforsaken place to negotiate a deal you couldn't get yourself? Why does that not sound so appealing to me?"

"Because that's not the situation. You're merely postponing your vacation for a couple of weeks to handle something for the family that, frankly, only *you* can do. Come on, you know your brothers. They're like bulls in a china shop. This deal is going to take a little more finesse. A more subtle approach, if you will."

Laurent was being fed a bowl of crap, but he nodded anyway. "And that's where I come in," he said, pointing to himself. "You know, something about this stinks. Where is this hotel?"

His father puffed up his chest and cleared his throat. "No deal I've ever tried to negotiate stinks! This is an opportunity for Martin Enterprises to own more than boutique hotels. We've talked about expanding into the medium-size hotel market for years, and that's what this chain will do for us."

"Where is the hotel?" Laurent asked with a little more bass in his voice this time.

Raising his chin and looking down his nose at his son, Thomas Martin let him know he didn't appreciate the tone. "It's in Danville, Kentucky. A short drive from Lexington."

Laurent tilted his head and blinked. "Where in the hell is that?"

"You've heard of the Kentucky Derby, haven't you?"

"Of course I have."

"Well, there's another horse track in Kentucky. Keeneland is in Lexington, and this place isn't too far from there. We can even relocate one of the hotels to Lexington to take advantage of the racing industry."

Laurent shook his head. "I knew it. So you're sending me to some little hick town while Marquis and Aubrey get the more appealing jobs. Why do I feel as if I'm being punished for my negotiating skills?"

The waiter returned to refresh Laurent's water. Thomas paused until he left to continue.

"You're not being punished. I've been watching you over the years, and I'm fully aware of the fact that you've wanted to put your own stamp on a property just as your brothers have done. So I'm going to offer you something better than what your brothers have. Son, you have a creative side to you that extends beyond the realm of business. I have no doubt that given the opportunity, any property you control will be a huge success. That's why I'm prepared to give you complete ownership of one of the hotels."

Everything inside Laurent's body screamed *yes*. His spine stiffened as he sat up straight and nodded. He needed to conceal his excitement until he heard all the details of his father's offer. The old man could be generous, but he could also be calculating.

"You don't have to thank me now, but a little show of appreciation wouldn't hurt. I'm giving you something both of your brothers would die to have."

"I do appreciate it. As a matter of fact, it sounds too good to be true, so I'm waiting for the other shoe to drop. What's the catch?"

Thomas shook his head. "None. You've earned this. All you have to do is return with a signed deal for the chain and you have your very own hotel to do with as you please. Of course, if you want input from me or your brothers, we're always here for you. Once it's yours, you can keep working with the current staff, or establish your own staff—it's up to you. But I need you in Danville next week."

Laurent couldn't contain the corners of his mouth as they turned up into a smile. How long had he expressed his desire to strike out on his own and establish something totally different from the luxury five-star hotels his family owned? Each hotel was a one-of-a-kind creation with its own personality based on the location. Abelle's, for example, with its French theme, served an elite clientele that demanded nothing but the best.

"Thank you. I think I'll be taking the first flight to

Danville on Monday morning." Laurent beamed with so much excitement he could hardly contain himself.

"You'll have to fly into Lexington and drive to Danville, but it's a short trip. When you arrive you can check in to the hotel like a regular guest. No need to alert anyone as to your intentions right away. Let's meet Monday morning to go over the current offer, then you can be on your way."

Laurent finished lunch with his father on a good note. This had to be the best lunch they'd ever shared.

Chapter 2

Laurent pulled up to the Rival Hotel in a rented, dark blue Hyundai Elantra. The car was a calculated choice for who he needed to be this weekend. His father had tried to work with Mr. Patel, the hotel's owner, with no success. No doubt it was his father's overconfidence, often mistaken for arrogance, that got in the way. Laurent had met with his father to go over all the particulars of the offer, which was very generous. However, after that meeting he postponed his departure until Friday, in order to do some of his own research. Mr. Patel had said he'd have to think it over and discuss it with his family, but he hadn't gotten back to Thomas.

Laurent's presence was to push those conversations along while making the family feel comfortable that they were getting the best deal possible.

He'd traveled in his athletic gear, another calculated choice, and left his Gucci luggage at home. He'd purchased a Samsonite duffel and an inexpensive suit bag especially for this trip. He got out of the car and looked up at the hotel, which was in need of a little TLC. The location in the middle of town was a plus, and probably what attracted his father in the first place. However, the building merely faded into the background, with very little curb appeal. Now he was curious as to the condition of the interior.

The front doors slid open as he carried his gear into the hotel lobby. The first thing that hit him was the overly perfumed smell. What were they trying to cover up? The hotel was about ten years old, but the choice of decor gave it a much older feel. For a Friday afternoon, things were kind of slow. There weren't very many cars in the parking lot, and only one person sat in the lobby reading a magazine. Laurent walked over to the front desk to check in.

"Good afternoon, sir, checking in?" A young, studious-looking Indian guy in thick wire-rimmed glasses greeted Laurent with a smile.

His plaid shirt didn't look like a hotel-issued uniform, which meant things were probably pretty lax at the Rival. Laurent returned the smile. "Yes, I am. Laurent Martin."

The young man glanced down at the computer, inputting information until he found Laurent's name. "I have you here, sir. Laurent Martin, a king room for a week. Is that correct?" he asked.

"It is," Laurent confirmed as he reached into his pocket for his license and credit card.

The clerk accepted his cards. "I'll be right back."

The minute he walked away, Laurent shook his head. The clerk shouldn't have to leave the front desk with the customer's information. That would have to change once he took over the hotel. He turned around and took another look at the uninviting lobby. Everything was square, with sharp edges and small bursts of colors. There seemed to be no theme at all, just some stiff furniture and a table that held what looked like brochures from local establishments.

"Hello, Mr. Martin!"

Laurent turned back around at the sound of his name spoken in a much deeper voice than the front desk clerk's. A taller man, also of Indian descent, with a thick mustache and eyebrows, greeted him with a huge smile on his face.

"I'm Raji Patel, but please call me Raji." He reached his arm across the counter to shake Laurent's hand. "My father informed me of your visit. He's looking forward to meeting with you."

Surprised, Laurent returned the handshake. "It's a pleasure to meet you, Raji. I'm looking forward to meeting with your father as well."

Raji reached back and took Laurent's identification from the desk clerk and handed the cards back to Laurent. "Here you go. I'm sorry, but our card reader out here isn't working at the moment."

Another situation Laurent would have to fix. He placed his cards back in his pocket. "No problem. I understand."

Raji finished checking Laurent in while the young

clerk moved over to help an older couple who'd just walked in.

"I'll get you your keys so you can check out your room. I'm sure you're tired after that long flight," he said as he smiled up at Laurent.

"It wasn't that bad. I practically live on airplanes, so I'm used to it," Laurent said as he accepted the room keys from Raji.

"Man, I couldn't take all that flying. I fly about two or three times a year because I have to check on our other hotels. Didn't experience any turbulence, did you?" he asked.

Laurent smiled and shook his head. "No, none."

"Good for you. My dad tells me your family owns a chain of hotels as well. Are you the head sales guy or something?"

"No, I'm VP of lifestyle brand management."

Laurent watched Raji's faraway look as he nodded his head. "In other words, I represent the company with regards to new developments, proposals and negotiations. I offer suggestions on brand and type best fit based on the proposed market and location. Along with managing guest satisfaction and a host of other responsibilities."

Raji nodded. "I started working for my dad right out of high school. Worked my way up to general manager."

Laurent smiled. "Will your father be around this evening?" he asked, wanting to get things started and over with as soon as possible.

"My dad probably won't be around until tomorrow afternoon. Along with my brother, Arjun. You'll meet them then. If you're up to it, I can give you a tour of the property once you've rested? All of the hotels have this same layout, but the decor is different."

"That would be great. Let me make a few phone calls and I'll be back down."

"Sure, take your time. I'll be in the office. Just ring the bell on the counter when you come back."

Laurent found his third-floor room and was pleasantly surprised by the clean design and decor. It wasn't fancy, but appropriate for the location. After checking out the room and making a few phone calls, he decided to return to the lobby for that tour. Before he could ring the bell, the younger desk clerk popped out from the back room.

"Raji will be right with you. He said to make yourself at home."

Laurent did just that and walked over to the couch and had a seat. He leafed through the current *People* magazine before Raji walked out to greet him.

"Well, that didn't take long at all," Raji pointed out.

Laurent stood up. "No, I'm kind of eager to check things out."

Raji began the tour by pointing out where breakfast was served every morning. There was a small gym down the hall, and a pool, which happened to be closed at the moment. Laurent made mental notes as Raji gave him an in-depth look at the property Thomas wanted so badly.

"This hall gets the most traffic." Raji pointed down a corridor with lots of closed doors. "Conference rooms. Almost every group in town meets here for one thing or another." He walked down the hall, calling out the names of the rooms.

Laurent looked at the well-traveled, outdated carpeting and wondered how any proprietor could let his property get this far out of hand.

"It might not be the Taj Mahal, but it's clean."

The irritated tone to Raji's voice let Laurent know he hadn't been able to hide the displeased look on his face. While he hadn't meant to insult, he was afraid he had just made a tactical error. Mistake number one.

After the tour, he found a pizzeria within walking distance of the hotel. He returned and settled in for the night. His cell phone rang while he was catching up on the news. He picked up the phone to see Marquis's name.

"So what do you think of the place?" Marquis asked, sounding as if he had a smile on his face.

"It's a dump. The location is perfect, but this place needs a major overhaul." Laurent adjusted the pillows against his back and grabbed the television remote to mute the sound.

"Of course. Once we take ownership, the entire chain will transform into something that's up to Martin Enterprises standards."

"You mean once I take ownership, don't you?" Laurent was certain his father had informed his brothers that he was giving him a hotel. He shared everything with them.

Marquis laughed. "That's right, this one's all yours. If you can pull it off, anyway. Have you seen your old fishing buddy yet?"

"What fishing buddy?" Laurent could count the number of times he'd been fishing on one hand.

"Sam Kane, your buddy from Berkeley? Didn't he used to take you guys out on a fishing boat all the time and come back empty-handed?"

Laurent laughed. "Yeah, we called it fishing, but every trip turned into a yacht party. It's hard to concentrate on fish with so many women on board." A brief picture of bikini-clad women dancing around the boat brought a smile to his face. "Man, I haven't seen Sam in years."

"When Dad told me you were going to Danville, I remembered running into Sam's father a couple of months ago. Sam met a girl from that area and moved to Kentucky. He's a professor at the local college in Danville. I wasn't sure if you knew that or not."

"I had no idea." He thought about how boring the town had looked on his drive in. "Why in the hell would he give up life in California for this place?"

"Hey, the love of a good woman will make you do some crazy things. I think he's married with kids and all. You should look him up."

Laurent shook his head. In college, Sam had had a different woman every semester. Sometimes more than one a semester. He loved to party and show everybody a good time. "I'm going to do that. But married with kids—man, I might not even recognize Sam."

"Tell him I said hello when you two hook up. Well, I just wanted to offer my assistance if you need anything. I know you've got these negotiations down pat, but I'm here for you if you need me."

"Thanks, Marquis, that means a lot." Marquis was a numbers man who could quickly provide Laurent with statistics on anything he needed in a matter of hours.

"No problem, bro. I'll be going back to Grand Cayman over the weekend, but I'm available by cell."

The Caribbean. Did he have to rub it in? "I don't think I'll have any problems, but if I need you, I'll reach out to you or your assistant."

"Oh, that would just make Lonnie's day. You know she has a crush on you. Every time you come to my office, it takes her several minutes to pull herself together after you leave."

Laurent laughed. "That is not the truth. But tell her I said hello anyway."

They shared playful laughter before Laurent ended the call and decided to call it a night. He'd skip looking over the hotel paperwork; he'd read enough on the plane. Instead, he'd hit the sack early and have a good run in the morning. That was the best way to see the surrounding area and survey what he was getting into. Then he'd have to look up his old buddy Sam. Hopefully, he hadn't changed too much and could still show him a good time while he was in town.

Tracee kept glancing in the rearview mirror at the boxes strapped into the back seat. She'd prepared a sample wedding cake along with a dozen cupcakes in various flavors for Melanie Jefferson's cake tasting this afternoon.

"Are you nervous?" Mae asked from the passenger's seat.

"As hell! I just hope he likes my cake. I know Melanie likes them, but if this fella of hers doesn't, we're sunk."

"Girl, don't worry—he'll probably like whatever she likes. I'm also eager to check out this space that you're wanting to lease."

"When the Rival Hotel first opened, my grandmother had a little coffee and pastry spot there. When she passed, my cousin Betty took over. The space grew into this small café, and she ran it until she passed a few years ago. So you can kind of say the space has been in my family for years. It has its own separate entrance and everything. After my cousin's passing, Mr. Patel closed the coffee shop's doors. I don't think it was ever very lucrative. I'd forgotten all about it until I was helping Corra and Tayler with one of their Color of Success events. The windows have this fancy paper on them so you can't tell what's inside. They opened the room to store some of the larger items for the event and I saw this space that would be perfect for our café—with a little remodeling, of course."

"And the location is perfect. We can take advantage of the hotel crowd as well as the downtown business community. I'm getting more and more excited about this venture."

"Me too," Tracee said after taking another glance at her precious cargo in the back seat. She pulled into the Rival Hotel's parking lot and found a space by the back door, which was closer to the hotel's small kitchen. She needed to store her baked goods in their refrigerator while she set up everything else for the meeting.

The front desk clerk unlocked the small meeting room she'd reserved and had the kitchen provide a side table with water and glasses. The room wasn't the most elegant of places to meet, but it did provide the privacy she needed and a backdrop for her to display her cakes without taking anything away from them. Within minutes, she and Mae had their brochures on display and had made sure the temperature in the room was just right.

Mae rubbed her palms together. "Time to bring in the cakes."

Tracee's heartbeat pounded in her chest. This was it. The moment she'd been waiting for. It was time to put her best foot forward. Mae's naturally flawless face and short curly hair always gave her a professional, polished look. She, however, had tried to tame her curls by pulling them back into a ponytail, but loose tendrils of hair were touching the sides of her face and neck.

They entered the kitchen and collected their cakes from the woman on staff. Tracee carried the sample wedding cake, while Mae followed her with the box of assorted cupcakes. Under her arm was a sleeve that held the cutting utensils Tracee liked.

The kitchen door opened into the corridor that led to the meeting rooms, the pool and the gym. Because her hands were full, Tracee turned around and, using her butt, pushed on the door. Immediately, something didn't feel right.

Chapter 3

Downtown Danville was about as slow as Laurent thought it would be. In some ways it reminded him of the small villages in Quebec he used to frequent with his mother when he was a child, only there were no French-speaking people here. He'd wanted to get up early for his run but overslept when he forgot to set his phone. His morning runs cleared his head and readied his mind for the work to come. Instead, he pulled on his running gear and went for a jog rather than eating breakfast.

With earbuds in, listening to his favorite play-list, he jogged his way back to the hotel. He wasn't sure what time Mr. Patel would be returning, but he planned to take a shower, dress and be ready for anything. Some community social group must have been having a meeting, because there were little old ladies mingling all around. Laurent caught the front desk clerk's attention and asked where he could find the closest vending machine. He needed a bottle of water. The clerk motioned down the hall, and said something about "toward the gym."

Switching the music on his cell phone to his cooldown playlist, he continued briskly down the hall toward the gym. There were several doors, but none of them had a vending sign. He started to say forget it and just go up to the vending machine on the third floor when he saw an unmarked door and a light coming from underneath it.

"This must be it," he said to himself. He reached for the doorknob and pulled it open, getting the surprise of his life.

A scream, followed by something flying over his head, ended with a pair of big, beautiful black eyes looking up at him. On reflex he'd grabbed the woman falling out of the door under her arms, just in time to keep her from hitting the floor. The light floral scent of her perfume tickled his nose, causing him to take a deep breath. Still inside the doorway, another woman stood with eyes bucked and mouth wide-open. That wasn't a good sign.

"Oh my God!" the woman in the doorway screamed.

As the woman in his arms struggled to right herself, Laurent tried to make sense of what had just happened. That wasn't the room with the vending machine. He helped her up before yanking the earbuds from his ears.

"Look at what you just did!" the woman yelled as she straightened to her full height.

When she set her eyes on Laurent, he stopped breathing for a second. She was beautiful. Her eyes could stop traffic, and those ruby-red lips were calling his name. Her hair was pulled back, but ringlets of curls had loosened as she'd fallen into his arms. His eyes followed her as she walked around him and over to something on the floor—a crushed white box. He needed to say something, but he was speechless.

"Oh, man, not my cake! Not now!" she screamed.

He found something of a voice. "I'm sorry, I didn't see you."

"Girl, is it okay?" Both women were in the hall now, as the beautiful one from his arms gingerly righted the box and examined the contents. A few of the older women from the lobby had come peeking down the hall to have a look.

Laurent had the sinking feeling he'd just ruined this beautiful woman's day.

She threw the top back. "It's ruined! My beautiful cake is ruined." She quickly turned to the other woman. "You have the cupcakes, don't you?"

"Right here." She held up a smaller, square box kept secure in her hands.

Both women took a deep breath before turning their fiery gazes on Laurent. He swallowed hard as he wrapped his earbuds around his cell phone. "Again, I apologize. I opened the door thinking I would find the vending machines."

The tall one with the red lips narrowed her eyes at

him, and he immediately felt worse. He had to offer to do something to fix the situation. He took a step toward them. "Let me buy you another cake," he offered. "Or two."

"You can't buy another one of those, son." The shorter, hippy sister tilted her head at him.

"Didn't you see the staff-only sign pasted above the door?" asked the tall woman, with her nostrils flared.

Laurent hadn't seen any sign on the door. But when he turned around and glanced up, sure enough there was a plaque just above the door that read Staff Only. Why in the hell wasn't it on the door instead of above the door? He quickly turned back to the women, who had "told you so" smirks on their faces.

"I'm sorry. I didn't see that. Just let me run upstairs and get my wallet—"

"This is a one-of-a-kind cake that can't be duplicated, you idiot. I have a meeting in less than fifteen minutes, and now I don't have a cake." She let out a nervous laugh. "This is crazy. The biggest meeting of my life, and you ruined it and my cake."

"Don't worry, girl, we still have the cupcakes." The shorter woman held up her box with a smile. "And even though the cake is smashed, maybe they can still taste it."

"I can't present that cake to anybody. Especially not Melanie."

Laurent wanted to return to his room and let these women resolve the situation themselves.

Then the taller one turned her wrath on him again, placing a hand on her hip. "Why are you walking through this place with those earphones on, anyway? You can't hear what's coming or going."

"I could ask why were you backing out of a room when you couldn't see what was on the other side. Like I said, I'm sorry, but I don't think I'm totally to blame here. Besides, I offered to purchase you another cake. I'm not sure what else I can do."

"You're right, you can't do anything else. You've already done enough." She turned to her friend. "I'm going to go in there and sell this, cake or no cake. Come on, Mae." Without another word they headed down the hall toward the conference rooms.

The minute she walked away, Laurent couldn't shake the feeling he should be going after her. Something about the look in those piercing eyes grabbed him by the throat and wouldn't let go. Who was she? He hadn't even gotten her name. Although at the moment, he doubted she'd want to give it to him. He stood there watching her confidently stride down the hall with a smile on his face.

Tracee's heart was pounding in her chest as she walked down the corridor. Her first official tasting was ruined unless she could quickly come up with something clever to save the day. Then again, she could just be honest with them and let them know how some jerk had caused her to lose her balance and ruin the sample cake. They still had a few minutes. When they reached the small conference room, Mae held the door open for her. Tracee took one look over her shoulder to see if that gym rat of a brother in shorts was still standing around. He wasn't.

"Girl, can you believe that dude," Mae said, following the direction of Tracee's gaze. "I bet he had that music blasting through his ears and wasn't paying attention to where he was going."

"That's obvious," Tracee said as she turned around and entered the room. "What I should have done was taken his money just on principle. If we don't get this gig, I'm going to find him and kick his butt."

Mae helped her display the cupcakes while they scrambled to come up with a story to save the day. Before they could agree on something, the door to the conference room opened, and a beautiful blonde followed by a shorter white guy entered the room.

"Melanie!" Tracee strode to the door to greet them.

"Hi, Tracee, it's so good to see you again."

"Same here." Tracee greeted Melanie with a cursory hug. They had gone to the same schools, although they hadn't been in the same classes, so Tracee felt as if they had something in common.

Melanie introduced her husband-to-be, and Tracee introduced Mae. Everyone had a seat at the round table full of brochures and cupcakes. Tracee couldn't help but notice the way Melanie's fiancé kept looking around the room. He made her nervous.

"So where's the cake?" he asked. "I thought this was going to be a cake tasting."

Tracee sighed and looked at Mae, who sat poised with her professional smile, leaving the explanation up to her. There was only one thing she could do. Tracee stood up and walked over to the side table where the smashed cake sat. In her book, honesty was the best policy.

* * *

When Laurent returned from his run, an envelope had been slipped under his door. Mr. Patel requested that he meet them at a nearby restaurant for lunch, which was just what Laurent had hoped for—a more relaxed atmosphere to discuss business. After he showered and changed into an outfit that made him look more like the average middle manager than a company VP, he was ready to meet with Mr. Patel and his sons. He grabbed his leather portfolio and set out to make magic happen.

He found the small Indian restaurant with no problem. Once inside, he was ushered to a back room, where a table filled with food, along with three men, waited for him. He assumed this was Mr. Patel and his sons.

The oldest of the three men walked toward Laurent with a slight limp in his gait. "Ah, you must be Laurent Martin?"

"Yes, sir. And you must be Mr. Patel." Laurent smiled and accepted the man's outstretched hand. Laurent towered over the shorter man, who was white headed with a salt-and-pepper mustache and beard. His face looked as if the years had taken a toll on him, but he smiled nonetheless. The tantalizing aromas and vibrant colors of the food on the table made Laurent's stomach growl. After his morning run, he was ready to eat, but he hoped they were also prepared to talk business.

"Call me Abeer. It's a pleasure to meet you after speaking with your father on so many occasions.

I'm sorry we could not come to an agreement, which would have saved you the trip."

"Well, let's hope you and I have better luck. My father has briefed me on everything, and I think we've included some incentives that you will find to your liking. Martin Enterprises is very interested in your properties, and in doing right by your family."

The older man had crossed his arms over his chest and glanced away, giving Laurent the impression that he wasn't interested in business. Mistake number two, Laurent said to himself. *He invited you to lunch—don't talk business yet. Let him lead the conversation.*

"Have you met my sons?" Mr. Patel asked as he waved them over. The two men at the other end of the table broke free of their conversation and joined them. "This is my son Raji, whom I believe you met yesterday."

Laurent nodded toward his tour guide and smiled. "Yes, I did. Thanks for the tour," he said as he shook Raji's hand.

"This is my eldest son, Arjun. He lives in Somerset and manages our hotel there."

Arjun was a slight man with a small frame. He offered Laurent a weak handshake with a closed-lip smile. He accepted the man's hand, to the sound of more people entering their private section of the restaurant. When Laurent turned around, a few women dressed in flowing saris, along with a few small children, entered the room. Arjun explained that the family would be joining them for lunch.

Mr. Patel patted Laurent on the back. "I hope you

like Indian food, and that you're hungry. A good friend of mine owns the restaurant, and he is an excellent cook. I didn't know what you'd like to eat so, as you see, we ordered a little bit of everything. Come on, let's eat."

Disappointed but not too surprised, Laurent smiled as he was introduced to the rest of the family before being told where to sit. He had truly been invited to lunch and not a business meeting, as he'd hoped. He understood now he had to gain Mr. Patel's trust before he'd speak numbers.

After a more than disappointing lunch with the Patels, where not a word of business was spoken, Laurent returned to his room and did a little digging to look up Sam Kane. Just as Marquis had said, he was a professor at Centre College. He got his old buddy on the phone.

"Man, I can't believe you're in Danville. Laurent, I haven't seen you since… I don't know man, when was the last time we were together?" Sam asked.

"Amsterdam, a year after graduation from Berkeley. We about shut the place down. That's why I almost fell out of my chair when Marquis told me you were married."

"A lot's changed since college, man. I met a woman who had the power to shut all that *partying* down. We've been married ten years now. Two kids, a boy, a girl, and a big-ass dog. Guess you can say I'm living the American dream."

Laurent shook his head. Happy for his friend, but surprised at the same time. "Man, that sounds wonderful, but somehow I thought you'd probably be practicing international law and living overseas. Thought you might follow in your old man's footsteps." *Like I did.*

"Law school really wasn't my thing. I thought about it, but after spending a few years studying abroad, I chose international relations instead. And now I'm teaching it."

"That's what I hear. Sam, the college professor. I'm proud of you, man. We have to sit down and get caught up while I'm in town."

"Definitely. How long are you going to be here?"

Laurent thought back to the lunch he'd assumed was going to be his first meeting. "A week or so, and then I'm taking a two-week vacation to someplace tropical."

"Man, we'll definitely have to get together. I want you to meet my wife. I used to tell her all about my old fishing buddies." They laughed together and went on to trade stories of fishing for women instead of fish. Sam's parties had been popular with all the beautiful women on campus.

"Say, I've got an idea. What are you doing tomorrow?" Sam asked.

It was Sunday and Laurent didn't know of a church to attend in the area. "Nothing. I'm all yours."

"My wife and I have reservations at this little bed-and-breakfast that does a wonderful Sunday brunch. It's kind of new, and we've been wanting to go for a while. Why don't you come and join us? That way we can catch up and you can meet my wife."

"Sure. Just let me know where to meet you."

"Great. I'll call and have them add one more. Is this your cell you're on? If so, I'll text you the address and time."

"Yep. You've got it."

"Fantastic! I can't wait to see my old fishing buddy."

"Me neither," Laurent said, chuckling at the way they used the term. He said goodbye, then pulled out his laptop. He was about to engage in the one thing he didn't like to do on a Saturday night—work.

Sunday brunch was another one of Tayler's ingenious ideas. Make it elegant, keep it simple and treat the guest like a VIP. Tayler knew how to take advantage of slow times and monopolize on them. Anyone who reserved a spot for Sunday brunch was offered a discounted rate for a midweek stay. Tracee was surprised by the number of folks who took advantage of the discounts. She especially liked the fact that she was able to grab a few more hours, since she hadn't been working Sundays.

This Sunday she was in a particularly good mood. Whoever said it doesn't pay to tell the truth was lying. After she'd confessed about her accident yesterday at the cake tasting, Melanie and her fiancé had still wanted to taste the smashed cake. They loved it so much that they looked through her portfolio of pictures and picked out the one they wanted. She had her first affluent client, which she hoped would lead to more business and greater revenue over time.

The kitchen was abuzz with Tayler, Corra and her aunt Rita all getting ready for the brunch crowd.

Tracee had baked a carrot cake and buttermilk panna cotta earlier that morning. Presently, there were only four guests staying at the bed-and-breakfast, with five reservations for brunch.

From the kitchen, Tracee could hear some of the guests had arrived and Tayler was welcoming them. Minutes later, Tayler entered the kitchen with orders of steak and eggs, breakfast pizza, French toast with berries, waffles and homemade jams. They also served a variety of cereals, muffins and other pastries.

Tracee backed out of the kitchen with a plate of French toast in one hand and a steak and eggs plate in the other. She turned toward the table full of handsome men and women with a smile.

"Who had the French toast?" she asked. A woman at the end of the table raised her hand. Tracee held the plates above their heads as she made her way to set the plate in front of a middle-aged black woman with beautiful salt-and-pepper hair. The hair was the first thing to catch her attention. She hoped as she grew older her hair would be so luscious.

"And how about the steak and eggs?" She held up the second plate.

"I believe that would be mine." A voice came from the other side of the table.

Tracee looked across the table and almost dropped the plate. The rude guy from the hotel yesterday looked up at her with raised brows. The corner of his lip turned up, and she realized he recognized her as well.

Chapter 4

Tracee shook the stupid look from her face and walked around the table to deposit his plate before him. "Your steak and eggs."

"Thank you. Would you happen to have any steak sauce?" he asked, glancing up at her.

There was something about the slow way his gaze traveled up her body before meeting her eyes that made her take a deep breath. She shook her head, then quickly changed directions. "I mean, yes. Of course we do. Does anybody else need anything?" she asked as she walked around the table. Everyone said no.

Tracee dashed into the kitchen and found the steak sauce in the pantry. She couldn't believe that guy was sitting in their dining room. He'd recognized her, but he hadn't said anything about yesterday. Steak sauce in hand, she returned to the dining room.

When she set the bottle on the table, he thanked her with a self-satisfied grin on his face.

"I hope everything went all right yesterday," he added before she walked away.

Tracee placed her hands on her hips. So, he wanted to acknowledge what he'd done.

"Luckily yes, everything was fine. Thank you for asking."

"Do you two know each other?" a man sitting across the table asked.

"I ran into her yesterday at the hotel. I believe you were on your way to a meeting?"

Mr. Rude had asked her that with squinted eyes. She gritted her teeth and smiled. "I was. A very successful meeting, I might add."

He smiled. "I'm glad to hear that. I don't believe I got your name?" he asked.

"And I don't believe I gave it." She let out a deep breath. "Tracee Coleman, and you're?"

"Laurent." He stood up halfway, holding the napkin in his lap, and offered his hand, knocking over his glass of iced tea at the same time.

Tracee jumped back as he quickly grabbed the glass before losing all of the contents. She wanted to laugh. He used his napkin to soak up the liquid from the table.

"I'm sorry about that," he said to the man sitting next to him, who'd managed to move his plate out of the way before any damage was done. Then Laurent turned his attention back to Tracee and extended his hand. "I'm clearly not making a good impression, but the name's Laurent Martin."

Tracee accepted his hand. "It's nice to meet you. Don't worry about that. I'll get you another tea. I don't believe I've seen you around here before. Do you live in the area?" she asked as she walked over to the sideboard for the pitcher of iced tea.

"No, I'm here on business."

"Laurent is an old fishing buddy of mine." The man next to Laurent put his arms around the woman sitting next to him. "I'm Sam Kane, and this is my wife, Janet."

Tracee nodded a hello to them.

"Laurent and I used to go fishing a lot in our college days."

Sam's wife elbowed him, while Laurent shook his head with a big smile on his face. Fishermen, huh? Tracee hated fishing. She ended this pleasant conversation by making sure everybody had everything they needed. She cleaned up the wet napkins and left the room to let the guests eat.

When she walked into the kitchen, her aunt Rita was pulling her carrot cake from the refrigerator and preparing to cut a few slices.

"How's it going out there?" she asked.

Tracee nodded. "Smooth as usual." She helped her aunt cut the cake and then started loading the dishwasher.

Tracee made a point not to return to the dining room for the rest of the brunch. Her aunt Rita handled the dessert, while Tayler cleared the table. Laurent Martin was an extremely handsome man. In his jogging clothes, or in casual attire, he had an unmistakable swag about himself. A swag that she wouldn't be able to resist, given the opportunity. Thankfully, she wasn't interested in somebody's old fishing buddy, no matter how hot he was.

Four days in town, and Laurent still hadn't been able to sit down with Mr. Patel to discuss business. In the meantime, he'd spent his days working remotely on projects that needed his attention, and looking over the Rival Hotel deal again. When he finally sat down with Mr. Patel, he would knock his socks off.

Meanwhile, he poured all his frustrations out on Sam as they sat at Nik's Place, drinking beer on a Tuesday evening.

"Thanks for coming out with me, man. Sitting in a hotel for the last couple of nights watching television is not what I had in mind when I flew over here."

Sam laughed. "Yeah, I know life in Danville is much slower than California, but I've gotten used to it. It's a pretty cool place actually. Great for raising a family." Sam cleared his throat. "You know, I have to admit that I'm surprised you're not married by now. Even though we all liked to party back then, you always struck me as the serious type. I mean, half the time you brought your girl on our fishing trips."

Laurent smiled and shrugged. "I don't know. I guess I just haven't found the right woman yet, or maybe I'm destined to be a bachelor—who knows. One day when the time is right, I'll slow down long enough to really get to know somebody."

Sam held up his beer bottle for a toast. "Well, enjoy the journey, my man."

They clinked bottles. The sound of women laughing from the other side of the restaurant caught Laurent's attention. The music was loud, but the women even louder. "Sounds like somebody's having a good time," he said. If Sam wasn't married, Laurent would suggest they check it out, but times had changed.

"It sure does," Sam replied as he turned in his seat to follow the ruckus with his eyes. Unfazed, he turned back around.

"So, how is married life?" Laurent asked. "Because man, I remember how you used to live for the weekends and parties. Remember how we used to drive up the coast partying with the girls up there? You were a beast, Sam!"

Sam smiled, but shook his head. "Man, I was searching for something and didn't even know it. Once I hooked up with my wife, I didn't even want to keep partying unless she was there with me. I'm telling you, man, she put something mighty powerful on me."

"Hell, I can see that. Look where she's got you. Not that this isn't a cool place, but Danville, Kentucky! Come on, Sam, you don't miss Cali at all? Or hanging out in the VIP room in Paris for a weekend?"

"Oh, I did at first. But I had my fill of a different woman every week. When you meet the right woman, your future will become crystal clear. Mark my words."

Laurent finished off his beer. "Okay, but what

does a single guy do around here for a good time? Because I haven't met that woman yet."

Sam shrugged. "He finds himself a good woman."

"Well, considering I'm going to be here for such a short time, that's not an option."

"Then how about a day at the racetrack? Keeneland's open all month for the fall meet. I don't have any classes on Wednesdays."

Laurent smiled. "Now that's what I'm talking about. A little horse racing while I'm here. Sure, let's make it happen." Laurent looked around. "Where's the men's room?"

Sam pointed. "Straight back on your left. Can't miss it."

"I'll be right back." Laurent walked through the restaurant toward the back. In a back corner, he found the group of loud women celebrating something. The table was decorated with balloons and gift bags everywhere. He only saw a few faces, but everyone seemed to be having a good time. He smiled to himself. He loved to see people enjoying life.

"Thank you all so much for remembering my birthday." Tracee gave Mae, who was sitting next to her, a hug. She was one of the true friends Tracee had since moving back into town. While Tracee was in Louisville learning how to become a pastry chef, Mae had been in business school. She'd met her husband and become a successful businesswoman before losing everything in their divorce. But with Tracee's help, she would bounce back.

"How could I not? The ladies of the book club wanted to surprise you."

Tracee looked around. "And you did. Great food, great friends—this was nice."

"And great liquor." Mae picked up her glass of wine.

"Don't talk about liquor. I need to run to the little girls' room." Tracee got up. "I'll be right back."

"Okay, but grab your jacket when you get back—we're taking our drinks up on the deck. The music's better up there."

Dinner and drinks with the girls was great. This wasn't the way Tracee usually celebrated her birthday, but money was tight now with Tracee's Cake World taking every dime she had. Every one of the women celebrating with her was a customer, and everyone in the restaurant potential customers, she thought as she walked to the restroom.

After checking her lipstick and washing her hands, she shouldered the door open. The corridor leading to the bathrooms was well lit, and a man had walked out of the men's room ahead of Tracee. Something about his body looked familiar.

He suddenly stopped and stepped back, stepping on her toe as two girls hurried past him headed for the bathroom.

"Ouch!" She jumped and pressed her hand against his back.

"Oh, excuse me."

Tracee hopped on one foot, while squeezing the other toes in her hand.

"I'm sorry, did I—?"

Mr. Rude. Tracee let go of her foot and straightened up. "Yes, you stepped on my toes." He smiled, and Tracee's heart fluttered. Why did he have to be so freaking handsome with those mesmerizing eyes and perfect lips?

"My apologies. I was trying to get out of the way. Looks like somebody had one drink too many the way they ran past." Then he gave her a quick head-to-toe glance.

He recognized her, but she'd bet he didn't remember her name. And she wasn't going to bail him out. Laurent Martin—she remembered his name. She tilted her head and smiled. *Either say something or get out of the way.*

"Tracee, we've got to stop meeting like this."

She crossed her arms. "So, you do remember my name. This is the third time in four days that I've seen you. Are you following me?"

His eyes widened, and he held his palms up. "No, ma'am. I'm just having a beer with a friend. I had no idea you'd be here." Then he raised a brow. "I might ask you the same thing. Are you following me?"

She laughed. "Absolutely not."

He lowered his hands. "If you say so."

The way he smiled at Tracee, slightly bobbing his head to the music in the bar, sent a shiver through her body. This brother had to know he was a head turner even in a casual black T-shirt, jeans and those fly boots. He was probably used to women tripping all over themselves to get to him. She was about to open her mouth to say something when he pointed toward her head.

"What's the occasion?"

She reached up and touched the crown she'd forgotten was pinned into the top of her hair. "Oh, it's my birthday. It's a book club thing. We pass the crown around for each person's birthday. Kind of silly, I know."

"That's not silly—it sounds fun. And happy birthday."

She nodded slowly. "Thank you."

"After you," he said, pointing back into the bar.

Tracee led the way out. After a few steps, she stopped and was just about to say goodbye and rejoin her friends when he leaned in closer to her.

"You'll have to let me buy you a birthday drink before you leave."

She held her chin up. "I just might do that." It would serve him right for ruining her cake if she ordered something expensive. "My friends and I are headed up on the deck if you'd like to join us. The music's better up there," she said, shocking herself. Why was she inviting this man to join her party when she didn't know anything about him other than he was fine as hell?

He glanced back at the bar, and for the first time she realized he might be with a woman.

"I'll see what Sam wants to do. You remember Professor Kane from Sunday brunch?" he asked.

Tracee looked around him and saw the professor sitting at the bar. His wife wasn't with him. "Oh, yeah. Your fishing buddy. Bring him, too. The more the merrier. But I'll warn you, my girls tend to get pretty lit up on the deck."

Laurent chuckled. "That sounds like the place to be." He glanced around him at the diners. "It's getting pretty dead around here."

"Then come on up," she said with a wave. *What the hell could it hurt? This little hen party is about to get turned up.*

His smile gave her life.

When she walked back into their section of the restaurant, some of the girls had already started packing things to go upstairs. Tracee had opened her presents and they'd finished dessert. This crew was ready to get their groove on, on a Tuesday night.

"Wasn't that the guy from the hotel Saturday morning?" Mae asked as Tracee reached the table.

Leave it to Mae not to miss a thing. "Yeah, that's him. The same guy that showed up at Sunday brunch."

"And he just happens to be in here tonight, too?" Mae asked, peeking around Tracee.

"Child, please, this makes the third time I've run into this guy. Coincidence, you think?" Tracee asked as she reached for her purse.

"Yeah, like maybe your paths were destined to cross. This is a small town, you know. Then again, he could be stalking you."

Tracee laughed. "Well, if he is, he's kind of cute, don't you think?"

"Kind of! Oh, he's very handsome. And he's got a certain sex appeal about himself. What were you guys talking about, anyway?"

Tracee shrugged. "Nothing really. He asked about the crown, so I invited him to join us on the deck."

Mae's head rocked back. "No, you didn't! The guy who ruined your cake?"

"Yep. Him and his professor friend. Come on, let's get up there."

Tracee slipped her jacket back on and followed the ladies to the deck, where there was music and an empty dance floor. Large heaters were placed around the perimeter to keep the chill away. Several tables were set up with a small bar and a DJ corner. One waiter sat talking to the DJ. All of Tracee's presents and the ladies' purses were deposited on one table while they hit the dance floor.

After a few minutes, more people from downstairs found their way up and joined in on the fun. Mr. Wood, who Tracee took all her dry cleaning to, even made it up with his wife. The middle-aged white couple were celebrating their tenth wedding anniversary. Then Tracee saw Laurent as he reached the top of the stairs nodding his head to the beat, and she lost all her rhythm.

Chapter 5

Tracee stumbled over her own feet and bumped into one of her friends.

"Tina, I'm so sorry," Tracee said with her hand over her mouth. She couldn't take her eyes off Laurent. Right behind him was his friend Sam, who was good-looking as well, but happily married. Together they looked like trouble—in a good way.

Afraid she'd stumble again and embarrass herself, she left the dance floor and walked over to Laurent and Sam. "I see you made it up."

Laurent gestured to his friend. "You remember Sam?"

Tracee accepted Sam's outstretched hand. "Yes, I do."

"Happy birthday," Sam said.

"Thank you."

A few more people came up the steps behind them.

"Maybe we should grab one of these tables before they're taken," Laurent said, as he walked over to the table next to Tracee's and pulled out a chair.

Was he pulling out a chair for her? Such a gentleman. She hesitated, because she didn't want her girls to think she was deserting them after all they'd done for her. Laurent merged the chairs, making one long table for six. She smiled and sat down.

One of her friends knew Sam, and they stood talking for a few minutes.

"What are you drinking?" Laurent asked as soon as Tracee sat down.

"I'll have a glass of white wine, thank you." She changed her mind about the most expensive thing on the menu.

"You're welcome." He walked over to the bar.

Two of her girlfriends came by to say good-night and give her another birthday hug. Tracee thanked them for everything.

Laurent returned with her glass of wine. "So, Tracee, tell me a little bit about yourself," he said as he set the glass in front of her.

"Well, you know I work at the Coleman House bed-and-breakfast."

"Yeah, Sam was telling me that's a family-run establishment. Did your parents own it?"

"No, my cousins' parents. Rollin and Corra, the owners, are my first cousins. I work there part-time, along with my younger sister, Kyla. As you've probably already guessed, I'm the pastry chef. I cook everything from desserts to side dishes."

Laurent lowered his head. "Yeah, about the cake. I know I've apologized numerous times, but I want to let you know how happy I was when you said it didn't ruin your presentation. How did you pull that off?"

"I told the truth. They thought it was funny and wanted to taste the cake anyway. Thank God it hadn't fallen out of the box. But all's well that ends well."

"So, you bake cakes for people outside the bed-and-breakfast?"

She reached into her purse, pulled out a business card and handed it to him. "Tracee's Cake World. I was on the way to my first 'official,'" she said, using air quotes, "cake tasting. And I needed that business. It's going to help me open my own store."

He read the card. "So you're a professional?"

"I'm a professional pastry chef, yes. But I can cook just about anything you want."

Laurent smiled at Tracee before turning up his beer bottle.

"So what do you do when you're not fishing?" Tracee asked Laurent.

Laurent lowered his head and chuckled. "I'm a hotel brand manager."

"What's so funny?" she wanted to know.

He shook his head. "Nothing, I was just thinking about how much Sam used to love to go fishing." Then he turned his seat around, facing her. "What do you do when you're not in the kitchen baking up something sweet?"

Tracee sipped her wine. "I'm always in the kitchen

baking something, or working on my business. But I also like to go to concerts in Lexington or Louisville."

"Really! Who do you like to see in concert?"

"Oh, I have really eclectic taste in music. You probably won't know anyone I name."

"Try me."

She set her wineglass down and gave him the side eye. She hadn't met a man yet who enjoyed her eclectic tastes in music. "Okay, how about Sabrina Claudio."

"Love her," he responded.

"Okay, that was easy—everybody loves her. How about Masego? Or French Kiwi Juice?"

Laurent leaned back in his seat, bringing his brows together. "What do you know about French Kiwi Juice?"

She smiled. "Oh, I know jazz. I know he's a multi-instrumentalist. I'm not too young to appreciate good music when I hear it."

"That's cool. Have you seen him perform live?"

"Unfortunately, no. Not yet, anyway. Have you?"

"I had the pleasure of catching his show in San Diego once. In a word, he's mesmerizing."

She smiled. "I can only imagine."

"I'm not as familiar with Masego, but I have heard the song 'Tadow,' featuring Masego. I like that one in particular."

"Oh, yeah, why?"

He shrugged. "I don't know—something about the groove reminds me of when my brothers and I used to play together. Growing up, we had ourselves a little band."

"Really! Where did you play?"

He laughed. "At home. We weren't actually good enough to leave the basement."

"Oh my God. I bet it was fun, though."

"It was. We listened to everybody and tried to mimic them. I'm particularly well versed in old-school music because my brothers are older than me. But I listen to a little bit of everything."

"What instrument did you play?"

"Guitar, a little bit of the keyboard."

"Wow that sounds fun. So, where are you from Laurent?"

"Palo Alto, California."

"What brought you to our little town?"

"I'm kind of working on the Rival Hotel's brand."

"Do you travel a lot, checking on hotels?"

He rocked his head from side to side before nodding. "I do, yeah."

"Well, you're staying in the second-best establishment in this town. The first one being the Coleman House bed-and-breakfast, of course," she said with a wink and smile.

Laurent rocked his head in time with the beat of the music and returned the smile. He was staring at her, which made her a tad uncomfortable.

"I like your hair," he finally said.

The compliment came out of the blue. On reflex she reached her hand up and touched the curls that couldn't be tamed today, so she'd just let them fly. "Thank you."

He pulled his chair closer and leaned in. "So, Tracee, why are you celebrating your birthday with your girlfriends and not your man?"

"If I had a man, do you think I would have invited you to join us?"

He straightened up. "No, I guess not. Or, I'd hope not."

She smiled and shook her head. "No, I wouldn't disrespect my man like that."

He grinned at her.

Sam joined them at the table. Two of Tracee's girlfriends had already grabbed chairs on the other side of her, while Mae hadn't stopped dancing.

"Lau, I'm gonna have to bounce. I'll give you a call tomorrow, bright and early," Sam said to Laurent as he turned up the rest of his beer.

"I'll be ready," Laurent said.

"You guys going fishing in October?" Tracee asked.

Sam almost choked on his beer and quickly jumped back to keep it from running down his shirt. He looked down at them, smiling. "I don't fish anymore."

"He's taking me golfing," Laurent said, before standing up and giving Sam some dap. "Get home safe, and tell the missus I hope to see her again before I leave."

Sam set his beer bottle on the table. "I'll do that. You guys enjoy your night."

Tracee checked her watch. It was only 9:00 p.m., and the restaurant wouldn't be closing until ten thirty.

"Would you like something else to drink?" Laurent asked after Sam left.

Tracee held her hand over her empty glass. "No, thank you. Maybe a glass of water."

"You got it." He stood up and returned to the bar.

Mae finally grabbed Sam's vacant seat. "I see you and Mr. Rude are hitting it off."

Tracee shrugged. "He's nice. And I'm just being friendly."

"Uh-huh. I know that seductive *friendly* look of yours."

Tracee shrugged. "What? He's cute."

Laurent returned with her water. They spent the next few minutes chatting it up about the new voices in R&B before Laurent asked Tracee if she wanted to dance.

"How about one dance with the birthday girl? Be forewarned, I'm not Fred Astaire, but I can hold my own."

She laughed. "Then maybe you can hold it for me, too. I'll try not to step on your feet."

Two more of Tracee's girlfriends danced over to her to say goodbye. They exchanged quick hugs before Tracee joined Laurent on the dance floor.

The DJ played a mix of pop and hip-hop, to Tracee's delight. Laurent moved out of one move into another with ease. He wasn't anything like her, black girl with no rhythm. "I thought you said you couldn't dance?" she asked him a few minutes later.

"I can't, but that doesn't stop me from trying."

After a few tracks, the DJ announced it was time to slow it down. Tracee thought she would scream when he played "Tender Love" by Force MDs, which was one of her favorites. But that was a slow jam, so she turned to walk away, but then Laurent took her hand.

"You're not leaving me, are you? This is a classic."

Her eyes widened. "I know, but I'm not really a slow dancer." She turned to walk away again, but he didn't let go of her hand. She glanced back at him.

"Let me teach you," he said.

The look in his eyes when he said that made her insides turn to jelly. He bit his bottom lip and raised a brow, waiting on her answer. She'd bet he could teach her a lot of things. The intensity of his gaze drew her like a bee to honey. "Okay, but don't blame me if I step on your feet."

He laughed and placed one arm around her waist while he kept holding her other hand. She tried to keep a little distance between them.

"How long did you say you were going to be in town?" she asked, merely to make conversation.

"Hopefully I'll be on a plane headed back to California by the weekend."

"Why do you say hopefully? What could stop you?"

"I have a business meeting this week that I should have had yesterday. If there's another delay, I could potentially be here a little longer."

She nodded, secretly hoping something trivial went wrong and she'd have another chance to see him. She closed her eyes and concentrated on the music for a minute when she felt Laurent pull her closer. They were really slow dancing now. She could feel the contours of his body pressed against hers, and she liked what she felt. The way he controlled her body and moved his hips said a lot about him. He could definitely hold his own, and yet she felt he was holding back.

"You're doing pretty damned good," he whispered in her ear. "I still have all my toes."

She whispered back, "Consider yourself lucky." Mr. Wood and his wife danced near them. He held his wife close, with her head on his chest. The love they had for one another came through in their dance. It was a beautiful thing to watch.

Tracee found herself wishing Laurent would wrap his arms around her body. She wanted him to run his hands up her back and grind into her like the boys used to do at high school basement parties. She could feel how hard and toned his body was, which made her weak in the knees. And his cologne smelled so masculine and tempting. Then the music slowly faded away. She opened her eyes and released her bottom lip that she hadn't realized she'd been squeezing.

Laurent let go of her hand and took a step back. He smiled down at her. "Thank you."

She sucked in a quick breath to keep from passing out—he was so fine. "No, thank *you*, that was nice." She spun around and wanted to shoot herself. Why did she have to say it was nice? As he followed her to the table, he placed his hand at the small of her back, and the muscles in her center contracted. Being around this man made her feel sexy.

Mae sat with an elbow on the table and her chin in

her palm, staring at them. "You guys looked great out there," she said as Laurent pulled out Tracee's chair.

Laurent held his chair back and looked down. "And she didn't step on my feet once." Everyone laughed as he sat down.

"While that was beautiful to watch, it reminded me that I need to go home and make a phone call before it's too late," Mae added, reaching for her purse. "Tracee, do you want me to help you put some of your gifts in the car?" she asked as she stood up.

It was time Mae called her boyfriend, John, before he went to sleep. Tracee looked at the gifts on the table and decided she only needed help with two of them. It was getting closer to closing for the restaurant and she should be leaving herself, but she wasn't ready to leave Laurent. "Uh, yeah. I guess it is getting late."

"Unless you want to finish your water and maybe Laurent can help you out?" Mae offered.

"Yeah, sure. When you get ready to go, I'll walk you to your car and help with anything you need. I was kind of hoping you'd stick around a bit. I'm enjoying your company."

Tracee looked from Mae's beaming face to Laurent, who held his bottom lip between his teeth, smiling. He was stunningly beautiful. "I think I will stick around for a bit. If you're sure you don't mind helping me out?"

"Not at all," he said, reassuring her with a smile.

Tracee stood and gave Mae a hug, thanking her for everything. Mae whispered in her ear, "Call me the second you get home." When Tracee released her, she winked at her. Tracee smiled at her best friend. "I'll do that."

When she sat back down, she noticed the party atmosphere they'd brought to the deck had vanished. Now there were only a few couples sitting close together enjoying the music and the ambience from the giant heaters, and the starlit sky.

"Thanks again for the dance, and sharing your birthday evening with me," Laurent said.

"I should be thanking you for livening up my night. Those are my book club sisters, and I love them, especially Mae, but they all have families or men to go home to. I take all my gifts to my lonely apartment." The minute she said that, she realized she'd just told a man she didn't know very well that she lived alone. How stupid of her.

"Well, good friends are hard to come by. Even harder than a man for some women, I'm sure. I can count the number of good friends I have on one hand. The men in this town are stupid if one of them is not at home waiting for you."

Tracee laughed. "You're right about having good friends. But I'm more focused on my business these days. I really don't have time for a man. Besides, I've been told my standards are too high."

"Ah, a woman with high standards," Laurent said.

"I think every woman should have high standards, don't you?"

He nodded. "I agree. So should a man."

"Is that why you're single? Or are you waiting for somebody who likes to go fishing with you?"

He laughed and tilted his head, staring at her. "How do you know I'm single?"

Tracee finished off her wine. "Because you're sitting here with me instead of lying across the bed in your hotel room talking to your girl on the phone."

He leaned forward and rested his forearms on the table. "You're right, there isn't a woman in my life right now. And I'm sitting here with you because I want to know more about you. I've never met a pastry chef who works at a bed-and-breakfast before. How do you like it?"

"I love it. I'm surrounded by my family all day, and people on vacation who are usually in a good mood. My cousin Rollin sets the example and goes the extra mile for his guests on a daily basis. He's very personable. And his wife, Tayler, she's the best. I've learned so much from her about business it's crazy. We have a U-pick store, where customers come out and pick their own organic vegetables. It was Tayler's idea to start selling some of my cakes and pies in there. And Tracee's Cake World grew from that."

"You sound very passionate about your work. I know that carrot cake on Sunday was the best I've ever had."

"Thank you." She hesitated a moment before posing a question. "Let me ask you something. Did you know I was going to be there on Sunday?"

He looked surprised. "No, why?"

She shrugged. "I don't know. The first thing that ran through my mind tonight when I saw you was how strange it seemed that I keep running into you in such a short time span. This town is not *that* small."

"If you're still questioning whether I'm following you, relax, I'm not. Sam suggested this place since it was close to the hotel, and I don't really know my way around. He also invited me to brunch Sunday with him and his wife. I had no idea you'd be at either place. But I'm glad you were. It gave me a chance to properly apologize for Saturday morning's incident."

Tracee waved him off. "Oh, let's not bring that up again. It's water under the bridge. Completely forgotten."

He nodded. "Thank you."

"Well, it looks like the DJ's ready to shut it down." The music had switched to piped-in jazz while the DJ started putting his equipment away. Only one other couple remained on the deck now. "I guess we'd better leave, unless we want to get locked up here."

Laurent stood up and helped Tracee with her chair. She started picking up gift bags and wrapping the balloons around her wrist. He grabbed the heavier bags and followed her downstairs and out of the restaurant. Tracee had backed her car in close to the front door. She reached in her purse and popped the trunk with her key fob.

After they placed the packages in her trunk, they walked around to the driver's door. She unlocked the door and leaned in to tie the balloons down so they would be out of her way. When she stood up, Laurent was standing there holding his car keys. "Where's your car?" she asked.

He pointed to a dark blue Elantra parked across the lot from hers. "It's a rental."

She nodded as they stood there awkwardly for a few seconds. She wondered if he was going to ask her out again before he left town. If he asked, she would definitely say yes.

Laurent held out his hand. "Well, Tracee, it was definitely a pleasure meeting you and celebrating your birthday with you. In fact, it was the highlight of my trip." He smiled, flashing his bright white teeth at her.

She shook his hand. "The pleasure was all mine." He held her hand a little too long, causing her to lose herself in his eyes. She hadn't even noticed him take a step closer to her until he leaned in. She smiled up at him. "Good night." The words sounded stifled coming out of her mouth.

"Good night," he said, slightly above a whisper.

He let go of her hand and eased his hand around her waist. Then he did it! He kissed her. A soft and gentle touch on the lips. She froze, so he came back for more. This time she closed her eyes and parted her lips, inviting his tongue inside. All the nerves in her body tingled with excitement. She needed to sit down. She could taste the beer on his breath and the desire in his mouth, and she didn't want him to stop.

When he released her lips and lowered his hand from her waist, she wanted to scream. Oh, God, she wanted more.

"A birthday present, from me to you," he said, arching a brow.

Be still, my beating heart! Her eyes fluttered. "And the best one I've received all night."

Laurent took a step back, laughing. "Get in the car. And do me a favor?"

She opened the car door. "Yes."

"Ring the hotel once you get home. I'm in room 319. Let me know you made it home safe."

"I'll do that." He held the door while she climbed inside. She closed the door and waved bye to the best-looking man she'd ever met. To a man who'd just kissed her and made her want to take her panties off right there in the parking lot.

Chapter 6

Laurent stood in the parking lot watching Tracee's car pull off. He wasn't ready to let her go, but he had no choice. When he licked his lips, he could still taste her. The smell of her perfume was still in his nostrils. Once her car was out of sight, he headed for his rental.

Inviting a woman back to his hotel didn't seem like the right thing to do, but the more he thought about it, the more he thought maybe he should have asked her up. It was her birthday and she'd probably be spending the rest of the night alone. He climbed in the car and started the motor. He shook his head, smiling to himself. If Tracee came anywhere near his room tonight, he'd make sure she wouldn't want to go home until tomorrow—if then.

His cell phone rang, interrupting the luscious thoughts he was having about Tracee Coleman. He glanced down at the caller ID. It was his father. He squeezed his eyebrows together and was tempted not to answer, but he put the phone to his ear as he pulled out of the parking lot.

"Hello, Dad."

"Laurent, imagine, if you will, me sitting in my den enjoying my afternoon cognac when I open this terribly disappointing report you sent me earlier."

Laurent shook his head. Time to get Tracee off the brain and talk business with his father, who had undoubtedly expected a miracle from him.

Thursday morning got off to a great start. Laurent went for a quick run before showering, then grabbed some breakfast. He'd dressed in a basic suit so as not to appear too overdressed for the clientele. This deal was sweeter than what his father had originally proposed, and according to their financials, the Patels would be fortunate to get what he offered. When Mr. Patel and his sons entered the room, Laurent was ready to do business. He'd waited long enough to lay his cards on the table.

Minutes into the meeting, however, something went wrong, and the entire mood shifted. Mr. Patel went from "I'm listening" to "now it's time for you to listen to me."

"Laurent, I understand everything you've shown me, and I appreciate the work you've put into this deal. However, the Rival Hotel is deeply rooted in the community of Danville. For starters, we're loyal to our employees, and in return they're loyal to us. I've only had to fire one person since the day we opened our doors. Do you know of another establishment that can say that after ten years in business?"

Laurent smiled. "No, sir, I don't."

"I've made one important promise to my employees. As long as they want to work here, I will have a job for them. And yet there is no mention at all of the existing staff in your deal."

Laurent licked his lips and sat a little taller, ready to address the older man's concern, when Mr. Patel started again.

"It's not just the staff I'm concerned about. We also host a number of community meetings, as well as social events, sometimes for free. Now, while we're not expecting you to promise us anything, we do want to sell this place to someone who understands its standing within the community, and who will continue the tradition we've set forth. I shared my concerns with your father earlier this year. I thought we had somewhat of an understanding in that regards." He pushed the papers Laurent had given him to Arjun, sitting next to him.

Laurent took a deep breath. "I understand your concerns and—"

"I don't think you do," Mr. Patel said, shaking his head. "Tell me what you know about our fair city."

Laurent had prepared for everything—except that question. He recited some information he'd read off the internet and talked about his experience over the last couple of days. It wasn't good enough.

Arjun spoke up. "My family owes a great deal to

this city. They have supported us and allowed us to flourish over the years. I believe what my father is trying to say is, he'd like to see a bid that's more inclusive with respect to the legacy we have built here. Not that you have an obligation to do so…but that is what he'd like to see."

Laurent nodded. "Anyone in the community will still be able to use the hotel in the same fashion as before."

Mr. Patel cleared his throat. "You mentioned that you had brunch at the Coleman House on Sunday. They're a small bed-and-breakfast that stays in business because of the great customer service and hospitality they provide. Everyone in the county and surrounding counties knows of their reputation. Well, the Rival Hotel has that same type of reputation in the community. We're not just a big-box hotel—we're a part of every family in this town. If you want to know how I know that, I'll tell you. Recently, I was diagnosed with cancer, and I don't know if we could have survived some of the rough times without the support of the people of Danville. When I walk away from this hotel, it will be to get some much-needed rest."

Laurent exchanged eye contact with every man sitting across from him before settling his gaze on Mr. Patel. He gave an understanding nod and used a gentler tone. "I'm truly sorry to hear about your diagnosis. I know that must have been a hard time for your family. I think I have a better perspective as to what you're looking for now. Give me a few days to talk this over with my family, and I'd love to sit down with you again."

The Patel men glanced at one another before Mr. Patel nodded.

Laurent hadn't fully understood what his father meant when he said they wanted someone a little more relatable. He'd assumed Martin Enterprises' power and wealth had gotten in the way of the deal, which was why he'd come dressed down. However, what Mr. Patel wanted was someone more in touch with the community they served, possibly on the same level as the community. What he'd anticipated to be a slam dunk seemed to have hit the rim and bounced off.

The oven buzzer sounded, and Tracee pulled herself from the chair and walked over to the stove. The kitchen of the bed-and-breakfast smelled of ginger and pumpkin as she pulled two tins of cupcakes from the oven and set them on a cooling rack. She'd spent the last two days baking and working on her business plan. Earlier when she detailed her time with Laurent to Mae, she told her she didn't expect to see him again, and that was the truth. The man could have left town by now for all she knew. Still, she couldn't believe she'd let him kiss her.

"Oh my God! Something smells good in here." Corra entered the kitchen with a couple of grocery bags in hand.

Tracee glanced over her shoulder while pulling containers from the cabinet for the muffins. "Cupcakes for dessert tonight."

"What are you still doing here? I thought you got off at noon today," Corra asked, setting the bags on the table.

"Aunt Rita's still a little under the weather, so I thought I'd hang out and help with dinner preparations." Two bags of candy slid from Corra's groceries as she began putting things away. "Isn't it kind of early to buy Halloween candy? It's three weeks away still." Tracee asked.

"Yeah but, we're having a party. Instead of letting the kids go door to door at home, I've decided to invite a few families out here, and we'll have a Coleman House bed-and-breakfast Halloween party."

"That's nice," Tracee said, as she found lids for her containers in another drawer.

"Is everything okay?" Corra asked.

Tracee nodded. "Yeah. Just fine, why?"

"Because you aren't your normal bubbly self. How was the party Tuesday night? I'm sorry I couldn't make it."

Tracee shrugged. "It was nice. We turned the deck up."

Corra stood by the counter and inhaled the aroma coming from the cupcakes. "Did you make enough for me to have one?" she asked.

"I made enough for everyone to have two." She popped one out and handed it to Corra, and then took another one for herself. She flopped down at the table to consume it. One thing Tracee had always prided herself on was not eating her own sweets. The more she baked, the less she ate. She missed her little sister, Kyla, who could eat her cupcakes and not gain a pound. She, on the other hand, was another story.

Corra sat down next to her. "Okay, what's up? Your sweets live on my hips, but it isn't often that you consume your own product. What's got you on the cupcake crack?" Corra asked.

Tracee smiled and shook her head. She loved her cousin. "Nothing, really. I was just thinking about this guy I met Tuesday night." She removed the paper from her cupcake.

"What about him?" Corra asked before biting into her treat.

Tracee shrugged, now wishing she'd never said anything. "He just seemed like a nice guy. He joined our little party on the deck."

"Did you get his number?"

Tracee shook her head. "No, he's from California. For all I know, he's probably gone back by now."

Corra shrugged while they sat in silence eating their cupcakes. Then Tracee's cell phone rang. She walked over and picked it up from the kitchen counter. The caller ID displayed a number she didn't recognize, but she answered it anyway.

"Hello," she said, with as much excitement as a slug.

"Hey, Tracee?"

Her eyes popped the minute she recognized Laurent's voice. "Yes."

"It's Laurent. I hope I didn't catch you at a bad time?"

"No, you didn't." She hadn't thought she'd ever see or hear from him again.

"Good. It looks like I'm going to be in town for a couple more days, so I thought maybe I could ask you for a tour of the city, and take you to dinner afterward?"

She smiled. He wanted to see her again. "I don't mind giving you a tour at all, but you've been here at least four days—haven't you gotten out?"

"Very little. But I'd like an insider's perspective. And if I'm being honest, I'd like to see you again."

She turned her back to Corra. "Sure, I'd like that, too. What day did you have in mind?"

"How about this afternoon when you get off work? Unless you have other plans."

Her hand immediately ran to her unruly hair. "I'm actually working late this evening, so how about tomorrow?"

"Great. When and where should I pick you up?" he asked.

"How about here at the bed-and-breakfast around 1:00 p.m. Do you remember how to get here?"

"It's in my GPS. So, I'll see you tomorrow?"

"I'll be waiting." Tracee set the phone down and turned back to Corra.

"Was that him?" Corra asked.

Tracee nodded. "He wants a tour of the town, from a local's perspective."

"Huh. Sounds like an excuse to ask you out. And I didn't mean to be listening, but did you say he's been here before?"

Tracee returned to the table. "He came to Sunday brunch with his friend Sam Kane and his wife.

Sam's one of a handful of black professors at Centre College."

"So, is your guy cute?" Corra asked with arched brows.

Tracee wrinkled up her nose and nodded fast. "Not to mention funny, and he's a gentleman. He walked me to my car at the end of the night and helped me with my packages." She stopped short of telling her about the kiss.

"Well, I can't wait to meet him. I'll be here tomorrow afternoon when he picks you up."

Tracee rolled her eyes. "You would be."

"Hey, I have to let Kyla know about this guy. We all know how picky you can be."

Tracee's mouth fell open. That old argument again. "I am not picky. I just have standards."

They debated Tracee's choice in men until Corra's daughter, Katie, burst into the kitchen to notify her mother that her brother, Jamie, had taken off on one of the bicycles the bed-and-breakfast had for guests—without asking permission.

Corra jumped up from the table. "That boy knows better." She turned back to Tracee before running out. "Well, maybe you didn't get his number, but I see he's got yours."

Tracee crossed her arms and poked out her bottom lip. *How did he get my number?*

As soon as Tracee finished working Friday afternoon, she went into the bathroom to freshen up before Laurent showed. A tour of the town wasn't exactly a date, but dinner afterward was. So, tonight she had a date with an attractive guy from California. In some ways, Laurent reminded her of her father. Before her parents lost their farm, her father had worn overalls most of the day, but when he took her mother out he had great taste in clothes. He never looked trendy, but he invested in classic pieces that never went out of style.

The bell over the front door jingled, and Tracee's hand froze in midstroke. That was Laurent. She quickly finished powdering her face and applied some lipstick. By her calculations, Tayler should be manning the front desk at this hour. She hurried into the back closet and grabbed her jacket. She turned down the hall and walked out into the lobby just as Corra walked through the front door.

Laurent turned from Tayler behind the reception counter to Tracee coming down the hall. She fought hard not to blush all over the place and give this guy a clue that she was excited to see him again.

"Oh, here she comes now," Tayler said as she gestured toward Tracee.

Not since Kyla was dating Jackson had Tracee seen such smiles on Tayler and Corra's faces. She introduced everyone before letting Tayler know she'd be returning later for her car. She was glad they got a good look at him in case he turned out to be some type of serial killer or something.

They walked out to Laurent's rental car, and he held the door open for her. He resembled the clean-cut, could-possibly-be-boring boy next door, but he was the finest boy next door she'd ever seen.

"This is a nice place, with a nice reputation," he said as he held the door.

"Looked us up, did you?"

"Before I came to brunch, I did a little research." He closed the door and walked around to the driver's side and climbed in.

"I'm glad you were impressed. My cousins have put a lot into the bed-and-breakfast and the organic farm. Their parents would be proud."

He started the car. "What happened to their parents?"

"They died years ago in a car accident. Rollin's sister, Corra, only joined the business two years ago. Now it's truly a family affair."

Laurent nodded as he drove down the long driveway from the bed-and-breakfast toward the main road. He stopped at the end of the driveway. "Which way?"

"Take a left. We'll start on Main Street."

"Near the hotel?" he asked.

"Unless you already know that area," she said.

"No, that's fine. I know very little about this town, other than what I found on the internet. But you know how that is—every city puts its best self on display. I'm looking for the inside scoop."

"What are you, an investigative reporter or something?" she asked, laughing.

He shook his head. "Nothing like that." Then he glanced over at her. "Like I said, my trip's been extended, and I wanted to see you again. What better excuse than to spend some time getting the lay of the land?"

She shrugged. "You could have just asked me out."

"I thought I did," he said.

"Not under the pretense of wanting a tour."

"But I really do want the tour. I'm interested in the town. So, show me everything."

Tracee laughed. "Okay, this should take all of a couple of hours."

Minutes later, Laurent drove down Main Street while Tracee pointed out important landmarks and fun places to dine and shop.

"I swear, your main street reminds me of a movie set—everything looks so pristine and quaint. The only things missing are the vintage cars. It's Norman Rockwellish, if you know what I mean."

She crossed her arms. "I do, but don't let the good looks fool you now."

"Oh, yeah?"

"Behind each and every one of these little shops, there's a story to tell. Some of the stories are scandalous, and some not so much. We have a lot of family-owned businesses in the area. And where there's family, there's drama."

"Intriguing! Family-owned businesses are pretty big in small towns, I'm starting to gather."

"In a lot of cases, there's not enough business for the big chains, so you're right. Then there's always a few people who don't want to stay in the family business. My brother, Gavin, used to work with my father on our small family farm. The way they lost the farm was dramatic for sure, but now Gavin's a technician at LSC Communications."

"How many brothers and sisters do you have?"

"One of each. Both younger than me."

"So, you're the big sister."

"That I am." She turned and glanced out the passenger side window. "Why don't you park along here somewhere? You can see downtown better on foot."

Laurent parallel parked in front of an antique-furniture store. They got out of the car and strolled leisurely along the quaint historic buildings. Tracee took him inside a shop that showcased works by local artists. It didn't take long to work their way up one side of the street and then down the other.

"I don't see a lot of us around here," he commented.

"And you won't. We do have an African American population, but probably nothing like what you're used to in California."

He nodded. "I see. So, what do you do around here for fun, other than hang at the pizza parlor?"

Tracee shrugged. "Around here we make our own fun. Then there's always Lexington or some of the other surrounding cities to visit."

"I guess Sam was right."

"About what?"

"I asked him the same thing. His reply was, find a good woman and settle down."

Tracee laughed. "It's not that bad. Small-town living is all about family. My parents live not far from me, and my brother and his family aren't that far, either. My little sister lives in Lexington. Do you live close to your family?"

"My brothers live in Santa Clara, which isn't far from me, but they travel a lot. My father lives in Palo

Alto, even closer to me, however, he recently remarried and, well, he's enjoying his new bride."

"Your parents are divorced?"

"No, my mom died when I was in high school."

Tracee stopped and looked at him. "I'm sorry."

"Thank you." Laurent looked up at the ice cream shop in front of them. "How about a scoop?"

Tracee looked into the window of the shop where one of her friends used to work. "Sure, come on. I've got a good story about this place."

Chapter 7

They sat and enjoyed ice cream while Tracee told him more stories about some of the people she knew who worked in downtown Danville. She hoped this was the type of inside scoop he wanted. After the ice cream shop, they finished the tour of downtown and made their way back to the car.

Tracee took him over to the Dr. Ephraim McDowell House for a guided tour of the home where the first American surgical procedure was performed. The little woman who led the tour was so sweet, and Tracee learned a thing or two herself. Then she walked him by Constitution Square and the original log post office that served as the first post office west of the Allegheny Mountains. By the time they finished with those spots, Tracee was starving.

Upon walking out of the little post office building, Laurent said, "As interesting as it all was, I think I've had about enough history for one day. I don't know about you, but I'm hungry."

"I'm famished," she replied.

"Cool, where can we grab a bite?"

"Do you like Cheddar's?" she asked.

He turned his head sideways. "I don't believe I've heard of it."

"It's American cuisine, with reasonable prices. I think you'll like it." If he enjoyed fish, he'd be able to get some there.

He smiled. "Okay, if you say so."

Within minutes, they were sitting in Cheddar's across the table from each other, enjoying an appetizer and a glass of iced tea.

"You know, from what I've seen so far, Danville seems like a quiet little town without a lot going on. Everybody's laid-back, and things move at a slower pace. So, how do businesses survive or even thrive at this pace?"

She shrugged. "We have something going on all the time. Out at the bed-and-breakfast, we celebrate every holiday, the change of seasons, harvest time— you name it. In town, they have a huge annual BBQ festival. And they have events for just about everything, as well."

The waiter arrived and took their dinner orders.

"Have you lived here all your life?" Laurent asked.

Tracee shook her head. "I was born and raised in Nicholasville, Kentucky, then I went to college in Louisville. I didn't move to Danville until years after I graduated."

"That's where the Kentucky Derby is, isn't it?"

"Yep, right up the road. I lived there for five years."

"If you don't mind me asking, what made you move to Danville? I mean, isn't Louisville a larger city?"

"It is. But sometimes even a big city can be too small for two people to live in."

He nodded. "I see. Man trouble?"

"Something like that." She lowered her gaze from his intense stare. She was not going down memory lane with this man. "But I don't regret moving here. I reconnected with my best friend, Mae, and I get to see my family every week. I have a niece and nephew that I adore, as well as another one on the way."

"Well, it's his loss, not yours. Every time I look at you, I'm amazed that you're single. I see an intelligent, sexy woman that some fool let get away."

She bit her bottom lip to keep from blushing. "I bet you say that to all the ladies," she said with a roll of her eyes.

He laughed. "No, I don't. And I consider myself very fortunate to have had you drop into my arms like you did."

Tracee held her chin up. What was he buttering her up for? "How long did you say you'd be in town?"

He shrugged. "A couple more days, at the most."

She smiled. "Well, we may have to extend this little tour. You're good for my ego. At one time, the Second Street area used to be a thriving African

American business district. We have some information at the bed-and-breakfast I'll get and show you tomorrow if you're interested?"

"Definitely."

"Great. Since my sister's out of town, I'm helping out at the farmers market in the morning. You can pick me up there."

After dinner, they climbed into Laurent's rental and headed back to the bed-and-breakfast.

"I'll say one thing, this countryside is beautiful. Especially with all the colorful foliage at this time of the year. And just look at that sunset."

Tracee glanced off in the distance at one of the things she truly appreciated—a perfect sunset. "If you don't have to be back at a certain time, there's a spot up the road where you have a perfect view of the sun setting."

"I've got nothing but time. Let's hit it."

Tracee had Laurent drive past the bed-and-breakfast entrance to a spot up the road where the tree line was lower and so the sun dropping off a cliff was visible.

"Nice… It's like a color explosion." Laurent turned the car off and opened his door.

Tracee got out as well and walked around to the front of the car. "This is the perfect time of year to witness the change in this spot. Is it like this in California as well?"

"Yes. But I'll have to admit, I'm hardly relaxed long enough to fully enjoy it." He leaned against the front of the car and crossed his legs at the ankle.

Tracee followed suit and cast her gaze out across the colorful foliage before her. Too bad Laurent wasn't sticking around—she could get used to him. He crossed his arms and turned his gaze to her.

"You come here often?"

She shook her head. "Not often, no."

He turned around to glance back over his shoulder. "This looks like what teenagers call a make-out spot. A policeman's not going to come along with a flashlight once it gets dark and tell us to move along, will he?"

Tracee laughed and reached out to punch Laurent on the arm. "Of course not. What kind of girl do you take me for?"

"One that knows how to have a good time. I enjoyed Tuesday night. I thought about it Wednesday night and I started to call you, but thought I'd better not."

"I was up to my elbows in sweet potato pies anyway. Two of my regular customers are nursing homes. They keep me pretty busy."

"I noticed there's a bakery in town. Isn't that competition for you?"

"Of course, but they can't duplicate my recipes. I've put my own spin on some of my grandmother's old recipes. I also modified recipes from the bakery I used to work for in Louisville. I've been told that my sweets are like crack. Once you get hooked, I've got you."

"From what I've tasted, I can believe that."

"Besides, I'm going to be leasing a prime spot downtown in the Rival Hotel."

Laurent turned toward her, resting his elbow on

the car hood. "You mean somewhere close to the hotel?" he asked.

"No, inside. There used to be a business connected to the hotel with an entrance from the inside and another from the outside. It's been closed for a while now, but I've been talking to the owner and I plan to reopen right there."

"Inside the Rival Hotel?"

"Yep."

He nodded. "Why not opt for your own spot downtown, or in a mall somewhere?"

"The hotel is kind of a special place for me. So it has to be there. Besides, I'm this close—" she held her index finger and thumb an inch apart "—to getting a small business loan."

He looked down at the car before turning back to the sunset, this time leaning his elbows back against the hood. She turned around and joined him, and they remained silent for a few minutes just enjoying the view.

"Can I ask you a question?" she said, breaking the silence.

"Sure," he responded.

"Why did you kiss me?"

He reached over for a lock of hair that had fallen across her face and tucked it behind her ear. "I don't know. Why does a guy kiss a girl? Because he wants to see what her lips taste like, or maybe because I didn't have a present for you and it was the only thing I could think of at that moment. Those red lips were calling my name." He cupped a hand around his mouth and called out to the wind. "Laurent, Laurent, kiss me."

"My lips said no such thing!" Tracee laughed.

He nodded. "Oh, yes, they did. They gave me that seductive pout that said, 'come hither, young man, and devour me. I've been waiting on you all night long.'"

Tracee held a hand over her mouth and laughed. If she'd given him that impression, maybe she'd had one glass of wine too many. "I don't pout," she said after she dropped her hand.

He pointed at her. "Yes, you do. Like now. Your lips are as beautiful as this sunset, far more inviting and begging to be kissed." He leaned in closer to her before reaching out and placing a hand behind her head.

Tracee's pulse quickened with the touch of Laurent's hand at the base of her neck. He gently pulled her closer and softly kissed her lips. Butterflies took flight inside her stomach, flying in every direction, as confused as she was. Should she return the kiss? She leaned against the car, letting him kiss her.

His lips were soft and moist, and she was having a fantasy of snuggling next to him in a warm bed. He released her and leaned back.

"Now this is officially a make-out spot," he said.

Saturday morning Laurent found the farmers market at the edge of town, just like Tracee said. After walking past booths of everything from organic produce to homemade soaps, he found the Coleman House Farm's booth. Tracee was in the middle of bagging a bunch of greens for two women who were trying their best to talk her down on the price. Laurent had tried to dress down in a pair of blue jeans, sneakers and a dark gray zip-up jacket, but he might have still been a little overdressed for this Saturday morning crowd. If he was going to be here much longer, he might have to do a little small-town clothes shopping.

The minute he made eye contact with Tracee, she checked her watch. He was early. It was eleven forty-five. After the ladies purchased their greens, they moved to the next booth.

"Ma'am, I wonder if you can help me pick out some greens," Laurent said as he picked up a bunch and water unexpectedly ran from the greens down his arm. He jumped back to keep the water from getting on his clothes.

Tracee grabbed a wad of paper towels and quickly exchanged them for the greens in his hand. He dried the water running up his sleeve. He couldn't believe the silly shit that happened to him when he was around this woman.

She came from behind the table, took the wadded paper towel from him and pitched it in a nearby garbage can. "I'm going to assume you wouldn't know how to cook those greens if I gave them to you."

"I wish you weren't right, but I'm afraid my skills in the kitchen could use a little work. I can make French toast, if that counts."

"Hey, not everybody can do that, so give yourself some credit. You have to get the proportion of egg and milk just right."

"Oh, I've perfected that. I also use a secret ingredient that just makes your mouth water."

She smiled. "I bet you do." Then she bit her bottom lip.

Laurent looked down at Tracee's snug jeans that stopped at her ankles and her white sneakers. Under a black vest, she wore a long-sleeved black T-shirt that hugged her hips. The Coleman House Farm logo was on the front in white letters. Her hair was pulled into a loose bun on the top of her head. And those silver hoop earrings were large enough they nearly touched her shoulders. Her casual appearance was sexy as hell.

"I know I'm a little early, but I didn't want to miss you."

"Not a problem. We were about to pack up. Just let me grab my purse."

"Laurent, I see you've found our farmers market."

He turned around at the familiar voice as Raji, Mr. Patel's youngest son, greeted him. Laurent didn't know why, but he hadn't expected to see him away from the hotel. They exchanged handshakes. A beautiful Indian woman stood beside him, smiling. "Don't tell me you sell vegetables, too?" Laurent asked.

Raji laughed. "No, but we do frequent the market. My wife likes to cook with fresh vegetables. This is my wife, Charmi."

Laurent nodded, and she nodded in exchange. "It's nice to meet you."

"So, what brings you to the market this morning?" Raji asked.

"I'm waiting for a friend. We're going to do a little sightseeing."

Raji grinned and nodded. "That's nice."

Laurent noticed him glancing toward the Coleman House truck.

"Miss Tracee is your friend?" Raji asked.

"Yes, she's my new friend, and my Danville tour guide."

"So, where are you two off to today?" he asked.

Laurent glanced over at Tracee. "I'm not sure yet. But I'm sure it will be something interesting."

"Well, you have beautiful weather for a tour. Enjoy your day."

"I will. You do the same." Laurent watched Raji and his wife as they strolled away.

"Okay, I'm ready," Tracee said as she walked up.

"Where are we off to?" Laurent asked.

"Yesterday I spoke to a member of the African American Historical Society who's going to be our guide for a brief tour of the African American business district and a few other historical landmarks I thought you might be interested in." Tracee looked down at her watch. "We're meeting him at the visitor's center in fifteen minutes."

"Sounds interesting. Have you taken the tour before?" Laurent asked.

Tracee shook her head. "No, believe it or not. I know Danville has an interesting African American history, but I've never felt compelled to take the tour. I guess I'll be learning right along with you."

Laurent was looking forward to his day with Tracee whether he learned anything to benefit him with the hotel deal or not. "Who knows—maybe before the day is over we'll teach each other something."

She smiled up at him in a way that weakened his knees, and he knew he was going to be in trouble today.

Chapter 8

After the African American historical tour, Laurent had gained more respect for the town of Danville, Kentucky. He'd learned some things that would serve as a marketing tool for him if they purchased the Rival Hotel.

"That was an amazing tour and a nice way to start the day," Laurent said to Tracee after they dropped off their tour guide and prepared for the next stop.

"It was, wasn't it? I'm surprised. To tell you the truth, I thought it was going to be a little boring, like yesterday, but it wasn't."

"Learning about your own culture's past is never boring," he said. "So, where to next?"

"You can't come to Kentucky without having a

horse-related experience, so I'm taking you horse-back riding."

Laurent's eyes widened. "I've never been horse-back riding."

"Well, you know what they say—there's a first time for everything. Come on, it's just a short ride up the road."

He was beginning to like this woman, but he didn't know if he liked her enough to climb on the back of some smelly horse. "You know, when I think of Kentucky I think of horses, but betting on them instead of riding atop one."

"Riding is better than betting, trust me. You never went horseback riding when you were young?" she asked.

"No, I didn't." The closest he'd come to a horse was dropping stacks of money at Belmont Park, a major Thoroughbred horse-racing track in New York, with a group of friends.

"Then this is going to be fun."

"If you say so."

On the way to the stables, they stopped at a farm-to-table restaurant for a quick lunch. Once they were back on the road, Laurent removed one hand from the steering wheel and placed it over his chest. "I know the tour's not over yet, but I want to say thank you. Your tour has turned into the best part of my trip. Who would have thought I'd find a beautiful woman to show me around and make me feel so welcome? I'm really enjoying your company." He glanced at her, watching her blush, before placing his hand back on the wheel.

"You might want to hold your compliments until after the horseback ride. If you've never ridden before, you might be walking a little bowlegged later."

He laughed, but she was the only person he wanted to see walking bowlegged. And he wanted to be the reason for that new stroll.

He drove the thirty minutes to the riding stables envisioning large stinky horses shooing flies with their tails and ears. Instead, he encountered a nice, clean stable with nothing but healthy-looking horses. He still wasn't sure this was something he wanted to do, but he was following Tracee's lead, and he'd enjoyed himself so far. Tracee introduced him to the woman who owned the stables, and she gave him a little tour of the facility before introducing him to his horse. A sickening feeling bubbled up in Laurent's stomach when the horse threw his head back and seemed to laugh at him.

"You're not scared, are you?" Tracee asked.

Laurent snorted and shook his head. "Of course not. I'm game for anything. Let's go." After a little instruction from the owner, Laurent stepped up onto the platform, hooked his foot into the stirrup and then swung his other leg over his horse.

"Okay, this here's Chester, and he's happy to meet you. Hold on to the reins there." The owner made sure Laurent was positioned correctly before she walked away.

Tracee and her horse trotted over to Laurent. Chester turned slightly to greet his buddy, and Laurent tightened his legs around the horse as he felt himself falling forward.

"You can sit up and relax. He's not gonna throw you," Tracee said as she and her horse circled around Laurent.

He inched himself up straighter but didn't like the feeling one bit.

Tracee laughed. "If you could see your face right now."

The instructor tapped Laurent on the knee. "You might want to ease up on your grip there, buddy. Your leg muscles will be sore for days gripping like that."

Laurent looked at Tracee and shook his head. He loosened his tense leg muscles. "Why did I let you talk me into this?"

"Oh, come on, I thought you were game for anything?"

His eyes widened. "So did I, until now."

Finally, they set off on a nice stroll following one of the young guides. Old Chester trotted right next to Tracee's horse, which Laurent was thankful for. Getting the hang of holding the reins and staying in the saddle wasn't really that difficult. After a few minutes, he fell into a steady rhythm.

"Did you grow up around horses?" Laurent asked Tracee once he could concentrate on something other than not falling off the horse.

"No, but my dad did, so he took us riding a couple of times a year."

Laurent enjoyed the view as they trotted along and he learned more about Tracee and her upbringing. Unfortunately, the saddle didn't get any more comfortable, and the smell of the horses as they used the open-air restroom made things worse. Chester had a fondness for grass, but the instructor asked Laurent not to let him eat grass. How he was supposed to keep this thousand-pound animal from doing so she didn't say.

As they headed back to the stable, the horses got a little happy and trotted over to the platform. Laurent didn't know what happened next, but Chester overshot the platform and kept going. He tried to stop him by pulling back on the reins, which obviously wasn't the thing to do. He could hear Tracee yelling his name and see the instructor running to catch up with him, but Chester had a mind of his own and tried to stand up on his hind legs.

Laurent leaned forward, determined to stay on the horse, but then old Chester came down and kicked out his back legs. The movement threw Laurent for a loop as he felt his body sliding off in one direction while trying to keep his grip on the reins.

A second later, he was lying on his back looking up at Tracee as she smiled down at him.

"Are you okay?" she asked.

He moved a little to make sure nothing was broken. "I don't think old Chester likes me," he said before coming to his feet.

"Something must have spooked him," the instructor said as she walked up with Chester. "You don't look none the worse for the wear, though," she said after looking Laurent up and down.

He brushed his pants and jacket off. "I'm fine. Maybe a little bruised ego, but I'll survive." To show he had no hard feelings toward the horse, he reached out and swatted old Chester on his hindquarter. The horse's tail swung up, and Laurent jumped back.

Tracee bent over laughing.

"Can we go now?" Laurent asked while biting his lip and trying not to laugh at himself. His ego couldn't take much more of this place. He thanked the owner and assured her again that he was all right. He couldn't wait to get back behind the wheel of the car—somewhere he felt as if he had control.

"Well, that was an interesting experience," Tracee said as she buckled her seat belt.

Laurent did the same, then started the car. "I like the horses at Belmont Park better," he said before glancing over at Tracee. She held a hand to her mouth, and they both opened up and laughed as loud as they could.

"I can't believe I actually fell off a damned horse and onto my ass out there."

"Oh, but you looked good up there. It's the dismount that was so entertaining." She started chuckling again.

As he pulled out of the parking lot, Tracee pointed him into the right direction.

"You're still laughing at me," he said playfully.

She put a hand over her mouth, shaking her head. "She said *old Chester*, like the most we'd get out of him was a trot."

"Yeah, that sucker almost broke out into a sprint with me on him. That was dangerous, you know. What if I'd been a kid who fell and hit their head?"

Tracee slowed her laughter until she stopped. "You're right, that was dangerous. I'm glad you didn't hurt yourself. Maybe old Chester needs to be retired."

"Or I need riding lessons, one or the other."

"Well, there's a little klutz in all of us," Tracee said.

He straightened his arms and gripped the wheel. "Not in Laurent Martin. I'm the most coordinated, balanced individual you'd ever want to meet."

"Uh-huh, like when you turned your drink over at brunch last Sunday?"

He nodded his head and sucked his teeth. "So, you wanna bring that up. How about you stumbling back into my arms?"

She turned in her seat and opened her mouth wide. "Ah! That wasn't my fault. You opened the door on me!"

He shook his head. "Yea, there's a little klutz in all of us."

After they enjoyed another good laugh, Laurent asked, "Okay, where to now?"

She sniffed the air. "Smells like we need a shower. Those horses rubbed off on us."

Laurent glanced over at her with nothing but explicit things on his mind. "That sounds like a good idea. Your place or mine?"

Tracee stepped out of the shower and reached for a towel to dry off. She had thirty minutes before Laurent returned. He'd gone to his hotel to shower and change, and then he'd be back for her. As she lotioned up, she thought about how much fun she'd had with Laurent in the last two days. If he lived in Danville, she'd have to give him a run for his money, but he was only in town for a short time. She couldn't remember what he said his business was, but whatever had delayed him, she hoped it kept him around a little longer. He was funny, good-looking and well educated—she could tell that from their conversations.

As she slipped into a fresh pair of jeans, the phone rang. She hoped it wasn't Laurent saying he wouldn't be able to make it back. She checked the caller ID before picking up her home phone.

"Hey, Mae, what's up?"

"I'm at the hospital, and I may have secured another corporate account for us. I'm going to check back with the director of food services later in the week."

"That's great! This afternoon I'm going to start on a few batches of cookies for the church. I volunteered to provide my lemon cookies for tomorrow's dinner service."

"Girl, you're going to get the church folk addicted to those cookies now. The last time I brought home a batch, John ate all but two and begged me to have you bake some more."

Tracee laughed. "And I did. Stop by tonight and I'll fix him a box."

"Thanks. So, what else you got up for today?"

Tracee held the phone between her ear and shoulder while she pulled a few tops from her closet, trying to decide on one. "Well, I have a dinner date with a very nice man."

"The guy from the hotel. What's his name?"

"Laurent," Tracee said in her best French accent.

"Yeah, him. You mean you've seen him since Tuesday night and didn't tell me?"

"I know how busy you've been. I was going to tell you. He called me yesterday for a tour of the town."

"Yesterday? I thought he was only in town for a couple of days."

"Whatever he's working on has been delayed, so he'll be here for a few more days. I'm not sure how long. I'll ask him tonight."

"It sounds like you're digging this guy."

"He's nice, and he makes me laugh," she said, settling on a thin black and white sweater.

"Well, enjoy him while you can. I'll drop by later to get those cookies."

Tracee said goodbye and ended the call, tossing the phone on her bed. She looked back at the clock on her nightstand. Laurent would be there any—

Her doorbell rang.

Laurent had changed into a dark gray sweater and black pants, which was perfect for where Tracee had in mind.

Minutes later, they entered Tracee's favorite pizzeria. "They have the best pizza in Danville," she told Laurent as they walked in. A little food, a little dancing and a little something to drink was what she had in mind. As the night rolled on, it seemed as if everyone in Danville had the same idea. The restaurant was so crowded they had to share tables, forcing Tracee to almost sit in Laurent's lap. His arm stretched around her shoulder, and his mouth was practically in her ear when he spoke.

"Any live music around here?" he asked.

She nodded. "Yeah, if you like country music," she said with her nose touching the lobe of his ear.

They were too close. The smell of his cologne made her whole body shiver.

He shook his head. "I'll pass."

The DJ at the pizzeria was going to have to do for tonight. He played top-forty pop, with a little hip-hop mixed in. Tracee managed to get Laurent to the dance floor a couple of times before they were afraid they'd lose their seat for good if they got up again. After the pizza, she was about to order some tiramisu when she remembered she had to whip up several batches of lemon cookies once she got home.

"Are you a dessert kind of man?" she asked.

He shrugged. "That depends. What did you have in mind?"

She put her lips as close to his ear as she could, again while resisting the urge to kiss his neck, and said slowly, "Rosemary-lemon shortbread cookies, from scratch."

He pulled back and stared down at her with wide eyes. "You're baking them?"

She nodded. "I need to bake four dozen before the night's over."

He tilted his head and put his lips to her ear. "Let's go."

Laurent paid the check, and they exited the noisy pizzeria and headed for the rental car.

On the ride to her condo, Tracee wondered if she was doing the right thing by inviting Laurent over. After spending so much time with him, she still didn't know very much about him. The one thing she did know was that she was extremely attracted to him, in a dangerous kind of way.

Chapter 9

The minute Tracee walked into her condo, she turned on the bright living room lights. She thought about texting Mae or somebody in her family to let them know Laurent was there, but she felt silly doing that. Besides, Mae would be swinging by later to pick up the cookies.

"Come on in." She tossed her purse and jacket on the couch before going into the kitchen, turning on all those lights as well.

Laurent walked in and followed her into the kitchen. "You have a nice place here."

"Thank you. I love to decorate."

He took a seat at the kitchen table. Tracee stepped into the powder room across from the kitchen and washed her hands. "Would you like something to drink?" she called out.

"Sure, if it's not too much trouble."

When she returned she noticed how relaxed he looked sitting there with his legs wide-open and his hands clasped in his lap. "Not a problem at all." From the cabinet she pulled down two wineglasses, holding them up. "Red or white?" she asked.

"White."

She set the glasses on the counter and opened the refrigerator. "The cookies won't take long to bake, and if you want you can turn on the television in the living room." She walked over to hand him a glass of wine.

"I'm cool right here. I'd like to watch the master at work."

She smiled and took a sip of wine. "Uh, if you stay in here, I might put you to work."

Laurent held his hands up. "Work me, baby. I'm all yours tonight."

Tracee glanced up at the ceiling for a brief moment. *If only.* Then she set her glass on the counter. "Okay, Mr. Martin, wash up and we'll get to baking."

Laurent jumped up and walked into the bathroom. Tracee proceeded to pull out her pans and the ingredients she needed from the refrigerator. She also started to preheat the oven.

"Okay, what do you need me to do?" Laurent asked when he returned.

"First, look inside that closet and get an apron out. You're going to get something on your sweater for sure."

He opened the closet door, pulled a large apron from the peg inside and tugged it over his head. Tracee watched him tie it in the back before joining her at the counter. He glanced down at the Eiffel Tower on the front and smiled.

"Nice apron," he said.

"Paris is my favorite place in the world."

"Have you ever been there?" he asked.

"Yes, I have. When I was in culinary school, I spent two weeks in Paris taking baking and cooking classes. It was wonderful. Isn't Laurent a French name?"

He nodded. "It is. My grandmother was French Canadian from Montreal. All the men in my family have French names."

"You want to lightly butter that pan for me?" she asked him. "You said you have two brothers, right?"

He pulled the paper back from the stick of butter and began working. "Yep, two older brothers. Marquis and Aubrey."

"Did you spend much time in Canada as a child?"

"Several holidays, but that's about it. My mother was happy to leave the cold for California, so my grandmother came to visit us more than we went there."

"Is your father from Canada, too?" she asked as she zested a lemon.

"No, Chicago. Evanston, Illinois, actually, north of Chicago."

Laurent reached over for a paper towel while Tracee turned on the food processor to pulse the lemon, sugar and rosemary. After wiping his hands, he walked over and picked up his wineglass. She continued to blend the butter, salt and vanilla.

"*Ça sent bon,*" Laurent said while leaning against the counter. "That smells good."

Tracee smiled. "Um, that sounded good. French is such a beautiful language. Are you fluent?"

He shook his head. "No, but I remember some things. Do your neighbors ever come over looking for something sweet? Because with smells like this going on, I'd be knocking on your door all the damned time."

She laughed. "Occasionally a neighbor will say, 'it smells mighty good up in there,' but no, no one has ever asked for something to eat." She turned off the food processor. Laurent stared at her with those mesmerizing eyes, and she almost missed the pan when she turned the dough out.

He quickly set his glass down and caught the pan, preventing it from sliding off onto the floor.

"Thank you. Now we need to make as many round balls as we can to fill up these cookie sheets."

"How many are you making?" he asked.

She cleared her throat. "*We* are making four dozen. Don't be shy, get your hands in there. You did say you were all mine tonight," she said, lowering her voice.

Laurent smiled and took a step back. "I did say that, didn't I? Well, I'd better get comfortable." He turned around and removed the apron before pulling his sweater over his head.

The hairs on Tracee's arms rose and her heart thumped hard against her chest. But she was slightly disappointed, because he had on a black T-shirt under the sweater.

"I hope you don't mind, it's getting a little warm," he said, standing there with his sweater in one hand and the apron in the other.

A tingle ran through her body. "No…not at all. It, uh…it is a little warm in here. The oven heats up the house after a bit." His short-sleeved T-shirt showed off his muscular arms and the frame of his chest.

He draped his sweater over the back of a chair before putting the apron back on. "Okay, where was I?" he asked, rubbing his palms together.

"You were about to dip your hands into this bowl and start making some lemon balls. Just place them on the sheet, like those." She'd formed a few already for him to follow.

He picked up the spoon she'd been using and scooped a spoonful into his hand. "Believe it or not, this is the most time I've spent in the kitchen in a long time."

"I hope you don't eat a lot of frozen dinners."

"No, but I dine out more than I should. Something like this intimidates the hell out of me."

"And this is easy. Once we're finished, we'll bake two sheets first for twenty-five minutes. While we wait, you can make the icing."

He wiped his hands again while she placed the pans in the oven.

Next, she let him help her with the icing before setting it in the refrigerator to chill.

She walked over and picked up her wineglass.

"Laurent, exactly what is it you're doing at the hotel?" she asked before taking a sip.

"I'm meeting with people and kind of assessing the hotel's brand."

"Okay, so how do you do that?" she asked.

"For instance, I conduct thorough property visits, look into labor trends, resolve staffing issues and stuff like that. Then I report back to our executive team."

She nodded again. "I see... So, what happens when you find a problem?"

"Well, it might be time for some new operational policies."

Tracee tilted her head. "Who do you work for again?" His job sounded more important than what she'd initially thought he did. It sounded interesting.

Laurent laughed. "Martin Enterprises. You look like I've confused the hell out of you. I promise I didn't mean to."

"You should have just said you were a hotel spy. That's what it sounds like."

Laurent shook his head. "I'm not spying on anybody. I'm very out in the open with my questions and observations. You'd be surprised how much knowledge you can gain just by asking questions."

Laurent retrieved his glass of wine before turning to Tracee. "What now?" he asked once they were finished.

"Now we wait. We can go back into the living room, away from the heat." She'd said it, but she doubted she could avoid the heat her body was giving off by being in his presence.

* * *

After Laurent saw Tracee's CD collection on her bookshelf, they took each other down memory lane. Tracee played CDs, and Laurent pulled up some of his favorites from his cell phone. When the first batch of cookies was complete, they took them out and put another batch in the oven before returning to the living room.

"What's this section over here?" Laurent asked, picking up a stack of CDs Tracee had set aside.

"Oh, that's my UK invasion stack. Are you familiar with any of the artists?"

Laurent leafed through the stack, nodding his head, then stopped. "Who's this?"

He handed Tracee the CD. "That's Labrinth. You've never heard of him?"

"Don't think I have."

"Then you have to let me play you something." She jumped at every opportunity to play her favorite music for someone. She played "Beneath Your Beautiful," by Labrinth, featuring Emeli Sandé, one of her favorite artists. She sat cross-legged on the floor listening to the lyrics hoping he could appreciate the beauty of the song as well. Tracee cut her eyes at Laurent, who was staring down at her from his side chair. She glanced away, wishing the nasty thoughts running through her mind would go away.

"That was beautiful," Laurent said after the song ended. "I like songs like that. About stripping down to who you really are and not putting on airs for somebody."

"And I like the part about not being perfect. That's

deep." She set the CD aside and looked around for another one of her favorites.

He grabbed his cell phone from the side table and slid down on the floor across from Tracee. "I've got one I bet you'll like. It's old-school. You may not know this group."

A slow-tempo song started, and Tracee liked the tune. "Who is it?"

He smiled. "Atlantic Starr, 'Let's Get Closer.' It's a classic. My brothers and I used to sing it when we had our band. The music was real easy."

Tracee took note as to how close Laurent was sitting to her on the floor during the song. "I like the music, and it does scream *old-school*."

He laughed. "Yeah, I told you I'm pretty well versed in that area. How about this one." He sat with his back against the chair and placed his phone on the floor between them.

Tracee immediately recognized Maxwell's voice. She smiled and closed her eyes.

"That one's 'Till the Cops Come Knockin','" Laurent said.

"Oh, I know that one," she said. Her body rocked in time with the music. Then she heard Laurent singing. She opened her eyes, surprised that he had a really smooth voice.

He stopped singing and looked at her.

"You have great taste in music," she said.

He smiled. "So do you. Play me another one."

Tracee selected a couple more CDs and continued to entertain Laurent with more of her favorites. She didn't know how it happened, but somehow she and Laurent ended up next to one another when he pulled up "Burn Slow" by Ro James.

Tracee's body leaned back into Laurent's chest, and she closed her eyes as he wrapped his arms around her. Their bodies moved in time with the groove, and she lost herself in his arms. The moment put a smile on her face. This man wasn't hers, but she wanted him. Maybe if only for tonight.

Laurent brushed her hair away from the side of her face and leaned down to kiss her on the temple. His kiss was soft and suggestive. She fought to keep her hands to herself, but he was making it difficult for her. She ran her hand along his forearm that embraced her. His hairy, strong arm was warm to the touch.

The song went off too soon, but the one that followed turned Tracee on even more. "Permission," another Ro James tune, had Tracee turning around in Laurent's arms. He released his hold on her body and brought both hands to her face. He held her face while he kissed her long and hard.

Tracee's body was on fire with desire. She wrapped her arms around Laurent and kissed him back with an unabashed shame and thirst like she'd never had for any man before. Her head spun as he released her lips and kissed a trail down to her neck. She threw her head back and bit her lip—his kisses were driving her crazy. He reached around and pulled her legs toward him and rested her head in the palms of his hands. She relaxed as he lowered her to the floor. Her breath caught in her throat as he gently bit at her nipples through her sweater. She shuddered as she caressed the back of his head.

In one fast move, he stopped and pulled her sweater over her head, tossing it onto the chair. Tracee lay on the floor staring up at this beautiful man with fire in his eyes. He then pulled his T-shirt over his head and tossed it with her top. He came down on one elbow and ran a hand along the side of her cheek, down her breast and around her waist. The music switched to another slow R&B song, and she could have sworn he'd set that up.

Tracee was soaking wet.

Then the oven buzzer went off.

Laurent jumped. "Oh, man." He exhaled before dropping his head between her breasts.

It took everything Tracee had inside her to not just let those cookies burn.

Chapter 10

Laurent sat up on his elbow, and his eyes met Tracee's. "The cookies?" he asked.

She closed her eyes and nodded.

He inhaled a deep breath and fell over on his back. Tracee lay still for a moment, waiting for the nerve endings in her body to stop tingling. She finally sat up as the music on his phone changed to the next track.

"I'll be right back." She got up and walked off to the hall bathroom.

Laurent closed his eyes and tried to steer his thoughts to something other than Tracee for a minute. But it was useless. He could see her big smile, her beautiful eyes and her curvy body against his eyelids. Whenever she laughed, it warmed something deep inside him. He was so comfortable with her he could lie on the floor with her all night sharing something special to the both of them.

He heard her moving around in the kitchen and opened his eyes. She had cookies to pack up, and he was keeping her from that. He sat up, forcing himself to remember that baking was her livelihood and at this point, he might be in her way. He reached for his T-shirt and decided it was best to leave before they went too far. After pulling his T-shirt and sweater back on, he picked up his phone and stopped the music.

"What are you doing?"

He turned around, and Tracee walked across the room in her jeans and that black lace bra that had captivated him so much a few minutes ago. He swallowed hard and hoped she'd stop before she reached him. If she touched him, he'd have a hard time doing what he knew he needed to do. "I think I better go."

"Why?" she asked with an innocent look on her face.

"I've taken up enough of your time, and I know you have things you need to do."

She stood close enough for him to pull her into his arms, but he clenched his jaw and kept telling himself to leave now, before it was too late.

She put her hands in the back pockets of her jeans and shrugged. "I'm finished with what I needed to do tonight, but if you have to leave, I'll understand." She walked past him, bumping against him in the process, and put on another CD. When she turned around, she ran her hands up and down her crossed arms.

He was going to leave, but he couldn't get his feet

to move toward the door. Instead, he stood there holding his phone in one hand and his keys in the other. She reached for her sweater, and he decided he couldn't let this moment pass, so he beat her to it. "Are you cold?" he asked as he held out the sweater.

She smiled and turned up her lips. "Yes, I am."

He tossed the sweater, along with his keys and phone, over onto the couch, farther away. Her mouth widened in surprise. "Let me keep you warm." He pulled her close, wrapping his arms around her body, and then whispered in her ear, "How's that?"

She let out a deep breath. "Perfect." She returned the hug, wrapping her arms around him as well.

"Look, Tracee, I don't know how long I'm going to be in town—"

"You're not leaving tonight, are you?"

He bit his lip and loosened his hold enough to look down at her. She stared up into his eyes, and his need for her grew stronger. He didn't say another word. He shook his head. They understood the stakes, and they still wanted one another.

She pulled out of his embrace and grasped the hem of his sweater. He raised his arms, and she pulled the sweater up and over his head. His T-shirt was next. If there was a chill in the air, he didn't feel it. His body was on fire again. While his clothes lay in a pile on the floor, Tracee reached for his hand and led him to what was no doubt the staircase to heaven.

At the top of the stairs was a room fit for a queen. Her bed had a tall headboard that, like the rest of the room, was draped in rich, royal colors and gold tones. She turned around, facing him when he reached out and tugged at the waist of her jeans. For a moment, he stared at her beautiful body, noticing her shiver. He stroked his hands up and down her upper arms. The heat in his hands quickly doused her chills as their gazes collided and her body relaxed.

Her lips parted, and his breath quickened. She lowered her gaze and slid her hands up his chest, forcing him to let go of her arms. Her fingers slowly traveled up his chest, and his breath caught in his throat.

"You have protection, don't you?" she asked.

"Yeah, I do."

She smiled up at him with big eyes. "Great."

She went for his belt, and in a matter of seconds they'd stripped their clothes off and lowered themselves to her bed. He tried to kiss every square inch of her body while she giggled with delight. When he brushed his lips across her nipples, he felt them harden. Her breasts rose and fell as she drew in quick breaths. He sucked a breast into his mouth, and she squirmed and moaned underneath his touch, causing him to go weak with need. He was hungry for her and spread her legs with one hand before caressing the velvety softness beneath his fingers.

"Oh, God, Laurent." She slid her hand around to caress the back of his head, while holding his mouth to her breast.

When he released her, he looked down at her hardened nipple and licked it until the throbbing between his legs forced him to stop. Heart pounding, he moved up and looked down at her succulent lips. "You're so beautiful," he whispered before capturing her bottom lip between his teeth.

He brought his hands around to her firm butt cheeks and squeezed. She kissed him hard, with a hunger that set him on fire. They clung to each other, stroking and sucking, desperate to douse the fire that had consumed them. He reached a point when he was so hard he couldn't take it any longer. He had to have her.

Tracee straddled him, his erection mere inches from where he wanted to be. He thrust his hips up, letting her know what he was ready for.

"Wait." She leaned closer and placed her palms on his chest as she caught her breath.

He looked up and met her gaze. He prayed she wasn't changing her mind. Not now.

"Where's the condom?"

He breathed a sigh of relief. "In my wallet."

"Don't you think now would be a good time to get it?"

He smiled. "I didn't forget it. I just want to look at your beautiful body for as long as I can."

She leaned closer with her smoldering eyes and kissed his chest, which nearly took him over the edge. Before he could climb out of bed and pull the condom from his pocket, the doorbell rang.

She sat straight up.

He looked up at her and tried to hide his crushed feelings. "Expecting company?"

"You know you're wrong for that," Mae said through the phone.

"Wrong for what?" Tracee asked, giggling. She

was straightening up the CDs she hadn't been able to put away last night.

"Shoving that box of cookies out the door at me. You could have at least let me say hello to the man."

"Child, please, you're lucky I answered the door."

Mae laughed. "I know that's right. Girl, I can't say that I wouldn't have left your ass out there ringing the bell my damned self. What time did he leave?"

"I don't know, sometime this morning. It was still dark out."

"And you made it to church this morning, after all that fornicating last night?"

"Let she who is without sin on this phone cast the first stone. And what did you and John do when you got home last night?"

"Okay, the both of us need to go to Bible study this week. I got horny just sitting there watching the two of you look at each other like you hadn't eaten in years."

Tracee laughed. "Was it that bad?"

"Hell yeah. So, what's up for today?"

"I need to deliver these cookies and then stop by Corra's to—"

"That's not what I'm talking about. Are you going to see Laurent today?"

"Oh, I don't know, we didn't make any plans. He might be doing something with his friend Sam." Tracee had enjoyed Laurent's company so much last night, but she understood it was a temporary thing. Any day now he would be returning to California. Besides, she wasn't trying to set herself up for another heartbreak.

"Did he say when he's leaving?"

"No, but maybe I'll see him again before he does. If I don't, I at least have something wonderful to remember him by."

Mae laughed. "Sure, if you say so. Girl, I know you're trying to have this nonchalant attitude, but I see through that shit. You might like to have a good time and all, but you let that man stay the night! The Tracee I know only does that when she's really feeling somebody. Which hasn't happened in a while."

Tracee hated to admit even to herself that Mae was right, but she was. And she didn't want to address any feelings she was having for Laurent. She wanted to be able to have a fling with this guy if she wanted to. "Whatever, Mae. Girl, this isn't anything serious. I'm just going to enjoy myself for a minute. Any law against that?"

"None whatsoever, I'm only making sure you don't get hurt."

"Child, please, he can't hurt me. He's something to do for a week or so, that's all."

"Uh-huh. Well, keep telling yourself that. Anyway, I'm in the car now headed to Richmond for the day, but there's another reason for my call. I know we're scheduled to meet with Mr. Patel tomorrow morning, but I'm not going to make it."

Tracee let out a deep sigh. "Mae, you missed sitting down with him last time. I looked forward to you making this meeting so he'll know my partner is in this with me."

"I know, and I'm sorry. But my boss asked me to head up a customer visit on his behalf. I'm flying to St. Louis first thing Monday morning. You'll do great, but I'll be with you in spirit."

"It's not the same thing," Tracee said with no enthusiasm. "But I totally understand. You have to do what you have to do. I'll call and update you after the meeting."

"I want an update on Laurent, too."

Tracee laughed. "Sure. If I see him again." She hung up hoping deep down in her heart that last night wasn't a one-night stand. She also tried to shake the growing uneasy feeling about Mae canceling on her. She prayed her friend was still as invested in the business as she was.

Monday morning, Tracee pulled up to the Rival Hotel and immediately looked around for Laurent's dark blue Elantra, but it wasn't there. She hoped he hadn't left town without saying goodbye.

Once inside, she met up with Raji, who happened to be an old classmate of Kyla's. He was dressed in a suit today, which was unusual for him. Seconds later, his father, Mr. Patel, came out and escorted her into a small conference room that was set up banquet style.

"Would you like a cup of coffee?" he offered politely.

"Sure," she said, as she set her purse and folder on the table before joining him at the coffee station against the wall. "Thank you for giving me a little time on your schedule this morning."

"Not a problem." He handed her a cup. "Decaf?"

"Yes, please." While he poured the coffee, she gathered her sweetener and cream. Once prepared, they took their cups to the table and sat down. She could sense a change in the air. Mr. Patel was more relaxed than she'd ever seen him. With her he was always professional, but he'd never offered her coffee before.

"So, how is everything with Tracee's Cake World?" he asked. "I thought your partner would be joining us today?"

She blew on her coffee and chose her words carefully. "Business is good. Sales were up this summer, and now I'm getting ready for the holiday season. Unfortunately, Mae had an emergency out of town, so I'm flying solo today."

"Well, I'm happy to hear that business is good. The unexpected does happen, so I understand."

"Mr. Patel, I want to thank you for everything you've done in support of our business. If you hadn't let us use your refrigerator a couple of times, I probably would have lost some of my biggest orders. And I more than appreciate the free meeting rooms."

He sipped his coffee. "I'm happy to do whatever I can to support you. I didn't see any reason to charge you for use of the room when you only want it for an hour or two. Little things like that I love to do for the community. The relationship we've had with the Coleman House over the years has been a beautiful one. This whole community has been very good to me and my family. I'm sure your café will be a great asset to the hotel." Then he cleared his throat.

She opened her folder, ready to talk business.

"Before you do that, there is something we need to discuss."

He set his coffee cup down and clasped his hands together on the table in front of him. Tracee swallowed the knot in her throat. She didn't like the serious change in his tone of voice.

"The future of the Rival Hotel will be changing. At this point in my life, I've decided to retire from the hotel business. I'm selling all of the locations except one."

Tracee's eyes widened. "You're kidding."

He shook his head. "I'm afraid not. I'm currently in negotiations with two separate companies. I'm sorry I couldn't have shared this information with you sooner, but we weren't close enough to a deal."

"And you are now?" she asked, with a sinking feeling in her stomach.

He smiled. "Yes, we're closer. Nothing has been signed as of yet, but negotiations are going well."

She took another sip of coffee, then pushed the mug aside. "I think I already know the answer to this, but will Tracee's Cake World be a part of the deal?" she asked.

He chuckled. "If that were possible, I'd do it. However, I'm afraid it's not."

She pressed on. "So, who are you considering selling to?"

He raised his brows. "I'd rather not share that information, considering we're still in negotiations. But I will mention the café when discussing the sale."

Tracee took a deep breath before taking one last sip of the coffee she was sure he had hoped would soften the blow. "Once you make a decision, I hope you will let me know, so I can approach the new owners about the space before someone else does."

He smiled. "Of course. And I'm very sorry I didn't have better news for you today."

"So am I. But all's not lost. I know you, Mr. Patel, and I'm sure you'll keep me posted."

He promised to do just that as they walked out of the conference room through the hotel lobby. The thought of the Rival Hotel being taken over by new ownership saddened Tracee. The hotel was a staple in the community and the only place outside the Coleman House she liked enough to consider doing business. Contrary to what she'd told Mr. Patel, there was no guarantee he'd keep her posted like he'd said. If she wanted that space, she'd have to do everything in her power to find the prospective buyers and approach them herself. She needed Mae with her now to shoulder the news. Wasn't that what partners were supposed to do?

Chapter 11

Tracee had missed her baby sister's presence at the Coleman women's discussions over breakfast. This morning, Kyla was back to tell everyone about her trip to Africa with her fiancé, Miles Parker.

The minute Tracee and Kyla were alone, Tracee filled her in on her current business situation.

Kyla set down her cup of tea. "Didn't Mr. Patel say the space was yours once you came up with the money? He knows someone in our family has rented that space ever since he opened. We expected to keep that tradition in the family."

"That's what I'm trying to do." Tracee shrugged and leaned back in her seat.

"If he won't tell you who the prospective buyers are, have you tried Raji? You know that boy can't keep his mouth shut. He gossips more than any woman I know."

"No, I haven't, but I don't know Raji like you. You guys went to school together, so maybe the next time you see him, you can poke around for me."

Kyla ran her fingers through her ponytail. "I'll just come out and ask him. Raji's like a kid. If he knows you want something and he has the answer, he can't keep it to himself."

"Thanks, Kyla. Business is really picking up, but I can't do the type of marketing I want to do until I have a signed lease on the space. I'm already servicing several downtown businesses."

"And I heard you landed Melanie Jefferson's wedding. That's a major feather in your cap, girl. Your unique cakes are such a huge hit. I can't wait until you create one for my and Miles's wedding."

Tracee sat up and clasped her hands together. "Me neither! But I do wish you were getting married here, since the bed-and-breakfast is famous for our weddings, too."

"I know, and I'm sorry." Kyla stuck out her bottom lip. "But Miles and I talked it over, and we want the ceremony performed in church."

Tracee stood up and walked around the table to hug Kyla. "I understand, and I'm so happy for you."

"Thank you." After they embraced, Kyla placed her hands on her hips. "So, what are you doing to make sure you get that space in the hotel?"

Tracee sat back down. "I had an idea for the potluck this weekend, so I invited Mae's cousin who's a photographer and writer for the paper."

"So, he's going to cover the potluck, but how does that help you?" Kyla asked.

Tracee smiled. "Oh, you'll see."

If anyone had told Laurent that at any point in his life he'd be in Kentucky attending a potluck dinner, he would not have believed them. However, the Coleman House Farm had some of the best fresh organic vegetables he'd ever put in his mouth. Plus, Tracee had invited him, and he didn't want to miss an opportunity to see her again. He'd seen her twice over the last couple of days, and like teenagers who'd discovered sex for the first time, they couldn't get enough of each other.

Tracee met him as he approached the house with her hair pulled into a long poufy ponytail cascading down her back. She had on a low-cut white top with a matching jacket and a pair of distressed jeans with some cute flats. The first thing that came to his mind was how well she would fit in in California. She greeted him with a kiss.

"How has your day gone so far?" she asked.

"Great." He eagerly returned the kiss, tasting some sort of cherry lip gloss. He wished they could skip the potluck and go back to her place. "My morning started with a good run. Thanks to you, my run is more interesting now that I have a better lay of the land. After that, I had a great conference call, which set the tone of the day."

The potluck was being held in the U-pick barn. Tracee led the way down the path to the big barn.

She smiled. "A conference call on a Saturday morning. My, my, you are a busy man."

"And now I'm a hungry man," Laurent said as they strolled inside the barn full of colorful people and flavorful smells. The barn was a tad drafty, but huge heaters strategically hung about kept it from being too cold.

Once inside, Tracee gave him what she called the potluck tour. She grabbed a couple of plates and escorted him around the table as they filled their plates with food from every color of the rainbow. At the same time, she introduced him to several of their neighbors.

"What are those crackers there with bacon wrapped around them?" He could feel his stomach growling but had to question some of the dishes.

Tracee smiled and elbowed him. "That's Joyce Ann's famous goat cheese and bacon creation. She brings them every month. Want to try one?" she asked with a raised brow.

The way she cocked her brow at him said it all. He cleared his throat and glanced away. "I think I'll pass. I'm excited to try these dishes prepared by the Coleman House cooks."

With full plates, they walked over to sit down across from Corra and her husband, Chris. Laurent found the dinner conversation enlightening. Chris was a businessman much like himself. They shared a passion for golf and football. Later, Tracee left the table and Laurent noticed her talking to a young man who was taking pictures of the dessert table she said she'd worked on most of the day.

Laurent hadn't realized how caught up he was in watching them until Corra pointed it out. "That table is amazing, isn't it?"

He tore his eyes away from them and turned to Corra. "It is. Tracee's an amazing pastry chef."

"Oh, she's more than that. Tracee is an artist. The title pastry chef doesn't begin to describe the designs she comes up with for cakes. And her theme parties and weddings are off the chain. We're going to hate to lose her once she opens her own place."

Laurent nodded in agreement with Corra. "In the little time I've been here, I've definitely come to understand that Tracee is a very special woman. She told me how she helped build your line of baked goods."

"She actually started the line. My aunt Rita bakes desserts for dinner and afternoon tea, but nothing on the scale of what Tracee started. She had us serving two to three different desserts with every meal. I am, however, proud to say we'll be her first regular customer. She has some recipes she'll reserve just for us."

Laurent turned his attention back to Tracee and the young man, who now held a tape recorder to her mouth. After a few minutes, Tracee walked away with her chin held high and a smile on her face.

After dinner, Laurent spent some time talking to Rollin and Chris before Rollin gave him a quick tour of the organic farm. The property was impressive, and he'd never met a brother who owned a farm and a bed-and-breakfast. Although Rollin confessed the women ran most of the bed-and-breakfast. The story of their humble beginnings reminded him of his father's rise in the boutique hotel industry.

After the farm tour, and when most of the guests had left, Laurent found Tracee sitting at a table looking less than enthused. A stark contrast from the happiness she'd displayed not long ago.

"Hey, what's up? Why are you sitting over here all alone?" he asked before he noticed she was looking down at her cell phone.

She shrugged. "I don't know. I'm just hoping my little plan pays off."

He sat down beside her. "What plan is that?"

She took a deep breath, sat up straight and placed her cell phone on the table. "Monday I found out some bad news, and I've started putting a plan in place to help myself."

He frowned. "Is it something you want to talk about?" He had to acknowledge that he was developing feelings for this woman, and he didn't like to see her hurt and sad.

"Well, you know I'm trying to open my own café in the Rival Hotel. So, I met with Mr. Patel Monday and found out he's selling the hotel. He wouldn't say to whom, but I'm not going down without a fight. I'm determined to find out who the prospective buyer is and have that space for my café."

Laurent jabbed his jaw with his tongue. Mr. Patel had shared information that Laurent had hoped he'd keep close until the deal was announced. From experience, Laurent knew to keep his mouth shut until he achieved his goal. Sometimes, a simple slip of the tongue could set you back and destroy all you'd worked so hard for.

He took one of Tracee's hands in his, and massaged her knuckles. "How do you plan to do that?" he asked, eager to hear her answer.

"I can't say, but I was texting somebody about that when you walked up. I also arranged this whole photo shoot today. I need to position myself as a great tenant to the new buyer. Although I don't know who the potential buyer is, a front-page story about me can't hurt. You know what I mean?"

The determined eyes that looked up at him sent a chill through his body.

"The minute you think things are looking up, somebody throws a boomerang at you and you're back at square one." She rested an elbow on the table and her forehead in her palm.

He looked down and caressed her long slender fingers. "I know I've asked you this before, but have you considered another location?"

She shook her head. "Nope. Remember me telling you the location was special to me?"

"Yeah, I do."

"Someone in my family has leased that space from him for years."

"Really? There's a connection to the Coleman House?"

"No, that's my father's side of the family. My mother's mother opened a coffee stand in the hotel not long after Mr. Patel open his doors. After a few years, she expanded the space to the size it is now. When she became ill, my cousin took over. She ran it until she got married and moved away. Mr. Patel has used it as storage space ever since. It took me a couple of years to get my finances straight, but now that I'm ready, he's ready to sell it off. My mother's family has lost a lot over the years, so I wanted to at least keep this tradition going."

Laurent nodded. "I understand. It has more sentimental value to you than anything."

"I don't even want to consider another spot."

Laurent hoped what he was about to say would be understood. He cleared his throat.

Tracee felt as if something wasn't right. Laurent squeezed her hand so hard it hurt. His palms were warm, and he kept rubbing her knuckles.

"Remember when you asked me what my business was in Danville?" he asked with his head down.

"Yeah, and you said you're a brand manager. Don't tell me that wasn't true?" She hoped to God he wasn't about to tell her he'd lied or something like that. A queasy feeling started in the pit of her stomach.

He chuckled, but his focus stayed on her hand.

Before he looked up into her eyes. "No, that's true, I am a branding manager. One of the things I handle is acquisitions. So, the reason I'm here is…uh—" he stalled before clearing his throat again. "I'm here to purchase the Rival Hotel."

"What!"

"Yeah, we're negotiating to buy the hotel chain."

A sudden coldness hit Tracee to her core. Her eyes

widened, and in her head she could hear herself yelling, *uh-uh. He did not say that!*

"We've assessed the business and made them an offer. Right now, I'm waiting on a few more particulars to be worked out, but after that we'll own the chain."

She couldn't believe what she was hearing. "So, all this time I've been talking about opening my business, you knew you were purchasing the hotel, or trying to?"

"I did, but I couldn't talk about it until the deal was completed. However, I see how distressed you are about possibly losing the space, and I don't want you to feel that way. Once I close the deal, your problem will be solved. I've seen the space you're referring to, and I think it will be great for a café. I can lease it to you."

She slid her hand from his. He looked so pleased and satisfied with himself, as if he'd just solved her problem. "Laurent, you haven't purchased the hotel yet, so I think it's a little premature to think you're the answer to all my problems."

He clasped his hands together. "Tracee, under normal circumstances I would have never said anything. But I think this is a done deal that I can have wrapped up by the weekend."

She leaned back in her seat and crossed her arms over her chest. "What makes you so sure of that?" she asked, wondering if he knew about the other prospective buyer.

"Mr. Patel likes my deal. We're ironing a few kinks out, but I'm sure by our next meeting everything will be to his satisfaction and he'll sign the papers."

No, he didn't know about a second buyer, and Tracee didn't think it was her place to tell him. If Mr. Patel had wanted Laurent to know, he would have told him. She pursed her lips and acted as if she knew nothing.

Laurent reached out and pinched her chin. "That's better. I like to see you smile."

"Laurent, I know you think you're my solution, but what if Mr. Patel doesn't like your offer? If it's all the same to you, I'd rather not put all my eggs in your basket." She pulled her hand back.

His shoulders dropped, and he clasped his hands together again. "What choice do you really have?"

She jerked her head back. "I have choices, and just like you, I prefer to keep them close to my chest for now."

"Tracee, come on. That came out wrong. I'm just saying that—"

"I know, you're the only option I have. But, Laurent, if I'd known you were trying to purchase the hotel, our friendship would have taken a much different turn. I would have had a choice in that matter. And my meeting with Mr. Patel where I learned about a surprise sale wouldn't have thrown me for a loop." She stood up to leave.

He stood up as well. "Tracee, let me just say I'm confident things will work out. Give it a couple of days—you'll see."

"I hope you like surprises, because you might be in for a big one." With her chin held high, she turned and headed out of the barn.

Chapter 12

Bright and early Saturday morning, Laurent met Sam and a few of his buddies at the nine-hole Sweetbrier Golf Course in Danville. The weather was perfect, the crowds were nonexistent and the fall foliage was absolutely breathtaking. Since college, both Sam and Laurent had improved their golf games. Sam's coworkers, also professors at the local college, were avid golfers as well. The course wasn't the best Laurent had played on, but it was sufficient to get a good workout. After about five holes, the conversation began to pique his interest.

"The landscape of downtown will definitely change once the Rival Hotel has been sold," Danny, an economics professor, said.

"I just hope they don't tear the place down, or turn it into an eyesore," Paul, another professor, replied.

Laurent and Sam shared a glance. Sam was aware of his interest in the hotel but kept that between them. He hadn't shared any pertinent details about Laurent with his colleagues.

"I don't think we have anything to worry about. If, or rather when, the hotel is sold, I'm sure the new owners will keep it right where it is. I know I'd hate to see too drastic of a change," Sam said, glancing at Laurent.

Danny walked over to switch out clubs. "I don't know, from what I hear, these companies specialize in mergers and acquisitions, then they destroy anything that resembles the original."

That wasn't true of Martin Enterprises, so Laurent wondered where this guy got his information.

"Do you know who's trying to purchase the hotel?" Laurent asked Danny.

"The Stephenson Group out of Lexington, and some other company from California. That's all I know right now. And I'm sure old man Patel is trying to squeeze them for everything he can get. He's a shrewd businessman."

The rest of Laurent's game went downhill. All he could think about was how he needed to get off that course and to a computer. He needed to find out all the details he could regarding a second buyer. Did his father know this bit of information? If so, why hadn't he told him?

"So the old man didn't say a word about negotiating with anyone else?" Sam asked Laurent as he placed his clubs in the trunk of his car.

"Not a word." Laurent set the clubs Sam had

loaned him into the trunk as well. "How can I be expected to compete when I don't even know there's a competitor? That might explain one thing, though."

"What's that?" Sam asked as he closed the trunk.

"Why he's stalling. He told me he wanted to sell to someone who understood their connection to the community. So I've spent the last week getting a feel for the community and how the Rival Hotel fits into the landscape. Now I'm curious to know if he's asked my competitor the same thing." Laurent climbed into the passenger's seat.

"You think he's trying to play the both of you to get a better deal?" Sam asked.

"Without question," Laurent replied. "Aside from him not feeling comfortable with my knowledge of Danville, he threw in several other stipulations that I'm trying to work out. But now I feel like I've wasted my time." Laurent looked out the window as Sam pulled away. There was only one good thing that had come out of him being in Danville so far. That was Tracee. But unless he could seal this deal, his efforts wouldn't pay off for her, either.

"Thanks for the invite this morning. This has been a very enlightening day, and it's going to make for a very exciting Monday." Laurent pulled out his cell phone and searched for his father's number.

Laurent realized Tracee was a little upset with him when he tried to make dinner plans with her for Saturday night. She was baking and meeting with Mae to work on their business plan. And Sunday after church, she would be busy working, as well.

He had to admit he was beginning to crave Tracee Coleman. Just hearing her voice made a difference in his day.

After he hung up with Tracee, he dialed Marquis. It was time to find out who his competition was and how to beat them.

"Hey, bro, I thought you'd be back here by now," Marquis said.

"I thought so, too. But this deal is taking a little longer. I found out some information today that you might be able to help me with."

"Sure, whatever you need."

"Do you still have that research team that works on a twenty-four-hour turnaround?"

"I do, what do you need?"

"Some dirt. I found out we're not the only one trying to purchase the hotel. What can you get me on the Stephenson Group out of Lexington, Kentucky?"

"How soon do you need it?"

"Is Monday morning too soon?"

"Not at all. Leave it to me. I'll need some information from you, so stick by the phone and I'll have someone call you in a minute."

"Thanks, and do me a favor. Don't mention this to anyone. Especially not Dad."

"Man, you know I wouldn't do that. I'll get back with you."

Laurent wasn't proud of himself for calling Marquis, but he knew his big brother could be discreet and get any information he needed. Laurent never asked where the information came from, and he didn't want to know now.

* * *

While Laurent patiently awaited the results from Marquis, he decided to see if Tracee was really working on her Sunday evening. From the driver's seat of the Elantra, he started to dial her number but quickly ended the call before it rang. If she was mad at him, she might tell him she was busy and hang up on him. But if he just showed up, he had a feeling he'd be welcomed. He decided to take a chance and cranked the engine.

During the less than fifteen-minute drive, he chastised himself for what he was about to do. He'd never been the type of guy to just show up on a woman's doorstep, but he couldn't stay away from Tracee. When he was around her, he forgot all about business and focused on her laugh and her arresting beauty.

He pulled up to her condo, and the lights were on inside. He hesitated after killing the engine. The last thing he wanted was for her to think his visit was all about sex. It wasn't. Although they had been doing a lot of that lately. He just needed to see her, to smell her and to have her voice put his mind at ease.

After he climbed out of the car, he turned the collar up on his coat. The brisk cold wind blew through his coat as if he didn't even have it on. He rang the bell while nibbling on his bottom lip. He didn't know what type of reception he was about to get, but he hoped it would be a warm one. After he rang the bell for a second time, the door opened.

A skeptical-looking Tracee, with a hand on her hip, took a step back and let him in. At least she didn't close the door in his face.

"I just happened to be in the neighborhood, so I thought I'd drop in to see if you were still mad at me." Laurent said with trepidation as he walked in behind her.

"I was never mad at you." She closed and locked the door behind him. "Just disappointed." She turned around and walked toward the kitchen. "I was about to eat dinner."

He turned down the collar of his jacket and shook off a chill. "I thought maybe you'd let me take you out for a bite."

"Take your jacket off. I made chicken marsala." She continued into the kitchen.

Laurent shrugged out of his jacket but couldn't take his eyes off her long legs or her curvy backside that, in black yoga pants, commanded his full attention. He realized now that he should have kept driving. He tossed his jacket on the couch and followed Tracee into the kitchen.

She pulled a second plate from the cabinet and set it on the table.

She'd left the Sunday paper on the counter, and he glanced down to see her beautiful face smiling back up at him. "Hey, I see that guy from the potluck got you in the paper," he said as he picked it up to read the article.

"Yep, that's what he was there for."

Laurent ignored her attitude and finished reading the article. The story covered the monthly potluck dinners the bed-and-breakfast put on and highlighted Tracee's Cake World. When he finished he returned the paper to the counter.

"Wash your hands."

Her harsh tone in Tracee's voice caught him off guard. She was more than disappointed. He let it go and stepped into her powder room to wash up. When he returned, she was sitting at the table with a glass of wine in her hand, swirling the white liquid around. His eyes transfixed on her glass. He'd dated enough women to know that look. He was in trouble. He pulled out a chair and sat down. "Are you okay?" he asked.

"Yeah, help yourself." She pointed to the platters of chicken and green beans on the table.

She'd already fixed her plate, and obviously waited on him. He fixed his plate, then poured himself a glass of wine. He reached for her hand to say the blessing, and to his surprise, she obliged.

They started eating in silence. A thick cloak of tension hung in the air like a rain cloud. Tracee kept her focus on her plate. After a couple of bites, Laurent braced himself for the shoe to drop.

"When were you going to tell me?" she asked.

He looked up at the stony expression on her face. "Tell you what?" He had no idea what she was talking about.

"That Martin Enterprises isn't just the name of the company you work for, but your family's business. That you aren't just a branding manager, but the VP of branding and an heir, along with your two brothers, to a multimillion-dollar business. That you're the much sought after son of Thomas Martin, founder of the exclusive Abelle hotel chain. For Christ's sake, Laurent, your hotels have butler service, spas and art galleries in the lobby!"

Laurent set his fork down and let her get it all out of her system.

"You're riding around town in an Elantra and eating at the pizzeria like it's something you do everyday. Martin is such a common name I never put two and two together. I thought you worked *for* Martin Enterprises, not that you *are* Martin Enterprises. You carry yourself more like a middle manager than a millionaire. This isn't your life. You're here pretending to be somebody you're not. But this is my life, Laurent, and that café is my future. You can play games with the Rival Hotel, but don't play games with me!"

"Tracee—"

She held out her palm to stop him. "I'm not done!"

Chapter 13

From across the conference table, Laurent studied the crease in Mr. Patel's brow as he read over the proposal Laurent had handed him. His rival, the Stephenson Group, wasn't who Mr. Patel thought they were, and Laurent hoped he could see that. Martin Enterprises, on the other hand, had a stellar reputation.

Mr. Patel slid the document to his son Arjun, on his left, while lifting his chin in Laurent's direction. In a smooth, placating voice, he said, "I see you've done your homework."

Laurent pulled his shoulders back and felt taller and stronger than he had during their last meeting. "A good businessman always does."

Raji, who was sitting to Mr. Patel's right, leaned

over and whispered something in his father's ear. Something that Laurent wished he could hear.

"Laurent, I don't know how you came upon this information, and I don't think I want to know." A stony expression took over Mr. Patel's face. "I've looked into the Stephenson Group myself, and I've heard nothing but good things about the company. They are very familiar with Danville and our commitment to the community." He paused and cleared his throat. "That's not to say I don't have a few reservations about them, or you wouldn't be here. However, this—" the older man broke eye contact with Laurent and tapped his index finger against the paper in front of his son "—is not California, and not the way we do business."

Laurent shook his head and leaned into the table. "Sir, I'm very aware of where I am. I've spent the last week getting to know your quaint little town and the wonderful people who live here. I've also gained a better understanding of what the Rival Hotel means to the community."

Mr. Patel pushed his chair back and slowly came to his feet. "Laurent, I have no doubt you put a lot into digging up this information, however, I feel like we're still not on the same page. I expressed interest in a few key areas during our last meeting that I don't think you picked up on. Getting in touch with key members of the *business* community would be more beneficial to you than with young women in the community."

Laurent exchanged eye contact with Raji, the only family member he was aware of who'd seen him with

Tracee. "Sir, I assure you that any *friendship* I've developed since being here has helped me to see Danville from an insider's perspective."

"I'm sure it has," Mr. Patel said with a forced smile before placing a hand on Arjun's shoulder. "Excuse me, but I'm not feeling so well right now, so Arjun here will have to conclude the meeting for me. If everything goes well, we may be ready to make a decision later in the week."

Laurent pressed his lips together in an attempt to hide the disappointment from his face. He'd hoped they'd complete the deal today. "Mr. Patel, I'm a very patient man, and I understand how important this negotiation process is to you. However, I think I've provided you with more than enough information to make a decision today. I would love to do business with you, but I am prepared to leave without a deal by the end of the week. You're not the only small chain hotel we have our eyes on. Martin Enterprises is in the hotel business and only the hotel business. Unlike my competition." As Laurent's grandmother used to say, it was time to crap or get off the pot.

"So he just left the room without another word?" Thomas Martin's voice came through the phone in a rushed tone.

Laurent had dreaded this phone call all afternoon. After last week's report back to his father that he hadn't completed the deal, he'd wanted the next call to be a reason for celebration. Instead, he had to report yet another delay.

"I made it clear that we're prepared to walk away

if a decision isn't made soon, but Mr. Patel wasn't feeling well, so I finished up the meeting with his sons." Although Laurent had issued the threat, he didn't want to walk away from this deal. This was his opportunity to have something for himself—and possibly help Tracee at the same time.

"You played your cards correctly. Although I want that chain, I'm prepared to walk away if he wants more than the twenty percent increase we've offered. We've made an effort, and that's all we can do."

Laurent had been throwing his dirty clothes in a laundry bag for the cleaners but stopped midtoss. "You're not serious, are you?" He had been bluffing, like he'd done numerous times before. And his father seldom walked away from anything.

"Laurent, you've been there for how many weeks now? I sent you because I had faith that you could work with Mr. Patel when I couldn't. However, it seems as if the man doesn't really want to sell his property. We've negotiated in good faith and had patience with him. Sometimes deals fall apart—that's part of doing business. You can't get too attached. Just walk away."

Laurent shook his head and sat down on the edge of the bed. "You can't be serious about walking away from this one. You dangled the ownership carrot in my face and now you want to take it back? I've done everything within my powers to get this deal. Believe me, after he fully looks over everything I provided, he'll be ready to sign the papers."

"Son, I hope so. I want this for you just as much as you want it for yourself."

Laurent hung up with his father and finished gathering his laundry. This trip wasn't going as smoothly as he'd expected. Forget his Caribbean vacation—now more than anything he wanted this hotel. Although his father had told him to pack it up, he wasn't a quitter. There was something about this deal and this town that he couldn't walk away from. Or maybe there was a certain woman who was the reason he couldn't walk away.

Tracee relaxed back into her father's broken-in recliner, kicking the footboard out. He'd brought the chair from their old home on the farm to their newer home in the city. The seat, which had contoured to his body, always gave her a safe and comforting feeling.

"You know Ernie says he can tell when you've been sitting in his chair." Paula Coleman, Tracee's mom, walked into the family room and sat in her chair next to Tracee and opposite the television.

Tracee ran her hands down the arms of the soft leather chair and inhaled. "How can he tell?"

"You leave your perfume behind. He says he can smell it a mile away."

Tracee's eyes widened. "What's he trying to say? My perfume's that strong?"

Paula shook her head and chuckled. "No, honey. I think it's more that he can tell the smell of each one of his children. So, what's going on with you?"

"Nothing, I just got off work so I thought I'd stop by to see how you guys were doing."

"Well, it's Tuesday, so your daddy's at the brotherhood meeting at church."

"Oh, I forgot all about that. What time does he come home?"

"Usually by four. So, what did you want to talk to him about?"

Tracee glanced over at her beautiful, brilliant mother, whom she could never put anything past. "Mama, what do you do when what you thought was the beginning to a bright future starts slipping through your fingers?"

"Baby, what's yours is yours. If it's meant for you, nothing can stop you from getting it. All you need is faith and patience."

Tracee let out a loud breath and sat up in the seat. "I've been patient for a long time. I want what's mine. I'm thirty-four years old with nothing but a part-time job and a side hustle."

Paula tilted her head and took a deep breath. "Tracee, you have a talent for creating and decorating cakes unlike anything I've ever seen. Be patient, baby. Maybe God has something bigger and better in store for you. But until that day comes, stay ready."

"I'm trying, Mama, but Satan keeps putting up roadblocks."

The doorbell rang.

Paula stood up to answer the door. "A roadblock is not a closed door. Remember that, baby."

Tracee's little sister, Kyla, joined them for a late lunch. Tracee was excited to know if Kyla had been able to get any information from Raji, but she held on to her excitement until after lunch.

"Don't worry about the dishes, Mom, I'll put them in the dishwasher." Kyla stood up and grabbed her mother's plate. "Tracee, you can get your own."

"Well, isn't that nice of you," Tracee said as she grabbed her plate and followed her sister into the kitchen. Once they were inside, Tracee handed Kyla her plate. "One more plate would have killed you?"

"Girl, I was trying to get you alone." After placing the saucers in the dishwasher, Kyla reached into her pants pocket. "I ran into Raji yesterday. I didn't know if you wanted Mama to know about this or not."

Tracee took the folded piece of paper from her and opened it up. "The Stephenson Group in Lexington," she read aloud.

"Ever heard of them?" Kyla asked.

Tracee shook her head. "No, but you'd better bet I'll know everything there is to know about them come tomorrow morning."

Tracee sat on her living room floor between the coffee table and the couch, staring into her computer screen. Beside her was a tablet with numerous notes she'd taken over the last couple of hours. After leaving her mom's, she couldn't wait to get home and start her research. The Stephenson Group was a holding company with a diverse portfolio including hotel real estate investments, financial services, automobile dealerships and asset management companies. Tracee gathered some names and switched to LinkedIn to do a more in-depth search.

She was deep in thought when the doorbell rang. *That has to be Mae.* She glanced at the clock on her computer before tearing herself away to answer the door. It was five thirty, and Mae had said she'd be over right after work.

Mae walked through the door like a business-woman on a mission. Today was going to be a good meeting. She hadn't gotten in good before Tracee started rambling about her findings.

"You won't believe what I found out this afternoon," she said.

"What's that?" Mae asked.

"The Stephenson Group. That's the name of one of the Rival Hotel's prospective buyers." Tracee closed the door and motioned Mae over to the couch, where her laptop sat on the coffee table.

"How did you find out?" Mae asked as she sat on the edge of the couch, still holding her purse.

"I didn't, Kyla did. She's been friends with Raji since high school. I think he had a crush on her at one time." Tracee resumed her seat on the floor with her back against the couch. "Anyway, I've been digging into this company all afternoon. They're a holding company and they own multiple businesses. I'm trying to narrow it down to who's in charge of the hotel acquisitions, but that's hard. I might have to make a few phone calls."

"Tracee, I need to talk to you about something."

Tracee snapped her fingers. "Oh, and I don't think I've told you about Martin Enterprises. That's going to blow your socks off." So much had happened in the last couple of days, Tracee was on information overload.

"Tracee, I need you to stop and listen to me."

Her friend's voice was shaky. Tracee glanced up at her—she was sitting as if she was about to leave. "What? Why are you sitting there like that? Take your coat off."

Mae cleared her throat. "I can't stay. But I didn't want to do this over the phone."

The hair on the back of Tracee's neck stood up. She put her pen down and got up from the floor to sit on the couch. "Girl, you're scaring me."

Mae lowered her shoulders. "I'm gonna have to bow out of the business."

Tracee's eyes widened. *I didn't hear that right.* She shook her head before studying her best friend and business partner. "What are you talking about?"

"I was offered the position of director of marketing this morning, and, Tracee, I can't turn that down. It's the position of a lifetime. I'll be the first African American female director with the company. That's the career path I was on before my divorce, when I had to put everything on hold."

Tracee was listening but felt a pain developing in the pit of her stomach at the same time. First the café itself, now her business partner. It seemed like the harder she tried, the more things fell apart.

"You've helped me get my head back in the game," Mae continued, "and I'm so grateful for that. I wanted to tell you the minute he made the offer, but I knew this was news I had to deliver in person."

Tracee nodded. "I understand—honestly, I do. I know it might not look like it, with my damp eyes and all, but I do. I'm just a little bummed right now, that's all. But I know what this position means to you, so I'm happy for you. Congratulations."

Tracee leaned over to give her friend a big hug. Mae deserved that job. As much as she hated to lose her as a partner, Tracee couldn't help but be happy for her. "Are you sure there isn't a way you can swing the job and be my part-time partner?" Tracee asked with a big smile after the embrace.

Mae frowned. "The job's in Memphis, Tennessee."

Tracee flinched, and her mouth fell open. She was on the verge of tears. "You really are leaving me, aren't you?"

"Not for a couple of weeks. I don't start until after Thanksgiving. Maybe until then I can help you find a new partner."

A wave of nausea found its way up the back of Tracee's throat. She moved back over to the couch and sat down. "I appreciate that, but get yourself ready to move. I'll find somebody, or I'll go it alone. Either way, I can't be stopped now." She wiped at her tears that threatened to spill over.

A huge smile broke out on Mae's face. "Girl, I've known you since junior high, and believe me, I know you'll find a way to open that café. Don't stop reaching for it. Never give up."

Tracee ran her hands through her hair and reminded herself to breathe. She blinked back tears as she quoted her friend. "Never give up! That's exactly what I plan to do."

Chapter 14

After Mae left, Tracee turned off the computer, turned on the television and balled up on the couch. She didn't care what was on the screen—she just wanted something to take her mind off her troubles for a few minutes. She needed to regroup and get herself together. The minute her head hit the couch, Laurent came to mind. Sunday night he'd surprised her by stopping by, and she'd surprised him by asking him to leave. Why hadn't he told her about his family's wealth? She'd thought he was just a fishing buddy of Sam's. Where was he right now? Would she ever see him again? She shut her eyes and fought the urge to reach for her cell phone.

In two weeks, Tracee had developed an unexpected fondness for Laurent. Now she needed to put some distance between them. If he became the new owner of the Rival Hotel, would he stay in town and run the hotel, or hire someone else and return to California? What about their friendship, which was turning into a relationship? She enjoyed having sex with him, but what if their intimacy had affected him leasing her the space like he said he would? Had she known about his pursuit of the hotel, she never would have gotten involved with him. Everything was so complicated right now she felt overwhelmed.

Her cell phone buzzed from the coffee table. She stared at it but didn't move. *Not now. I don't want to talk to anybody right now.* Maybe it was Mae calling to see if she was okay? She was, so there was no reason to answer the phone. Then she thought about the way she'd kicked Laurent out Sunday night and the fact that he might be leaving any day now. She reached for the phone and turned it over. The display read Laurent Martin, so she answered it.

"Hello."

"Hey…it's Laurent, were you busy?"

She swung her legs off the couch and sat up. "I know who it is, and no, I'm not." Her tone was void of enthusiasm, and he probably thought it was all about him.

"Feel like some company?"

She hesitated, covering her face with her hand. What had she just thought about putting some distance between them? If he came over, no doubt they would end up in her bed; she couldn't help herself. She could see the strong structure of Laurent's jawline, his perfect nose and the beautiful bow of his top lip that made her want to kiss him every time she was with him.

"Hello? You didn't hang up on me, did you?"

Her eyes popped open. "No, I'm here. Sure, come on over. We need to talk anyway." Her thoughts went from losing the space to Laurent's deception, and now the loss of her business partner. She might be down, but she wasn't out. She was just as determined to have her café as Laurent was to own the hotel. Instead of being mad at him, maybe she needed to take him up on his offer and work with him.

It took fifteen minutes for Laurent to get there, walk in and pull Tracee into his arms. She closed her eyes and inhaled. What she needed right now was a hug, and Laurent's hello hugs were everything. She didn't want him to let go, but he did.

Laurent held her at arm's length, clasping her forearms. "I'm sorry. If there was a way I could have told you more about me without discussing the deal, I would have. I could have handled Sunday night a little better as well. I have so much pressure on me right now to finalize this deal that—"

Tracee let out a loud sigh. "I accept your apology. We do need to talk, though, because now I feel like I don't know who you are."

He held one hand to his chest. "You know me, Tracee. I just didn't give you all of my background, but I wasn't pretending to be somebody I'm not. I'm just a guy from California who loves music and my work. My family's French Canadian and African American. You know I have two brothers, Aubrey and Marquis, a father, Thomas Martin, and a stepmother who thinks she's Marie Antoinette. I have family in Evanston, all over California and in Montreal that I don't see that often because of my work. I have an MBA from Berkeley. My blood type is O positive, and—"

"Stop it!" she said, laughing. "TMI. Nobody asked for all that."

"Well, I want you to know who I am and what I'm about." He let go of her other arm. "In more ways than one, I'm a musician trapped in a businessman's body. You know my love for music is real."

She nodded as he spoke. "I know that."

He smiled. "Thank you for letting me come over. You said we need to talk, and I agree with you."

Tracee reached for Laurent's jacket and placed it on the arm of the chair before walking back over to the couch to reclaim her spot. He followed and sat next to her.

"Would you like anything to drink?" she offered.

"Naw, I'm good."

She felt like she could use a bottle of wine, but she knew what one glass would do to her on an empty stomach, so she let the wine stay where it was.

Laurent leaned forward, resting his forearms on his thighs. "What did you want to talk about?"

She crossed her legs. "I received some pretty bad news today, so I need to know what you think your chances are with Mr. Patel."

He took a deep breath. "What kind of bad news?"

"Mae came by earlier, and she's pulling out of the business."

Laurent sat up and frowned. "Why?"

"She's moving to Memphis." Tracee told him everything she knew about Mae's promotion and how she was going to miss her business partner and best friend.

He leaned over, scooting closer to her, and pulled her into his arms. "Baby, I'm sorry. I know you two had big plans for the future," he said softly in her ear.

She closed her eyes and allowed herself to be comforted for about a nanosecond, then she pulled back out of his embrace. "So, I'm back to square one." She held her hands up and started counting off. "I don't have enough money. I have no partner and no location. But that's not going to stop me. I'll find a new partner." With her elbows bowed out, she placed her palms on her thighs and gave Laurent a serious look. "What I don't want to do is find another location."

He nodded. "I know you don't. I can't say what's going to happen, but either I'll have a deal or I'll be going home by the weekend. That's why I wanted to see you."

Tracee's chest tightened as Laurent gazed over at her with a dismal expression on his face. She'd known this day was coming sooner rather than later, but she hadn't realized the impact those words would have on her. It felt as if someone had punched her in the gut. She couldn't respond. They sat staring at one another while the television blared on, unnoticed.

She controlled the quiver in her voice long enough to ask, "So you came to say goodbye?" His eyes squinted, and her insides began to melt.

"I have to get back or my family might start looking for a new brand manager."

"Don't leave yet. I'm not ready to let you go." Tracee couldn't control the trembling of her bottom lip as she placed a hand against Laurent's chest, feeling the loss already.

The corners of his mouth slowly turned up, and he arched a brow. "You're not?"

She bit the inside of her cheek, feeling vulnerable for a moment, but wanting him to know how she felt. "No. Right now I'm thinking about how bad I want you to kiss me."

"Funny, I was thinking the same thing." His head lowered, and his lips met hers.

The softness of his lips warmed Tracee down to the bone. She snuggled closer to him. He wrapped his arms around her, and the thought of him taking his hugs away saddened her.

He backed up slightly and glanced down at her before planting a soft kiss on the tip of her nose. She closed her eyes and experienced the most gentle, sensual thing he'd ever done to her.

His voice lowered to a whisper when he pressed his lips against her ear. "I need to hold on to you."

She hardly recognized the thick voice coming from Laurent. His words and lips were coated with desire as he planted kisses from her earlobe down her neck. His kisses sent hot, sensual flames throughout her body. She needed more air. She leaned her head back on the couch, still holding on to Laurent's shirt. He slid a hand around her back and lowered her down to the couch. His lips branded her neck and her chest before making their way back up to her lips.

The need to touch and explore Laurent's body again was so overwhelming for Tracee. She'd never wanted a man as much as she wanted this man right here. She couldn't control when he left, if he left or if he ever came back, but she could control tonight. He was hers tonight.

The cologne Laurent wore was enough to send her over the edge any day, but tonight his scent tickled her senses and made her want to come out of her panties. He ran his hand down her body, and she ached to feel him against her skin. She let go of his shirt and pushed hard until he sprang back and stared down at her. His brows furrowed, and she watched him try to bring his breathing under control.

"You're not leaving me tonight," she whispered.

He stood up, bringing Tracee to stand with him. He stared down into her eyes before pressing his palm lightly against her cheek. She closed her eyes and leaned into his hand.

"Tu es si belle," he whispered.

Tracee opened her eyes before narrowing them at him.

"You are so beautiful," he said in a soft voice.

She smiled. "I love it when you speak French." Then she took his hand and led him to her bedroom.

Laurent's hand trembled slightly as he unhooked Tracee's bra and slid the straps down her shoulders. He leaned down and kissed her there. She dropped her head back into his chest, wanting to savor every moment of his touch. He brought his arms around her stomach and squeezed tight.

There was something different about the connection between them tonight. Tracee didn't know if Laurent could feel it or not, but she wasn't her usual playful self. He wasn't her man, and she knew it, but tonight she needed him to make love to her as if he was. When he released her, she finished removing her bra and tossed it on the chair before leading him to her bed.

When they reached the bed, he turned her around and took her face between his palms. She waited for him to say something, but he never did. Those big brown eyes were talking to her, telling her how much he wanted and needed her, but nothing came out of his mouth. She could say *I love you*, but it was too soon. She didn't want to scare him away. If he left her tonight before making love to her, she'd cry herself to sleep.

Laurent lowered his head and kissed her forehead, the tip of her nose and then her lips. She wanted a man to look at her the way he was gazing into her eyes right now for the rest of her life.

Without warning, he bent down and picked her up. She wrapped her legs around his waist and her arms around his neck. He walked across the room until her back was above her bed, and then he bent over and tossed her onto the bed. He smiled down at her as he stripped off his shirt, then unbuckled his belt.

She watched him look at her, and her body began to tremble with anticipation. She knew what was coming, but still she bubbled over with excitement.

Chapter 15

Laurent took his time when he made love to Tracee, and expressed with his body what he wanted to say but hadn't. Something was different about Tracee tonight. After two weeks he'd begun to fall in love with this woman. There was strong chemistry between them that he couldn't deny.

In the warm afterglow of lovemaking, Laurent's body was still on fire. He pulled her closer as she snuggled against him. She'd ignited every part of him, and yet he wanted more. Her curls brushed against his neck and chest, and he could feel his erection returning. With his arms wrapped around her, he cupped her breast in the palm of his hand and squeezed.

"Where's your phone?" Tracee asked him.

"Downstairs, why?"

"I wanted to play you a song."

He smiled. "How about I sing for you instead." He cleared his throat. "Let me take you back to some old-school." The song Laurent knew she would recognize was "I'll Make Love to You," by Boyz II Men.

He squeezed her a little tighter and serenaded her with his best rendition of the Boyz II Men vocals.

Laurent had sung that song so many times when he and his brothers performed at family and friends' weddings that he usually went into autopilot mode. But not tonight. Tonight, for the first time, the song meant something to him. When he finished, he kissed the top of her head.

"That was beautiful," she said in a soft voice.

"Thank you."

"I'm surprised you didn't pursue singing as a full-time career."

"We played around growing up, but we were never serious musicians. It was fun, and I guess a way for my parents to keep us out of trouble. My mom loved to hear us perform. Then I went off to college and kind of lost interest in music for a little bit."

"Don't tell me that's when you met Sam and turned into a fisherman?"

Laurent laughed and released Tracee's breast while still holding her close to him. "I'm going to let you in on a little secret. I've never held a fishing pole in my life."

Tracee pulled away from him and turned around, grimacing. "So, why all the joking about fishing?"

"Sam's dad had a yacht. So we called it 'going

fishing' whenever he threw a party and invited a lot of women. The yacht was our bait."

Her mouth fell open. "So you were fishing for women?"

Laurent held his palms up. "Sam was, not me. I was just along for the ride."

She twisted her lips. "Sure you were."

He laughed and pulled her back into his arms.

"I didn't think you, nor Sam, looked like the outdoorsy type. I bet you guys were a couple of playboys in college."

Laurent cupped her breast and gently massaged. "I've never been the playboy type. I had a lot of female friends, but strictly platonic relationships. Plus, I work too hard to have time for that type of lifestyle. Besides, I'm a one-woman man."

"Oh, yeah! Then you need to buy that hotel so you can stay right here in Danville. As a matter of fact, I'm thinking about locking you in. Have you ever been kidnapped before?"

Laurent threw his head back laughing. "No, I haven't. But I promise I won't put up a fight. I might even enjoy it."

"You would." She laughed and turned in his arms, resting her cheek against his chest.

"You could make me your love slave. Force me to have sex with you every hour."

Tracee pushed herself up and flashed him an openmouthed smile. "You're enjoying this, aren't you?"

"Immensely." The anticipation of making love to her was enough to get him hard again. He reached down and pulled her up until she straddled him. He wanted to feel her warm flesh.

Tracee settled snugly against him, placing her arms around his neck and kissing his face. Her sweet lips against his skin made him smile. He closed his eyes and grasped her hips as she rocked back and forth against him.

"Laurent, what if I pay Mr. Patel a visit and try to persuade him to go with your deal? He likes me—he might listen to reason."

Laurent opened his eyes. "Thank you, baby, but I can't let you do that."

"But if you don't get it, I'll be forced to deal with somebody else."

He smiled at her sheer dogged determination. She would have her café in that spot no matter who owned the hotel. Her ambition was inspiring, and he had no doubt she'd succeed. But so would he.

He brushed her hair back from her cheek and pulled her forward to kiss her tempting lips. "He's retiring, so yes, he's going to sell to somebody. But he won't get a better deal than the one I gave him. For two weeks he's had me jumping through hoops, only to find out he's been playing me this whole time."

"You didn't know another company was trying to purchase the hotel?"

"No, I didn't. He didn't like the initial deal my father proposed, so I was sent to negotiate a better deal. Then he tells me he wants to sell to someone who understands the hotel's place in the community. He led me to believe that if I made an effort to understand Danville and the people who live here, we'd have a deal. But that wasn't good enough. We negotiated a few more points that I had no problem with, but then I learned that I have some competition. This whole time he's been juggling both companies to see who he could get the best deal from."

"So what do you know about the competition?" she asked.

"I did a little digging around, and they are not the type of company he wants to deal with. He didn't like the fact that I researched my competition, but I'm sure once he checks into everything I said, he'll thank me. After all, I've jumped through all his hoops, and I doubt that the other company has."

"So, was calling me for a tour a part of jumping through his hoops?"

He pondered her question for a few seconds. She had a confused look on her face. "In a way, but you helped me get a perspective I couldn't have gotten otherwise. And in the process, I got to know you."

She sat back and stared at him a moment before swinging her leg around and shifting her body until she sat next to him on the bed, reaching for the covers. What the hell had he said wrong?

"Did you use me?" she asked, her voice a pitch higher than before.

Laurent faced her, leaning on one elbow. "Of course not." He didn't like the way she put that, but had it not been for Mr. Patel's request, he might not be lying here with her right now.

"I'll send him a thank-you card. But if he hadn't asked you to learn more about the community, you still would have called me?"

"I like to think that I would have, but I can't say. Initially, I'd only planned to stay in town for a couple of days. I told you that."

She turned and regarded him with puzzled eyes. "In other words, no. I did introduce you to a lot of people and give you that 'insider's perspective' you were looking for. Was this a perspective you wanted to get as well?" She pointed between herself and him. "All a part of becoming one with the community?"

He reached out and pulled her back into his arms. "Of course not." A cool breeze sailed through the room, as if someone had opened a refrigerator door. All the warmth between them vanished, along with his erection. Laurent could feel her slipping away from him. "You already know the answer to that. You've been on my mind ever since I ran into you at the hotel. Then, when we kept bumping into each other, I knew I was supposed to connect with you."

She chuckled as she threw the covers back, swinging her long legs over the edge of the bed. "I hear what you're saying and I know you're right, but somehow I still feel a little used."

"Tracee, don't feel that way. Those tours, and you, are the best thing that's happened to me in a long time. It may look as if I used you in some form, but I didn't."

"How about the potluck? You met my whole family and got to meet a lot of the people who live out here. What do you call that?"

"I called it spending time with a beautiful young lady who *invited* me to the bed-and-breakfast's potluck dinner. She introduced me to her family and I had a great time. The next day, she had me do something I'd never done before. I went horseback riding."

"I'm not saying you didn't enjoy yourself. Hell, I enjoyed myself. I'm just saying maybe you were attracted to me for some manufactured reason, not because you were interested in me. Then the sex got good, and here we are."

He shook his head. "If it wasn't for Mr. Patel, I wouldn't have had the pleasure of learning more about this town, or you. Maybe I should thank him instead of being upset with him. Because whether he sells to us or not, I walk away with something more valuable than just good sex."

She shrugged and stared at him as if trying to detect if he was being truthful or not, which he was. If nothing else came out of this trip, he'd found a woman he wanted to be with. He didn't know how, but he wanted to be with Tracee. He reached out to stroke her cheek, but she turned her head.

"I'm gonna need to think about this. Yeah, I thought we were having a great time, and then I started falling for you, but now I don't know how I feel." She stood up.

Laurent threw back his covers. "Tracee, where you goin'? Come back to bed." He looked around at the glowing clock on her nightstand. It was 2:35 in the morning.

"I'll be back. I need to use the bathroom," she muttered before disappearing behind the bathroom door.

He lay back on the pillows and ran his hands over his face. Tonight couldn't end like this—he wouldn't let it. She'd admitted she was falling for him, and the feeling was mutual. Which was why he wanted to be up front with her. He didn't play games with women.

When Tracee returned, Laurent patted her side of the bed. "Come here, let me talk to you for a minute."

She stared at him, leery of his motives. He patted her side of the bed again, and she walked over to join him.

"You're not really upset over this, are you?"

Tracee snorted. "I know I shouldn't be, but I can't help thinking that if Mr. Patel hadn't played you against the Stephenson Group this whole time, we wouldn't be having this conversation right now. It's not like you would have reached out to me anyway."

To hear that name come out of Tracee's mouth made the hair on the back of Laurent's neck take notice. He'd been careful *not* to mention the name of his competition, but somehow she already knew. "How did you know who the other company was? I never mentioned them."

"I have my resources."

"How long have you known?" he asked, curious now that maybe *she* was trying to play him, too. Had she known from the moment he met her?

"Why? That's not important."

"It's important to me," he said, with a little more bass in his voice than he'd intended. Had she contacted anyone from that company?

She got out of bed again. "It's important to me that I get my lease. You're not the only one who knows how to do a little research. I'm going to take a shower."

Laurent sat there thinking. Could she be in contact with someone from the Stephenson Group? Was that why she had such an attitude? To what lengths would she go to secure that lease?

He climbed out of bed and reached for his clothes.

The next morning, Laurent threw on his running gear and grabbed his earbuds. When he opened the door to his hotel room, he got the shock of his life. Standing on the other side of the door with his fist up, poised to knock, was his father, Thomas Martin.

"What are you doing here?" The words spewed out of Laurent's mouth at a speed that made his father blink his eyes. He frowned and pushed past Laurent.

"I might ask you the same thing. What the hell's going on?" he asked as he walked in.

In his signature Ralph Lauren business suit, his father looked around the room as if he expected someone else to be there. Laurent closed the door and removed the earbuds. "I told you what's going on. You've gotten my reports. The deal is taking longer than I anticipated. Now I've discovered there's another buyer in line."

Thomas Martin shook his head. "So what? You've never let something like that stop you before." He walked over and put his hand on Laurent's shoulder. "This isn't like you, Laurent. You're a shrewd negotiator, or you used to be. What's happened to you, son? I thought you wanted this deal."

Laurent pulled away from his father's condescending tone. "I do! But you need to give me a little more time."

His father walked over and looked out the window at the city below. He stood there shaking his head before turning back around to face Laurent. "I gave you a few days, which is all it should have taken. So I'll meet with Mr. Patel myself and discuss this new discovery. Go for your run. I'll fill you in when you get back."

Like hell you will. Thomas Martin was a fair man, but if you squandered an opportunity he'd given you, there might not be another one. Laurent saw the disappointment in his father's slack face and heard it in his lifeless words. He'd let him down. The family's troubleshooter and master negotiator wasn't living up to his reputation.

He dropped his phone and earbuds on the table. "Wait a minute. I'm getting dressed. This is still my deal."

Chapter 16

Standing in front of a mirror in what used to be Kyla's room the summer she lived at the bed-and-breakfast, Kyla helped Tracee try on a Wonder Woman costume. "I think this thing is too tight, don't you?" Tracee asked as she studied the strapless one-piece that showed off her curvy figure, but might be too much for a kids' party.

"No tighter than this stupid jester costume you talked me into. Now be still while I get all this damned hair under your headband."

"I'm glad Corra decided to throw a Halloween party this year. I prefer partying over waiting on some kids to ring my bell so I can toss them a few pieces of candy. Besides, the kids don't come by like they used to anymore."

"Yeah, I know." Kyla took a step back and looked at her handiwork. "Wait until they get a look at you, superhero, in your over-the-knee boots and bright red lipstick. That shade matches the top of the suit perfect."

"I look like a hooker," Tracee said, glaring back at herself.

"No you don't. Wonder Woman's an Amazonian warrior. That's what you look like."

Tracee didn't agree with her little sister, but since she'd gone to all the trouble of bringing the costume from Lexington, she appeased her. "So, is Miles coming to the party next week?"

"I think so. He said he would be in Lexington on the thirty-first, so I'm sure he'll come. If he does, I might not wear this lame costume—we'll get matching ones."

"Oh, that's so cute. I love to see couples all matchie-matchie."

"Why don't you and Laurent get matching outfits?" Kyla asked.

"Please, Laurent and I aren't a couple. Besides, he'll probably be gone by then."

"Didn't you say he was trying to purchase the hotel?"

"Yeah, but he might finish his deal and be out of here before Halloween."

"But if he does purchase the hotel, won't he be in town a lot more? I mean, if he's going to run it, maybe he'll relocate here."

Tracee shook her head. "I don't think Laurent has any intention of moving to Danville."

Kyla placed her hands on her hips. "Did he say he wasn't?"

Tracee shrugged and realized something for the first time. They'd never talked about what would happen once, or if, he purchased the hotel. He never said who would run it or if he'd be back in town to do anything. "He didn't, but it's not something I think will happen."

"And you're okay with that? Don't try to tell me you don't have feelings for that man, because I know you do. It's not just a sex thing like you want me to believe."

You could fool some of the people some of the time, but she could never fool Kyla. "So what if I like him. When his business is over here, he'll go back to California. I'm just hoping he buys the hotel and leases me the space. I'm working on lining up a new partner."

Kyla stood next to Tracee and started laughing as they looked at themselves in the mirror.

Tracee grabbed Kyla's hand. "Come on, let's go show Corra."

Kyla snatched her hand away. "I'm not going out there like this. I look like a clown. We have guests."

"Girl, nobody's hanging out in the lobby. Who's going to see us but Corra? Come on, she's working on the computer at the front desk."

Tracee took Kyla by the hand and pulled her out of the spare bedroom, down the hall and out into the lobby. Kyla begged her not to and laughed all the way. The minute they walked through the lobby entrance, a tall, distinguished older black man who stood at the counter turned toward them.

Tracee heard Corra say, "Ah, here's Tracee now. Ladies, uh…this is Mr. Thomas Martin. He's looking for Tracee."

She dropped Kyla's hand as a rush of adrenaline tingled through her body. Did Corra say Thomas Martin, as in Laurent's father? Kyla turned around and retreated back into the family quarters. Tracee wanted to run away as well, but he'd already seen her.

Mr. Martin stared at her boots and worked his way up to her red lips, with raised brows. "Tracee Coleman?" he asked.

"Yes, I'm Tracee. You'll have to forgive the costume—we're getting ready for our first big Halloween party." The suffocating suit made her breasts look as if they were ready to pop. And from the disapproving look on Mr. Martin's face, she was sure he thought the same thing.

He offered his hand. "I'm Thomas Martin, Laurent's father. Would it be possible to speak with you alone for a moment?"

His grip was firm, and the words in her mouth froze. She did not want to meet Laurent's father dressed like this. Costume or not, he might get the wrong impression of her.

Corra came from behind the counter. "Tracee, you might want to step into the library for a little privacy." She motioned them in that direction before turning the opposite way. "I'll be in the office if you need anything, okay, Tracee?"

Tracee nodded, unable to verbalize a response. What was Laurent's father doing in Danville? And how did he know to come looking for her at the bed-and-breakfast? Mr. Martin took a step back, and Tracee pulled herself out of the daze she'd sunken into. She smiled as she walked into the library. "We can talk in here."

He walked in behind her, and she closed the pocket doors. She turned around to find his focus on the books. She breathed a sigh of relief.

"You're probably wondering why I'm here," he said as he turned around to set his disapproving gaze on her again.

She crossed her arms over her chest, feeling the coldness in his eyes. She sensed that this man did not like her. "Are you looking for Laurent?"

"No. I've come to speak to you."

She uncrossed her arms and placed a hand over her heart. "Me!"

"Yes. I believe you're the young lady who's been occupying my son's time since he's been in town." That wasn't a question, but more of a statement, which he followed up with a curt smile.

She shivered. There was something not so nice about this man. "I gave him a tour of the town and we've spent some time together, yes."

"And there lies the problem." He walked away and ran his fingers across some of the books. No doubt looking for dust, the way he had his nose all up in the air. "You see, Laurent was tasked with closing a very important deal. It should have taken him a couple of days at the most." He stopped and turned back to Tracee. "However, he's been here for over two weeks."

Tracee dropped her smile. "Yes, I know. He told me about it."

"Well, you see, Tracee…may I call you Tracee?" She nodded. "Sure."

"Tracee, I know my son. He's never let anything get in the way of negotiating a deal. He's a Martin— it's what he does. But he's young, and the only thing I can think of that would distract him from taking care of business is a beautiful young lady such as yourself."

Tracee wanted to smile, but the quick head-to-toe glance he gave her Wonder Woman costume let her know that wasn't exactly a compliment. He'd come to insult her.

"I'm sorry, but are you trying to insinuate that I'm the reason Laurent couldn't close that deal?" It was insane, she knew, but that sounded like what he was saying.

"On the contrary. I'm sure you helped him in numerous ways, and I thank you for that. Unfortunately, Laurent has a fondness for beautiful women. So when I received his report about a delay, I knew a woman was involved somewhere."

"And you came to Danville to tell me that?"

He left the bookshelf and strode closer to her. "I came into town to finish the deal. Once I learned of your existence, I wanted to meet you myself. I wanted to see the woman who could cost my company millions of dollars. The woman who'd stolen my son's heart."

Was that what she'd done? "Mr. Martin, your son has stolen my heart also. In the short amount of time

Laurent has been here, I have to admit I've grown very fond of him."

He smiled down at the floor before glancing back up at her. "Of course you have. Laurent is a very sought-after bachelor. A young woman would be lucky to be seen with any of my sons. Laurent didn't come to Danville looking for a woman. He had a job to do, and I thank you for helping him. But in a few days the deal will be complete and Laurent will return to California. I wanted to make sure you understood that."

She bit her bottom lip. Laurent's daddy was telling her to back off his son. "Sir, I'm well aware that Laurent won't be staying in Danville."

Mr. Martin smiled and clasped his hands together. "Good, we have an understanding. In the next couple of days we'll be closing this deal, and I'd appreciate it if you could manage to stay away from Laurent during that time. He works better without the distraction."

He walked toward the library door, and Tracee was too flabbergasted to open her mouth. She just stood there with her arms crossed and her heart breaking.

Mr. Martin opened the doors before turning back to Tracee. "Ms. Coleman, it was a pleasure meeting you. As I said, you are a lovely young lady, and I hope we have an understanding?" He smiled like a Cheshire cat, waiting on her to answer him.

All Tracee could do was nod her head.

"Good, and I'll see myself out, thank you."

He left, and she wanted to run and slam the door behind him. She wanted him to get the hell out of there and never come back.

Tracee still stood in the same spot minutes later when Kyla and Corra walked into the library. She couldn't move. Her conversation with Mr. Martin had stunned her.

"Tracee, you okay?" Kyla asked as she touched Tracee's shoulder.

"What did he want?" Corra asked.

Tracee closed her eyes; she could see Laurent lying in her bed and feel his arms around her as she cuddled up next to him. He always kissed the top of her head, and she thought that was the most romantic thing. But did he do that with every woman? His father said he was sought after. Did that mean he had lots of girlfriends in California?

"Snap out of it, girl," Kyla said with a snap of her fingers in Tracee's face.

Tracee blinked and looked at her little sister, who'd taken off her costume and put her khakis and polo shirt back on, the Coleman House Farm uniform. She was waving her hand in Tracee's face. Tracee swatted at Kyla's hand. "Get your hand out of my face."

"Well, what the hell happened? You're standing here looking crazy and he just took off. What did he say? What did he want?" Kyla asked.

"He wants me to stay away from his son, that's what he wants."

"Say what?" Corra asked.

The stunned looks on her family's faces summed up Tracee's own feelings. She still couldn't believe that man came into town, then drove out there, all to ask her to stay away from Laurent. He could have done that shit over the phone. How did he even know they had been seeing one another? Had Laurent told him about her?

"Who does he think his son is?" Kyla asked.

Tracee took a few steps back and sat on the couch behind her. "He's Laurent Martin, son of millionaire Thomas Martin, who's the owner of Abelle, a five-star boutique hotel chain that caters to the wealthy. They have hotels in Canada, France, the US and Italy, too, I think."

Kyla and Corra came to sit on the couch on either side of Tracee.

"No shit!" Corra said.

"Tracee, how long have you known that?" Kyla asked.

Tracee shrugged. "I found out when I was doing research on the Stephenson Group. I researched Martin Enterprises, too. Laurent never told me he worked in the family business. Not that it makes a difference, because now I'm in love with the guy. But after what his father just said to me, I don't know that I'll ever see him again."

Corra leaned back and crossed her arms. "Okay, tell us everything he said. Nobody comes into my home and insults my family."

Tracee fell back onto the couch and covered her

eyes with her hands. "I should have taken off this suit before coming out into the lobby. He probably thinks I'm some type of a floozy or something. I made a bad first impression."

Kyla pulled Tracee's arms down. "Tracee, what did the man say?"

Tracee relived the worse fifteen minutes of her life to her family members. Afterward, Corra and Kyla were ready to find out where Mr. Martin was staying and ride over to give him a piece of their minds.

"I was right. Laurent used me. He can have any woman he wants—why would he be interested in me?" Tracee dropped her face into her palms again and felt sorry for herself for a few seconds.

"You mean, why wouldn't he be interested in you?" Corra stood up. "Tracee, Laurent was lucky to have met you, and he knows it. Don't listen to his father. I've seen you guys together, and believe me, he has strong feelings for you as well. And I don't for one minute believe he used you."

Kyla stood up, too. "Come on, Tracee, don't let him get you down on yourself."

Tracee dropped her hands and leaned back into the couch again. She took a deep breath and shook her head. "It's not just him. Mae had to pull out of the business, I don't know who Mr. Patel is going to sell the hotel to and Laurent and I had something like a fight the other night. I might not see him again anyway. Nothing is going right. Things should be coming together instead of falling apart."

Kyla and Corra flopped back down on the couch opposite Tracee for a group hug.

"I wish I'd known he was Laurent's father when he walked in," Corra said. "I'd have told him we were closed until hell freezes over."

Tracee looked at Corra, who rolled her eyes, and the three of them burst out laughing.

Chapter 17

Laurent spent most of Thursday morning on his cell phone. He'd neglected a few of his ongoing projects and had to put in the time to make sure they weren't totally going south. Through conference calls, his direct reports had kept him on top of anything critical, but some issues he had to attend to himself. For now, a phone call would have to suffice, but soon he'd have to get back to his life and his job.

He was deep in thought when his brother Marquis called.

"The old man told me he was going to Lexington on business, but I know a line when I hear one. How's it going?" Marquis asked.

"He has his way of doing things, and I have mine. He's getting in my way. Yesterday he insisted on a meeting with Mr. Patel, only to make me look like a fool. I had to sit there while he went on and on about Martin Enterprises' esteemed reputation."

Marquis's robust laughter came through the phone and Laurent shook his head, smiling to himself. "Man, you should have been here. He put on a show."

"Relax, little bro, you know that's how he is. I can see him with his chest poked out now. Martin Enterprises hotels have been awarded five stars by *Forbes Travel Guide*, *Business Insider* and every other important publication in the world. We offer experiences, not just a room to sleep in."

Laurent sat back in his hotel chair, laughing at the way Marquis had his father down to a tee. "Man, I think you *were* there."

"I've been there enough," Marquis answered.

"Well, for what it's worth, I believe he impressed Mr. Patel's sons, if no one else. He's staying in Lexington, thank goodness. After the meeting he said his wife is dragging him to some function there."

"Maybe that's the business he had to attend to. If you're lucky he'll stay in Lexington and let you handle your business. What happened with the information I gave you?"

"Yeah, we need to talk about that. I'm gonna need someone who can corroborate those findings."

Marquis made a sucking-air-through-his-teeth sound. "Not sure if I can do that, little bro."

"Yes, you can. You're a Martin, and we make the impossible possible. And I need contact information before tomorrow."

"What?" Marquis asked, raising his voice.

"This deal is mine, and it's going down tomorrow. The old man wants me to play hardball, so that's what I'm going to do. You've got about eighteen hours to get back with me."

Marquis let out a deep breath. "Stay by the phone. I'll see what I can do."

"Thanks, bro. I'm nothing without you—you know that, don't you?"

"Yeah, yeah, whatever. Butter me up. You know I've got your back."

Laurent hung up, eager to add an addendum to his deal before his last meeting with Mr. Patel. He needed a yes from the old man. He had big plans for the hotel that he hadn't shared with anyone, and walking away wasn't a part of his plan.

Laurent worked until his eyes blurred from staring at his laptop screen. He sat back to take a break when he realized he hadn't eaten anything since breakfast and it was past dinnertime. He leaned back and stretched, trying to figure out what he wanted to eat tonight. He could go for anything besides pizza. He closed his computer, disconnected his cell phone from the charger and grabbed the Elantra's keys.

He drove through town trying to decide on a restaurant. The urge to pick up the phone and ask Tracee to have dinner with him was strong, but he fought it. She was upset with him, and he knew he needed to give her a little time. He'd have to pick something out himself. He pulled into the nearest Speedway gas station to fill the tank. About the only thing he did like about the rental was the gas mileage. This was his first fill-up since arriving.

His mind wandered back to Tracee as he pumped the gas. He hadn't noticed a truck pulling up across from him until he heard someone call his name.

"Laurent?"

He turned to see a young woman close the truck door and walk over toward him. A sign on the side of the truck read Coleman House Farm. Then he recognized the face. "Hey, you're Tracee's sister, Kyla, right?"

She stopped at the trunk of his rental. "Yes, I am."

The gas handle clicked, and Laurent turned around to top it off at an even amount. The way Tracee's sister's eyes were narrowed and she crossed her arms over her chest, he had a feeling this wasn't going to be a pleasant conversation.

"It's nice to see you again," he said as he waited for his receipt.

"When's the last time you spoke to Tracee?" she asked.

Laurent pocketed his receipt and joined her at the trunk of his car. She looked like she was about to drill him about something.

"Tuesday night, why?"

"Did you know your father stopped by the bed-and-breakfast yesterday?" she asked as she leaned against the trunk of the Elantra.

Laurent's brows rose as he took a step back. *Impossible.* "My father?" he asked in disbelief.

She nodded. "Yes, Mr. Thomas Martin."

Laurent felt his heartbeat increase along with

a ripple of anger that ran through him. *No, Dad wouldn't do that. Why would he do that?* His father had returned to Lexington after the meeting yesterday, or so he thought. "Did he say what he wanted?"

"He came to speak to Tracee."

His chest muscles tightened. His father had spoken to Mr. Patel and his sons, who'd undoubtedly told him about his relationship with Tracee.

"What did he say to her?" Now he leaned against the Elantra.

"Let's just say he wasn't so nice. He accused her of costing you a deal that stood to be worth millions, I believe."

Laurent lowered and shook his head. *Damn, how could he!* He didn't know what had gotten into his father lately. It wasn't like him to show up and interfere with Laurent's deal, and it definitely wasn't like him to seek out Tracee in that way. "That's not true, you know?"

"I didn't think so. But he tried to sell it. Right before he asked her to stay away from you in order for you to complete the deal."

What the hell! His father was sticking his nose somewhere it didn't belong.

"I'm sorry. I don't know what's gotten into him. He flew in yesterday for a quick meeting. He had no business bringing Tracee into this. I guess she's upset with me now, huh?"

Kyla nodded. "I'd say so. I didn't hear what your father said, but he upset my sister something awful."

"Damn." Laurent had to get that man on the next flight back to California. "I'll talk to him, and I promise you it won't ever happen again. I apologize on his behalf. He's just a little hyped about this deal, that's all. I'll reach out to Tracee."

Kyla pulled away from the car. "I don't know you, really, but do know that Tracee has strong feelings for you. So strong that your dad really got under her skin."

Laurent's heartbeat pounded in his chest as he also pushed away from the car. The anger inside him was building so, he wanted to strangle his father. "Thank you, Kyla."

Another car pulled up behind Laurent, waiting for him to move since all the other pumps were full.

Kyla took a few steps backward. "Whatever you do, don't hurt my sister. She deserves a good man."

He nodded. "I know, and I have no intentions of hurting her."

Kyla turned around and went to fill up the truck. Laurent climbed in the car and took off. Now he wanted to see Tracee. He needed to talk to her and make everything all right again. He pulled out his cell phone and dialed her number. The call went straight to voice mail. He didn't want to, but he left a message asking her to call him as soon as she could. But something told him he wouldn't get a call back. Then he dialed his father. He answered on the first ring.

"Hello, and I know why you're calling," Thomas Martin said in a commanding tone.

Laurent ignored his father's "you know I'm the father" voice. "What kind of game are you playing with me? You give me this deal, then you interfere in the worst way possible. What did you say to Tracee?"

"See, I was right. She is the problem. Son, don't let a woman open your nose so wide you can't focus on the business at hand. I sent you down here to close a very important deal."

"Where are you?" Laurent didn't want to hear another word from his father. He only wanted him gone.

"We're in Lexington."

"At what hotel?"

"Laurent, I'll be back in the morning."

"No, you won't. I'm on my way there now. We need to talk."

Instead of finding a local dinner spot, Laurent hit the highway headed to Lexington, thirty minutes away. He needed to sit down with his father and put an end to his meddling. Having Thomas Martin step in at closing for any other deal would be a feather in his cap, but not this one. His father had promised him this hotel if he could close the deal, and that was exactly what he was going to do. After handling his father, he would have to make amends with Tracee. He wasn't about to let her, and the deal, slip from his grasp.

Friday morning after his run, Laurent showered and dressed for his 11:00 a.m. meeting with the Patels. Thomas Martin and his wife were on a flight back to California. Marquis had come through late yesterday with the name and number of a businessman who could corroborate his findings regarding the Stephenson Group. Before Laurent left Lexington, he'd met a gentleman eager to provide all the information he needed.

He placed a quick call to a local florist and had a dozen red roses sent to Tracee at the Coleman House, where he knew she'd be this morning. Then he sat down to send her a text message and attached the perfect song, "Get You" by Daniel Caesar. Music was how he expressed himself, and with this song she'd know how he felt.

He needed to talk to her, and he would after he'd taken care of his business. He hadn't gotten much sleep last night, unable to get Tracee off his mind. Whatever move he made next, he wanted her to be a part of it. Whether he purchased the hotel or not, he didn't want his relationship with her to end. He wanted them to take it to the next level.

At 11:00 a.m. Laurent walked into the conference room at the Rival Hotel with the confidence of his father, his brothers and the entire Martin Enterprises team at his back. No matter what, he was his father's son, and this was what he did best.

Thirty minutes into the meeting, Laurent had Mr. Patel eating out of his hand. He detailed his assurances that the current staff could stay on after renovations, if they so desired. He'd noted that the established community involvement aspect of the hotel was intact, along with an added outreach to the local college offering a place for returning graduates and visiting parents, as well as people doing business locally.

"I'm also aware that before you decided to sell,

you were going to lease the space downstairs to Tracee's Cake World. I want to give her that lease alongside a small jazz café that I plan to open."

For once, Mr. Patel didn't look at his sons with dissatisfaction. Instead, he smiled at Laurent and gave him an assuring nod. "I think time has shown you what this place means to me. And I appreciate you going the extra mile."

"Thank you, sir. I also have someone I'd like you to speak with." He pulled out his cell phone. "You were skeptical about the information I gave you regarding the Stephenson Group, so I reached out to the former owner of Hotel VanDee in Lexington. Mr. Robert VanDee would like to share some information with you."

"Didn't they sell that property a few years ago and reopen under another name?" Raji asked.

Laurent shook his head. "No, but I'll let Mr. VanDee explain why." He FaceTimed with Mr. VanDee, who explained how the Stephenson Group had purchased his hotel, only to tear it down and build another business—after promising to renovate and keep him on as a consultant. Laurent let Mr. Patel and Mr. VanDee talk before ending the call.

Afterward, he left the family to talk among themselves. While he waited, he walked down to the lobby and dialed Tracee's number. The call went straight to voice mail again, and he left another message. "Hey, Tracee, I need to talk to you when you have a few minutes. I ran into your sister yesterday and… I'm real sorry about what happened. I don't know how to explain my father's behavior, but I'm going to try. I hope you got the song I sent you. I'll talk to you later." He hung up, shaking his head.

"Excuse me, Laurent?"

He looked up at the sound of Raji's voice. "Yes?"

Raji stood against the rail from the mezzanine level looking down at Laurent with a smile on his face. "We're ready to resume."

Laurent bit his lip and tried not to read anything into that smile. He slipped his phone into his pocket and headed back to the conference room.

Chapter 18

Friday night Tracee wanted to let her hair down and get Laurent off her mind. She hadn't answered any of his calls, nor listened to his voice mail. His father had helped her realize how hard she'd fallen for him in such a short time. She'd even admitted it to Kyla and Corra, something she wished she hadn't done. Now the three of them sat in the pizzeria, eating, drinking and doing whatever she could to get Laurent off the brain.

"Would you like to dance?" A voice came from behind Tracee.

She turned around, and a young man all in black with a mustard-colored jacket and an array of heavy chains around his neck smiled at her. A college student. She smiled back. "Sure."

Before getting up, she turned to Kyla and Corra, who'd been nursing the same drink for the last hour. "It's time to have some fun, ladies." When she turned around, the college guy took her hand and led her to the pizzeria's small dance floor.

As it turned out, he was a pretty good dancer, and the DJ's selection of hip-hop music was good as well. But neither one could keep Tracee from thinking back to her birthday night when she'd danced with Laurent. He invaded her every thought while she fought hard to concentrate on her dancing partner. It was time to turn it up.

Laurent rang Tracee's doorbell a couple of times before giving up and getting back into his car to head for the bed-and-breakfast. Since she wouldn't answer his calls, he'd have to track her down. He hit his second strike when Tayler informed him that Tracee had gone with Corra and Kyla to their favorite Friday night spot—the pizzeria.

Minutes later, he walked into the pizzeria and found Corra and Kyla sitting at a pub table with a half-eaten pizza propped in the middle.

"Did you save me some?" he asked as he approached the table.

Surprise! Corra looked up at Laurent with her mouth wide-open. Kyla, on the other hand, slowly turned up the corners of her mouth, as if she'd expected him to show up.

"If you like veggie pizza, help yourself," Kyla said as she pointed to the leftover slices.

"Mind if I join you?" he asked.

"Please do." Corra turned her stunned expression into a soft smile.

Laurent pulled out a chair and sat down.

"I'll pass on the veggie pizza, but I will take a look at the menu." He hadn't eaten since breakfast, because he hadn't really had an appetite. "Where's Tracee?"

The women gave each other wide-eyed looks before Kyla turned her gaze to the dance floor.

Laurent followed her gaze, and that's when he spotted Tracee. She was working up a sweat with what looked like a group of young college kids on the small dance floor of the pizzeria. He could tell she was enjoying herself. Her curls were loose, big and bouncing freely all over the place.

"Here you go." Kyla handed him a menu. "Their calzone's good."

Laurent looked the menu over but couldn't concentrate on anything he read. When he glanced up at the dance floor, the music had changed, and Tracee was still dancing.

"So, Laurent, Tracee said you may be leaving soon. Is that true?" Corra asked.

"Yes, in a few days. But I'll be back soon, though."

"Oh! Good news?" Kyla asked.

Laurent gave the ladies a little smile. "Yeah, that's actually what I want to talk to Tracee about. If she's not too upset with me."

As if on cue, Tracee danced her way over to the table without making eye contact with Laurent. "Ladies, you have to get out there—the music is good and there are plenty of dance partners. Those guys belong to a fraternity at Centre College."

Laurent looked at Tracee and wondered how long she was going to keep pretending she didn't see him. After a few beats, he concluded she was going to be stubborn.

"Hello, Tracee," he said, above the music.

She turned to him with cold eyes, clenching her jaw. He wanted to walk over and put his arms around her. He wanted to take away any pain that he or his father had caused.

"Hi. I thought you'd be on your way back to California by now," she said before picking up her drink and playing with the straw.

He slowly shook his head. "No, not yet."

"Uh-huh," she muttered before turning away. "So, ladies, why so quiet? Let's order another drink. Where's the waiter?"

"None for me," Corra said.

"Me neither," Kyla added.

Laurent forgot about eating and focused on what he'd come here for. He set the menu down and stood up. "Tracee, can I talk to you a minute?"

She looked up with a polite smile on her face. "I think your father said enough for the both of you." With her drink in hand, she turned her back to him, giving her attention to the dance floor.

He leaned into the table and said, "Excuse me, ladies," to Corra and Kyla before walking around to get Tracee's attention. She sipped her drink, and her gaze wandered everywhere but on him.

Laurent leaned into her, placing his hand on the

table behind her and his mouth close to her ear. "I'm sorry. I didn't know he was coming, but give me a minute to explain what happened."

Tracee threw a hand up, palm out. "There's nothing to explain. I totally understand and I won't interfere with your business."

He wrapped his hands around hers, getting her attention. "Can you follow me, please, so we can talk?"

"Tracee."

The both of them turned at the sound of Kyla's voice.

She held out Tracee's jacket. "It's kind of loud in here," she said with a wink.

Laurent let go of Tracee's hand in order for her to put her drink down and accept the jacket from her sister. He wanted to thank Kyla. When Tracee turned to him, he stifled a smile and gestured toward the door. He placed his hand at the small of her back as they exited the restaurant.

Once outside and a few steps away from the door, Tracee whirled around on Laurent. "I'm not supposed to be distracting you," she said with her hands on her hips. "Your father and I have an understanding, or didn't he tell you?"

Laurent rolled his shoulders and let out a heavy sigh. "That was an asshole move by my father, but he doesn't speak for me."

"He seems to think he does. Or maybe it's the business's best interest he had in mind." She shoved her hands into her jacket pockets.

Laurent reached out to touch her, but she pulled away. "Okay, I'm so sorry my dad showed up and

The Sweetest Affair

showed out like that. His presence here surprised the hell out of me, too. He wanted to meet with Mr. Patel, and as far as I knew, after the meeting on Wednesday he went back to Lexington, which is where he was staying. I had no idea he even knew who you were, let alone that he came out to the bed-and-breakfast. He's gone now. He and my stepmother took a flight back to California this morning."

Tracee zipped her jacket up all the way and turned up the collar. "Your father's a grown man—no need to apologize for him. He spoke his mind. Did he tell you he came to see me?"

"No. I ran into Kyla yesterday at a gas station."

"She shouldn't go around telling my business."

"Well, I'm glad she told me, since neither you nor my father were likely to say anything. Tracee, I know he didn't mean it."

"No, maybe he was right, and I was right. Maybe you did use me and it backfired on you. The same way your research backfired on you." She crossed her arms and stared him down.

Laurent wanted to pull her into his arms, but he didn't want to get smacked, so he kept his hands in his pockets. He hoped the good news he was about to share with her would turn her attitude around.

"Tracee, it's cold out here. Let's get in the car and talk?"

She looked over her shoulder toward the parking lot, and then back at him. He could see the conflict going on in her head. She wanted to be with him, but she wanted to continue to be mad at the same time.

"Please. I have something I need to tell you."

Surprisingly, she didn't protest. They walked over to the Elantra, and he opened her door. She held on to the door and looked up at him. "This won't take long, will it?"

He shook his head and grinned. She was stubborn. "Get in the car, Tracee."

Again she complied without an argument. He closed the door and walked around to the driver's side to climb in. She sat there with her arms crossed looking straight ahead. As much as Tracee tried to put on a brave front, Laurent knew she was hurt. He'd seen it in her eyes, and it was killing him. He started the engine.

"What are you doing?" she asked, unfolding her arms.

"Turning on the heat. You're cold." He reached over and stroked her arm while taking a deep, calming breath. "Tracee, I want you to pay close attention to everything I'm about to say. I never intentionally used you. I don't care who says otherwise. From the moment you fell into my arms at the hotel, I was eager to meet you and find out who you were. Yes, I called you for a tour *after* my discussion with Mr. Patel, but I could have chosen another route to get information on the town. I chose to call you because I wanted an excuse to see you again."

He reached over and placed his hand under her chin, turning her head to face him. "I kept calling because I wanted to be with you. You inspire me. You're a talented, determined, beautiful woman with a bright future. And if you let me, I want to be a part of your growth. I want to lift you up and support you in any way that I can. Not that you actually need my help, because the fire you have inside you will take you wherever you want to go, I'm sure of that."

She unzipped her jacket, and he reached over to turn the heat down. She looked like she wanted to say something, but he stopped her. He had a lot to say before he told her the outcome of his deal.

"Tracee, I want you to be that special woman in my life. Maybe I wasn't looking for a woman on this trip, but I thank the Lord that I found you. You brighten my day, and I think we're good together."

Her posture had relaxed, and her hands rested in her lap. He had her full attention now. A need to touch her and make love to her again consumed him. The sexy way she bit her lip and glanced up at him was more than enough to make him want to take her back to his hotel room and make love to her, but he had news to deliver.

"You know, when my father offered me this deal I jumped at it. I admit I wasn't excited about it being in Danville because I didn't think there was anything here. But I was wrong. My future is here."

Tracee let go of her lip and shook her head. "Laurent, don't do this to me. I know you're going back to California."

The look on her face was squeezing his heart. "Hey, I don't know how we're going to work this out, but we will. Tracee, if our love is meant to be, and I think it is, I know we'll find a way."

"So, you're not going back?"

"I am, but I'll be back real soon. I closed the deal

with Mr. Patel this morning. Martin Enterprises just purchased all four of the Rival Hotels."

Tracee's mouth fell open, transforming her sad face into a beautiful smile. "Wow! That's wonderful, Laurent."

She must have forgotten all about being mad at him, because she leaned over and gave him a big hug. He didn't want to let her go, but he did.

"Despite my father's interfering ways, Mr. Patel said yes to my deal. So you're looking at the new owner of the Rival Hotels."

She brought a hand to her mouth. "Oh my God, does that mean what I think it does?"

He nodded. "It means more than you think it does. I've planned for a café in the new hotel."

She blinked several times and looked confused. "You're doing what?"

"When I agreed to broker this deal, my father promised me sole ownership of a single hotel of my choosing. This is fulfillment of a lifelong dream for me. I get to have my jazz club, and you can have your café. I'm renovating and I've planned on space for your café. Or, how about a café by day and a music spot by night? That is, if you're still interested in working with me?"

Laurent thought Tracee was going to pull him from the driver's seat, she reached out and wrapped her arms around his neck so hard. He heard her crying before he felt the tears against the side of his face. "I guess that's a yes!" he said.

She released him and sat back, wiping her eyes. "That's a hell yes! The minute it seemed as if everything in my life was falling apart, I got down on my knees and prayed. I prayed you'd get the hotel and that everything would work out between us. Lord knows I wasn't ready for you to walk out of my life."

"Tracee, we're just getting started."

She cleared her throat. "What will your father say?"

Laurent laughed. "My father won't be a problem, you'll see."

"I don't know, Laurent. He did ask me to stay away from you."

"And I'm asking you to stay with me. To become my partner in business, and in life, so we can fulfill our dreams together."

"Laurent, this is more than I could have ever imagined. Are you sure you want to do this?"

"I wrote it into my proposal. I'm sure."

Someone tapped on the window, startling the both of them. Laurent looked behind Tracee to see Kyla and Corra peering into the car.

"Is everything okay in there?" Corra asked.

Tracee released his neck. "Can I tell them?" she asked.

He nodded. "Sure."

The car door flew open, and Tracee jumped out. "I've found my new partner!" she screamed.

Epilogue

Six months after Thomas Martin had asked Tracee to stay away from his son, he was now sitting at the dining room table of the Coleman House bed-and-breakfast with his wife and son enjoying Sunday brunch. Today's brunch was reserved for family. Rollin had added a leaf to the dining room table in order to accommodate Tracee's parents as well as her siblings. She looked around the table and couldn't keep the smile off her face. They were like one big happy family—husbands, wives and children.

Laurent's parents had flown into town for the grand opening of their son's new hotel, Hotel Nicholas. With the opening of the hotel, Laurent had found another way to honor his mother, who'd given all of her boys the same middle name—Nicholas.

After the deal closed, he'd spent the last six months renovating the old Rival Hotel into a piece of artwork that the whole town was excited about. He'd had a soft opening two weeks ago in order to make sure everything was perfect for the grand opening. But first, Laurent had insisted his father spend some time getting to know Tracee and her family.

"Laurent, did I ever tell you my parents had a little garden out back when I was growing up?" Thomas Martin asked.

Laurent arched a brow and turned to wink at Tracee before answering. "No, that's news to me."

"Yeah, my old man liked to grow his own food as well. I guess you could say we had our own organic farm. He grew lettuce, tomatoes, onions, cucumbers, potatoes and some other vegetables. I'd almost forgotten about that."

"Everybody had some type of garden back in the day," Tracee's father added.

Tracee felt Laurent squeeze her thigh under the table. She reached over and found his hand. They held on to one another, expressing how happy they were at the moment. In a few hours, they would be celebrating the achievement of dreams come true.

The kitchen door swung open, and Rita, followed by Tayler, entered the room carrying with them platters of what smelled like heaven on earth.

"Um, something smells wonderful," Laurent said.

"That would be my multigrain blueberry pancakes," Rita said as she placed two platters in the middle of the table. "This here's family style, so help yourself. We got more coming." She returned to the kitchen for more food.

Rollin said the blessing, and then everybody dug in as Tayler and Rita returned with more plates. Tayler came around with pitchers of iced tea and water.

"Sir, would you like tea, water, or can I fix you a mimosa?" Tayler asked, standing next to Mr. Martin.

Tracee sat directly across the table from Laurent's father, who when he glanced up at her looked embarrassed and a little ashamed. They'd spoken once since the last time he entered the bed-and-breakfast, and all he said then was, "Hello, it's nice to see you again." Laurent told her he'd had numerous conversations with his father about her over the last six months. His father had apologized to Laurent for his behavior and promised to make it up to Tracee. She was waiting on that apology.

"I'll have some sweet tea, thank you," Thomas Martin said to Tayler, before flashing a smile toward Tracee.

Plates were clinking and glasses were being thumped against the table. Then silence filled the room while everyone enjoyed their food too much to engage in conversation.

Minutes later, Thomas Martin broke the silence. "These are the best pancakes I've ever had. And I don't know the last time I've had grits, but they're wonderful as well. I need to fly a few of my chefs in for cooking lessons. We might need to add a little southern flair to the menu."

The fact that Laurent's father had eaten in some of the best restaurants in the world, yet he praised

Rita's cooking, pleased everyone on the Coleman staff. Tracee loved the beaming smiles on Rollin, Corra and Tayler's faces.

Corra responded by adding, "Aunt Rita is the best cook in Boyle County."

"And don't forget about Tracee," Tayler added. "You know she's the best pastry chef in the county and we're going to hate to see her go. But I'm more than happy for her at the same time." Tayler held a glass of orange juice up to salute Tracee.

Tracee held her glass up in return, blushing, and winked at Tayler.

"So I've heard," Thomas Martin said, smiling at Tracee. "I hope we get to sample some of your work today."

Tracee was surprised that he spoke directly to her. Laurent squeezed her hand under the table again. "As a matter of fact, I baked a carrot cake and a golden cake with buttercream frosting for today's brunch."

"And her cakes are to die for," Rollin added. "At least that's what the girls say, right?" He gestured to Tayler and Corra before Tayler blew him a kiss.

"That's right. When the U-pick store was open, we couldn't keep Tracee's desserts on the shelf. And I'm sure that will continue now that we'll be your number-one customer," Corra said to Tracee.

"As long as you pay your bill every month, you'll always be my number one," Tracee replied.

Everyone at the table got a good laugh out of Tracee's response.

Finally, Rollin stood up and tapped his fork

against his glass. "Folks, I'd like to make a toast before we all get scattered around."

Tracee gave Laurent a thin-lipped smile, not sure what her cousin was about to say.

"First of all, I want to say thank you to Laurent for building such a nice hotel that is likely to steal some of my customers."

Everyone laughed again, and Laurent shook his head.

Rollin continued. "No, really. Hotel Nicholas is going to be a tremendous asset to the community. The whole town is excited about what you're doing. And we're excited about you making Tracee's Cake World a part of that excitement. I see nothing but good things in the future for you two. Here's to a successful grand opening celebration tonight. Oh, and don't forget to take a stack of our brochures to keep in your lobby."

Tayler yanked at Rollin's shirt, laughing, while he held his glass high. "To Hotel Nicholas."

The minute everyone took a sip, Laurent pushed his chair back and came to his feet.

"Keep your glasses up. I'd like to say a few words also." He cleared his throat and glanced around the room at everyone, stopping at his father. "I'd like to thank my parents for taking the time out of their schedules to fly down for the grand opening." He nodded at his parents.

"Wouldn't miss it for the world," his father said.

Laurent continued, "And for coming a day early in order to join this Sunday brunch. I told you it was going to be some of the best food you'd ever put in your mouth."

Thomas Martin nodded first to Laurent, then in Rollin's direction.

"And Rollin, you keep doing what you're doing. I don't think you'll have a thing to worry about as far as customers are concerned. If there's one thing I learned in researching Danville and its residents, is that the Coleman House farm and bed-and-breakfast has a stellar reputation. If anything, you might want to send your overflow my way."

Rollin gave Laurent a wide-eyed look before nodding.

"Seriously, I want to thank everyone for the hospitality you've shown me from that first Sunday brunch I attended here over six months ago, to assisting me with making some choices in regards to the grand opening. I've bragged about you to everyone I know, and I'm happy to call you friends. I look forward to entertaining you tonight, so here's to having a good time."

After the last toast, everyone finished their meals and Tracee helped Rita and Tayler serve dessert. Rollin had started a conversation with Laurent's father when Rita reentered the room with a camera.

"Mr. and Mrs. Martin, if you don't mind, may I have a picture for my wall?" She pointed to the pictures above the sideboard of the celebrities and local heroes who'd eaten or stayed at the bed-and-breakfast.

Laurent's father stood up, smoothing his tie down

the front of his chest before helping his wife up. "Of course, we're honored that you asked."

"Well, it's not every day that we have the president of a five-star hotel chain dining with us. Tracee showed me your hotels on the internet. Very impressive!"

Thomas Martin grinned as if he'd been complimented by the queen of England.

After pictures and dessert, Rollin offered Laurent's parents a tour of the property. Thomas Martin said he hadn't spent time on a farm since his childhood growing up in Evanston, Illinois. A fact that he repeated a few times before the day was over.

Tracee stepped out on the front porch and took a seat in one of the white rockers to get some air and to pinch herself. She couldn't believe everything that was going on inside. Everyone was happy, peaceful and enjoying one another. This was turning into the perfect day. The front door opened, and Laurent's father stepped outside.

"Here you are, Ms. Tracee." He walked over and took a seat in the rocker a table away from her. "I owe you an apology. The first time we met, I was an obnoxious blowhard. I said some unkind things to you, and I hope you've forgiven me for my bad behavior."

Tracee had been scared of Laurent's father, thinking he'd never apologize to her because he might have thought it beneath him. But he was just a man like every other man in there. "Thank you, sir. I was scared to talk to Laurent after you left. But we talked it over, and I think I understood the pressure you were under. So, you're more than forgiven."

Mr. Martin smiled. "Well, we're lucky that Laurent never listens to me. He's headstrong and capable of making his own decisions. What frightened me was the fact that he hadn't settled the deal, and I knew this was his future. All of my hotels will be left to my sons when I pass on. But an Abelle hotel isn't what Laurent wants for himself. I know him. Don't tell my other sons, but he's the most creative and talented of the three of them. He needs to express himself in his own way, with his own property. He's young, but Laurent is ready for ownership, and I hope you are as well. He shared his plans for Café Amour with me."

She tried not to show every tooth in her mouth as she smiled. "Yes, sir, I'm more than ready. You see, having my own business is a lifelong dream for me. My grandmother opened a coffee stand in the Rival Hotel years ago, and my cousin carried on the tradition until she passed. Now in that same spot I want to take her dream to the next level. I want to make my family proud as well."

Mr. Martin smiled. "I admire your drive, and I see why my son has fallen in love with you. You're not just a pretty face."

Tracee tried her best not to blush. "No, sir. I'm not."

"Sometimes It Snows in April," according to Prince, but not today. The weather was perfect, and the trees and flowers had begun to bloom.

Laurent's original plan had been to purchase the Rival Hotel, return to California and hire a project manager to oversee the renovations. However, after developing a relationship with Tracee, he'd decided to take up residency in Danville and handle the renovations himself. After all, Hotel Nicholas was his!

For the grand opening, he'd hired a local DJ to play old-school music all night. All of the hotel's staff played a part, from serving hors d'oeuvres to giving tours and greeting guests with gift bags that included samples from Tracee's Cake World. Local business owners and event planners, along with newspaper and magazine people from the surrounding counties, were in attendance. Everybody wanted to see what the new hotel looked like.

Laurent walked through the crowd greeting and welcoming everyone. In the corridor leading to the gym he ran into Sam and his wife, Janet.

"Laurent, this place is absolutely magnificent. Man, you've created a unique brand experience with the new hotel, and we love it."

"Thanks, man." Laurent pumped shoulders with Sam, before kissing Janet on the cheek. "I appreciate that, really I do."

"So we see you've found something to do around here for fun," Janet said.

Laurent laughed at her reference to him being bored when he first arrived in Danville. "Yeah, I found something and someone. Like Sam said—" he reached out and grasped Sam by the shoulder "—find a good woman and settle down. And I've been having nothing but fun ever since."

"Looks like we spoke her up. Here comes Tracee now," Sam said.

Laurent turned around as the woman who'd completely turned his world upside down sashayed toward them. Tracee looked stunning with her hair swept back from her face into a long ponytail running down her back. Her little black cocktail dress was a traffic stopper. It hugged every curve of her body, showing off her beautiful figure. When she smiled at him, his heart filled with warmth and nothing but love for her. Before leaving California, he'd made sure his father knew that one day Tracee would be a part of their family.

Walking alongside her was her best friend, Mae. They might not be business partners, but their friendship remained intact.

"Hey, guys, what are you doing standing out here? Café Amour is open and Tracee's Cake World is serving up dessert." Tracee hugged and kissed Sam and Janet before motioning them toward the café.

"Now this I'm looking forward to," Sam said. "You've created a sweet spot and a jazz spot under one roof. I think I'm going to have a new hangout."

"That's right, we have all your pastry needs during the day, then stick around for some smooth jazz in the evenings from Thursday through Sunday. I might even play a little something from time to time," Laurent added.

"Now you're talking. Thank you both for sharing your gifts with us. We'll be customers for sure," Sam said, smiling at his wife.

"And you know I've already reserved a table for John and me for this Friday night," Mae added before reaching out to give Laurent a hug.

After all the well wishes, Sam, his wife and Mae left them and went to check out the café.

Laurent took the moment they were alone to pull Tracee into his arms and kiss her inviting red lips. "You look so beautiful tonight—ready for the red carpet."

She snapped her fingers. "That's what we should have done. Rolled out the red carpet. Everyone from the local press is here. We're going to be on the front page tomorrow, you know."

He smiled. "I know. I've given a few interviews, but I have a feeling we'll be giving a few more before the night's over. I just want to take this moment to say thank you for entering my life and being there when I needed you most. Tracee Coleman, I love you so much."

She smiled. "I should be thanking you. Remember, I was the one who had the boring life until this good-looking guy from California showed up. A couple of days turned into a couple of weeks, and I was hooked. I love you back, Laurent Martin."

The hotel lights began to flicker, indicating it was time for everyone to assemble in the lobby for a speech from the new owner.

Laurent walked into the circle his staff had assembled for him and looked around at everyone in attendance with awe. Tracee's entire family was there. His parents were there, and his brother Marquis had arrived just in time for the reception. His other brother, Aubrey, sent his well wishes and apologized for not being able to get back from Hong Kong for the opening.

Butterflies were dancing in Laurent's stomach as he delivered his thank-you speech. He wasn't nervous about the speaking, but the little box in his jacket pocket had his heart beating double time. After he thanked everyone, he asked Tracee to join him. He introduced her to anyone who didn't already know who she was. Then, as if on cue, the DJ played her favorite song, "Why I Love You" by Major.

Tracee turned and smiled at the DJ, who was posted up in the corner. When the crowd gasped, she turned back around—Laurent had pulled the box from his pocket and gotten down on one knee. Her hand flew over her mouth.

Laurent reached out for her hand. "Tracee, I feel as if the stars have all aligned and God brought you to me. I love you with everything inside me, and I want to be there for you until the end of time. I want us to grow this thing together. I love you, I need you and I want you to be my partner in life. What do you say? Will you marry me?"

Tears streamed down Tracee's cheeks as she looked down at Laurent smiling up at her with wide eyes, waiting for her answer. She closed her eyes, wanting to savor the moment for just a second longer. This man was everything she'd ever wanted, even when she didn't know it. She loved him more than anything and couldn't bear to be without him. She opened her eyes and removed her hand from her mouth. *"Yes!"* she screamed and held up her shaking hand for Laurent to slide a beautiful engagement ring on her finger.

The applause sounded like thunder in her ears

while Laurent stood up and kissed her before wrapping his arms around her and giving her the best hug yet. She cried some more, thankful that she'd never have to go without his hugs ever again.

* * * * *

IF YOU CAN'T STAND
THE HEAT...

JOSS WOOD

For their love and support, I have so many friends to thank. Old friends, new friends, coffee friends and crying friends. Friends who know me inside out and friends I've just met. But, because we share a friendship based on raucous laughter, craziness, sarcasm, loyalty and love, this book is especially dedicated to Tracy, Linda and Kerry.

CHAPTER ONE

'ELLIE, YOUR PHONE is ringing! Ellie, answer it now!'

Ellie Evans grinned at her best friend Merri's voice emanating from her mobile in her personalised ring tone, then eagerly scooped up the phone and slapped it against her ear.

'El?'

'Hey, you—how's the Princess?' Ellie asked, sorting through the invoices on her desk, which essentially meant that she just moved them from one pile to another.

'The Princess' was her goddaughter, Molly Blue, a six-month-old diva who had them all wrapped around her chubby pinkie finger. Merri launched into a far too descriptive monologue about teething and nappies, interrupted sleep and baby food. Ellie—who was still having a hard time reconciling her party-lovin', heel-kickin', free-spirited friend with motherhood—*mmm*-ed in all the right places and tuned out.

'Okay, I get the hint. I'm boring,' Merri stated, yanking Ellie's attention back. 'But you normally make an effort to at least pretend to listen. So what's up?'

Her friend since they were teenagers, Merri knew her inside out. And as she was her employee as well as her best friend she had to tell her the earth-shattering news. Sitting in her tiny office on the second floor of her bakery and delicatessen, Ellie bit her lip and stared at her messy desk. Panic, bitter and insistent, crept up her throat.

She pulled in a deep breath. 'The Khans have sold the building.'

'Which building?'

'This building, Merri. We have six months before we have to move out.'

Ellie heard Merri's swift intake of breath.

'But why would they sell?' she wailed.

'They are in their seventies, and I would guess they're tired of the hassle. They probably got a fortune for the property. We all know that it's the best retail space for miles.'

'Just because it sits on the corner of the two main roads into town and is directly opposite the most famous beach in False Bay it doesn't mean it's the best...'

'That's exactly what it means.'

Ellie looked out of the sash window to the beach and the lazy ocean beyond it. It had been a day since she'd been slapped with the news and she no longer had butterflies about Pari's, the bakery that had been in her family for over forty years. They had all been eaten by the bats on some psycho-drug currently swarming in her stomach.

'Why can't we just rent from the new owners?'

'I asked. They are going to do major renovations to attract corporate shops and intend on hiking the rents accordingly. We couldn't afford it. And, more scarily, Lucy—'

'The estate agent?'

'Mmm. Well, she told me that retail space is at a premium in St James, and there are "few, if any" properties suitable for a bakery-slash-coffee-shop-slash-delicatessen for sale or to rent.'

After four decades of being a St James and False Bay institution Pari's future was uncertain, and as the partner-in-residence Ellie had to deal with this life-changing situation.

She had no idea what they—she—was going to do.

'Have you told your mum?' Merri asked quietly.

'I can't get hold of her. She hasn't made contact for ten days.

I think she's booked into an ashram…or sunning herself in Goa,' Ellie replied, her voice weary. Where she *wasn't* was in the bakery, with her partner/daughter, helping her sort out the mess they were in.

Your idea, Ellie reminded herself. *You said she could go. You suggested that she take the year off, have some fun, follow her dream…* What *had* she been thinking? In all honesty it had been a mostly symbolic offer; nobody had been more shocked—horrified!—than her when Ashnee had immediately run off to pack her bags and book her air ticket. She'd never thought Ashnee would leave the bakery, leave *her*…

'El, I know that this isn't a good time, especially in light of what you've just told me, but I can't put it off any longer. I need to ask you a huge favour.'

Ellie frowned when she picked up the serious note in Merri's voice.

'Anything, provided that you are still coming back to work on Monday,' Ellie quipped. Merri was a phenomenal baker and Ellie had desperately missed her talent in the bakery while she took her maternity leave.

The silence following her statement slapped her around the head. Oh, no…no, no, *no*! 'Merri, I need you,' she pleaded.

'My baby needs me too, El.' Merri sounded miserable. 'And I'm not ready to come back to work just yet. I will be, but not just yet. Maybe in another month. She's so little and I need to be with her…please? Tell me you understand, Ellie.'

I understand that I haven't filled your position because I was holding it open for you—because you asked me to. I understand that I'm running myself ragged, that the clients miss you…

'Another month?' Merri coaxed. 'Pretty please?'

Ellie rubbed her forehead. What could she say? Merri didn't need to work, thanks to her very generous father, so if she forced her to choose between the bakery and Molly Blue the bakery would lose. *She* would lose…

Ellie swallowed, told herself that if she pushed Merri to come back and she didn't then it was her decision…but she felt the flames of panic lick her throat. They were big girls, and their friendship was more than the job they shared—it would survive her leaving the bakery—but she didn't want to take the chance. Her head knew that she was overreacting but her heart didn't care.

She had too much at stake as it was. She couldn't risk losing her in any way. She'd coped for over six months; she'd manage another month. Somehow.

Ellie bit her top lip. 'Sure, Merri.'

'You're the best—but I've got to dash. The Princess is bellowing.' Now Ellie could hear Molly's insistent wail. 'I'll try to get to the bakery later this week and we can talk about what we're going to do. Byeee! Love you.'

'Love you…' Ellie heard the beep-beep that told her the call had been dropped and tossed her mobile on the desk in front of her.

'El, there's someone to see you out front.'

Ellie glanced from the merry face of Samantha, one of her servers, peeking around her door to the old-fashioned clock above her head, and frowned. The bakery and coffee shop had closed ten minutes ago, so who could it be?

'Who is it?'

Samantha shrugged. 'Dunno. He just said to tell you that your father sent him. He's alone out front…we're all heading home.'

'Thanks, Sammy.' Ellie frowned and swivelled around to look at the screens on the desk behind her. There were cameras in the front of the shop, in the bakery and in the storeroom, and they fed live footage into the monitors.

Ellie's brows rose as she spotted him, standing off to the

side of a long display of glass-fronted fridges, a rucksack hanging off his very broad shoulders. Week-long stubble covered his jaw and his auburn hair was tousled from finger raking.

Jack Chapman. Okay, she was officially surprised. Any woman who watched any one of the premier news channels would recognise that strong face under the shaggy hair. Ellie wasn't sure whether he was more famous for his superlative and insightful war reporting or for being the definition of eye candy.

Grubby low-slung jeans and even grubbier boots. A dark untucked T-shirt. He ran a hand through his hair and, seeing a clasp undone on the side pocket of his rucksack, bent down to fix it. Ellie watched the long muscles bunching under his thin shirt, the curve of a very nice butt, the strength of his brown neck.

Oh, *yum*—oh, stop it now! Get a grip! The important questions were: why was he here, what did he want and what on earth was her father thinking?

Ellie lifted her head as Samantha tapped on the doorframe again and stood there, shuffling on her feet and biting her lip. She recognised that look. 'What's up, Sammy?'

Samantha looked at her with big brown eyes. 'I know that I promised to work for you tomorrow night to help with the *petits fours* for that fashion show—'

'But?'

'But I've been offered a ticket to see Linkin Park and they are my favourite band…it's a free ticket and you know how much I love them.'

Ellie considered giving her a lecture on responsibility and keeping your word, on how promises shouldn't be broken, but the kid was nineteen and it *was* Linkin Park. She remembered being that age and the thrill of a kick-ass concert.

And Samantha, battling to put herself through university, couldn't afford to pay for a ticket herself. She'd remember it for for ever...so what if it meant that Ellie had to work a couple of hours longer? It wasn't as if she had a life or anything.

'Okay, I'll let you off the hook.' Ellie winced at Samantha's high-pitched squeal. 'This time. Now, get out of here.'

Ellie grinned as she heard her whooping down the stairs, but the grin faded when she glanced at the monitor again. Scowling, she reached for her mobile, hastily scrolling through her address book before pushing the green button.

'Ellie—hello.' Her father's deep voice crooned across the miles.

'Dad, why is Jack Chapman in my bakery?'

Ellie heard her father's sharp intake of breath. 'He's there already? Good. I was worried.'

Of course you were, Ellie silently agreed. For the past ten years, since her eighteenth birthday, she'd listened to her father rumble on and on about Jack Chapman—the son he'd always wanted and never got. 'He's the poster-boy for a new generation of war correspondents,' he'd said. 'Unbiased, tough. Willing to dive into a story without thinking about his safety, looking for the story behind the story, yet able to push aside emotion to look for the truth...' Yada, yada, yada...

'So, again, why is he here?' Ellie asked.

And, by the way, why do you only call when you want something from me? Oh, wait, you didn't call. I did! You just sent your boy along, expecting me to accommodate your every whim.

Some things never changed.

'He was doing an interview with a Somalian warlord who flipped. He was stripped of his cash and credit cards, delivered at gunpoint to a United Nations aid plane leaving for Cape Town and bundled onto it,' Mitchell Evans said in a clipped voice. 'I need you to give him a bed.'

Jeez, Dad, do I have a B&B sign tattooed on my forehead?

Ellie, desperate to move beyond her default habit of trying

to please her father, tried to say no, but a totally different set of words came out of her mouth. 'For how long?'

God, she was such a wimp.

'Well, here's the thing, sugar-pie…'

Oh, good grief. Her father had a *thing*. A lifetime with her father had taught her that a thing *never* worked out in her favour. 'Jack is helping me write a book on the intimate lives of war reporters—mine included.'

Interesting—but she had no idea what any of this had to do with *her*. But Mitchell didn't like being interrupted, so Ellie waited for him to finish.

'He needs to talk to my family members. I thought he could stay a little while, talk to you about life with me…'

Sorry…life with him? What life with him? During her parents' on-off marriage their home had been a place for her mum to do his laundry rather than to live. He'd lived his life in all the countries people were trying to get out of: Iraq, Gaza, Bosnia. Home was a place he'd dropped in and out of. Work had always been his passion, his muse, his lifelong love affair.

Resentment nibbled at the wall of her stomach. Depending on what story had been consuming him at the time, Mitchell had missed every single important event of her childhood. Christmas concerts and ballet recitals, swimming galas and father-daughter days. How could he be expected to be involved in his daughter's life when there were bigger issues in the world to write about, analyse, study?

What he'd never realised was that he was her biggest issue…the creator of her angst, the source of her abandonment issues, the spring that fed the fountain of her self-doubt.

Ellie winced at her melodramatic thoughts. Her childhood with Mitchell had been fraught with drama but it was over. However, in situations like these, old resentments bubbled up and over.

Her father had been yakking on for a while and Ellie refocused on what he was saying.

'The editors and I want Jack to include his story—he *is* the brightest of today's bunch—but getting Jack to talk about himself is like trying to find water in the Gobi Desert. He's not interested. He's as much an enigma to me as he was when we first met. So will you talk to him?' Mitchell asked. 'About me?'

Oh, good grief. Did she have to? Really?

'Maybe.' Which they both knew meant that she would. 'But, Dad, seriously? You can't just dump your waifs and strays on me.' He could—of course he could. He was Mitchell Evans and she was a push-over.

'Waif and stray? Jack is anything but!'

Ellie rubbed her temple. Could this day throw anything else at her head? The bottom line was that another of Mitchell's colleagues was on her doorstep and she could either take him in or turn him away. Which she wouldn't do…because then her father wouldn't be pleased and he'd sulk, and in twenty years' time he'd remind her that she'd let him down. Really, it was just easier to give the guy a bed for the night and bask in Mitchell's approval for twenty seconds. If that.

If only they were *normal* people, Ellie thought. The last colleague of her father's she'd had to stay—again at Mitchell's request—had got hammered on her wine and tried to paw her before passing out on her Persian carpet. And every cameraman, producer and correspondent she'd ever met—including her father—was crazy, weird, strange or odd. She figured that it was a necessary requirement if you wanted to chase down and report on human conflicts and disasters.

Mitchell's voice, now that he'd got his own way, sounded jaunty again. 'Jack's a good man. He's probably not slept for days, hasn't eaten properly for more than a week. A bed, a meal, a bath. It's not that much to ask because you're a good person, my sweet, sweet girl.'

My sweet, sweet girl? Tuh!

Sweet, sweet sucker, more like.

Ellie sneaked another look at Mr-Hot-Enough-to-Melt-Heavy-Metal. He did have a body to die for, she thought.

'Have you met Jack before?' Mitchell asked.

'Briefly. At your wedding to Steph.' Wife number three, who'd stuck around for six months. Ellie had been eighteen, chronically shy, and Jack had barely noticed her.

'Oh, yeah—Steph. I liked her...I still don't know why she left,' Mitchell said, sounding plausibly bemused.

Gee, Dad, here's a clue. Maybe, like me, she hated the idea of the man she adored being away for five of those six months, plunging into the situation in Afghanistan and only popping up occasionally on TV. Hated not knowing whether you were alive or dead. It's no picnic loving someone who doesn't love you a fraction as much as you love your job.

She, her mother and Mitchell's two subsequent wives had come second-best time after time...decade after decade. And she'd repeated the whole stupid cycle by getting engaged to Darryl.

She'd vowed she'd never fall in love with a journalist and she hadn't. But life had bust a gut laughing when she'd become engaged to a man she'd thought was the exact opposite of her father, only to realise that he spent even less time at home than her father had. That was quite an accomplishment, since he'd never, as far as she knew, left London itself.

She'd been such a sucker, Ellie thought. Still was...

Maybe one of these days she'd find her spine.

Ellie looked down at her mobile, realised that her father hadn't said goodbye before disconnecting and shrugged. Situation normal. She glanced at the monitor again and saw the impatience on Jack's face, caught his tapping foot. The muscles in his arms bulged as he folded them across his chest. Although the feed was in black and white she knew that his eyes were hazel…sometimes brown, sometimes green, gold, always compelling. Right now they were blazing with a combination of frustration, exhaustion and a very healthy dose of annoyance.

He was different from the twenty-four-year-old she'd met a decade ago. Older, harder, a bit damaged. Ellie felt an unfamiliar buzz in her womb and cocked her head as attraction skittered through her veins and caused her heartbeat to fuzz…

She tossed her mobile onto her desk and pushed her chair back as she stood up and blew out a breath.

It didn't matter that he was tall, built and had a sexy face that could stop traffic, she lectured herself. Crazy came in all packages.

'Jack?'

Jack Chapman, standing in the front section of the bakery— aqua stripes on the walls, black checked floors, white cabinets, a sunshine-yellow surfboard—whirled around at the low, melodious voice and blinked. Then blinked again. He knew he was tired, but this was ridiculous…

He'd been expecting the awkward, overweight, shy girl from Mitch's wedding not this…*babe*! This tropical, colourful, radiant, riveting, dazzling babe. With a capital B. In bold and italics.

Waist-length black hair streaked with purple and green stripes, milk-saturated coffee skin, vivid blue eyes and her father's pugnacious chin.

And slim, curvy legs that went up to her ears.

'Hi, I'm Ellie. Mitchell has asked me to put you up for the night.'

His pulse kicked up as he struggled to find his words. He eventually managed to spit a couple out. 'I'm grateful. Thank you.'

Whoa! Jack dropped his pack to the floor and resisted the

impulse to put his hand on his heart to check if it was okay. With his history…

You are not *having a heart attack, you moron! Major over-reaction here, dude, cool your jets!*

So she wasn't who he'd been expecting? In his line of work little was as expected, so why was his heart jumping and his mouth dry?

Jack rocked on his heels, looked around and tried not to act like a gauche teenager. 'This is a really nice place. Do you own it?'

Ellie looked around and the corners of her mouth tipped up. 'Yep. My mum and I are partners.'

'Ah…' He looked at the empty display fridges. 'Where's the food? Shouldn't there be food?'

Her smile was a fist to his sternum.

'Most of the baked goods are sold out and we put the deli meats away every night.' She fiddled with the strap of her huge leather tote bag. 'So, how was your flight?' she asked politely.

Sitting on the floor of a cargo plane in turbulence, with bruised ribs and a pounding headache? Just peachy. 'Fine, thanks.'

The reality was that he was exhausted, achingly stiff and sore, and his side felt as if he had a red-hot poker lodged inside it. He wanted a shower and to sleep for a week. His glance slid to a fridge filled with soft drinks. And he'd kill someone for a Coke.

Ellie caught his look and waved to the fridge. 'Help yourself.'

Jack grimaced. 'I can't pay for it.'

'Pari's can afford to give you a can on the house,' Ellie said wryly.

The words were barely out of her mouth and he was opening the fridge, yanking out a red can and popping the tab. The tart, sugary liquid slid down his throat and he sighed, knowing the sugar and caffeine would give him another hour or two of energy. Maybe…

He swore under his breath as once again he realised that he was stuck halfway across the world. He couldn't even pay for a damn soft drink. He silently cursed again. He needed to borrow cash and a bed from Ellie until his replacement bank cards were delivered. He grimaced at the sour taste now in his mouth. Having to ask for help made him feel…out of control, helpless. Powerless.

He hated to feel beholden, but he reminded himself it would only be for a night—two, maximum.

Jack finished his drink and looked around for a bin.

Ellie took the can from him, walked behind the counter and tossed it away. 'Help yourself to another, if you like.'

'I'm okay. Thanks.'

Ellie's eyebrows lifted and their eyes caught and held. Jack thought that she was an amazing combination of east and west: skin from her Goan-born grandparents, and blue eyes and that chin from her Irish father. Her body was all her own and should come with a 'Danger' warning. Long legs, tiny waist, incredible breasts…

Because he was very, very good at reading body language, he saw wariness in her face, a lot of shyness and a hint of resignation. Could he blame her? He was a stranger, about to move into her house.

'Funky décor,' he said, trying to put her at ease. Hanging off the wall next to the front door was a fire-red canoe; its seating area sprouting gushing bunches of multi-coloured daisy-like flowers. 'I don't think I've ever seen surfboards and canoes used to decorate before. Or filled with flowers.'

Ellie laughed. 'I know; they are completely over the top, but such fun!'

'Those daisy things look real,' Jack commented.

'Gerbera daisies—and I don't think there's a point to flower arrangements if they aren't real,' Ellie replied.

He'd never thought about flowers that way. Actually, he'd never thought about flowers at all. 'What's with the signatures on the canoe?'

Ellie shrugged. 'I have no idea. I bought it like that.'

Jack shoved his hand into the pocket of his jeans and winced when the taxi driver leaned on his horn. Dammit, he'd forgotten about *him*. He felt humiliation tighten his throat. Now came the hard part, he thought, cursing under his breath. A soft drink was one thing...

'Look, I'm really sorry, but I've got myself into a bit of a sticky situation... Is there any chance you could pay the taxi fare for me? I'm good for it, I promise.'

'Sure.' Ellie reached into her bag, pulled out her purse and handed him a couple of bills.

Jack felt the tips of his fingers brush hers and winced at the familiar flame that licked its way up his arm. His body had decided that it was seriously attracted to her and there was nothing he could do about it.

Damn, Jack thought, as he stomped out through the door to pay his taxi fare. He really didn't feel comfortable being attracted to a woman he was beholden to, who was his mentor's beloved daughter and with whom he'd spend only two days before blowing out of her life.

Just ignore it, Jack told himself. *You're a grown man, firmly in control of your libido.*

He blew air into his cheeks as he handed the money over to the taxi driver and rubbed his hand over his face. The door behind him opened and he turned away from the road to see Ellie lugging his heavy rucksack through the door. Ignoring his burning side, he broke into a jog, quickly reached her and took his pack from her. The gangster bastards had taken his iPad, his satellite and mobile phones, his cash and credit cards, but had left him his dirty, disgusting clothes.

He would've left them too…

'Here—let me take that.' Jack took his rucksack from her.

'I just need to lock up and we can go,' Ellie said, before disappearing back inside the building.

Jack waited in the late-afternoon sun on the corner, his rucksack resting against an aqua pot planted with hot-pink flowers. He was beginning to suspect—from her multi-coloured hair and her bright bakery with its pink and purple exterior—that Ellie liked colour. Lots of it.

Mitchell had mentioned that Ellie was a baker and he'd expected her to be frumpy and housewifey, rotund and rosy—not slim, sexy and arty. Even her jewellery was creative: multi-length strands of beads in different shades of blue. He could say something about lucky beads to be against that chest, but decided that even the thought was pathetic…

He heard the door open behind him and she reappeared. She pulled the wooden and glass door shut, then yanked down the security grate and bolted and locked it.

Jack looked from the old-style bakery to the wide beach across the road and felt a smile form. It was nearly half-past six, a warm evening in summer, and the beach and boardwalk hummed with people.

'What time does the sun set?' he asked.

'Late. Eight-thirty-ish,' Ellie answered. She gestured to the road behind them. 'I live so close to work that I don't drive… um…my house is up that hill.'

Jack looked up the steep road to the mountain behind it and sighed. That was all he needed—a hike up a hill with a heavy pack. What else was this day going to throw at him?

He sighed again. 'Lead on.'

Ellie pulled a pair of over-large sunglasses from her bag and put them on, and they started to walk. They passed an antique

store, a bookstore and an old-fashioned-looking pharmacy—
he needed to stock up on some supplies there, but that would
raise some awkward questions. He waited for Ellie to initiate
the conversation. She did, moments later, good manners over-
coming her increasingly obvious shyness.

'So, what happened to you?'

'Didn't your father tell you?'

'Only that you got jumped by a couple of thugs and were
kicked out of Somalia. You need a place to stay because you're
broke.'

'Temporarily broke,' Jack corrected her. Mitchell hadn't
given her the whole story, thankfully. It was simple enough.
He'd asked a question about the hijackings of passing ships
which had pushed the warlord's 'detonate' button. He'd gone
psycho and ordered his henchman to beat the crap out of him.
He'd tried to resist, but six against one…bad odds.

Very bad odds. Jack shook off a shudder.

'So, is there anything else I can do for you apart from giving you a bed?'

Her question jerked him back to the present and his instinctive answer was, *A night with you in bed would be great.*

Seriously? *That* was what he was thinking?

Jack shook his head and ordered himself to get with the
programme. 'Um…I just need to spend a night, maybe two.
Borrow a mobile phone, a computer to send some e-mails,
have an address to have my replacement bank cards delivered to…' Jack replied.

'I have a spare mobile, and you can use my old laptop. I'll
write my address down for you. Are you on a deadline?'

'Not too bad. This is a print story for a political magazine.'

Ellie lifted her eyebrows. 'I thought you only did TV work?'

'I get the occasional assignment from newspapers and mag-
azines. I freelance, so I write articles in between reporting for
the news channels,' Jack replied.

Ellie shoved her sunglasses up into her hair and rubbed her eyes. 'So how are you going to write these articles? I presume your notes were taken.'

'I backed up my notes and documents onto a flash drive just before the interview. I slipped it into my shoe.' It was one of the many precautionary measures he took when operating in Third World countries.

'They let you keep your passport?'

Jack shrugged. 'They wanted me to leave and not having a passport would have hindered that.'

Ellie shook her head. 'You have a crazy job.'

He did, and he loved it. Jack shrugged. 'I operate best in a war zone, under pressure.' He loved having a rucksack on his back, dodging bullets and bombs to get the stories few other journalists found.

'Mitchell always said that it's a powerful experience to be holed up in a hotel in Mogadishu or Sarajevo with no water, electricity or food, playing poker with local contacts to the background music of bombs and automatic gunfire. I never understood that.'

Jack frowned at the note of bitterness in her voice and, quickly realising that there was a subtext beneath her words that he didn't understand, chose his next words carefully. 'Most people would consider it their worst nightmare—and to the people living and working in that war zone it is—but it *is* exciting, and documenting history is important.'

And the possibility of imminent death didn't frighten him at all. After all, he'd faced death before...

No, what would kill him would be being into a nine-to-five job, living in one city, doing the same thing day in and day out. He'd cheated death and received a second swipe at life... and the promise he'd made so long ago, to live life hard and fast and big, still fuelled him on a daily basis.

Jack felt a hard knot in his throat and tried to swallow it down. He was alive because someone else hadn't received the same second swipe...

'We're here.'

Ellie's statement interrupted his spiralling thoughts and Jack hid his sigh of relief as she turned up a driveway and approached a wrought-iron gate. Thank God. He wasn't sure if he could go much further.

Ellie looked at the remote in her hand, took a breath and briefly closed her eyes. He saw the tension in her shoulders and the rigid muscle in her jaw. She wasn't comfortable... Jack cursed. If he had been operating on more than twelve hours' sleep in four days he would have picked up that the shyness was actually tension a lot earlier. And it had increased the closer they came to her home.

'Look, you're obviously not happy about having me here,' Jack said, dropping his pack to the ground. 'Sorry. I didn't realise. I'll head back to the bakery—hitch a lift to the airport.'

Ellie jammed her hands into the pockets of her cut-offs. 'No—really, Jack...I told my father I'd help you.'

'I don't need your charity,' Jack said, pushing the words out between his clenched teeth.

'It's not charity.' Ellie lifted up a hand and rubbed her eyes with her thumb and index finger. 'It's just been a long day and I'm tired.'

That wasn't it. She was strung tighter than a guitar string. His voice softened. 'Ellie, I don't want you to feel uncomfortable in your own home. I told Mitch that I was happy to wait at the airport. It's not a big deal.'

Ellie straightened and looked him in the eye. 'I'm sorry. I'm the one who is making this difficult. Your arrival just pulled up some old memories. The last time I took in one of my father's workmates I was chased around my house by a drunken, horny cameraman.'

He sent her his I'm-a-good-guy grin. 'Typical. Those damn cameramen—you can't send them anywhere.'

Ellie smiled, as he'd intended her to. He could see some of her tension dissolve at his stab at humour.

'Sorry, I know I sound ridiculous. And I'm not crazy about talking about my relationship with Mitchell for this book you're helping him write—'

'I'm *helping* him write? Is that what he said?' Jack shook his head. Mitchell was living in Never-Never Land. It was *his* book, and *he* was writing the damn thing. Yes, Mitchell Evans's and Ken Baines's names would be on the cover, but there would be no doubt about who was the author. The size-able advance in his bank account was a freaking big clue.

'Your father...I like him...but, jeez, he can be a pain in the ass,' Jack said.

'So does that mean you don't want to talk to me about him?' Ellie asked, sounding hopeful and a great deal less nervous.

Jack half smiled as he shook his head. 'Sorry...I do need to talk to you about him.'

He raked his hair off his face, thinking about the book. Ken's fascinating story was all but finished; Mitch's was progressing. Thank God he'd resisted all the collective pressure to get him to write his. Frankly, it would be like having his chest cracked open without anaesthetic.

He was such a hypocrite. He had no problems digging around other people's psyches but was more than happy to leave his own alone.

Jack looked at Ellie, saw her still uncertain expression and was reminded that she was wary of having a strange man in her house. He couldn't blame her.

'And as for chasing you around your house? Apart from the

fact that I am so whipped I couldn't make a move on a corpse, it really isn't my style.'

Ellie looked at him for a long moment and then her smile blossomed. It was the nicest punch to the heart he'd ever received.

CHAPTER TWO

JACK LOOKED UP a lavender-lined driveway to the house beyond it. It was a modest two-storey with Old World charm,
wooden bay windows and a deep veranda, nestled in a wild
garden surrounded by a high brick wall. The driveway led up
to a two-door garage. He didn't do charming houses—hell, he
didn't do *houses*. He had a flat that he barely saw, boxes that
were still unpacked, a fridge that was never stocked. In many
ways his flat was just another hotel room: as impersonal, as
bland. He wasn't attached to any of his material possessions
and he liked it that way.

Attachment was not an emotion he felt he needed to become
better acquainted with…either to possessions or partners.

'Nice place,' Jack said as he walked up the stairs onto a
covered veranda. Ellie took a set of keys from the back pocket
of those tight shorts. It *was* nice—not for him, but nice—a
charming house with loads of character.

'The house was my grandmother's. I inherited it from her.'

Jack glanced idly over his shoulder and his breath caught
in his throat. *God, what a view!*

'Oh, that is just amazing,' he said, curling his fingers
around the wooden beam that supported the veranda's roof.
Looking out over the houses below, he could see a sweeping
stretch of endless beach that showed the curve of the bay and
the sleepy blue and green ocean.

'Where are we, exactly?' he asked.

Ellie moved to stand next to him. 'On the False Bay coast. We're about twenty minutes from the CBD of Cape Town, to the south. That bay is False Bay and you can see about thirty kilometres of beach from here. Kalk Bay is that way—' she pointed '—and Muizenberg is up the coast.'

'What are those brightly coloured boxes on the beach?'

'Changing booths. Aren't they fun? The beach is hugely popular, and if you look just north of the booths, at the tables and chairs under the black and white striped awning, that's where we were—at Pari's.'

'It's incredible.'

'Your room looks out onto the beach and the bathroom has a view of the Muizenberg Mountain behind us. There are some great walks and biking trails in the nature reserve behind us.'

Ellie nudged one of two almost identical blond Labradors aside in an attempt to get close enough to the front door and shove her key in the lock. Pushing open the wooden door with its stained glass window insert, she gestured for Jack to come into the hall as she automatically hung her bag onto a decorative hook.

'The bedrooms are upstairs. I presume that you'd like a shower? Something to eat? Drink?'

He probably reeked like an abandoned rubbish dump. 'I'd kill for a shower.'

Jack had an impression of more bright colours and eclectic art as he followed Ellie up the wooden staircase. There was a short passage and then she opened the door to a guest bedroom: white and lavender linen on a double bed, pale walls and a ginger cat curled up on the royal purple throw.

'Meet Chaos. The *en-suite* bathroom is through that door.'

Ellie picked up Chaos and cradled the cat like a baby. Jack scratched the cat behind its ears and Chaos blinked sleepily.

Jack thankfully dropped his backpack onto the wooden

floor and sat down on the purple throw at the end of the bed while he waited for the dots behind his eyes to recede. Ellie walked to the window, pulled the curtain back and lifted the wooden sash to let some fresh air into the room.

He dimly heard Ellie ask again if he wanted something to drink and struggled to respond normally. He was enormously grateful when she left the room and he could shove his head between his knees and pull himself back from the brink of fainting.

Because obviously he'd prefer not to take the concept of falling at Ellie's feet too literally.

Ellie skipped down the stairs, belted into the kitchen and yanked her mobile from her pocket.

Merri answered on the first ring. 'I know that you're upset with me about extending my maternity leave...'

'Shut up! This is more important!' Ellie hissed, keeping her voice low. 'Mitchell sent me a man!'

Merri waited a beat before responding. 'Your father is procuring men for you now? Are you *that* desperate? Oh, wait... yes, you are!'

'You are so funny...not.' Ellie shook her head. 'No, you twit, I'm acting as a Cape Town B&B for his stray colleagues again, but this time he sent me Jack Chapman!'

'The hottie war reporter?' Merri replied, after taking a moment to make the connection. She sounded awed and—gratifyingly—a smidgeon jealous. 'Well?'

'Well, what?'

'What's he like?' Merri demanded.

'He's reluctantly, cynically charming. Fascinating. And he has the envious ability to put people at ease. No wonder he's an ace reporter.' When low-key charm and fascination came wrapped up in such a pretty package it was doubly, mind-alteringly disarming.

'Well, well, well…' Merri drawled. 'It sounds like he has made *quite* an impression! You sound…breathy.'

Breathy? No, she did not!

But why did she feel excited, shy, nervous and—dammit—scared all at the same time? Oh, she wasn't scared of *him*—she knew instinctively, absolutely, that Jack was a gentleman down to his toes—but she was on a scalpel-edge because he was the first man in ages who had her nerve-endings humming and her sexual radar beeping. And if she told Merri *that*…

'You're attracted to him,' Merri stated.

She hated it when Merri read her mind. 'I'm not…it's just a surprise. And even if I was…'

'You are.'

'He's too sexy, too charming, has a crazy job that I loathe, and he'll be gone in a day or two.'

'Mmm, but he's seriously hot. Check him out on the internet.'

'Is that what you're doing? Stop it and concentrate!' She gave Merri—and herself—a mental slap. 'I have more than enough to deal with without adding the complication of even *thinking* about attraction and sex and a good-looking face topping a sexy body! Besides, I'm not good at relationships and men.'

'Because you're still scared to risk giving your heart away and having to take it back, battered and bruised, when they ride off into the sunset?'

Merri tossed her own words back at her and Ellie grimaced.

'Exactly! And a pretty face won't change anything. My father and my ex put me through an emotional grinder and Jack Chapman has the potential to do the same…'

'Well, that's jumping the gun, since you've just met him, but I'll bite. Why?'

'Purely because I'm attracted to him!' Ellie responded in

a heated voice. 'It's an unwritten rule of my life that the men I find fascinating have an ability to wreak havoc in my life!'

They dropped in, kicked her heart around, ultimately decided that she wasn't worth sticking around for and left.

Merri remained silent and after a while Ellie spoke again. 'You agree with me, don't you?'

'No, don't take my silence for agreement; I'm just in awe of your crazy.' Merri sighed. 'So, to sum up your rant: you are such a bum magnet when it comes to men that your rule of thumb is that if you find one attractive then you should run like hell? Avoid at all costs?'

'You've nailed it,' Ellie said glumly.

'I want to see how you manage to do this when the man in question has moved his very hot self into your rather small house.'

Ellie disconnected her mobile on Merri's hooting laughter. Really, with friends like her...

Returning to the spare bedroom with towels for his bathroom and a cold beer in her hands, Ellie heard a low groan and peeked through the crack in the door to look at Jack, still sitting on the edge of the bed, his hands gripping the bottom of his shirt, pale and sweating.

Hurrying into the room, she dumped the towels on the bed, handed him the beer and frowned. 'Are you all right?'

Jack took a long, long drink from the bottle and rested the cold glass against his cheek. 'Sure. Why?'

'I noticed that you winced when you picked up your backpack. You took your time walking up the stairs, and now you're as white as a sheet and your hands are shaking!'

Jack rubbed the back of his neck. 'I'm a bit dinged up,' he eventually admitted.

'Uh-huh? How dinged up?'

'Just a bit. I'll survive.' Jack put the almost empty beer bottle on the floor and gripped the edge of his shirt again.

Ellie watched him struggle to pull it up and shook her head at his white-rimmed mouth.

'Can I help?' she asked eventually.

'I'll get there,' Jack muttered.

He couldn't, and with a slight shake of her head she stepped closer to the bed, grabbed the edges of his T-shirt and helped him pull it over his head. A beautiful body was there—somewhere underneath the blue-black plate-sized bruises that looked like angry thunderclouds. He had a wicked vertical scar bisecting his chest that suggested a major operation at one time, and Ellie bit her lip when she walked around his knees to look at his back. She couldn't stifle her horrified gasp. The damage on his back was even worse, and on his tanned skin she could see clear imprints of a heel here and the toe of a boot there.

'What does the other guy look like?' she asked, trying to be casual.

'Guys. Not as bad as me, unfortunately.' Jack balled his T-shirt in his hand and tossed it towards his rucksack. 'The Somalians decided to give me something to remember them by.'

Jack sat on the edge of the bed, bent over and, using one hand and taking short breaths, undid the laces of his scuffed trainers. When they were loose enough, he toed them off.

Jack sent her a crooked grin that didn't fool her for a second. 'As you can see, all in working order.'

'Anything broken?'

Jack shook his head. 'I think they bruised a rib or two. I'll live. I've had worse.'

Ellie shook her head. 'Worse than this?'

'A bullet does more damage,' Jack said, standing up and slowly walking to the *en-suite* bathroom.

Ellie gasped. 'You've been *shot*?'

'Twice. Hurts like a bitch.'

Hearing water running in the basin, Ellie abruptly sat down. She was instantly catapulted back in time to when she'd spent a holiday with Mitchell and his mother—her grandmother Ginger—in London when she was fourteen. He'd run to Bosnia to do a 'quick report' and come back in an ambulance plane, shot in the thigh. He'd lost a lot of blood and spent a couple of days in the ICU.

It wasn't her favourite holiday memory.

Jack didn't seem to be particularly fazed about his injuries; like Mitchell he probably fed on danger and adrenalin... it made no sense to her.

'You do realise that you could've died?' Ellie said, wondering why she even bothered.

Jack walked back into the room, dried his face on a towel he'd picked up from the bed and shrugged. 'Nah. They were lousy shots.'

Ellie sighed. She couldn't understand why getting hurt, shot or putting yourself in danger wasn't a bigger deterrent. She knew that Jack, like her father, preferred to work solo, shunning the protection of the army or the police, wanting to get the mood on the streets, the story from the locals. Such independence ratcheted up the danger quotient to the nth degree.

There was a reason why war reporting was rated as one of the most dangerous jobs in the world. Were they dedicated to the job or just plain stupid? Right now, seeing those bruises, she couldn't help but choose *stupid*.

'So, before I go...do you want something to eat?'

Jack shook his head. 'The pilot stood me a couple of burgers at the airport. Thanks, though.'

'Okay, well, I'll be downstairs if you need anything...' Ellie couldn't resist dropping her eyes to sneak a peek at his stomach. As she'd suspected, he had a gorgeous six-pack—but her attention was immediately diverted by a mucky, bloody sanitary pad held in place by the waistband of his jeans.

She pursed her lips. 'And that?'

Jack glanced down and winced. With an enviable lack of modesty he flipped open the top two buttons of his jeans, pulled down the side of his boxer shorts and pulled off the pad. Ellie winced at the seeping, bloody, six-inch slash that bisected the artistic knife and broken heart tattoo on his hip.

'Not too bad,' Jack said, after prodding the wound with a blunt-edged finger.

'What is that? A knife wound?'

'Mmm. Psycho bastards.'

'You sound so calm,' Ellie said, her eyes wide.

'I *am* calm. I'm always calm.'

Too calm, she thought. 'Jack, it needs stitches.'

'This is minor, Ellie.' Jack looked mutinous. 'I'm going to give it a good scrub, slather it in the antiseptic I always carry with me and slap another pad on it.'

'Who uses sanitary pads for *this*?'

'It's an army thing and it serves the purpose. I'm an old hand at doctoring myself.'

Ellie sighed when Jack turned away to rummage in his rucksack. He pulled out another sanitary pad, stripped the plastic away and slapped the clean pad onto his still bleeding wound. She saw his stubborn look and knew that he'd made up his mind. If she couldn't get Jack to a hospital—he was six-two and built; how could she force him?—she'd have to trust him when he said that he was an old hand at patching himself up.

'When my bank cards arrive I'll go down to the pharmacy and get some proper supplies,' Jack told her.

Ellie sucked in a frustrated sigh. 'Give me a list of what you need and I'll run down and get it. I'll be back before you're finished showering.' She held up her hand. 'And, yes, you can pay me back.'

Jack looked hesitant and Ellie resisted the impulse to smack the back of his head. 'Jack, you need some decent medical supplies.'

Jack glared at the floor. She saw his broad shoulders dip in defeat before hearing his reluctant agreement. Within a minute he'd located a notebook from the side pocket of his rucksack and a pen, and he wrote in a strong, clear hand exactly what he wanted. He handed her the list and Ellie knew, by his miserable eyes, that he was embarrassed that he had to ask for her help. *Again.*

Men. Really…

The mobile in her pocket jangled and Ellie pulled it out, frowning at the unfamiliar number. Answering, she heard a low, distinctively feminine voice asking for Jack. Ellie's brows pulled together… How on earth could anyone know that Jack was with her? She had hardly completed that thought before realising that the jungle drums must be working well in the war journalists' world. Her father was spreading the news…

Ellie handed her mobile to Jack and couldn't help wondering who the owner of the low, subtly sexy voice was. Lover? Colleague? Friend?

'Hi, Ma.'

Or his mother. Horribly uncomfortable with the level of relief she felt on hearing that he was talking to his mother, Ellie scuttled from the room.

Jack lifted the mobile to his ear on an internal groan. He just wanted to go and lie down on that bed and sleep. Was that too much to ask? Really?

'I haven't been able to reach you for a week!' said his mother Rae in a semi-hysterical voice.

'Mum, we had an agreement. You only get to worry about me after you haven't spoken to me for three weeks.' Jack rubbed his forehead, actively trying to be patient. He understood her worry—after all that he'd put her and his father through how could he not?—but her over-protectiveness got very old, very quickly.

'Are you hurt?' his mother demanded curtly.

He wished he'd learnt to lie to her. 'Let me talk to Dad, Mum.'

'That means you're hurt. Derek! Jack's hurt!'

Jack heard her sob and she dropped the phone. His father's voice—an oasis of calm—crossed the miles.

'*Are* you hurt?'

'Mmm.'

'Where?'

Everywhere. There was no point whining about it. 'Couple of dents. Nothing major. Tell Mum to calm down to a mild panic.' Jack heard his mum gabbling in the background, listened through his father's reassurances and waited until his father spoke again.

'You mother says to please remind you to visit Dr Jance. Does she need to make an appointment for you?'

He'd forgotten that a check-up was due and he felt his insides contract. He did his best to forget what he'd gone through as a teenager, and these bi-yearly check-ups were reminders of those dreadful four years he'd spent as a slave to his failing heart. He tipped his head back in frustration when he heard Rae demand to talk to him again.

'Jack, the Sandersons contacted us last week,' she said in a rush.

Jack felt his heart contract and tasted guilt in the back of his throat. Abruptly he sat down on the edge of the bed. Brent Sanderson. He was alive because Brent had died. How could he *not* feel guilty? It was a constant—along with the feeling that he owed it to Brent to live life to the full, that living that way was the only way he could honour his brief life, the gift he'd been given...

'In six weeks it will be seventeen years since the op, and

Brent was seventeen when he died,' Rae said with a quaver in her voice.

She didn't need to tell him that. He knew *exactly* how long it had been. They'd both been seventeen when they'd swapped hearts.

'They want to hold a memorial service for him and have invited us…and you. We've said we'll go and I said that I'd talk to you.'

Jack stretched out, tucked a pillow behind his head and blew out a long stream of air. He tried not to dwell on Brent and his past—he preferred the *it happened; let's move on* approach— and he really, really didn't want to go. 'It's a gracious invitation but I'm pretty sure that they'd be happy if I didn't pitch up.'

'How can you say that?'

'Because it would be supremely difficult for them to see me walking around, fit and healthy, knowing that their son is six feet under, Mum!'

They'd given him the gift of their son's heart. He'd do anything to spare them further pain. And that included keeping his distance…

'They aren't like that and they want to meet you. You've avoided meeting them for years!'

'I haven't avoided them. It just never worked out.'

'I'll pretend to believe that lie if you consider coming to Brent's service,' Rae retorted.

His mother wasn't a fool. 'Mum, I'll see. I've got to go. I'll visit when I'm back in the UK.'

'You're not in the UK? Where are you?' Rae squawked.

Jack gritted his teeth. 'You're mollycoddling me, and you know it drives me nuts!'

'Well, your career drives *me* nuts! How can you, after fighting so hard for life, routinely put yourself in danger? It's—'

'Crazy and disrespectful to take such risks when I've been given another chance at life. I'm playing Russian Roulette with my life and you wish I'd settle down and meet a nice girl and give you grandchildren. Have I left anything out?'

'No,' Rae muttered. 'But I put it more eloquently.'

'Eloquent nagging is still nagging. But I do love you, you old bat. Sometimes.'

'Revolting child.'

'Bye, Ma,' Jack said, and disconnected the call.

He banged the mobile against his forehead. His parents thought that guilt and fear fuelled his daredevil lifestyle. It did—of course it did—but did that have to be a bad thing? They didn't understand—probably because he could never explain it—but playing it safe, sitting behind a desk in a humdrum job was, for him, a slow way to die. At fourteen he'd gone from being a healthy, rambunctious, sporty kid to a waif and a ghost, his time spent either in hospital rooms or at his childhood home. He'd just *existed* for more years than he cared to remember, and he'd vowed that when he had the chance of an active life he'd live it. Hard and fast. He wanted to do it all and see it all—to chase the thrills. For himself and for Brent. Being confined to one house, person or city would be his version of hell. His parents wanted him to settle down, but they didn't understand that he wouldn't settle down for anything or anyone. He had to keep moving—and working to feel alive.

Jack switched off the bedside light and stared up at the shadows on the ceiling, actively trying not to think about his past. As per normal, his job had thrown him a curveball and he'd landed up in a strange bed in a strange town. But, he thought as his eyes closed, he was very good at curveballs and strange situations, and meeting Mitch's dazzling daughter again was very much worth the detour.

On his second night in Ellie's spare room, Jack put aside the magazine he'd been reading, rolled onto his back and stared at the ceiling above his bed. The air-conditioning unit hummed softly and he could hear the croaky song of frogs in the garden, the occasional whistle of a cricket. It wasn't that late and his side throbbed.

Knowing that he wouldn't be able to sleep yet, he flipped back the sheet and stood up. After yanking on a pair of jeans he quietly opened the door and walked to the stairs. Navigating his way through the dark house, he walked into the front lounge, with its two big bay windows, leaned against the side wall and looked through the darkness towards the sea. Through the open windows he could hear the thud of waves hitting the beach and smell the brine-tinged air.

Ellie's distinctively feminine voice drifted through the bay window, so he pulled back the curtain. He looked out and watched her walk up the stairs to the veranda, mobile to her ear and one arm full of papers and files. She looked exhausted and he could see flour streaks on her open navy chef's jacket. Jack glanced at the luminous dial of his watch…ten-thirty at night was a hell of a time to be coming home from work.

'Ginger, my life is a horror movie at the moment.'

Ginger? Wasn't that Mitchell's mother? Ellie's Irish grandmother?

'Essentially I need Mum to come back but it's not fair to ask her. I'm chasing my tail on a daily basis, it's nearly month-end, I have payroll and I need to pay VAT this month. And I need to move the bakery but there's nowhere to move it to! And, to top it all, your wretched son has sent me a house guest!'

So she wasn't as sanguine about having him as a guest as she pretended to be. Jack watched as she balanced the stack of papers and two files on the arm of the Morris chair.

'No, he's okay,' Ellie continued. 'I've had worse.'

Only okay? He was going to have to work on that.

Ellie used her free hand to dig into her bag for her house keys and half turned, knocking the unstable pile with her hip.

The files tipped and the papers caught in the mild evening wind and drifted away.

'Dammit! Ginger—sorry, I have to go. I've just knocked something over.'

Ellie threw her mobile onto the seat of the Morris chair, then started to curse in Arabic. His mouth fell open. His eyes widened as the curses became quite creative, muddled and downright vulgar.

Jack thought that she could do with some help so he stepped over the sill of the low window directly onto the veranda and started to collect the bits of paper that were scattered all over the floor.

'Do you actually know what you're saying?' he demanded, when she stopped for ten seconds to take a breath.

Ellie sent him a puzzled look. 'Daughter of a donkey, son of a donkey, your mother is ugly, et cetera.'

Uh, no. Not even close. 'Do me a favour? Don't ever repeat any of those anywhere near an Arab, okay?'

Ellie slowly stood up and narrowed her eyes. 'They are rude, aren't they?'

He didn't need to respond because she'd already connected the dots.

'Mitchell! He taught me those when I was a kid.' It was so typical of Mitch's twisted sense of humour to teach his innocent daughter foul curse words in Arabic. 'I'm going to kill him! I take it you speak Arabic?'

'Mmm.' He'd discovered that he had a gift for languages while he was a teenager, when he'd been unable to do anything more energetic than read.

Ellie sent him a direct look. 'So, do you speak any other languages?'

Jack shrugged. 'Enough Mandarin to make myself understood. Some Japanese. I'm learning Russian. And Dari…'

'What's that?'

'Also known as Farsi, or Afghan Persian. Helpful, obviously, in Afghanistan.'

Ellie stared at him, seemingly impressed. 'That's incredible.'

Jack shrugged, uncomfortable with her praise. 'Lots of people speak second or third languages.'

'But not Farsi, Russian or Mandarin,' Ellie countered. 'I'm useless. I can barely spell in English.'

'I don't believe that.'

'You can ask Mitchell if you like. Nothing made him angrier than seeing my spelling test results,' Ellie quipped. 'Besides, English is a stupid language...their and there, which and witch, write, right, rite.'

'And another wright,' Jack added.

'You're just making that up,' she grumbled.

'I'm not. It's one of the few four-word homophones.' Jack's grin flashed. 'W.R.I.G.H.T. Someone who constructs or repairs things—as in a millwright.'

'Homophones? Huh.' Ellie heaved an exaggerated, forlorn sigh. 'Good grief, I'm sharing my house with a swot. What did I do to deserve that?'

Jack laughed, delighted. 'Life does throw challenges at one.'

After they'd finished collecting the papers Ellie sat down on the couch, rolling her head on her shoulders.

Jack sat on the low stone wall in front of her. 'Tough day?' he asked, conversationally.

Ellie slumped in the chair. 'Very. How can you tell?'

Jack lifted his hands. 'I heard you talking to your grandmother.'

'And how much did you hear?'

'You're pissed, you're stressed, something about having to move the bakery. You've had worse house guests than me.'

Even in the dim light he could see Ellie flush. 'Sorry.

Mitchell tends to use me as his own personal B&B… I didn't mean to make you feel unwelcome.'

'Am I?'

Ellie threw her hands up and sent him a miserable look. 'You're not. I'm more frustrated at Mitchell's high-handedness than at the actual reality of a house guest, if that makes sense.'

Jack nodded, hearing the truth in her statement, and relaxed. 'Mitch does have a very nebulous concept of the word *no*,' he stated calmly.

'And he's had twenty-eight years to perfect the art of manipulating me,' Ellie muttered. 'Again, that's not directed at you personally.'

Jack laughed. 'I get it, Ellie. Relax. Talking about relaxing…' Jack walked back into the house, found a wine rack and remembered that he'd seen a corkscrew in the middle drawer when he was looking for a bread knife earlier. He took the wine and two glasses back to the veranda. 'If I ever saw a girl in need of the stress-relieving qualities of alcohol, it's you.'

'If I have any of that I'll fall over,' Ellie told him, covering a yawn with her hand.

'A glass or two won't hurt.' Jack yanked the cork out, poured the Merlot and handed her a glass.

Ellie took the glass from him and took the first delicious sip. 'Yum. I could drink this all night.'

'Then it would definitely hurt when you wake up.' After a moment's silence, he succumbed to his curiosity. 'Tell me what that conversation was about.'

Ellie cradled the glass in her hand and eyed Jack across the rim. Shirtless, and with bare feet, he was a delectable sight for sore eyes at the end of a hectic day. 'You're very nosy.'

'I'm a journalist. It's a job requirement. Talk.'

She wanted to object, to tell him he was bossy—which he was—but she didn't. Couldn't. She needed someone to offload on and maybe it would be easier to talk to a stranger who was leaving... When *was* he leaving? She asked him.

Jack grinned. 'Not sure yet. Is it a problem if I stay for another night or two? I like your house,' he added, and Ellie's glass stopped halfway to her mouth.

'You want to stay because you like my house? Uh...why?'

'Well, apart from the fact that we haven't yet talked about Mitch, it's...restful.' Jack lifted a bare muscled shoulder. 'It shouldn't be with such bright colours but it is. I like hearing the sea, the wind coming off the mountain. I like it.'

'Thanks.' Ellie took a sip of wine. It would be nice to know if he liked her as much as he liked her house, but since she'd only spent a couple of hours with him what could she expect? Ellie couldn't believe she was even thinking about him like that. It was so high school—and she had bigger problems than thinking about boys and their nice bodies and whether they liked her back.

Jack topped up her wine glass and then his. He squinted at the label on the bottle. 'This is a nice wine. Maybe I should go on a wine-tasting tour of the vineyards.'

'That's a St Sylve Merlot. My friend Luke owns the winery and his fiancée Jess does the advertising for the bakery.'

'And we're back full circle to your bakery. Talk.' Jack boosted himself up so that he sat cross-legged on the stone wall, his back to a wooden beam.

His eyes rested on her face and they encouraged her to trust him, to let it out, to *talk* to him...

Damn, he was good at this.

Ellie's smile was small and held a hint of pride. 'Pari's Perfect Cakes—'

'Who was Pari, by the way?' Jack interrupted her.

'My grandmother. It was her bakery originally. It means "fairy" in India.' Pain flashed in her eyes. 'As you saw, Pari's is a retail bakery and delicatessen, with a small coffee shop.'

'It doesn't look like a small operation. How do you manage it all?'

'Well, that's one of my problems. We have two shifts of bakers who make the bread and the high turnover items, and Merri, my best friend, used to do the specialised pastries. I do special function cakes. My mum did the books, stock and payroll and chivvied us along. It all worked brilliantly until recently.'

Jack held up his hand. 'Wait—back up. Special function cakes? Like wedding cakes?'

'Sure—but any type of cakes.' Ellie picked up her mobile and quickly pressed some buttons. 'Look.'

Jack put his glass of wine next to him on the wall and leaned forward to take the device. He flipped through the screens, looking at her designs.

'These are amazing, Ellie.'

'Thank you.'

He looked down at her mobile again. 'I can't believe that you made a cake that looks exactly like a crocodile leather shoe.'

'Not any shoe—a Christian Louboutin shoe.'

Jack looked puzzled. 'A what?'

'Great designer of shoes?' Ellie shook her head.

'Sorry, I'm more of a trainers and boots kind of guy.' Jack handed the mobile back to her. 'So, what went wrong at the bakery?'

'Not wrong, exactly. Merri had a baby and started her maternity leave. She told me yesterday that she's extending it.'

'She *told* you?'

Ellie heard the disbelief in Jack's voice and quickly responded, 'She asked…suggested…kind of.'

Jack frowned. 'And you said yes?'

'I didn't have much of a choice. She doesn't need to work and I didn't want to push her into a corner and…'

'And you couldn't say no,' Jack stated with a slight shake of his head.

'And I suppose you've never said yes when you wanted to say no?' Ellie demanded.

'I can't say that I've never done that. I generally say what I mean and I never let anyone push me around...'

'She didn't...' Ellie started to protest but fell silent when she saw the challenging expression on Jack's face. This wasn't an argument she would win because—well, she *did* get pushed around. Sometimes. Would he understand if she told him that, as grown-up and confident as she now was, she still had intense periods of self-doubt? Would he think her an absolute drip because her habit reaction was to make sure everyone around her was happy? And if they were they would love her more?

'What else?' Jack asked, after taking a sip of wine.

Ellie swirled the wine in her glass. 'My mother has taken a year's sabbatical. She always had this dream to travel, so for her fiftieth birthday I gave her a year off. A grand gesture that I am deeply regretting now. But she's in seventh heaven. She's got a tattoo, has had at least one affair and has put dreadlocks in her hair.'

'You sound more upset about the dreadlocks than the affair.'

Ellie shrugged. 'I just want her home—back in the bakery. She managed the place, did the paperwork and the accounts, the payroll and just made the place run smoothly.'

And while I say that I want everyone to be happy I frequently resent the fact that she left, that Merri left—okay, temporarily—and I have to carry on, pick up the pieces. When do I get to step away?

'So, you're stressed out and doing the work of two other people?'

'And none of it well,' Ellie added, her tone sulky.

Jack smiled. 'Now, tell me about having to move.'

Ellie gave him the rundown and cradled her glass of wine in her hands. She felt lighter for telling him, grateful to hand over the problem just for a minute. She didn't expect him to solve the problem, but just being able to verbalise her emotions was liberating.

And, amazingly, Jack just listened—without offering a solution, a way to fix it. If he wasn't ripped and didn't have a stubble-covered jaw and a very masculine package she could almost pretend he was a girlfriend. He listened like one. *Keep dreaming*, she thought. Not in a million years could she pretend that Jack was anything but a hard-ass—literally and metaphorically—one hundred per cent male.

Ellie yawned, curled her legs up and felt her eyes closing. She felt Jack take the glass from her hand and forced her eyes open.

'Come on. You're dead on your feet.' Jack took her hands and hauled her up.

He'd either overestimated her weight or underestimated his strength because she flew into his chest and her hands found themselves splayed across his pecs, warm and hard and...*ooooh*... Her nose was pressed against his sternum. She sucked him in along with the breath she took...man-soap, man-smell...*Jack*.

She felt tiny next to his muscled frame as his hands loosely held her hips, fingers on the top of her bottom. A lazy thumb stroked her hipbone through the chef's jacket and Ellie felt lust skitter along her skin. She slowly lifted her head and looked at him from beneath her eyelashes. There was half a smile on his face, yet his eyes were dark and serious...

He lifted his hand and gently rested his fingers on her lips. She knew what he was thinking...that he wanted to kiss her. Intended to kiss her.

Ellie just looked up at him with big eyes. She felt like a deer frozen in the headlights, knowing that she should pull away, unable to do so. She could feel his hard body against hers, his rising chest beneath her palms. His arms were strong, his shoulders broad. She felt feminine and dainty and…judging by the amount of action in his pants…desired.

He stepped back at the same time as she pushed him away. She shoved her hands into her hair, squinting at him in the moonlight. This was crazy… She was adult enough to recognise passion that could be perilous—wild, erratic and swamping. But lust, as she'd learnt, clouded her thinking and stripped away her practicality. Lust, teamed with the brief emotional connection she'd felt earlier, when she'd opened up a little to him, had her running scared.

Bum magnet.

Jack cocked his head. 'So, not a good idea, huh?'

Ellie bit her lip. 'Really not.'

Jack lifted a shoulder and sent her a rueful smile. 'Okay. But you're a very tempting sight in the moonlight so maybe we should go in before I try to change your mind.'

When she didn't move, Jack reached out and ran a thumb over her bottom lip.

'You can't just stand there looking up at me with those incredible eyes, Ellie. Go now, before I forget that I am, actually, a good guy. Because we both know that I could persuade you to stay.'

Ellie erred on the side of caution and fled inside.

CHAPTER THREE

EVERY TIME HIS foot slapped the pavement a hot flash of pain radiated from his cut and caused every atom in his body to ache. It was the morning after almost kissing Ellie, and he was dripping with perspiration and panting like a dog.

He placed his hand against his side and winced. He shouldn't be running, he knew that, but running was his escape, his sanity, his meditation. And, thinking about things he shouldn't be doing, kissing Ellie was top of the list. Why was he so tempted by his blue-eyed hostess? Especially since he'd quickly realised that she wasn't into simple fun and games, wasn't someone he could play with and leave, wasn't a superficial type of girl. And he didn't do anything *but* superficial.

But there was something about her that tweaked his interest and that scared the hell out of him.

He started to climb the hill back home and—dammit! He *hurt*. Everywhere. *Suck it up and stop being a pansy*, he told himself. *You've had a heart transplant—a cut and a beating is nothing compared to that!*

Jack pushed his wet hair off his forehead and looked around. Good Lord, it was beautiful here...the sea was aqua and hunter-green, cerulean-blue in places. White-yellow sand. Eclectic, interesting buildings. He was lucky to be here, to see this stunning part of the world...

Brent never would.

Brent never would. The phrase that was always at the back of his mind. Intellectually he knew it came from survivor's guilt—the fact that he was alive because Brent was dead. In the first few months and years after the op he'd been excited to be able to do whatever he wanted, but he knew that over the past couple of years the burden of guilt he felt had increased.

Why? Why wasn't he coming to terms with what had happened? Why wasn't it getting easier? The burden of the responsibility of living life for someone else had become heavier with each passing year.

The mobile he'd borrowed from Ellie jangled in his pocket and he came to an abrupt stop. Thankfully he was back at Ellie's place. He didn't think he could go any further.

'So, what do you think of Ellie?' Mitchell said when Jack pushed the green button on the mobile and held it up to a sweaty ear.

'Uh…she's fine. Nice.'

She was…in the best sense of the word. A little highly strung, occasionally shy. Sensitive, overwhelmed and struggling to hide it. Sexy as hell.

'So, have you talked to her about me yet?'

Jack lifted his eyebrows at Mitchell's blatant narcissism and felt insulted on Ellie's behalf.

'Ellie's well, but over-worked. Her bakery is fabulous; she's running it on her own as her mum is overseas,' he said, his tone coolly pointed as he answered the questions Mitch should have thought to ask.

'Yeah, yeah… But how far have you got with the book? Did you get my e-mail? I sent it just now.'

His verbal pricks hadn't dented Mitchell's self-absorbed hide. Jack wished he could reach into the phone and slap Mitchell around the head. Had he always been so self-involved? Why hadn't he noticed before? Jack sighed and looked at his watch. It wasn't quite seven yet. Far too early to deal with Mitchell.

'Firstly, my laptop is still in Somalia, and, contrary to what you think, I don't hover over my laptop waiting for your e-mails,' Jack said as he made his way into the house, up the steps and into his room. Jack heard Mitchell splutter with annoyance but continued anyway. 'And, by the way, why did you teach Ellie such crude Arabic insults when she was a little girl? They are, admittedly, funny as hell, because she gets them all mixed up, but really…'

'She still remembers those, huh?'

Jack pulled his T-shirt over his head, walked into the bathroom and dropped it into the laundry basket. Yanking a bottle of pills out of his toiletry bag, he shook the required daily dosage into his hand, tossed them into his mouth and used his hand as a cup to get water into his mouth.

Those pills were his constant companions, his best friends. He loved them and loathed them in equal measure.

'And why did you tell Ellie that I'm *helping* you write this book?'

As per normal, Mitch ignored the questions he didn't want to answer. 'So, have you spoken to Ellie yet about *me*?'

'No. The woman works like a demon. I haven't managed to pin her down yet.' Jack frowned. 'And she's not exactly jumping for joy at the prospect.'

Mitchell didn't answer for a minute. 'Ellie and I have had our ups and downs…'

Ups and downs? Jack suspected that they'd had a lot more than that.

'She didn't like me being away so much,' Mitchell continued.

Jack rolled his eyes at that understatement. As he walked over to the window his eye was caught by two frames lying against the wall, behind the desk in the corner. Pulling them out, he saw that they were two photographs of a younger Ellie and a short blond man in front of the exclusive art gallery

Grigson's in London. Jack asked Mitch who the man in the photograph was.

'Someone she was briefly engaged to—five, six years ago.' Jack heard Mitchell light a cigarette. 'She wanted to get married. He didn't.'

Jack felt a spurt of sympathy for the guy. He'd had two potential-to-become-serious relationships in the past ten years and they'd both ended in tears on his partner's face and frustration on his. They'd wanted him to settle down. He equated that to being locked in a cage. He'd liked them, enjoyed them, but not enough to curtail his time or freedom for them.

'Jack? You still there?' Mitchell asked in his ear.

'Sure.'

'I spoke to most of our commissioning editors today and told them that you've been injured. They will leave you alone for three weeks. Unless something diabolical happens—then all bets are off,' Mitchell stated.

That was enough to yank his attention back, and fast. Jack felt his molars grinding. 'You do know I get very annoyed when you interfere in my life, Mitchell?'

Mitchell, never intimidated, just laughed. 'Oh, get over yourself! You haven't taken any time off in two years and we all know that leads to burnout. You've been flirting with it for a while, boyo.'

'Crap.'

'If you don't believe me, check your last couple of stories. You've always been super-fair and unemotional, but there's a fine line between being unemotional and robotic, Jack. You are drifting over that line. Losing every bit of empathy is every bit as problematic as having too much.'

'Again...crap,' Jack muttered, but wondered if Mitchell had a point. He remembered being in Egypt six weeks ago and watching a paramedic work on a badly beaten protester.

He'd been trying to recall if he'd paid his gas bill. Maybe he was taking the role of observer a bit too far.

'I'm going to courier you my notebooks, my diaries,' Mitchell told him. 'Get some sun, drink some wine. But if you don't get cracking on my book…'

Mitch repeated the most gruesome of Ellie's Arabic curses from the night before and Jack winced.

Jack tossed the mobile onto the bed, slapped his hands on his hips and stared at the photographs he'd replaced against the wall. Ellie… Maybe he should think about leaving, and soon. Almost kissing her last night had been a mistake…

Sure, he was attracted to her—she was stunning; what man wouldn't be? If she was a different type of girl then he could have her, enjoy her and then leave. Unfortunately he wasn't just physically attracted, and he *knew* that mental attraction was a sticky quagmire best avoided. And, practically, while Mitch wouldn't win any Father of the Year awards he might not approve of them hooking up, and he didn't want to cause friction between him and his subject, mentor and colleague.

Ellie, with her cosy house and settled lifestyle—the absolute opposite of what he liked and needed—was also far more fascinating than he generally liked his casual partners to be. Because fascination always made leaving so much harder than it needed to be.

'Morning.'

Ellie jumped as he entered the kitchen, looking tough and rugged and a whole lot of sexy. She could see that his hair had deep red highlights in the chocolate-brown strands. He'd scraped off his beard and the violet stripes under his eyes were almost gone. He did, however, still have that glint in his eyes—the one that said he wanted to tear up the bedcovers with her.

Ellie cursed when she felt heat rising up her neck.

'Can I get some coffee?'

Jack's question yanked her out of her reverie and she nodded, reaching for a mug above the coffee machine to give her hands something to do.

'You're up early,' she said when she'd found her voice.

Jack took the cup she handed him and leaned against the counter, crossing his legs at the ankles. 'Mmm. Good coffee. I went for a run this morning along the beachfront. It was… absolutely amazing. It's such a beautiful part of the world.'

'It is, but should you be exercising yet?'

'I'm fine.'

Yeah, she didn't think so—but it was his body, his choice, his pain. Ellie shook her head, picked up her own cup and sipped. She echoed his stance and leaned against the counter. Tension swirled between them and Ellie thought she could almost see the purple elephant sitting in the room, eyebrow cocked and smirking.

Maybe it would be better just to get it out there and in the open. But she couldn't get the words out… How she wished she could be one of those upfront, ballsy girls who just said what they felt and lived with the consequences.

She was still—especially when it came to men—the shy, awkward girl she'd been as a teenager.

Jack's eyebrows pulled together. 'The wariness is back in your eyes. Why?'

'Uh…last night. Um—' Oh, great. Now her tongue was on strike.

Jack, no slouch mentally, immediately picked up on what she was trying to say. 'The kiss that never happened?'

Ellie blushed. 'Mmm.'

'Yeah—sorry. I said I wouldn't hit on you and I did.' His tone didn't hold a hint of discomfort or embarrassment.

Ellie bit the inside of her lip. That wasn't what she'd expected him to say. Actually, she had no idea *what* she'd thought he'd say. The purple elephant grinned. 'I just… It's just that…'

Jack scratched the underside of his jaw and looked at her with his gold-flecked eyes. 'Relax, Ellie,' he said. 'It won't happen again...'

Ellie lifted her eyes to meet his and swallowed. In his she could read desire and lust and a healthy dose of amusement... as if he could read her thoughts, understand her confusion.

'Well...' he drawled as his finger gently pushed back a strand of hair that had fallen over her left eye. 'Maybe I should clarify that. I'll try not to let it happen again. You're very, very kissable, Ellie Evans.'

Ellie's eyes narrowed. She might not be the most assertive person in the world but that didn't mean he could look at her with those hot eyes and that smirky expression. Or presume that whatever happened between them would be solely *his* decision. Ellie narrowed her eyes, gripped the finger that had come to rest on her cheek and bent it backwards.

Hating personal confrontation, but knowing she needed to do this for the sake of her self-respect, she took a deep breath and forced the words out. 'There's only one person who will decide what happens between us and that will be me—not you.'

Jack grimaced and yanked his index finger out of her grip. He shook his finger out and sent her a surprised look. But, gratifyingly, there was an admiration in those hazel eyes that hadn't been there before and she liked seeing it there.

Jack sent her an approving smile. 'Good for you. I was wondering if you could stand up for yourself.'

Ellie narrowed her eyes. 'When I need to. No casual kissing.'

'Can we do *non*-casual kiss...?' Jack held up his hands at her fulsome glare. 'Joke! Peace!'

'Ha-ha.' Ellie rolled her shoulders. 'Would you like to go to work for me today?' she asked, blatantly changing the subject. 'I could do with a day off.'

'Okay—except my sugar icing and sculpting skills are sadly lacking. I can, however, make a mean red velvet cake.'

Ellie lowered her cup in surprise. 'You can bake?'

Ellie thought she saw pain flicker in his eyes. When he spoke his voice was gruff.

'Yes, I can bake. Normal stuff. Not pastries and croissants and fancy crap.'

Fancy crap? Well, that was one way to describe her business.

'Who taught you?' Ellie asked, openly curious.

'My mother.'

Ellie lifted her eyebrows. 'Sorry, I can't quite picture you baking as a kid. On bikes, on a sports field, camping—yes. Baking…no.'

Jack placed his cup on the counter and turned his face away from her. 'Well, it wasn't from choice.'

He sipped his coffee and when he looked at her again his face and eyes were devoid of whatever emotion she'd seen. Fear? Anger? Pain? A combination of all three?

This time it was Jack's turn to change the subject. 'So—breakfast. What are we having?'

Ellie looked at her watch and shook her head. 'No time. I need to go. I was supposed to be at work an hour ago.'

Jack shook his head. 'You should eat.'

'I'll grab something at the bakery.'

Well, she'd try to, but she frequently forgot. There just wasn't time most days. Ellie sighed. One of these days she'd have to start eating properly and sleeping more, but it wouldn't be any time soon. Maybe when Merri came back she could ease off a bit…but she probably wouldn't.

After all, she had a business to save.

Ellie looked at Jack, who was pulling eggs and bacon out of her fridge. Her mouth started to water. She'd kill for a proper fry-up…

Ellie pulled her thoughts away from food. 'So, I've given you keys to the house and I've just paid the deposit for you to hire a car. It should be delivered by eight so you won't be confined to the house any more.'

'The receipt for the deposit?' Jack sent her a level look.

Ellie rolled her eyes. He was insistent that she kept receipts for everything she spent so that he could repay her. 'In the hollow back of the wooden elephant on the hall table. With all the others.'

The annoying man wouldn't even allow her to buy milk or bread without asking for a receipt.

'Thanks.'

Jack slit open the pack of bacon and Ellie whimpered. She really, really didn't have time. She picked up her keys and bag, holding her chef's jacket in one hand.

'Pop down to the bakery later. I'll show you around. If you want to,' she added hastily.

Jack's smile had her melting like the gooey middle of her luscious chocolate brownies.

'I'll do that. See you later, then.'

Ellie bravely resisted the arc of sexual awareness that shimmered between them and sighed as she walked out of the kitchen.

In your dreams, Ellie. Because that was the only place making love to Jack was going to happen.

And even there her heart wasn't welcome to come to the party. Her heart, she'd decided a long time ago, wasn't allowed to party with *anyone* any more.

Later, dressed in denim shorts, flip-flops and an easy navy tee, Jack slipped through the front door of Pari's and looked over Ellie's business.

There were café-style tables outside, giving patrons the most marvellous view of the beach while they sipped their coffee and ate their muffins, and more wrought-iron tables inside, strategically placed between tables piled with preserves and organic wines, ten different types of olive oil and lots of other jars and tins of exotic foods with names he barely recognised. The décor was bohemian chic—he'd noticed that before—and all effortlessly elegant. Huge glass display fridges held a wide variety of pastries and cakes, and in another layer thick pink hams, haunches of rare roast beef and dark sausages.

It looked inviting and happy, and there was a line of people three deep at the wide counter, waiting to be served. The place was rocking, obviously extremely popular, and Jack suddenly realised what effort would be needed to move the bakery. If Ellie could find a place to move it to...

'Jack!'

Jack whipped his head up and saw Ellie approaching a table in the back corner of the room, a bottle of water in her hand. A good-looking couple sat at the table and Ellie motioned him over. Jack threaded his way through tables and people and ended up at the table, where a fourth chair was unoccupied.

'Paula and Will—meet my friend Jack. Take a seat, Jack,' Ellie said.

After shaking hands with Will, Jack pulled out the chair and sat down.

'I'm just about to chat to them about their wedding cake, but before we start does anyone want coffee?' Ellie continued.

Jack wasn't sure why he was sitting in on a client consultation, but since he didn't have anything better to do decided to go with the flow. He ordered a double espresso and noticed that Will was frowning at him.

'Do I know you?' Will asked, puzzled.

This was one of the things he most liked about Cape Town—the fact that people hardly recognised him. While he wasn't famous enough to attract paparazzi attention in the UK, his face was recognisable enough to attract some attention.

'I have one of those faces,' he lied.

Ellie sent him a grin. 'I'm just going to run through some ideas with Will and Paula, then I'll show you around.'

She placed her notebook on the table and switched into work mode, outwardly confident. Jack listened as the couple explained why they now wanted a Pari's cake—their cake designer had let them down at the last moment—and watched, amazed, as Ellie took their rather vague ideas and transformed them into a quickly sketched but brilliantly drawn concept cake. He sampled various types of cake along with the couple, and when they asked for his opinion confirmed that he liked the Death by Chocolate best. Though the carrot ran a close second. Or maybe the fudge…

If he hung around the bakery more often Jack decided he'd have to add another couple of miles to his daily run to combat the calories and the cholesterol.

Ellie watched her clients go as she gathered her papers and shoved a pencil into the messy knot of hair behind her head.

'Today is Monday. Their wedding is on Saturday. I'm going to have to do some serious juggling to get it done for them.' Ellie rubbed her hand over her eyes.

'So why are you doing it, then?' Jack asked, curious.

'They are a sweet couple, and a wedding cake is important,' Ellie replied.

'Sweet? No. But they sure are slick.'

Ellie looked puzzled. 'What do you mean?'

She might be confident about her work but she was seriously naïve when it came to reading people, instinctively choosing to believe that people put their best foot forward.

Jack leaned his forearms on the table and shook his head. 'El, they were playing you.'

'What are you talking about?'

'They decided to come to you for their wedding cake— but it wasn't because their cake designer let them down. They knew there was no chance you'd make their cake at such late notice if they didn't have a rock-solid reason and they appealed to the romantic in you.'

'But why would you think that? I thought they were perfectly nice and above-board.'

'She doesn't blink—at all—when she lies, and his eyes slide to the right. Trust me, they were playing you.'

'Huh...' Ellie wrinkled her nose. 'Are you sure?'

Of course he was. He'd interviewed ten-year-olds with a better ability to lie. 'So, what are you going to do?'

Ellie stood up and shrugged. 'Make them their cake, of course. Let's go.'

Of course she was. Jack sighed as he followed her to the back of the bakery. She was going to produce a stunning, complicated cake in five days and their guests would be impressed, not knowing how she'd juggled her schedule to fit it in.

'I'm beginning to suspect you're a glutton for punishment,' Jack told Ellie as she pushed through the stable door leading to the back of the bakery. And a sucker too. But he kept that thought to himself.

She threw a look at him above her shoulder. 'Maybe—but did you notice that they didn't ask for a price?'

He hadn't, actually.

'And that order form they signed—at the bottom it states that there is a twenty-five per cent surcharge for rush jobs. Pure profit, Jack.'

Well, maybe not so much of a sucker.

Ellie walked over to a stainless steel table and tossed her sketchpad onto it. She scowled at the design they'd decided on. 'There's a standard surcharge for rush jobs,' she admitted. 'But I really don't need the extra profit.'

'And now you're angry because they played you?' Jack commented.

'I was totally sucked in by Paula's big blue eyes, the panic I saw on her face. Will played his part perfectly as well, trying to reassure her while looking at me with those *help me* eyes!'

'They were good. Not great, but good.'

'*Arrgh!* I need the added pressure of making a wedding cake in five days like I need a hole in my head!'

'So call them up and tell them you can't do it,' Jack suggested.

That would mean going back on her word, and she couldn't do that. 'I can't. And, really, couldn't you have given me a heads-up *before* I agreed to make their damn cake?'

Jack cocked his head. 'How?'

'I don't know! You're the one who is supposed to be so street-wise and dialed-in... Couldn't you have whispered in my ear? Kicked my foot? Written me a damn note?'

Jack's lips quirked. 'My handwriting is shocking.'

'It is not. I've seen your writing!' Ellie shoved her hands into her hair. Her shoulders slumped. 'Useless man.'

'So I've been told.' He reached out and laid a hand on her shoulder, his expression suddenly serious. 'Sorry. It never occurred to me to interfere.'

She looked at him, leaning back against the wall, seemingly relaxed. But his eyes never stopped moving... He hadn't said anything to her because he was an observer. He didn't get involved in a situation; he just commentated on it after the fact. She couldn't blame him. It was what he did. What journalists did.

She would have appreciated a heads-up, though. *Dammit.*

Ellie heard a high-pitched whistle and snapped her head up, immediately looking at the back section of the bakery, where the production area flowed into another room. Elias, one of her head bakers, stood at the wide entrance and jerked his head. Something in his body language had Ellie moving forward, and she reached her elderly staff member at the same time Jack did.

'What's wrong, Elias?' Ellie asked when she reached him.

Ellie felt Jack's hand on her lower back and was glad it was there.

Elias spoke in broken English and Ellie listened carefully. Before she had time to take in his words, never mind the implications, Jack was also demanding to know what the problem was.

'One of the industrial mixers is only working at one speed and the other one has stopped altogether,' she explained.

'That's not good,' Jack said.

'It's a disaster! We have orders coming out of our ears and we need cake. *Dammit!* Nothing happens in the bakery without the mixers... Elias, how did this happen?'

Elias shifted on his feet and stared at a point behind her head. 'I did tell you, Miss Ellie...the mixers...they need service. Did tell you...bad noise.'

Ellie scrubbed her face with her hands. He was right. He *had* told her—numerous times—but she'd been so busy, feeling so overwhelmed, and the mixers had been working. It had been on her list of things to do but it had kept getting shoved to the bottom when, really, it should have been at the top.

Ellie placed her hands over her face again and shook her head. What was she going to do?

When she eventually dropped her hands she saw that Elias was walking out of earshot. Jack had obviously signalled that they needed some privacy. He placed his hands on the mixer and lifted his eyebrows at Ellie.

'Dropped the ball on this one, didn't you?' he remarked.

Ellie glared at him, her blue eyes laser-bright. 'In between juggling the orders and paying the staff and placing orders for supplies, I somehow forgot to schedule a service for the mixers! Stupid me.' She folded her arms across her chest as she paced the small area between them.

'It was, actually, since this is the heartbeat of your business.'

Did he think she didn't know that? 'I messed up. I get it... It's something I'm doing a lot of lately.'

'Stop feeling sorry for yourself and start thinking about how you're going to fix the problem,' Jack snapped.

She felt the instinctive urge to slap him...slap *something*.

'You can indulge in self-pity later, but right now your entire production has stopped and you're wasting daylight.'

His words shocked some sense into her, but she reserved the right to indulge in some hysterics later. 'I need to get some-one here to fix these mixers...' Ellie saw him shake his head and she threw up her hands. 'What have I said wrong now?'

'Priorities, Ellie. What are you going to do about your or-ders?'

'You mean the mixers,' Ellie corrected him.

Jack shook his head and reached for the paper slips that were stuck on a wooden beam to the right of the mixers. 'No, I mean the orders. Prioritise the orders and get...what was his name...Elias...to start hand-mixing the batter for the cakes that are most urgent.'

That made sense, Ellie thought, reluctantly impressed.

Ellie took the slips he held out and a pen and quickly pri-oritised the orders. 'Okay, that's done. I'll get him working on these.'

Jack nodded and looked at the mixers. 'Are these under guarantee or anything?'

'No. Why?'

'Got a toolbox?'

'A toolbox? Why? What for?'

'While Elias starts the hand-mixing I'll take a look at these mixers. I know my way around machines and motors. It's prob-ably just a broken drive belt or a stripped gear.'

'Where on earth would you have learnt about machines and motors?' Ellie demanded, bemused.

'Ellie, I spend a good portion of my life in Third World

countries, on Third World roads, using Third World transportation. I've broken down more times in more crappy cars than you've made wedding cakes. Since I'm not the type to hang about waiting for someone else to get things working, I get stuck in. I can now, thanks to the tutelage of some amazing bush mechanics, fix most things.'

Ellie shut her flapping mouth and swallowed. 'Okay, well... uh...there's a basic toolbox in the storeroom and a hardware store down the road if you need anything else.'

Jack put his hands on his hips. 'And get on that phone and get someone here to service those mixers. I might be able to get them running but they'll still need a service.'

Ellie looked at him, baffled at this take-charge Jack. 'Jack—thank you.'

'Get one of the staff to bring me that toolbox, will you?' Jack crouched on his haunches at the back of one of the machines and started to work off the cover that covered the mixer's motor. 'Hell, look at this motor! It's leaking oil...it's clogged up...when was this damn thing last serviced?'

Ellie, who thought that Jack wouldn't appreciate hearing that she hadn't the faintest clue, decided to scarper while she could and left Jack cursing to himself.

CHAPTER FOUR

ELIAS LAUGHED WHEN Jack messed up the traditional African handshake—again—and slapped him on the shoulder. 'We'll teach you yet, *mlungu*.'

'Ma-lun-goo?' Jack tested the word out on his tongue.

'"White man" in Xhosa,' said the old Xhosa baker.

'Ah.' Jack stared at Elias and a slow grin crossed his face. 'I heard you talking Xhosa earlier. I love the clicking sound you make. If I were staying I would want to learn Xhosa.'

'If you stay...' Elias grinned '...I teach you.'

'There's a deal,' Jack said, before bidding him goodnight and turning back to the rear entrance of the bakery.

Ellie looked up as he walked towards her and ran the back of her hand over her forehead. 'Bet you're regretting ambling down the hill this morning,' she said with a grateful smile.

'It's been an...interesting day,' Jack said, conscious of a dull headache behind his eyes. 'A baptism by grease, flour, sugar and baking powder...'

'I never expected you to help with either the fixing or the mixing, but thank you.'

He'd resurrected one of the mixers, and when a part arrived for the other mixer in the morning he'd have that up and running within an hour. While he'd been working on the mixers he'd watched Elias and his assistant falling further and further behind on the orders, and had instantly become their best friend when he'd got the one mixer working.

'Elias really battled physically to do that hand-mixing.'

Ellie cocked her head. 'So that's why you stepped in to help him?'

He shrugged. 'I thought he was going to have a heart attack,' Jack admitted.

He'd mixed the batter for more than a hundred and twenty cupcakes and, under Elias's beady eye, also mixed the ingredients for two Pari's Paradise Chocolate cakes and more than a few vanilla sponge cakes. His shoulders ached and his biceps were crying out for mercy...

'He's stronger than he looks. He should've retired years ago, but he doesn't want to and I can't make him.' Ellie sighed. 'He's worked here since the day the bakery opened. It's his second home, and as long as he wants to work I'll let him. But maybe I should try to sneak in another assistant.'

'Sneak in?'

'It took me six months to get him to accept Gideon in his space.' Ellie grinned. 'He's a wonderful old gent but he has the pride of Lucifer. I'm surprised he let you do anything.'

'Yeah, but I *did* get his beloved mixer working.'

'That you did,' Ellie agreed. 'And I'm so grateful. You worked like a dog today.'

Which raised the question...*why* had he bust his gut to help this woman he barely knew? He was an observer, not a participator, and her bakery wouldn't have gone into bankruptcy if they'd waited for a mechanic to fix the mixers. But he'd felt compelled to step up and get stuck in, to help her, to...

Aargh! He must have taken a blow to the head along with the stabbing and the beating, because this wasn't how he normally rolled.

Jack, frustrated at not recognising himself, thought that he'd kill for a beer or two. He stood next to Ellie's table and leaned his shoulder against a wall, watching her work. She'd been in the bakery for nearly twelve hours and she was still working on another cake. The nightshift of two more bakers were starting their shift and Ellie would probably be there to see them off in the morning.

She might tend to panic when she hit a snag but he admired her work ethic.

And her legs... Who would've thought that a chef's jacket over shorts and long tanned legs could look so sexy? Jack swallowed, uneasy at the realisation that he wanted...no, *craved* her.

He'd never had this reaction to any woman before. Generally it was easy come, easy go. Nothing about Ellie so far had been easy, and he suspected that nothing would be. Jack shifted on his feet as desire flared. It would be easy to seduce her, but that would make leaving in a couple of days that much more complicated. Because somehow he instinctively knew that he couldn't treat her as a casual encounter. There was something about Ellie that tugged at him—some button that she pushed that made him suspect that this was a woman worth getting to know...

And that was more terrifying than being caught in the crossfire in any hot zone anywhere in the world. They had yet to make flak jackets to protect against emotional bullets.

Ellie looked up from the bare cake in front of her, which had been cut into the vague shape of a train and was covered in rough white icing. She sent him a tired smile. 'I'm wondering what I can give you for supper.'

Jack pried himself off the wall and walked away from the table she was working at. 'Something simple...let's order pizza.'

Ellie sighed and Jack saw relief flicker on her face.

'Okay. I just need to finish this and we can go home. Or you can go home and I'll follow in a bit.'

Jack hooked a stool with his foot and rolled it towards him, sinking down onto it with a groan. 'I'll wait for you.'

Ellie pulled out a ball of fire-engine-red dough from a container and started to knead it with competent hands.

Jack stretched out his legs. 'What are you making with that red dough?'

'It's not dough. It's fondant icing. It's for a train cake,' Ellie explained. She gestured to what looked like a big pasta roller on the table next to hers. 'It goes in there to flatten it out, then I'll drape it over the cake.'

'Does it have to be done tonight?'

'It should be. Luckily, I can make this in my sleep.' Ellie slapped her hand into the fondant and caught his look. 'What? Why are you looking at me like that?'

'I was just thinking about your business, what you do here.' He hadn't been, but he suspected that she wasn't ready to hear what he'd really been thinking…which involved her being naked and sliding all over him.

Oh, Lordy-be, there was that smile that made her womb vibrate. It was a combination of schoolboy naughtiness and sex-on-a-stick, and Ellie thought that stronger women than her would have trouble resisting it. She opened her mouth to ask what he was smiling about and practically bit her tongue in half to keep the words from escaping.

The hell of it was that while she'd initially thought that Jack might be all flash, today he had proved that he was more than just a hot body with a reasonably sharp brain. How many men of her acquaintance would have jumped in to help, tinkering with a motor and getting splattered with grease and then patiently mixing endless batches of batter—a thankless, back-breaking, horrible job to do by hand—without a word of complaint?

Ellie smoothed icing over the front of the train. The ability to give without asking for something in return, to jump into a situation and offer help when it was most needed, was a rare quality and unfortunately deeply attractive. Even more so than his hot body and masculine face.

Ellie's hand stilled on the cake as a panicked thought jumped into her head. She wanted him to go—now—tonight. She wanted him to go before she started imagining him in her bakery, in her life…before she started dreaming of a clear mind to keep her focused, a steady hand to prod her along, a hard body to touch and taste, then to curl up against at night.

Ellie fisted her hand and had to stop herself from punching the cake. She was suddenly ridiculously, outrageously angry at herself. Why was she even letting thoughts like those into her head? Considering what-ifs and maybes? Yes, he was a good-looking guy who gave her a buzz, a man nice enough to help her out, but there was no call to start thinking that he was anything more than a transient visitor. He was nothing but her father's friend, a brief acquaintance, and realistically she wasn't his type.

Oh, she was attractive enough for a brief fling, but she wasn't stupid enough to believe that she could ever be more than that. *Nobody will give up their freedom and time for monogamy with you…*

Jack had got up, rested his hand on her clenched fist and forced her fingers open.

Ellie twisted her lips and blew out a breath, but kept her eyes fixed on the cake.

'I think that's enough for now. We need pizza and beer and to chill,' he said.

Ellie pulled her hand out from beneath his and brushed her hair off her forehead with the tips of her fingers, leaving a trail of red icing on her forehead. 'This cake…'

'Will still be here tomorrow.' Jack took her hand again and pulled her away from the table. He leaned forward and his voice was low, seductive and sexy in her ear. 'Beer. Pizza.'

Ellie looked at the half-white, half-red train. Beer, pizza and conversation with an interesting man versus a stupid train cake...? No contest.

The woman amazed him, Jack thought. Twenty minutes ago Ellie had looked as if she was about to collapse, but now, sitting across from him at a table on the deck of an admittedly fake, slightly scruffy Italian restaurant, she looked sensational. She'd pulled her hair back into a sleek ponytail which highlighted her amazing cheekbones and painted her lips a glossy soft pink. She'd sorted out the smudged make-up around her eyes and she looked and smelled as if she'd just stepped out of a shower.

He, on the other hand, felt as if he'd spent the day hauling hay and cleaning out stables. He took a long sip of his beer and sighed as the bittersweet liquid slid down his throat. The night was warm, the surf was pounding, he had a beer in his hand and a pretty girl across the table from him.

The only scenario that sounded better was if he'd had pizza in his belly and the girl was naked beneath him.

'There's that smile again,' Ellie murmured.

'Huh? What smile?'

Ellie rested her chin in the palm of her hand. 'You get this secretive, naughty, sexy smile...'

'Sexy?' The light on the deck was muted but Jack grinned as he saw her blush.

'Yeah, well...anyway. So, I'm starving.' Ellie looked around, not trying to hide the fact that she was looking to change the subject. 'Where's that pizza?'

Jack decided to let her off the hook—mostly because flirting caused his pants to wake up and start doing its happy dance.

He looked around and narrowed his eyes. 'Have you had any more thoughts about the bakery?'

Ellie wrinkled her nose. She took a sip from her glass of wine and glanced at the ocean. 'Moving it, you mean?'

'Mmm.'

'I have an idea that I'm working on,' Ellie said mysteriously.

His curiosity was instantly aroused. 'You can't leave me hanging!' Jack protested when she didn't elaborate.

Ellie smiled. 'There might be a property that could work.'

'You don't have much time,' Jack pointed out.

'I know. Six months.'

Under the table Jack felt Ellie crossing her legs and he heard her sigh.

'I want to hyperventilate every time I think about it.'

'Call your mother and tell her to come home. It's her business too, El. You don't have to carry this load alone. Tell her about having to move. Tell her that you need help.'

'I can't, Jack. She's been working in that bakery for ever, never taking time off. Now she's living her dream and having such a blast. I can't ask her to give that up. Not just yet. And…and I feel that if I do I'm admitting failure. That I need my mummy to hold my hand.'

Jack shook his head. 'So you'd rather work yourself to a standstill, knocking yourself out, instead of asking your friend to come back to work and your mother to come back and help you?'

'Making sure that the people I love are happy is very important to me, Jack.'

'Not if it comes at too high a price to *you*.'

She'd inherited Mitchell's irritable, don't-mess-with-me stare.

'You're really sexy when you're irritated,' he commented idly, unfazed.

'I suspect that you can be annoying…' she paused for a beat and bared her teeth at him '…all the time.'

Jack grinned at her attempt to intimidate him. She looked as scary as a Siamese cat with an attitude disorder.

Ellie rubbed her temple with her fingertips. 'Can we not talk about the bakery tonight? I'd like to pretend it's not there for five minutes.'

Jack agreed and sighed in relief when he saw a waiter heading their way with pizzas. It wasn't a moment too soon. He thought his stomach was about to eat itself.

'So, why war reporting?' Ellie asked, when they'd both satisfied their immediate hunger.

Ellie wound a piece of stray cheese around her finger and popped it into her mouth. Jack nearly choked on the bite of pizza he'd just taken. *Hell...* He quickly swallowed and pulled his mind out of the bedroom. She was getting harder and harder to resist. And he *had* to resist her...mostly because she *was* so damn hard to resist.

Ellie repeating her question wiped the idea of sex—only temporarily, he was sure—from his brain.

'When I was about fifteen I watched a lot of news, and Mitch and other war reporters were reporting from Iraq. I was fascinated. They seemed larger than life.'

'He was. Is.'

'Then he was interviewed and he spoke about the travelling and the adrenalin and I thought it was a kick-ass career.' Jack bit, swallowed and grinned. 'I still think it is.'

Ellie's eyes were a deep blue in the candlelight and Jack felt as if she could see into his soul.

'How do you deal with the bad stuff you've seen? The violence, the suffering, the madness, the cruelty? How do you process all of that?'

Jack carefully placed his slice of pizza back down on his plate. He took a while to answer, and when he did he was surprised to hear the emotion in his voice. 'It took some time but I've programmed myself to just report on the facts. My job is to tell the story—hopefully in a way that will facilitate change. I observe and I don't judge, because judgement requires an emotional involvement.'

'And you don't get emotionally involved,' Ellie said thoughtfully. 'Does that carry over into other areas of your life?'

Jack stiffened, wondering where she was going with that question. 'You mean like relationships and crap like that?'

'Yeah—crap like that.' Ellie's response was bone-dry.

He had to set her straight. Right now. Just in case she had any ideas...

'Like your father, my life doesn't lend itself to having a long-term relationship. Women tend to get annoyed when you don't spend time with them.'

'Yep, I know what that feels like. Any woman who gets involved with a war reporter is asking to put her emotions through a meat-grinder,' Ellie replied. 'God knows that's exactly what Mitchell did to me.'

She didn't give him time to respond and was frustrated when she changed the subject.

'So, how is the book coming along?'

Ellie pushed her plate away and Jack frowned. She'd barely managed to eat half her medium pizza and he had almost finished his large. 'Well, apart from the fact that I can't get a certain reporter's daughter to sit down and answer my questions, fine.'

He saw guilt flash across her face. 'Oh, Jack, I'm so sorry! You probably want to leave, head home, and I'm holding you up—'

Jack shook his head. Where did this need to blame herself for everything come from? She was so together and confident in some ways—such a train wreck when it came to her need to please.

'Ellie, stop it!' Ellie's mouth snapped shut and Jack thought that was progress. 'Firstly, if I wanted to leave I would've made a plan to go already. Secondly, as I said, I like your house, I like this area, and when I start feeling pressurised for time I'll tell you and we'll get down to it. As long as you do not want me out of your house we're good. *Do* you want me to leave?'

'No, you're reasonably well house-trained,' Ellie muttered. Jack grinned.

'So, why aren't you prepared to write your story? Mitchell said that you were asked to.' Ellie picked up the thread of their conversation again.

Because my story isn't just my story and it's a lot more complicated than people think. Jack swallowed those words and just shrugged.

Ellie picked an olive off her pizza and popped it into her mouth. They sat in a comfortable silence for a while, until Ellie spoke again. 'I think I know why you are reluctant to tell your story.'

This should be good. A little armchair analysis. 'Really? Why?'

'In light of what you said earlier, digging into your own story, analysing your life choices, would require emotional involvement. You can't stand back and just observe your own life. You can't be objective about yourself. Then again, who can?'

It was Jack's turn to stare at her, to feel the impact of her insightful words. He couldn't even begin to start formulating an argument. There wasn't one, because her observation was pure truth.

Jack drained the last inch of beer in his bottle and threw his serviette onto the table. 'You ready to go?'

Ellie nodded, pushed her chair back and pulled her purse out of her bag. He ground his teeth as she placed cash under the heavy salt cellar. Where the hell were his new bank cards? He was sick of not having access to funds.

He stopped at the cashier on the way out and asked for a

receipt, and he knew without looking at Ellie that she was rolling her eyes at him.

'Jack, you worked in the bakery. I'll pay for dinner.'

'No.' Jack took the printed bill from the manager and shoved it into his pocket.

'Stop being anal.'

Jack gripped her ponytail and tugged gently. 'Stop nagging. I thought we agreed that if I'm living in your house then I'll pick up the tab?'

She tossed her head. 'We never agreed on anything!'

Jack's grin flashed. 'It's easier if you just do it my way.'

'In your dreams.'

It was shortly after six the following evening when Jack returned from a trip to Robben Island, the off-coast prison that had housed Nelson Mandela for twenty-four years, and his mind was still on the beloved South African icon when he walked into Ellie's kitchen.

He kicked off his shoes, dumped the take-away Chinese he'd picked up on the way on the kitchen table and tossed his brand-new wallet containing his brand-new bank cards onto the table. Inside was enough cash to reimburse Ellie for everything she'd paid for so far. Thinking about Ellie, he wondered where she was.

Jack walked back into the hall and stood at the bottom of the stairs, calling her name. Her bag was on its customary hook and her mobile sat on the hall table. Jack walked back to the kitchen, onto the back deck, and finally found her, sprawled out on a lounger in the shade of one of the two umbrellas that stood next to her pool.

She was asleep, with an open sketchbook on her bare, flat stomach and a piece of charcoal on the grass below her hand. She was dressed in a tiny black and blue bikini and he spent many minutes examining her nearly-but-not-quite naked body.

Her long damp hair streamed over her shoulders and across the triangles that covered her full breasts. She had a flat, almost concave stomach, slim hips and long, smooth legs with fine muscles. The tips of her elegant feet were painted a vivid pink that reminded him of Grecian sunsets.

Very alluring, very sexy, Jack thought, sinking to the grass next to her chair. In order to stop himself from undoing those flimsy ties keeping those tiny triangles in place, he picked up the sketchpad and flipped through the pages.

The sketches were rough, jerky, but powerful, full of movement. She'd sketched her house, capturing its fat lines and bay windows, and there was a sketch of her dog, head on paws, his eyes soulful. There was a rather bleak landscape of cliffs and shadows which oozed sadness and regret.

Jack gasped at his likeness, grinning up at him from another white page. She'd captured his laugh and, worse, the attraction to her he'd thought he was hiding so well.

'Snoop.'

Jack snapped the book closed and looked up into her face. Her eyes were still closed and her eyelashes were ink-black on her face.

'I thought you were still asleep. I was trying to be quiet.'

'I'm a really light sleeper,' Ellie said, and held out her hand for her sketchpad.

Jack reluctantly handed it over. 'These are good—'

'It's something I do to pass the time.' Ellie tossed the pad on top of a box of charcoal sticks and sat up, covering her mouth as she yawned. 'Talking of which, what *is* the time?'

Jack looked at his watch. 'Half-six.'

Ellie looked horrified. 'I went for a swim around five and thought I'd take fifteen minutes to chill… I must've dozed off.'

Jack drew his thumb across the purple shadow under her eye. 'It looks like you needed it. What time did you finish last night? I saw your light was still on after midnight.'

'One? Half-one? I finished the VAT return and paid some creditors.' Ellie swung her legs off the sunchair, her feet brushing Jack's thighs. 'I've got a couple of hours' work tonight and then I'll be caught up. I shouldn't have fallen asleep…I meant to work after my swim.'

Jack clenched his fists in an effort not to reach for her. She looked so tired, so young, so…*weary* that all he wanted to do was take her in his arms and ease her stress. He shoved his hand into his hair. *She tries to hide it*, he thought, *but she's wiped out in every way she can be by the responsibilities of her business.* He wished there was something he could do for her. Dammit, was he starting to feel protective over her? He didn't know how to handle her, deal with her. He was used to resilient, emotionally tougher women, and Ellie had him wanting to shield her, shelter her.

'I need to think about what to make for supper,' Ellie said as she stood up, unfurling that long, slender body.

Her voice was saturated with exhaustion and he felt irritation jump up into his throat. 'Ellie, I am *not* another one of your responsibilities!' he snapped.

Ellie blinked at him. 'You don't want me to make supper?'

'No. For a number of reasons. The first being that I bought supper—Chinese. My replacement bank cards arrived,' he explained when she looked at him enquiringly. 'Also, I really think you need to learn that the world will not stop turning if you stop for five minutes and relax. You never stop moving, and when you do you're so exhausted that you can't keep your eyes open.'

Ellie picked up a sarong and wound it around her hips. 'Jack, please. I really don't want to argue with you.'

Jack nodded. 'Okay, I won't argue. I'll just tell you what to do. You're going to change into something that doesn't stop traffic and then we're going for a walk. On the way we'll stop and have a beer at one of the pubs on the beachfront. Then

we'll come home, eat Chinese, of which you will have a reasonable portion, and then you're going to bed. Early.'

'Jack, it's hot. I don't feel like a walk and I can't take the
time—'

'Yeah, you can,' Jack told her. 'And I know you're hot.
You're standing there in a couple of triangles cooking my
blood pressure. So this should help both of us cool off.'

Jack scooped her up, ignored her squeal and stepped, still
dressed, into the deep end of her gloriously cold, sparkling
blue pool.

CHAPTER FIVE

'IT'S SUCH A stunning evening. Would you like to take the long route to the beachfront?' Ellie asked him as they stepped onto the road outside her house. 'It's a ten-minute walk instead of a five-minute walk but I'll show you a bit of the neighbourhood.'

'Sure,' Jack agreed, and they turned left instead of right.

He walked next to Ellie, his hands loose in the pockets of his shorts. The sea in front of them was pancake-flat and a patchwork quilt of greens and blues. It was make-your-soul-bump beautiful. The temperature had dropped and she was cool from the swim and the light, short sundress she was wearing.

She was really looking forward to an icy margarita and Jack's stimulating, slightly acerbic company.

A little way away from the house Jack broke their comfortable silence. 'By the way, I was contacted today by the Press Club. They've heard that I'm in town and have invited me to their annual dinner. I'd like you to go with me, but I know how busy you are. Any chance?'

Ellie's heart hiccupped. A date! A real date! *Whoop!* She did an internal happy dance. 'When is it?'

'Tomorrow. Tomorrow *is* Friday, right? It's black tie, I'm afraid.'

A date where she could seriously glam up? Double *whoop!*

'So, do you think you can leave work early for a change?' Jack enquired. 'It's a hassle going to these functions on my own.'

In a strange city where he knew no one of course it would be. And the world wouldn't stop turning if she left work a little earlier than normal. Besides, Merri would come in for an hour or two.

'Sure. That sounds like fun.'

'Great.' Jack moved between her and a large dog that was walking along the verge of a house with its gates left open.

Ellie appreciated his innate protectiveness but she knew Islay. He was as friendly as he was old.

Jack cleared his throat. 'Ellie, I was only supposed to spend one, maybe two nights in your house...'

'And tonight will be your fourth night,' Ellie replied quietly. 'Do you want to leave?'

Jack shook his head. 'Just the opposite, actually. Mitch, being Mitch, has put the word out to the network editors that I'm hurt and need some time off.'

Ellie flicked a glance at his hip. 'You *are* hurt.'

'Superficially.' Compared to what he'd gone through, his stab wound was minimal. 'Anyway, I'm off for a few weeks unless—'

She knew the drill. Journalists were only 'off' until the next story came along. 'Unless some huge story breaks.'

Jack nodded his agreement. 'So, I thought I'd stay in Cape Town for a bit longer.'

'In my house?' Ellie heard the squeak in her voice and winced. She sounded like a demented mouse.

'Well, I could move into a hotel, but I spend enough time in hotels as it is and I'd rather pay you.'

Ellie stopped in her tracks and turned to look at him. 'You'd pay to live with me?'

What exactly did he mean by that? What would be included in that deal? Not that she believed for one minute that he'd make her an offer that was below-board, but she just wanted to make sure… And really, how upset would she be if he suggested sleeping together? Since she was constantly thinking about sex with him…not very.

His grin suggested he knew exactly what she was thinking. 'It's a simple transaction, Ellie. Someone has to get paid to put my butt into a bed and I'd prefer it to be you and not some nameless, faceless corporation.' Jack stepped forward and his thumb drifted over her chin. 'A bed, food, coffee. No expectations, no pressure.' Damn.

'Oh.' Ellie dropped her head and thought she was an idiot for feeling disappointed. *You don't want to get involved, on any level, with any man—remember, Ellie?* Especially a man like Jack. Too good-looking, too successful, too much. Rough, tough, unemotional and—the big reason—never around.

But she wanted him. She really did.

Jack dropped his hand and Ellie was glad, because she didn't know for how much longer she could stop herself reaching up and kissing him, tasting those firm lips, feeling the rasp of his stubble under her lips, her fingers. She watched him walk away and after two steps he turned and looked back at her.

He must have seen something on her face, because his steps lengthened and then his hands were on her hips, yanking her into him. His mouth finally touched hers sweetly, gently, before he allowed his passion to explode. His quick tongue slipped between her lips, scraped her teeth and tangled with her own in a long, deep kiss that had no end or beginning.

One hand held her head in place and the other explored her back, her hip, the curves of her bottom, the tops of her thighs. Ellie slid her hand up his back, under his loose T-shirt, and acquainted herself with his bare flesh, the muscles in his back, that strip of flesh above his shorts and the soft leather belt. He was heat and lust and passion in its purist, most concentrated form; causing her nipples and her thighs to press together to subdue the deep, insistent throbbing between them.

He kissed her some more.

Ellie wasn't sure how much time had passed when he finally lifted his head and rested his forehead against hers. 'I'm burning up, on fire from wanting you. That's why I haven't kissed you before this.'

'Why did you kiss me now?' Ellie whispered back, her hands gripping his sides.

'Because you looked like you wanted me to—really wanted me to.'

She really had. And she wouldn't object to more.

Jack stepped back, linked his hands behind his head. The muscles in his arms bulged. 'I can't take you to bed... I mean of course I *can*. I want to. Desperately. But it would be the worst idea in the world.'

It didn't matter that she agreed with him. She wanted to know why he thought so. 'Why?'

Jack's mouth twisted. 'I'm not good for you. I'm hard and cynical, frequently bitter. I have seen so many bad things. You're arty and creative and...innocent. Untainted.'

'No, I'm not.' Ellie pursed her lips. He made her sound like a nun. 'You're not a bad man, Jack.'

'But I'd be bad for *you*.' Jack dropped his arms and stared out to sea. 'I am not a noble man, Ellie, but I'm trying to do the right thing here. Help me out, okay?'

Ellie lifted her hands in puzzlement. 'How am I supposed to do that?'

Jack glared at her. 'Well, for starters you could stop looking at me as if you want to slurp me up through a straw. Sexy little dresses like that don't help—and you're *very* lucky that you kept possession of that thing you call a bikini this afternoon. Short shorts and tight tops are out too...'

'Would you like me to walk around in a tent?' Ellie asked

sarcastically, but secretly she was enjoying the fact that she could turn him on so quickly. It was a power she'd never experienced before, a heady sensation knowing that this delicious man thought that she was equally tasty.

'That might work,' Jack replied.

Ellie pulled in a breath as he stepped forward and took her much smaller hand in his. His expression turned sober.

'El, I like you, but I think you have enough going on in your life without the added pressure of an affair with me. I need to write your father's life story and I don't know how objective I'm going to be if I am sleeping with his daughter.'

Ellie kept her eyes on his and gestured him to continue. Everything he'd said so far had made sense, but she could still feel his lips on hers, his big hands on her skin. Taste him on her lips.

'It's been a long time since I just liked a woman, enjoyed her company. Can we keep this simple? Try to just be friends? That way, when I leave, there won't be any...stupid feelings between us.' Jack stared down at her fingers. 'You know it's the smart thing to do.'

Ellie sighed and wished she could be half as erudite as he was. Sure, words were the tools of his trade, but he made her feel as thick as a peanut butter sandwich when it came to expressing herself. Only two words came to mind, and neither were worthy of this conversation.

'Yeah, okay,' she muttered.

Jack smiled and ran his thumb over her knuckles before dropping her hand. 'So, will you go to the camping store for a tent or shall I?'

'Make sure it's a pink one.' Ellie looked around and her expression softened. 'Oh, we're here!'

'Where?' Jack asked as she grabbed the edge of his shirt and tugged him across the road.

Ellie walked up to some wrought-iron gates and wrapped

her fingers around the bars, looking at the dilapidated double-storey building.

Jack tugged on the chain that held the gates together. 'What *is* this place?'

'It was a library at the turn of the century, then it was turned into a house, but it's been empty a couple of years. I've heard a rumour that old Mrs Hutchinson is finally considering selling it. Restored, this building would be utter perfection. Two storeys of whimsy, with balconies and bay windows galore. Its irregular shape reminds me of a blowsy matron in a voluminous skirt and a peculiar hat. Romantic, eccentric and very over the top.'

Jack immediately picked up where she was going with this. 'You're thinking of this place for the bakery?'

'It's just around the corner from the present location, with ample parking space. I took a box of cupcakes to the Town Planning office and...well, bribed them into letting me take a look at the building plans. There is a lot of space, but not too much...enough to hold the bakery, the delicatessen and a proper breakfast and lunch restaurant.'

Jack put his hands on his hips. 'It's difficult to comment without seeing the place. Let's go in.'

Ellie pointed at the sign on the fence. '"No Trespassers".'

'If I obeyed those signs I'd never get a story,' Jack said, and pulled at a rusty iron post on the fence. It moved, and he gestured Ellie through the gap he'd created. 'You're slim enough to climb through here.'

'And you?'

Jack grabbed the top of the fence with his hands, yanked himself up and held his body weight while he swung his legs onto the railing. Within seconds he was on the other side and his breathing hadn't changed.

Ellie shook her head as she slipped through the fence. 'If

you've split open your cut you're going to the emergency room,' she told him.

'Yes, Mum.' Jack grinned and led her up to the huge front door. He pursed his lips at the lock. 'No breaking in through *this* door.'

'We're not breaking in through any door!' Ellie stated as he pulled her away from the front door and around the house. 'Seriously, Jack, that's a crime!'

Jack peered through a window. 'Relax, there's nothing to steal, so if we get caught we can plead curiosity. I'm good at talking my way out of trouble.'

'Jack!'

Jack stopped at a side door. 'Good. Yale lock. Pass me a hairpin, El.'

'You are not going to… Hey!' Ellie slapped her hand against her head where Jack had yanked the pin from her hair. 'That hurt!'

'Sorry.' Jack opened the pin, inserted it into the lock and jiggled the handle. Within a minute the door swung open to his touch. 'Bingo.'

'I cannot believe that you picked that lock! Who taught you that?'

'You really don't want to know.'

Ellie looked curious. 'No, tell me. Who?'

'Your father, actually.'

Ellie rolled her eyes and Jack just grinned as he placed a hand on her lower back and pushed her inside.

'I *so* didn't need to know that!' she muttered.

'Relax.' Jack placed his hands on his hips and looked into the room to his right. 'Kitchen through here—an enormous one, but it needs to be gutted. God, Ellie, the ceiling is falling down!'

'I never said it didn't need work. Look at these floors, Jack. Solid yellow-wood.'

Jack looked at the patch of direct sunlight on the warped wood and at the hundreds of holes in it. 'White ants, Ellie, white ants. I bet the house is infested with them.'

'Are you always this pessimistic?' Ellie asked as she opened doors on either side of the passage.

'I just think you should slow down to a gallop. I can see the look in your eye. If you could you'd slap the deposit down,' Jack said. He picked at a piece of wallpaper and a strip came off in his hand. 'Before you even consider doing that I suggest you get an architect to look at the place, and a civil engineer to check that it's not going to fall down.'

It was sensible, unemotional advice—but sensible was for later. Right now she wanted to feel, sense, imagine.

Jack ducked his head into another room and Ellie heard what she swore was a screech. 'Did you squeal?' she called.

Jack hurried out of the room. 'Girls squeal. Men...don't. A rat nearly ran over my shoe! I hate rats!'

'Well, you squeal like a girl, and I'd rather have rats than white ants,' Ellie replied as they stepped into a massive hall-way which was dominated by a two-storey-high ceiling and a thoroughly imposing staircase. Coloured sunshine from the stained glass inserts next to that imposing front door threw happy patterns onto the wooden floor.

'Okay, this is amazing,' Jack admitted.

'It's unbelievable,' Ellie said, falling hard.

Nothing had prepared her for the immediate visceral connection she felt to this property. She walked to the bay window behind the staircase and looked out onto the wilderness beyond, with its overgrown shrubs and trees. She could easily imagine the rambling, once stunning gardens that surrounded the house, like carefully chosen accessories on a red-carpet dress. Ellie walked the area downstairs and quickly established that the place could, without a huge amount of construction, be adapted to house the bakery.

It just took imagination—and she had lots of that.

'Why hasn't someone converted it into a restaurant? A bed and breakfast? An art gallery?' Jack asked when she rejoined him in the hall.

'Many have tried. Many have failed. Mrs Hutchinson hasn't ever been prepared to sell. She doesn't need the money and this building was her childhood home.' She shrugged at Jack's enquiring face. 'Basically, she's bats. The town fruitcake. She's refused offers—huge offers—for stupid reasons. Perceived lack of manners, not polishing your shoes. One man wore too much jewellery.'

'She sounds bonkers,' Jack said.

'That's one way of putting it,' Ellie said briskly, and tipped her head to look up at him. 'Let's finish with the breaking and entering. I could murder a drink.'

Jack followed her down the passage back to the side door, which he yanked open for her. 'Technically, it was only entering. We didn't break anything.'

'Semantics,' Ellie said as he pulled the door shut behind him and they headed back down the winding driveway to the road.

'You really are a bit of a pansy, aren't you?' Jack leapt over the fence and jammed his hands in his pockets as he waited for her to climb back through the gate.

She was just straightening up when she heard a car approaching and slowing down. Ellie looked up and straight into the eyes of the driver, who was looking at her curiously.

'Oh, *dammit.*'

Jack looked from her to the disappearing Toyota. 'Problem?'

Ellie slapped the palm of her hand against her forehead. 'That was Mrs Khumalo, the busiest of St James's busybodies. Soon it will be all over town either that I am having secret trysts with a married man, or that I am buying the property, or that I'm joining a cult and this is going to be its headquarters.'

Jack laughed as she stomped down the road. 'Cool. As the great Oscar Wilde said, "There's only one thing in the world worse than being talked about, and that is *not* being talked about".'

'Grrr.'

They fell into an easy silence on their walk home from the pub, and Ellie enjoyed the fact that they could be quiet together, that neither of them felt the need to fill the space with empty words.

Jack took the keys from her hand and opened the front door for her, nudging the dogs out of the way with a gentle knee so that she could walk in first. In the hallway Ellie dropped her bag on the side table and placed her hands on her back, stretching while Jack examined the life-size nude painting of a blonde on a scarlet velvet couch on the opposite wall. She wore only her long hair and a waist-length string of pearls… and a very come-hither grin.

'I can't stop looking at this painting.'

Since it was a nude painting of a gorgeous woman, Ellie wasn't surprised. Most men had the same reaction.

'Who *is* that?'

'My best friend Merri.'

Jack stepped up to the portrait and lightly touched the canvas with the back of his knuckle. 'I meant the artist. The way he's captured the blue veins in her pale skin, her inner glow… God, he's amazing!'

Ellie felt a spurt of pure, unadulterated pleasure. 'Thanks.'

Jack's mouth fell open. '*You* painted this?'

'Mmm. I studied Fine Art at uni and lived in London for a while, but I couldn't support myself by selling my art so I came home and started work at the bakery.'

'It's brilliant. But you left out quite a bit between uni and coming back to Cape Town.' He touched the frame with his fingertips. 'And this is more than something you pass time with.'

Ellie felt the familiar stab, the longing to immerse herself in a big painting that sucked her into a different dimension. 'It used to be my passion. It isn't any more.'

'Why not?'

'I painted that just before I went to the UK. I'd finished uni and was going to conquer the world. I was so in love with art, painting, creating. I was...*infused* by art.'

Jack sat on the bottom stair and patted the space next to him. Ellie sat down and rested her arms on her knees, looking at Merri's naughty smile.

'Were you always arty?'

Ellie shrugged. 'I think I started when I was about six. I remember the first time I fell into a drawing.'

'Tell me.'

Ellie felt her voice catch. 'Mitchell was home. He'd just come back from somewhere in Africa. He was working in his study—nothing strange there—and the door was open. He was reading aloud an article he'd written...he did that. He read all his articles aloud.'

'He still does.'

'It was a report on the genocide happening in Rwanda—Burundi—somewhere like that. The report was graphic, horrific...' Ellie shuddered and felt Jack's strong arm around her waist, his hand on her hip. This time there was nothing sexual about his touch. It was pure comfort. 'Mitchell called it like he saw it: women, old people, children. Severed heads, limbs...'

'I know, sweetheart. Skip that part. Tell me about the art.' Jack rested his chin on her hair, shaken by the idea of a little girl hearing that. Damn Mitch and his stupidity. The man was a talented journalist, but as a father...useless.

'I couldn't get the pictures his words conjured out of my brain and the only thing I could think of to do was draw.

Happy things—butterflies, princesses. I had nightmares for a while, and I'd wake up and hit my desk to paint or colour.' Ellie sighed. 'Mitchell could never censor himself. He had no conception of sensibility—that young kids didn't need to know that sixteen Afghan rebels had been executed and their decapitated heads paraded through the streets as a warning and that he'd witnessed it. It drove my mother mad that he couldn't keep his mouth shut in front of me.'

'But you had your art?'

'I did. He reported on brutality and war, violence, and I tried—still try—to counter that by producing beauty. It used to be through oils. Now it's through cake and icing.' Ellie shrugged and managed a smile.

Jack saw her staring at Merri's portrait and caught the pain and sadness in her eyes. There was more to this story or he wasn't a journalist. 'Why did you give it up?'

'Can we skip this part?' Ellie asked with a wobble in her voice.

'I'd really like to know.' Jack lowered his voice, made it persuasive.

'You ask me all these questions but you won't talk about yourself,' Ellie complained.

True. 'I know. I'm sorry. But tell me anyway.'

'Short story. He was the owner of an exclusive art gallery in Soho.' Grigson's, Jack remembered. The short blond from that photo in his room. 'He offered me an exhibition, told me I was the next big thing. I fell deeply, chronically in love with him. I found out later that was his *modus operandi*. I wasn't the first young artist he'd seduced into bed with that promise.'

Jack winced.

'I was swept away by him. He dealt in beauty and objects of art. He was a social butterfly—had invitations to something every night of the week. But he never took me along to anything. Like my father, he dropped in and out of my life. I kept asking him about the exhibition, spending time with me, taking me along, but he kept fobbing me off.'

'Bastard,' Jack growled.

'I told him that I wanted to break it off and he responded by proposing. I thought that meant that he'd change, but nothing did. I saw less of him than ever.'

'So what precipitated the break-up?' Jack briefly wondered why he was so interested in her past, why he felt the need to find the jerk and put him into a coma.

'I told him that I was done with waiting around for him. He responded by telling me that I was a mediocre artist who'd never amount to anything. That he'd just wanted to sleep with me occasionally but I wasn't worth the hassle…that it was, essentially, not worth my being around, him trying to keep me happy.'

Forget the coma. He now had the urge to put the guy six feet under. When Mitch had mentioned him he'd initially felt sorry for him, because he'd thought that she must have been pushing him into marriage, but he was the one who'd messed *her* around, messed her up. No wonder she tried so hard to be indispensable to the people she loved; she thought she had to try harder to be loved.

The two men she'd loved the most had hurt her, damaged her the most. God, the ways that love could mess up people. Just another reason why he wanted nothing to do with it…

'Anybody since then?' Jack asked, although he knew there hadn't been.

'No.'

Needing to move, to work off his anger, Jack jumped up and jogged up the stairs to inspect another painting. He placed his hands on his hips and looked around at the art covering the walls.

'Good grief, Ellie, some of these paintings are utterly fantastic. I'm trying to work out which ones are yours, because not all of them are.'

'Some are by fellow art students; others I've picked up along the way,' Ellie said, pride streaking through her voice. 'You like art?'

'I love art. Sculpture. Architecture,' Jack confirmed, quickly moving up the stairs to examine a seascape.

He placed a hand on his hip and winced at the movement. Ellie watched his body tense. His face was illuminated by the spotlight above his head. The violet shadows beneath his eyes were back and his face was pale beneath his slight tan.

Jack Chapman, she decided, had no concept of how to pace himself. He'd recently suffered a horrendous beating, had a nasty knife wound, and yet he'd spent the day sightseeing. She could see that he was exhausted and in pain, and she knew that he was one of those men who would carry on until he fell down.

He came across as easygoing and charming but there was a solid streak beneath the charm, a strength of character that people probably never saw beneath the good looks and air of success. His thought-processes were clear-headed and practical. While he'd challenged her decisions and her actions she didn't feel as if he was judging *her*.

He'd coaxed her past out of her and he was a fabulous listener. He listened intently and knew when to back away from the subject to give the guts-spiller some time to compose themselves.

Ellie caught his slight wince as he walked back down the stairs and she shook her head at him. 'For goodness' sake—will you sit down before you fall down?'

Jack's strong eyebrows pulled together. 'I'm fine.'

'Jack, you're not fine. You're exhausted and your body is protesting. Take a seat in the lounge, watch some TV. Do you want something to drink?'

Jack raked his hand through his hair. 'Nothing, thanks. Mind if I veg out on the veranda for a while?'

'Knock yourself out,' Ellie said. 'I'll plate up the Chinese.'

'Hey, El?' Jack called.

Ellie poked her head around the kitchen door. 'Yes?'

Jack rattled off an Arabic curse and Ellie wrinkled her nose. 'Something...something donkey. Sorry...what?'

'I just called your ex a bleeping-bleeping horse's bleeping ass.'

Ellie laughed. *Nice, Jack.*

After supper they headed back to the veranda and watched as dusk fell over the long coastline. Lights winked on as they sipped their red wine, sharing the couch with their bare feet up on the stone wall. Jack placed his arm along the back of the couch and Ellie felt his fingers in her hair. She turned to look at him but Jack was watching her hair slide between his fingers.

'It's so straight, so thick.'

Ellie felt his hands tug the band from her hair and felt the heavy drop as her hair cascaded down her back, could imagine it flowing over Jack's broad hand. She heard his swift intake of breath, felt his fingers combing her hair.

'I love the coloured streaks. They remind me of the flash of colour in a starling's wing.'

There was that creative flair again—this time with words. And there was that sexual buzz again. Ellie licked her lips. 'They're not my real hair.'

'Still pretty.' Jack lifted a strand of her hair and because it was so long easily brought it to his nose. 'Mmm...apple, lemon...flour.'

Ellie could not believe that she was so turned on by a man sniffing her hair. 'Jack...'

His eyes deepened, flooded with gold. He drifted the ends

of her hair over his lips before dropping it and sliding his big hand around her neck. 'Yeah?'

Ellie dropped her eyes. 'We weren't going to do this, remember?'

'Shh, nothing is going to happen,' Jack said.

He dropped his arm behind her back, wrapped it around her waist and pulled her so that she was plastered against his hard body. Ellie swung around and rested her head against his chest, deeply conscious of his warm arm under her breasts.

'Did you submit your piece on that Somalian pirate-slash-warlord?' Ellie asked, to take her mind off the fact that she wanted to move his hands to more deserving areas of her body. Her breasts, the backs of her knees, between her legs.

'Yes. I didn't get as much information from him as I wanted to, but it was okay.'

'Have you worked out what you said that set him off?'

She felt Jack shake his head. 'Nah. I think he was high... and psychotic.'

'That might be it.' Ellie rested her hands on his arm, feeling the veins under his skin. 'Tell me about yourself. Mother? Father? Siblings?'

'Like you, I was an only child. I'm not sure why,' Jack replied.

Ellie half smiled. 'Tell me what you were like as a kid.'

She felt him stiffen at her question. 'At what age?'

Strange question. 'I don't know...ten?'

Jack's laugh rumbled through his chest. 'Hell on wheels. Maybe that's why my folks didn't have another kid. They probably despaired in case they'd have another boy.'

Ellie laughed. 'You couldn't have been *that* bad.'

'I was worse. Before I was eight I'd broken a leg, had three lots of stitches and lost most of my teeth.'

Ellie's mouth fell open. 'How on earth did you manage to do that?'

'The broken leg came from ramping with my BMX. The ramp I'd built myself collapsed. The teeth incident was from a fight with Juliet Grafton. I called her ugly—which she was. She was also built like a brick outhouse and her father was a boxing champion. Her mean right hook connected with my mouth. Stitches—where do I start? Falling off bikes, roofs, rocks...'

Ellie raised an eyebrow.

'But I was cute. That counted for a lot.'

She wanted to tell him he was still cute, but she suspected he already knew that, so instead she just watched night fall over the sea.

CHAPTER SIX

ELLIE WALKED INTO the ballroom on Jack's arm and looked around the packed space, filled with black-suited men and elegant women. His appearance caused a buzz and Ellie felt the tension in Jack's arm as people turned to watch their progress into the room. To them he was a celebrity, and well respected, and a smattering of applause broke out.

Jack half lifted his hand in acknowledgement. When he spoke, he pitched his voice so that only she could hear him. 'Those are the most ridiculous shoes, Ellie.'

Ellie grinned at the teasing note in his voice. He'd already told her that he liked her shimmery silver and pink froth of a cocktail dress, and she knew that her moon-high silver sandals made her calves look fantastic. She *felt* fantastic; she was sure it had a lot to do with the approval in Jack's expressive eyes.

'And, as I said, that is a sexy dress. Very you. Bright, colourful, playful.'

Ellie looked around and half winced. 'Most women are wearing basic black.'

'You're not a basic type of girl. And colour suits you.' He touched the hair she'd worked into a bohemian roll, with curls falling down her back. 'Gorgeous hair...make-me-crazy scent...'

'So I'll do?'

Jack took her hand and his words were rueful. 'Very much so.'

Ellie smiled with pleasure, then lifted her eyebrows as a tall blonde with an equine face stalked up to Jack, took his hand and kissed his cheek. Jack lifted his own eyebrows at her familiarity as she introduced herself as the Chairperson of the Press Club. Ellie forgot her name as soon as she said it.

'I have people who'd like to meet you,' she stated in a commanding voice.

'I'd like to get my date a drink first,' Jack said, untangling himself from her octopus grip.

'Ellie?'

Ellie turned at the deep voice and looked up into laughing green eyes in a very good-looking face. 'Luke? What are *you* doing here?'

'St Sylve is one of the club's sponsors,' he told Ellie, after kissing her on the cheek. He held out his hand to Jack. 'Luke Savage.'

'You drink Luke's wine all the time at home, Jack,' Ellie told him after they'd been introduced. 'Where's Jess, Luke?'

Luke looked around for his fiancée and shrugged. 'Probably charming someone for business.'

'Jack, I really *must* take you to meet some people.'

The blonde tugged on Jack's sleeve and Ellie caught the irritation that flickered in his eyes.

Jack looked at Ellie and then at Luke. 'Will you be okay?'

Ellie smiled at him. 'Sure. I'll hang with Luke and Jess and see you at dinner.'

Jack nodded and turned away.

Ellie looked up at Luke and pulled a face. 'We're going to be placed at some awfully boring table, I can tell, with Horse Lady neighing at Jack all night.'

Luke grinned. 'Well, we're sitting with Cale and Maddie—'

Ellie squealed with excitement. 'They're here too?'

'Cale *is* a sports presenter and journalist, El.'

'I *so* want to sit with you guys!' Ellie fluttered her eye-lashes up at him.

Luke winked at her. 'We'll just have to see if we can make that happen.'

Ellie felt a feminine arm encircle her waist and turned to look into her friend's laughing deep brown eyes.

'Are you flirting with my husband-to-be, Ellie Evans?'

Ellie laughed and kissed Jess's cheek. ''Fraid so.'

'Can't blame you. I flirt with him all the time. Now, tell me—why and how are you here with the very yummy Jack Chapman?'

Luke had somehow organised that they were all at the same table, and Jack felt himself relaxing with Ellie's charming group of friends. They were warm and down-to-earth and Jack was enjoying himself.

He leaned closer to Ellie and lowered his voice. 'How do you know all these people?'

Ellie sent him a side-glance out of those fabulous eyes. 'Maddie and I went to uni together. I met Luke through her, and Cale—he and Cale are old schoolfriends. But I've known Jess for years and years—before she and Luke met. Her company does Pari's advertising.'

'So, El,' Luke said as he picked up a bottle of wine from the ice bucket on the table and topped up their glasses with a fruity Sauvignon, 'what's this I hear about you having to move your bakery?'

Ellie wiped her hands on a serviette and pulled a face. 'I have to find new premises in less than six months.'

'And have you found anything?' Cale asked.

'Maybe. There's an old building close to the bakery that might work. It's supposed to be on the market, but I need to find an architect—someone who can look at the house and tell me if it's solid and if I can do the alterations I'm thinking of—before I put in an offer.'

Luke looked at Cale and they both nodded. 'James.'

'Another friend from uni?' Jack asked with a smile on his face.

Luke and Cale laughed, but didn't disagree with him. Luke told Ellie that he'd send her his contact details and the rest of the table moved onto another subject.

'Are you seriously considering that building for the bakery?' Jack asked Ellie, resting his cheek on his fist.

'Maybe. Possibly.' Ellie fiddled with her serviette. 'I'll speak to James and see what he says. Then I'll have to run it by my mum.'

'Understandable, since Pari's will be paying for it.' Jack saw something flash across her face and frowned. '*You're* paying for it? How would you...? Sorry—that has nothing to do with me.'

'How would I pay for it? It's fine. I don't mind you asking. Ginger—my grandmother—set up a trust for me when I was little and she's pretty wealthy. Pari's would pay me rent. That's if I actually decide to buy and renovate the building.'

There it was again—that lack of confidence in her eyes. 'Why do you doubt yourself?'

'It's a lot of money, Jack.' Ellie twisted the serviette through her fingers. 'What if it's a disaster? What if I end up disappointing my mother, Merri, my grandmother Pari's memory...? God, my *customers*?'

'That's a lot of disappointing, El. And a lot of what-ifs.' Jack placed his hand on hers and held them still. 'You love that building. Yours eyes light up when you talk about it. When are you going to start trusting yourself a little more?'

Ellie bit that sexy bottom lip—the one he wanted so badly to taste again.

'Merri says that I'm too much of a people-pleaser. That I have this insane need to make the world right for everyone.'

He didn't think Merri was wrong. 'You need to start listening to yourself more and to underestimate yourself less.'

Ellie twisted her lips. 'And not to think that I'm indispensable and the world will stop turning if I say no... I'm a basket case, Jack.'

Jack sent her an easy grin. 'We're all basket cases in our own way. You're just a bit more...vulnerable. Softer than most.'

'I need to grow a bit more of a spine.'

'I think you're pretty much perfect just as you are.'

Jack sighed as the Master of Ceremonies started to talk. He'd much rather talk to Ellie than listen to boring speeches. He heard the MC introducing him and grimaced. His was probably going to be the most boring speech of all. He felt Ellie's hand grasp his knee and a bolt of sexual attraction fizzed straight through him.

'You didn't tell me that you were making a speech!' she hissed.

He stood up, buttoned his jacket and looked down at her. 'Yeah, well, for some reason they find me interesting.'

'Weird. I simply can't understand why,' Ellie teased.

Jack swallowed his laughter before moving away from her and heading for the podium, thinking that he could think of a couple of things he'd rather be doing than giving a speech. Top of the list was doing Ellie. In the pool, in the kitchen, in the shower...

Jack reached the podium, looked at the expectant faces and let his eyes drift over to his table. Luke raised his glass at him. Maddie rested her arms on the table and sent him a friendly smile. Ellie, being Ellie, pulled a quick tongue at him and he swallowed a grin.

There wasn't much wrong with the world if Ellie was in it, making him laugh.

* * *

It had been heaven to be in Jack's arms, even if it was just for a couple of slow dances around the edge of the dance floor. In her heels she'd been able to tuck her face into his neck, feel his warm breath in her hair, on her temple. There had been nothing demure about their dancing. They'd been up close and personal and neither of them had been able to hide their desire. Her nipples had dug into his chest and her stomach brushed his hard erection. Their breaths mingled, lips a hair's breadth apart. She was certain that someone would soon notice the smoke and call the fire brigade.

The music had changed now, from slow to fast, and Jack's broad hand on her lower back steered her back to their empty table. He pulled out a chair for her and looked from her to a hovering waiter.

'What can I get you to drink? G&T? A cocktail? Or do you feel like sharing a bottle of red wine?'

'That sounds good.'

Ellie crossed her legs as Jack took the chair next to her and flipped open the wine list he'd been handed. He held it so that Ellie could scan the selection with him.

Ellie tapped the list with her finger. 'I don't really care as long as it has alcohol and is wet. Any of Luke's wines are good. St Sylve's.'

She sounded nervous, Jack thought. So she should, even if she had only a vague idea of how close she'd come to being ravished on the dance floor.

Jack rubbed his forehead. *Ravished.* Only Ellie could make him think of such an old-fashioned word. Pulling himself together, he ordered the wine, then slipped off his suit jacket before loosening the collar on his white dress shirt and yanking down his tie in an effort to get more air into his lungs. Now, if only he could sort his tented pants out.

'That's better.'

Ellie touched her hair and smiled wryly. 'I wish I could do that to my hair.'

He wished *he* could do that to her hair. He'd spent many hours thinking about that hair brushing his stomach, about wrapping it around his hands as he settled himself over her... Jack shifted in his chair. What was *with* this woman and her ability to short-circuit his brain? He dropped his eyes to her chest, where the fabric of her dress flirted with her cleavage and showed just a hint of a lacy pink bra.

Kill me now, Jack thought.

Ellie draped a leg over a knee and looked across the room. He could see her rapidly beating pulse at the base of her neck and knew that she was just as hot for him as he was for her. Not that he needed any confirmation. The little brush of her stomach across his body on the dance floor had been a freaking big clue.

Their wine was delivered and their conversation dried up. Jack didn't care. He just wanted to drink her in, lap her up... He gulped his wine, thoroughly rattled at how sexy he found her. Deep blue eyes, that sensual mouth, the scent of her sweetly sexy perfume. She had such beautiful skin, every inch of which he wanted to explore, taste, caress...

Sitting there, looking at her, he became conscious of something settling inside of him... To hell with being sensible and playing it safe. He knew what he wanted and he was damn well going to ask for it.

He reached over and lightly rested the tips of his fingers on the inside of her wrist, smiling wryly when he felt her pulse skitter. He lifted his hand, pushed a strand of hair that had fallen over her eyes behind her ear.

He leaned over and spoke in her ear. 'I can't do this any more. I've tried everything I can to resist you but enough is enough. Let's go home. Let me take you to bed.'

He saw the answer in her eyes and didn't wait for her nod

before taking her hand and leading her—wine, function and friends forgotten—out of the room.

Jack waited while she locked the front door and then backed her up against it, his body easily covering hers. He'd removed his jacket and she could feel the heat from his body beneath his shirt. His chest flattened her breasts and her breath hitched in response. This was so big, she thought, so overpowering...

His hands were large and competent, stroking her waist and skimming her ribcage in a sensual promise of what was to come. His hands skirted over her bottom and he lifted her up and into him, forcing her to wrap her legs around his waist. His hands held her thighs, steaming hot under the frothy skirt of her favourite dress. One heel dropped to the floor and it took a slight shake of her other foot for her remaining shoe to drop as well. Jack's mouth finally brushed hers and his tongue dipped into her mouth in a long, slow slide.

Jack walked with her to the stairs and at the first step allowed her to slip down him. He cradled her head in his hands and rested his forehead on hers.

'Upstairs?' he whispered, and Ellie felt the word and his breath drift over her face.

She nodded, ordered her legs to move and lightly ran up the stairs. She turned into her darkened bedroom and realised that Jack was a second behind her. He yanked her to him and walked her backwards to her big double bed. She felt the mattress dip under her weight, and dip some more as she was pushed on her back and Jack crawled over her.

She felt one of the straps of her dress fall down a shoulder and Jack's lips on her smooth skin. He was everything she'd ever wanted, she thought: strong, sexy, amazingly adept at making heat and lust pool in her womb. She'd never felt so intimately invested in a kiss, an embrace...so desperate to have his mouth on her, his fingers on her, to touch him, explore him, know him.

This could mean something, Ellie thought. This could mean something…huge.

Jack sat back on his haunches and pulled her up, kissing her as his hands looked for the zip at the back of her dress. Cool air touched her fevered skin as his hands wandered and soothed, danced over her skin, while his tongue did an erotic tango with hers.

Then her dress fell to her waist and she half sat, half lay in her strapless bra, her torso open to his hot gaze.

It had been so long. She'd half forgotten what to do. Should she undo the buttons of his shirt, pull it over his head? Let him do it himself? Could she do that? Should she do that? Ellie brushed her hand over his hip and felt the padding of his dressing. Another thought dropped into her scrambled head. Should he even be doing this? What if he pulled the skin apart and he started bleeding again?

'Your cut…' Ellie murmured, sitting up in an effort to escape those searing eyes.

'Is fine,' Jack replied, stroking her from shoulder to hand.

Ellie rested her forehead on his collarbone and sighed. She wanted this, wanted to immerse herself in this experience with him, but suddenly her mind was jumping around like a cricket on speed, playing with thoughts that were not conducive to inspiring or maintaining passion. Thoughts like, What did this mean to him? To her? With all her previous lovers—okay, all two of them—she'd felt and given love and thought that that love was reciprocated to a degree. There was nothing like that with Jack. They had nothing more between them than a burgeoning friendship and a searing, burning passion.

It had been so long since Darryl, and she was so out of practice. Would she be enough for him? She had enough pride to want to get this right. Was she knowledgeable enough, sexy enough, passionate enough to make this something that he'd remember?

Jack pulled her dress over her head and ran his index finger above the edge of her bra, his finger tanned against her creamy skin. Ellie looked down at his finger and closed her eyes, confused and bemused. She wanted him, but she wasn't wholly convinced that she was ready...

She should say no. She needed to say no...

Jack looked down at her breasts spilling over her frothy bra and thought that he'd never seen anything as beautiful in his life. Her skin had a luminosity that he'd never seen before—the palest blush on a creamy rose. Her ribcage was narrow, her arms slim, and her fingers were still on his hip. He could feel the heat in them through his pants, as tangible as her very sudden, very obvious mental retreat.

Going, going...oh, crap...*gone*.

Jack knew that he could kiss her, could stoke those fires again, but if she wasn't as fully in the moment with this as he was—had been—then it wasn't fair to her or—*dammit*—to him. He wanted her engaged, body, mind and soul. He could have physical sex with other women. He wanted, *expected* more from Ellie. Why and how much more he wasn't sure, but still...

Jack ran his hand over her head and sat back, his knees on either side of her legs. Ellie looked at him with big, wide eyes the colour of blue moonlight and ran her tongue over her top lip. He really wished she wouldn't do that...it made him think of the plans he'd had for that tongue. Hot, wicked, sexy plans.

Dammit... He sighed.

There were a bunch of reasons why he shouldn't be doing this, he thought. All of them valid. He was here for a limited time and she wasn't the type of girl who indulged in brief affairs. They were already living in the same house, so if they slept together they'd step over from friendship into sex-coloured friendship which was the gateway for affection, which led to attachment and a myriad of complications.

And what if that happened and he found himself liking living with her and not wanting to leave? How could he reconcile that with the promise he'd made to himself and to others that he'd live life to its fullest? His hard, fast, take-no-prisoners lifestyle—a life spent on planes, trains and hotel rooms—was not conducive to a full-time lover and invariably led to disappointment and sometimes to disaster.

'Jack?'

Jack blinked and lifted his eyebrows. 'Mmm?'

'You're a bit…heavy,' Ellie said in a small voice.

Jack immediately moved off her legs and sat on the edge of the bed. 'Sorry,' he muttered.

'No, it's okay. Just…um…need to get my blood circulating,' Ellie said in a jerky voice.

Jack sat sideways on the bed and thought that Ellie looked breathtaking in the low light that spilled into the room from the passage. Her mouth was soft and inviting and her hair was mostly out of its elaborate style, falling in waves over her shoulders.

Jack, all concerns forgotten, started to lean forward, intent on kissing the life out of her, but he made the mistake of looking into her eyes. They were round and slightly scared—and utterly, comprehensively miserable. He wondered how long it would take for her to call it quits, how far she'd take him down the road before she realised that she wasn't mentally ready to sleep with him.

It turned out not to be long at all…

'I'm sorry.' Ellie's voice was jerky and full of remorse. 'I really can't do this.'

So, she did have guts. Good to know, Jack thought. And at least she was honest.

'Okay.'

Jack saw Ellie cross her arms over her chest so he stood up and walked over to her bedroom door, unhooked her dressing gown. He passed it to her and moved on to stand at her open window, looking out at the dark night. When he turned around again Ellie's gorgeous body was covered, chest to knee, in a silky wrap that was almost as heart-attack-inducing as the dress she'd worn earlier.

He had to get out of her room before he did something he would regret. Like haul her back into his arms.

So he walked over to her and dropped a kiss on her temple. 'It's late. Maybe we should get some sleep.'

He thought it was a tragedy when Ellie didn't try to stop him when he walked out of the room.

Ellie woke, dressed and stumbled down the stairs half asleep. The noise of the television from the lounge jerked her fully awake and immediately caused memories of the previous night to rush back with the power of a sumo wrestler. She groaned. Jeez, she'd had all the sophistication of a pot plant. It had been so long, and she'd been so nervous, so self-conscious and hadn't been able to stop the weird thoughts buzzing around her head. She'd been worried about him seeing her naked and she'd stressed about whether he would stay the night with her, how much foreplay he expected and whether he was enjoying himself.

She'd been unable to let go, and if she was so attracted to him shouldn't she be able to lose herself in him? Wasn't that what lust-filled lovers did?

Ellie stood in the doorway to the lounge and stared at her wooden floor.

'Morning,' Jack said from the corner of the room, where he sat in a violet chair, leaning forward, his hands loose between his knees.

Elle lifted her head and squinted at him. 'Morning. How long have you been up?'

'Not too long.'

Ellie rested her hand on the doorframe. 'I'll go and make coffee.'

Jack nodded to a steaming cup of coffee that stood on the coffee table. 'I heard you moving around as I came down the stairs so I made you a cup.'

'Thanks.' Ellie walked across the room to pick up her cup and wrapped her hands around it. The purple elephant was back and was laughing like a maniac. But she wasn't going to consider raising the subject. It was embarrassing enough thinking about it. Talking to him about it would be absolutely impossible!

And that was even before she realised how preoccupied and distant Jack looked.

'I thought I'd get caught up with what's happening in the world. Do you mind?' he said.

'No.'

He gestured to the TV. 'Your dad is in Kenya, reporting on the riots.'

Okay, she'd go with world politics if that was all he had. 'They are having elections soon,' he added.

She *so* didn't care. She wanted to know what he was going to do now, how she was supposed to act. Ellie bit her lip, walked further into the room and looked at her father's familiar face on the screen.

'He's looking tired.' Ellie sat down on the couch and tucked her legs up under her as Mitchell answered questions from the anchor in New York.

'He texted me earlier. He thinks there's big trouble brewing.'

Jack turned up the volume on the TV set and she listened with half an ear as Mitchell spoke about the situation in Kenya.

He's nearly sixty, Ellie thought, wondering whether he had any thoughts about retiring. Because that wasn't something he'd ever discuss with *her*.

'I'm going there.'

Ellie took a moment to assimilate his statement. 'Going where?'

'To Kenya. A massive bomb was found and defused and the country is on a knife edge. I have contacts there,' Jack explained. He lifted his cup. 'I'm going to head out as soon as I've finished my coffee.'

'Ah...'

'I'm the closest reporter, and if I can get on a flight now I'll be with Mitch within a couple of hours. He's going to need help covering this.'

'Why?'

Jack frowned. 'It's news, Ellie, and news is my job. I know Nairobi. I want to be there.'

Ellie's heart sank. Of course he did. It didn't matter that he was beaten up, hurt and tired, or that he'd kissed her senseless, there was a story and he needed to follow it. It was the nature of the beast.

The fact that she was acting like a nervous, awkwardly shy Victorian nerd was also a very good excuse for him to run from her—fast and hard. Could she blame him?

Ellie refocused as Jack answered his ringing mobile. 'Hey, Andrew. No, I managed to get a seat on the next flight out to Nairobi. I'll be at the airport in—' he looked at his watch '—an hour. In the air in three.'

It took forty-five minutes to get to the airport, which left fifteen minutes for him to pack up and walk out of her life, Ellie thought. Last night she'd been lost in this man's arms and this morning he was making plans to walk out through the door without giving her a second thought.

And that just summed up all her experiences with war re-porters. Nothing was more important than the story…ever.
Ever.

Jack leaned forward in his seat. He really didn't want to be on this plane, was unenthusiastic about going to Kenya, but all through the night, unable to sleep, he'd known that he couldn't stay with Ellie, that he needed to get some distance. From her…from the feelings she pulled to the surface.

Last night, for the first time in years, he'd allowed himself to become mentally engaged with a woman, and in doing so he'd caught a glimpse of all that he was missing by not al-lowing that intimate connection. The warmth of her smile, the richness of her laughter, her enjoyment of being with him all added another layer to the constant sexual buzz that took it from thrilling to frightening.

They'd been emotionally and physically in sync and he'd loved every second of the previous evening—even if she had called a halt to it. Hell, he'd loved every minute of the past few days. He could, if he let himself, imagine a lifetime of evenings drinking wine on the veranda, taking evening walks with her, making love to her.

Brent had never got to experience anything like this….

The thought chilled him to the bone. *Brent.* And, dear God, he needed to make a decision about going to that memorial service, to face his family…to face his demons, the never-ending guilt of being alive because that teenage boy was dead.

Jack rubbed his face. If he hadn't had a heart transplant, if he'd grown up normal, what would his life be like? Where would he be? What would he be? Would he be married yet? Have kids?

How much of his reluctance to get involved was his own reticent nature and how much was driven by guilt? Was he avoiding love and permanence not only because he felt that his job didn't allow it but also because he felt he didn't deserve it? That if Brent couldn't have it why should he?

He already had his heart—was he entitled to happiness with it as well? Jack let out a semi-audible groan.

The elderly lady next to him, with espresso eyes and cocoa skin, laid an elegant hand on his arm.

'Are you all right, my dear?'

Jack dredged up a smile. 'Fine, thanks.' He saw doubt cross her face and shrugged. 'Just trying to work through some stuff.'

She rattled off a phrase in an African language he didn't recognise.

'Sorry, I don't understand.'

'African proverb. Peace is costly but it is worth the expense.'

Indeed.

CHAPTER SEVEN

ELLIE SNAPPED AT one of her staff and, after apologising, realised that she desperately needed a break from the bakery.
Taking a bottle of water from the fridge, she walked out
through the front door into the strong afternoon sunlight.
Checking for cars, she walked across the street and sat on the
concrete wall that separated the beach from the promenade
and stretched out her bare legs. She flipped open the buttons
of her chef's tunic and shrugged it off, allowing the sea breeze
to flow over her bare shoulders in her sleeveless fuchsia top.

It had been four hellish days since Jack's abrupt departure.
She had the concentration span of a flea and her thoughts were
a galaxy away from her business and her craft.

His memory should have faded but she could still remember, in high definition, her time spent with Jack. The way his
eyes crinkled when he smiled, the flash of white teeth, those
wizard-like eyes that made you want to spill your soul.

She missed him—really missed him. Missed his manly way
of looking at a situation, his clear-headed thought-processes,
and she missed bouncing ideas about Pari's off him. She missed
her friend.

But more than missing him she was also now seriously irritated. Furious, in fact. Partly at Jack, for whirling out of her
house like a dervish, but mostly at herself. How stupid was

she to think that she could rely on him, that he wouldn't drop her like a hot brick for a story, for a situation?

The men she was attracted to always ran out on her, so why had she thought it would be different with Jack? He'd been in her life for under a week and she was livid that, subconsciously at least, she'd come to rely on him in such a short time. For advice, for a smile, for conversation and company at the end of a long day. How could she have forgotten, even for one minute, that war reporters always, *always* left, usually at a critical time in her life?

She couldn't help the memory rolling back—was powerless against the familiar resentment. She'd been fourteen and she'd entered a drawing of a lion into a competition in a well-known wildlife magazine. Out of thousands of entries throughout the country she'd won the 'Young Teenager' category. She'd been due to receive her prize at a prestigious televised awards ceremony. She'd spent weeks in a panic because Mitchell was on assignment, and the relief she'd felt when he'd arrived back home three days before the ceremony had been overwhelming.

Everything had been super-okay with her world. The thought of going up onto that stage in front of all those people had made her feel sick, but her handsome dad would be in the audience so she'd do it. She would move mountains for him.

Then someone had got assassinated and he'd flown out two hours before the event…which she'd been too distraught to attend.

Ellie straightened her shoulders. She was no longer that broken, defeated, sad teenager who'd flung her arms around her father and begged him not to go.

She sipped her water and narrowed her eyes. She'd looked up the political situation in Kenya, and while it was tense it wasn't exploding. Jack hadn't needed to high-tail it out of her house. He was running from her—probably looking for an excuse to get away from her hot and cold behaviour, her lack of confidence in that sort of situation and her disastrous bedroom skills. If Jack had bailed just because of that, if she never saw him again—and who knew if she would, since *she hadn't heard from him since he'd left*—then good riddance, because then he was an idiot. As angry and...she searched for the word...*disappointed* as she felt, she knew that she was worth far more than just to be some transient woman who provided him a bed and some fun in it.

Ellie heard a long wolf whistle and looked up to see Merri leaving Pari's, two bottles of water in her hand. She'd obviously left Molly Blue with someone in the bakery—probably Mama Thandi—and was sauntering across the road as if she owned it.

Merri handed her another bottle of water and sat next to her, stretching her long body. A car passing them drifted as the driver gaped at her sensational-looking friend. Merri, as per normal, didn't notice. Ellie was quite certain that the majority of motor car accidents in Muizenberg were somehow related to Merri and the effect she had on men's driving.

'Now, tell me, why are you looking all grumpy and sorry for yourself?'

Ellie cracked open the second bottle of water and took a long swallow. How did she explain Jack to Merri?

The best way was just to blurt it all out. 'I nearly slept with Jack.'

'Good for you!' Merri gaped at her. 'Wait...did you say *nearly*? What is wrong with you, woman?'

There was no judgement in Merri's voice, and Ellie knew that her 'almost sleeping with Jack' story wouldn't even create a blip on her shock radar. Merri was pretty much unshockable.

Unlike her, Merri was a thoroughly modern woman. Not a drip.

'Do you want to talk about it?' Merri asked.

Ellie shook her head. 'Yes. No. Maybe. Still processing. Very confused.'

'So it wasn't just sex, then?'

'We didn't get that far. I said that I wasn't ready and he backed off.'

'Nicely?'

'What do you mean?'

'Was he nice about it? No tantrums, accusations, saying you led him on?'

Ellie shook her head. 'Of course not. He just passed me my dressing gown and said goodnight.'

'Huh. I *really* have to start dating nicer guys,' Merri stated thoughtfully. 'So why couldn't you go through with it?'

Ellie looked out to sea and wondered if she could escape this conversation. As if sensing her thoughts, Merri hooked her arm in hers and kept her in place.

'It was fine—great. I was totally in the moment and then—' Ellie snapped her fingers '—like that, my brain started providing a running commentary.'

'Oh, I hate it when it does that,' Merri agreed. 'I remember being so caught up in the intensity of being with this one guy, and then he took off his shirt and he had a pelt of chest hair. And back hair. It was like he was wearing a coat...*ugh*. My brain started making jokes at his expense. Does Jack have back hair?'

'Uh...no.'

'Did he make animal sounds?'

'No.'

'Talk dirty?'

'No.'

'Have a really small—?'

'Merri!' Ellie interjected, cutting her off. 'He's fine— gorgeous, in fact! He didn't do anything wrong!'

'Then what was the problem?' Merri asked, puzzled. 'He's

gorgeous, nice, and you were into him.' She looked Ellie in her eyes and twisted her lips. 'Ah, *dammit*, Ellie!'

'What?' Ellie demanded.

'When you told me that Jack was staying with you we talked about you getting emotionally entangled with him.' Merri shook her head in despair. 'And you have, haven't you?'

'I'm not entangled with him. Or at the very least I'm trying not to get emotionally attached to him. When we were getting it on I had this thought that he could become a big thing if I let him.'

'And how is that *not* getting emotionally involved with him?' Merri demanded.

'The key phrase is *if I let him*,' Ellie protested.

Merri was silent for a while, and her voice was full of hope when she spoke again. 'Are you not just getting lust and feelings mixed up? Sometimes sex is just sex and it doesn't always have to be more.'

'I know that…and I tried to think that. Unfortunately I can't just think of him as a random slab of meat.'

'Try harder.' Merri sighed forlornly. 'Have I taught you nothing?' She narrowed her eyes in thought. 'Maybe you need to practise the concept of casual sex a bit more? I have a friend who is always up to…helping the cause.'

Ellie hiccuped a laugh at Merri's outrageous suggestion. 'Thanks, but no. Really.'

They both heard Merri's name being called, and across the street Mama Thandi stood with Molly in her arms, her face wet with tears. 'I'm coming!' Merri called back as she stood up.

She bent and kissed Ellie goodbye and a nearby jogger nearly ran straight into a lightpole.

Merri was right. She had to wrap her head around the concept of casual sex. And if—big if!—Jack came back, then she'd have to decide whether she could separate sex and emotion, because becoming emotionally attached to Jack would be a disaster of mega proportions.

They were fire and water, heaven and hell, victory and defeat. Maybe there *was* something fast and hot between them sexually, but fast and hot weren't enough to sustain a relationship. Relationships needed time and input, and at the very least for the participants within said relationship to be on the same continent for more than a nano-second.

Like Mitchell, Jack was the ultimate free spirit: an adventurer of heart and soul who needed his freedom as he needed air to breathe.

Apart from the fact that she didn't want to—was too damn scared to—become emotionally involved with a man who was just like her father, Ellie knew that she wasn't exciting enough, long term, for someone as charismatic as Jack. Darryl had put her childhood fears and suspicions into words five minutes before he'd left her life for good.

'You need to face facts, Ellie. You're not enough—not sexy enough, smart enough, interesting enough—for a man to make sacrifices for. Nobody will give up their freedom and time for monogamy with you. Nobody interesting, at least.'

It was something she'd suspected all her life, and having someone—him—verbalise it had actually been a relief. Even if it had hurt like hell.

Ellie watched the afternoon crowds walk down the promenade, smiling at the earnest joggers, the chattering groups of women walking off their extra pounds. Kids on bicycles weaved through the crowds and skateboarders followed in their wake. It was a typical scene for a hot day in the summer.

Ellie saw a taxi pull up across the road just down the street from the bakery before she half turned to look at the sea. A number of cargo ships hovered on the horizon and a sailboat zipped by closer to shore. Reaching for her bottle of water, she looked back at the bakery and saw a man climb out of the taxi, his hand briefly touching his side. His broad shoulders and long legs reminded her of Jack…but this man had short hair, wore smart chinos, a long-sleeved white shirt with the cuffs rolled back and dark, sleek sunglasses. Then the sun picked up the reddish glints in his hair…

Jack?

Ellie yelped and dropped her water bottle as he paid the driver and pulled that familiar black rucksack from the boot of the taxi.

Jack… Jack was back.

Oh, good God… Jack. Was. Back.

As if he sensed her eyes on him Jack straightened and looked across the road. Ellie folded her arms and bit her lip. There was no way that she was going to run across the road like a demented schoolgirl and hurl herself into his arms…as much as she wanted to.

Ellie gnawed on her bottom lip as he lifted his rucksack with one hand, dropped it over his shoulder and slowly walked across the road. When he reached her he dropped the rucksack at her feet and sent her a small grin.

'Hi, El.'

Ellie's stomach plummeted and twisted as her name rolled off his tongue. She tucked her hands into the back pockets of her jeans and rocked on her heels.

'You're back. And you cut your hair…' Ellie stuttered and her heart copied her voice.

The corner of Jack's mouth lifted as he brushed his hand over his short back and sides. 'Seems like it.'

'I thought you would've headed home…' Ellie said, wishing she could hug him and also that she could finish a sentence. What *was* it about this man who had her words freezing on her tongue?

His eyes didn't leave hers. 'I have a flat in London but it certainly isn't home.' His mouth lifted in that teasing way that she'd missed so much. 'Besides, I paid you for three weeks' board and lodging and I'd like to get my money's worth.'

Ellie grinned. 'That sounds fair.' She could smell him from where she stood: sandalwood and citrus, clean soap and sexy male. Ellie breathed him in and again wished she were in his arms.

She looked up into his face and sighed at the stress in his eyes, the deeper brackets around his mouth. 'Rough trip?'

He shrugged. 'I've had worse.' He took her hand and raised her knuckles to place a gentle kiss on them. 'I'm sorry I didn't call...I wasn't sure what to say.'

Ellie's eyes narrowed as she remembered that she was supposed to be cross with him. 'I have to say that when it's required you can vacate a house at speed.'

Jack pushed his hair off his forehead. 'Yeah, sorry. I'm not used to explaining my actions... I've been on my own for too long and I'm not good at stopping to play nice.'

Ellie pulled her hand out of his and tapped her finger against her chin. 'How's my dad?'

'He's fine.' Jack went on to explain what he'd done in Kenya, the outcome of the contact he'd made with his numerous sources. His words were brief and succinct but Ellie could hear the tension in his voice, saw pain flicker in and out of his eyes and wondered what he wasn't telling her.

'Something else happened. Something that rocked you.'

Shock rippled across Jack's face. Then those shutters fell over his eyes and he dropped his gaze from hers, looking down at the pavement. When he lifted his head again his expression was rueful. 'The sun is shining; it's a stunning afternoon. I want to go home, climb into my board shorts and hit the surf. I just want to forget about work for a while.'

Ellie wished she could join him but gestured to the bakery. 'I still have a couple of hours' work to do.'

'Of course you do. I'll meet you back here at closing time.'

Jack picked up his rucksack and slung it over one shoulder. 'It's good to be back, El.'

Ellie watched him cross the street and turn the corner for home. Jack was back and the world suddenly seemed brighter and lighter and shinier.

That couldn't, in *any* galaxy, be good.

'So, he hasn't made a move on you again?'

'No, not even close. Then again, he's barely spoken to me,' Ellie answered Merri, who was in for the afternoon, helping her make Sacher Torte for an order to be picked up that evening.

Princess Molly Blue, as beautiful as her mother, was fast asleep on Mama Thandi's back, held in place by a light cotton shawl wrapped around her back and Mama's chest. Ellie looked at Mama, who was quickly plaiting strips of dough for braided bread; it really was a very efficient way to carry on working and let your baby be close to you. Ellie hoped Merri was taking notes.

'What do you mean?'

'He's been back for two days and I've barely seen him.' Ellie shrugged. 'We eat supper together and then he disappears to his room to work.' She tightened the ties of her apron and frowned. 'There are friends, lovers and acquaintances. Jack left as a friend, was briefly—sort of—a lover, and he's come back as the last.'

Merri split a vanilla pod and scraped out its insides with a knife. 'What changed? Do you think it was because you said no?'

Ellie separated the whites and yolks of eggs as she considered the question. 'I don't know. Maybe.'

'If that's the reason then he's a jerk of magnificent proportions,' Merri stated, adding the vanilla to butter and sugar and switching on the beater.

'He might as well be a guest in my B&B, except that he packs the dishwasher, makes dinner if I'm working late and even, very kindly, did a load of my laundry with his own. I just want my friend back,' Ellie added.

'No, you don't. You want to sleep with him,' Merri said in a cheerful voice.

'No! Well, yes. But I can't. Won't.'

'Uh…why?'

'Because, as you said, I can't seem to separate the emotion and the deed,' Ellie admitted reluctantly. 'If I sleep with him I risk—'

'Caring for him, falling in love with him. Why would that be the worst thing that could happen to you?'

Ellie viciously tipped the egg whites into another mixing bowl and reached for a hand-beater. 'I don't want to talk about this any more.'

'Tough.'

Ellie shut off the hand-beater and checked on the chocolate that was melting in a *bain-marie*. 'We don't have enough time for me to list the reasons…'

'Yes, we do. Spill.'

'He has a job I hate. He's never around. I don't have time for a relationship—'

Merri pointed a wooden spoon at her. 'Quit lying to yourself, El. The biggest reason you are so scared is because he doesn't need you, and we all know that you live to be needed.'

Ellie looked at her, shocked. 'That's so unfair.'

'Ellie, you take pride in being indispensable. You *need* people to need you. You need to love more than you need love, and you recognise that Jack doesn't need your love to survive, to function. You're terrified of being rejected…'

'Aren't we all?' Ellie demanded.

'No. Some of us realise that you can't force someone to love you just because you want him to.'

'Bully for you,' Ellie muttered mutinously.

Merri stared at her, her eyes uncharacteristically sombre.
'I don't think I ever realised until this moment how much
your father's lack of attention and Darryl's scumbag antics
scarred you.'

Ellie wanted to protest that she wasn't scarred, that she was
just being careful, but she knew it wasn't true. She'd suspected
for a long time that she was emotionally damaged, and Merri's
words just confirmed what she'd always thought.

So maybe it was better that she and Jack kept their distance,
kept the status quo.

'Can we talk about something else? Molly Blue? Is she
teething yet?'

Merri grinned at her. 'No, I don't want to talk about my
baby.'

She'd been talking about Molly for six months straight
and she didn't want to talk about her now? How unfair, Ellie
thought.

'I still want to talk about you. Let's talk about your inabil-
ity to say no...'

Ellie, past the point of patience, threw an egg at her.

Ellie rolled over and looked, wide-eyed, at the luminous hands
of her bedside clock. It was twelve-seventeen and she wasn't
even close to sleep. Throwing off her sheet, she cocked her
head as she heard footsteps going down the stairs.

It seemed she wasn't the only person who was awake.

Ellie pulled a thigh-length T-shirt over her skimpy tank.
It skimmed the hem of her sleeping shorts. Deciding against
shoes, she flipped her thick plait over her shoulder, left the
room and walked down the darkened stairs. She knew where
he'd be: standing on the front veranda, looking out to the
moonlit sea.

He wasn't. He was sitting on one of the chairs, dressed in

running shorts and pulling on his trainers. Ellie hesitated at the front door and took a moment to watch him, looking hard and tough, as he quickly tied the laces in his shoes. It was after midnight—why was he going for a run? It made no sense...

'What are you doing?' she asked, stepping through the open door.

Jack snapped his head up to look at her and she caught the tension in his eyes. 'Can't sleep.'

'So you're going for a run?'

Jack shrugged. 'It's better than lying awake looking at the ceiling.'

Ellie folded her arms and looked at the top of his head. For the past four days he'd been quiet, and tonight at dinner he'd said little, after which he'd excused himself as usual to do some work. Despite hoping that he'd come back downstairs, she hadn't seen him since he'd left the table.

Jack stood up and started to stretch, and Ellie wondered if this was Jack's way of expelling stress and tension. She might indulge in a good crying jag but he went running. Maybe, just maybe, she could get him to try talking for a change.

She crossed her arms as she stepped outside, then walked up to him and nudged him with her shoulder.

'Why don't you talk to me instead of hitting the streets?'

'Uh—'

'C'mon.' Ellie boosted herself up on the stone wall so that she faced Jack, her back to the sea. 'What's going on, Jack? Has something happened?'

Jack placed his arm behind his head to stretch out his arms and Ellie noticed his chest muscles rippling, his six-pack contracting, that nasty scar lifting. She forced herself to take her mind off his body and concentrate on his words.

'Nothing's happened...'

Dammit, he simply wasn't going to open up. Ellie felt a spurt of hurt and disappointment and hopped off the wall.

'Okay, Jack, don't talk to me. But don't treat me like an idiot by telling me that nothing happened!'

Ellie headed for the front door and was stopped by Jack's strong arm around her stomach.

'Geez, Ellie. Cool your jets, would you?'

Ellie whirled around, put her hands on his chest and shoved. Her efforts had no impact on him at all. 'Dammit, I just want you to talk to me!'

'If you gave me two seconds to finish my sentence then you'd realise that I am trying to talk to you!' Jack dropped his arms and pointed to the Morris chair. 'Sit.'

Ellie sat and pulled her feet up to tuck them under her, her expression mutinous. She'd give him one more chance, but if he tried to fob her off with 'nothing happened' again she'd shove him off the wall.

Jack sat on the edge of the wall. 'Kenya was a fairly routine trip in that nothing *unusual* happened. I hit the streets, found my contacts, got some intel, reported. I worked, hung out with the rest of the press corps.'

Ellie pulled a face. 'Sorry.'

Jack placed his hand behind his ear. 'What was that?'

Ellie glared at him. 'You heard me. So if the trip was fairly routine, then what's bugging you?'

'Exactly that...the fact that the trip felt so routine. Unexciting, flat.'

Ellie scratched her forehead. 'I'm sorry, I don't understand.'

'I'm not sure if I understand either. There are certain reasons I do what I do. Why I do it. I need the adrenalin. I need to feel like I'm living life at full throttle.' Jack must have seen the question on her face because he shook his head. 'Maybe some day I'll tell you why but not now. Not tonight.'

Not ready yet. She could respect that. 'Okay, so you need the thrill, the buzz of danger...'

'Not necessarily danger—okay, I like the danger factor

too—but in places or situations like that there's always a buzz, an energy that is so tangible you can almost reach out and taste it. I feed on that energy.'

'And there wasn't any this time?'

Jack closed his eyes. 'Oh, there was—apparently. Everyone I spoke to said that there was something in the air, a sense that the place was on a knife edge, that violence was a hair's breadth away. The journalists were buzzing on the atmosphere and I didn't pick up a damn thing. I couldn't feel it. I felt like I was just going through the motions.'

'Oh.'

'There are different types of war correspondent. There are the idealists—the ones who want to make a difference. There are the ones who, sadly, feed off the violence, the brutality. There are others who use it to hide from life.' Jack scrubbed his hands over his face. 'I report. Full-stop. Right from the beginning I knew that it wasn't my job to save the world. That my job was to relay the facts, not to get involved with the emotion. I have always been super-objective. I don't particularly like making judgement calls, mostly because I can always see both sides of the story. Nobody is ever one hundred per cent right. But I always—*always!*—have been the first to pick up the mood on the street, the energy in the air.'

'Do you ever take a stand? Get off the fence?' Ellie asked him after a short silence. 'Make a judgement call?'

Jack thought about her question for a moment. 'Personally or professionally?'

'Either. Both.'

'When it comes to political ideologies I am for neutrality. Personally, I've experienced some stuff…gone through a lot… so when bad things happen I measure it up against what I went through and frequently realise that it's not worth getting upset about. So I don't get worked up easily, and because of that I probably don't get involved on either side of anything either.'

Whoa! Super-complicated man. 'Okay, so getting back to Kenya...'

'I made an offhand comment to Mitch about feeling like this and that led to a discussion about me. He said that I've become too distant, too unemotional, too hard. He used the word "robotic". *Am* I robotic, El?'

Ellie stood up, sat on the wall next to him and dropped her head onto his shoulder. 'I don't think you are, but to be fair I haven't seen you in that situation or seen you report for a long time—six months at least.'

'He also said that I'm desensitised to violence, that I don't see other people's pain. That I'm becoming heartless.'

That was rich, coming from her father, Ellie thought, the King of Self-Involvement. Except her father was very good at what he did, so he might have a point. But Ellie didn't believe that Jack was as callous as he or her father made him out to be. It was more likely that he used his emotional distance as a shield.

'Is not caring just a way to protect yourself from everything bad you've seen?'

Jack shrugged. 'I have no idea. Mitch said that I'm burnt out, that it's affecting my reporting, that I'm coming across as hard. He said that I need to get my head in the game, take some time off to fill the well. We had a rip roaring argument...'

'He sent you home?'

Jack looked rebellious. 'As much as he likes to think he does, Mitchell doesn't *send* me anywhere. I left because there wasn't much more to report on except for rehashing the same story.' Jack stared at his feet.

'Is he right? *Are* you burnt out?' Ellie asked quietly, keeping her temple on his shoulder.

'I don't know.'

'I think you need to give yourself a break. You were beaten up in Somalia, stabbed, kicked out of the country. You've just come back from a less than cheerful city. When did you last take a proper holiday, relax…counter all the gruesome stuff you've witnessed with happy stuff?'

'Happy stuff?'

'Lying on a beach, surfing, drinking wine in the afternoon sun. Napping. Reading a book for pleasure and not for research. Um…sleeping late. In other words, a holiday?'

'Not for a while. Not for a very long time,' Jack admitted, placing his broad hand on her knee.

'Thought so. Maybe you should actually do that?'

'I don't know how to relax, to take it easy. It's not in my nature. I like moving, working, exploring. I need to keep moving to feel alive.'

'Maybe that's what you've conditioned yourself to feel… but it's not healthy.' Ellie yawned and reluctantly lifted her head off his arm.

Jack stood up and ran a gentle hand over her hair. 'Get some sleep, El. There's no point in us both being exhausted.'

Ellie didn't think about it. She just stood up, wrapped her arms around his waist and laid her cheek on his bare chest. 'Don't beat yourself up, Jack. Mitchell might think he's always right, but he's not.'

'I kind of think he might be this time.'

'Well, I hope you didn't tell him that. You'll never hear the end of it.' Ellie placed her forehead on his chest and kept one hand on his waist.

Jack stood ramrod-straight and for the longest minute Ellie held her breath, certain that he would push her away. Eventually his arms locked around her back and he buried his face in her hair. Ellie rubbed her hands over his back, met his miserable eyes and ran her hand across his forehead, down his cheek to his chest. Her hands dropped, brushed the waistband of his shorts, and she felt tension—suddenly sexual—skitter through his body. She moved her hands to put them on his hips and felt his swift intake of air.

'I missed you,' he said, his voice gruff.

'I missed you too.'

Jack closed his eyes and his arms tightened and his lower body jumped in reaction to her words. She could feel his heat and response through her light cotton shirt and sleeping shorts and she wanted him...

She didn't want to want him. She couldn't afford to want him.

She forced herself to say the words. 'I need to go to bed, Jack.'

Jack immediately released her and she suddenly felt colder without his heat.

'Go on up. I'm going for a run.'

Ellie nodded. 'Thanks, by the way.'

One eyebrow rose. 'For...?'

'Talking to me. I thought you were mad at me, so it was a bit of a relief. Sorry I jumped to the wrong conclusion in the beginning.'

Jack sent her a small grin. 'Next time you jump to conclusions I won't give you a second chance.'

Ellie patted his chest. 'Yes, you will.'

'I'm afraid you're probably right,' Jack said softly, and jogged down the stairs.

The night was warm and the streets were deserted, and the sea was his only companion as he ran along the promenade, his feet slapping against the pavement. Sweat ran down his temples and down his spine into the waistband of his shorts. His body felt fluid but his mind was a mess.

God, it felt good to run. Apart from the fact that it kept his heart working properly, it was easier to think when he was running.

He hadn't lied to Ellie—he *hadn't* connected with the story or the atmosphere in Kenya and that worried him—but he certainly hadn't told her the whole truth. How could he? How could he explain to her that he'd spent his days in Kenya missing her, thinking about her? He'd never allowed anyone to distract him from the job at hand, yet she had. He'd be walking the streets, seeing an old man whittling away at a piece of wood, and he'd think Ellie would crouch down next to him and demand to know what he was creating. He'd drink his morning coffee at the hotel and wish he was standing on her veranda, watching the endless blues and greens of the sea.

His nights were a combination of fantasy and frustration, thinking about what he wanted to do to and with her amazing body.

When he'd seen her on the wall that afternoon he'd come back his thumping heart had settled, sighed. And he'd known he had the potential to fall deeper and deeper in trouble. Emotional trouble.

He'd known her for only days and she'd stirred up all these weird feelings inside him. Why? What was it about her that made him feel as if he'd stepped outside of himself? He could talk to her. He wanted to talk to her. Take this evening, for example. He would never have spoken to any of his previous girlfriends like that…hell, he'd barely *spoken* to them. He'd just flown in from wherever, climbed into bed, kept said girlfriend in bed until he needed to leave and then left. He didn't know how to act as part of a couple on an on-going basis, and before he'd landed in Cape Town he'd never come close to being tied down by anyone or anything. He excelled in saying goodbye and never looking back. He'd had a second chance at life and he'd made a promise to live it hard, because he'd always believed it would be an injustice to live a small life… to confine himself to a humdrum job…to be shackled by a house or a lover.

His beliefs, so firmly held for so long, were starting to waver.

And that was why he'd scuttled out of Ellie's house last week. He hadn't needed to go to Kenya but it had been a damn good excuse to put some distance between them.

Jack stopped and, breathing heavily, placed his hands on his hips. In the low light of the sodium streetlights he stared out to the breaking waves as clouds scuttled across the moon. Little in life made sense any more… He could easily have gone back to London after Kenya but he'd headed south instead. What was happening to him?

He'd been shot, beaten up and stabbed. He'd sneaked behind enemy lines, walked into the compounds of drug cartels, through whorehouses filled with the dregs of humanity who'd slit his throat just for the fun of it—just to get a story. He'd seen the worst of what people could do to each other and yet he'd never felt fear like this before…

He was terrified he was becoming emotionally involved with her—would do practically anything to stop that happening. Ellie had hit the nail squarely in one of their many conversations; he was an observer, not a participator. Involvement with her would require a decision, taking a stand for her, sticking around, partaking in a life together.

He didn't want to do that—wasn't ready to do that. Wouldn't do that. He needed to find some perspective, reconnect with his beliefs, reaffirm his values. Jack nodded at the sea. He had to make sure that he kept some emotional distance, guarded against any deepening of their relationship. It was the sensible decision—hell, it was the only decision.

And while he was making major decisions he really needed to decide what he was going to do about Brent's memorial service. Go or not? He was starting to feel that he needed to, that he needed to honour Brent, to say thank you for the gift of his life. But would seeing him make the Sandersons' day worse? Would being there deepen the guilt he felt?

Maybe he shouldn't go.

Jack swore as he resumed running. This was why it was better not to examine his thoughts and emotions too closely. It just confused him. And, talking about being confused, what had Ellie meant when she'd said she had thought that he was angry with her? Why would she think that?

Jack intended to find out.

CHAPTER EIGHT

JACK POUNDED UP the steps and flung open her bedroom door. He knew she wouldn't be asleep and she wasn't. She was sitting up in bed, working on her computer. Didn't she ever give work a rest?

'Why are you working?' he demanded crossly.

'I'm not. I'm catching up with friends.'

'At one in the morning?'

'Excuse me, at least *I'm* not the one running after midnight!' Ellie closed the lid of her computer and tapped her finger against it. 'Did you just burst in here to give me a hard time generally or was there a specific reason?'

Jack walked into the room and stood at the end of her bed. 'You said that you thought I was mad at you. Why, Ellie?'

Ellie plucked the sheet with her fingers and felt her face flaming in the dim light of her lamp. 'It's not important.'

Jack sat on the edge of the bed and placed his hand on her knee. 'I think it might be. Talk to me, El.'

Ellie shook her head and placed her computer on her bedside table. 'Jack, it really doesn't matter since you haven't made any…since we're not…'

'Sleeping together?' Jack sounded puzzled. 'Are you upset that I'm *not* sleeping with you?'

'Yes…no. I don't know. I thought you'd changed your mind about…me.'

Jack's expression was pure confusion. 'Let me try and de-code that from girl-speak. Firstly, I couldn't run out of your house, not call you, then come back and expect to jump into bed with you. I thought we needed some time, and I've been dealing with all this other crap, so...' Jack rubbed the back of his neck. 'I changed my mind...? Hold on a sec—did you think that I didn't want to sleep with you? Why on earth wouldn't I want to sleep with you?'

'Good grief, Jack, you can't expect me to verbalise it!' Ellie cried.

'Well, if you want me to understand what's going on in that crazy head of yours, *yes*! Because I am lost!'

'I wasn't any good and it couldn't have been much fun for you,' Ellie mumbled. 'And I backed off midway.'

There was a long silence and Ellie felt Jack staring at her head. When he eventually spoke Ellie could hear the regret in his voice.

'Have you been worried about that since I left?'

'Mmm.'

Jack swore. 'And I left here with a rocket on my tail, not even thinking... Dammit!'

Ellie looked up at him. 'So you weren't mad that I said no?'

'Disappointed? Yes. Cross? Absolutely not.'

'Oh.'

Jack played with her fingers. 'Why *did* you stop, by the way? What happened?'

'My brain started a running commentary as soon as we got to my bedroom. I started to second-guess what we were doing—what I was doing. And whether I was getting it right.'

Jack cradled her cheek with his hand. 'Making love is not a test to be graded, sweetheart. Come on—cough it up. What else were you worrying about?'

'Whether I was enough for you. Whether I was practiced

enough. Cellulite…other crazy girl stuff.' Ellie stared at a point beyond his shoulder.

'You don't have a centimetre of cellulite, and if you do I *so* don't care. And if we're trading thoughts about that night then I should tell you that I'm sorry if I went too fast for you. I'd thought about having you so many times, in so many ways… and I guess I was nervous too.'

'Why were you nervous? You've had lots of sex before.'

'Yes, but I've never had sex with *you*!' Jack exclaimed. 'What? I'm not allowed to be nervous? I finally get the girl I've been fantasising about in bed and suddenly I'm a stud? It doesn't work like that, Ellie. The first time you make love to someone it's *always* the first time. I'm also worried about pleasing you. It never works out perfectly. We don't know each other's bodies, what the other person likes and/or doesn't like. It falls into place with time.'

Ellie continued to stare at her bedclothes.

'Sweetheart, I really need you to talk to me, to tell me what you're thinking,' Jack said quietly, his voice persuasive.

Ellie lifted her head and looked at him with sad eyes. 'Thank you for that—for saying all of that. And you're probably right. We just need time.'

'Exactly.'

Ellie held his gaze. 'But we have a problem. By my calculations, and from everything you've told me, you're staying another week at the most. Then you'll leave…probably around about the time we can start making mountains move. So my two questions are: how fair would that be to either of us? And, really, what would be the point?'

'It doesn't have to be love, Ellie. It doesn't have to be for ever. It can just be two people who are attracted to each other giving each other pleasure and company. The point can be…' Jack encircled her neck with his hand and smoothed his thumb over the tendons in her neck '…this.'

He touched the corner of her mouth with his.

'So sweet. Spicy.' He stroked her jaw and placed his lips on the spot between her jaw and her ear. 'Soft. The point can be that I think you have the most beautiful skin.'

Jack moved and dropped his other hand onto her bottom. In a movement that was as smooth as it was sexy, he pulled her onto his lap so that she straddled his thighs.

As sparks bolted down her inner thighs Ellie dimly remembered that she had to be pressing on his knife wound and tried to scramble off him. Jack's hand on her thighs kept her firmly in place.

'Nuh-uh—where are you going? I like you here,' he said.

'Your cut,' Ellie protested, her head dropping so that their noses were practically touching.

'I'm fine and you feel great,' Jack informed her, lifting his head to nibble on her mouth. 'I love your mouth…' he murmured. 'Love your eyes…fantastic skin…'

He lifted his hands from her thighs and placed them on her chest, holding the weight of her breasts in his hands. Ellie moaned as he thumbed her nipples into gloriously sensitive peaks.

'As for these…these are simply a point of their own.'

Ellie couldn't find any words, was drenched in the wet heat of his voice. She arched her back and rolled her neck as she pushed into his hands seeking more.

'You are so beautiful…' Jack dropped his hands down to her waist.

She shook her hair out and it spilled down her chest, over her brief tank top. Jack leaned back and just looked at her, his caress as bold as his eyes.

'Take it off,' he said, his voice hoarse. 'Let me look at you.'

Somewhere in some place deep inside her Ellie knew that she should probably say no, that she should climb off his lap and be sensible, but instead she arched her back, pulled her shirt over her head and held the garment in place against her chest. She hadn't thought it was possible for Jack's eyes to darken with passion, but they did and she saw his jaw clench.

She felt feminine and powerful and wondrously, wickedly wanton.

'You're killing me here, woman,' Jack growled and he lifted his hand to yank the shirt away. His nostrils flared as he took in her creamy skin now flushed with arousal. He held her face in his hands. 'Trust me, El. I'm going to show you exactly what the point of this is...'

Ellie walked into the bedroom from the bathroom, wrapped in a towel from waist to mid-thigh and towel-drying her hair. She looked from the clock to Jack, who was lying crossways across the bed, spread out on his stomach. 'We've wasted a good portion of the morning.'

'Hush your mouth, wench. A morning in bed is never wasted,' Jack said as he stood up and stretched. He was totally self-confident about his body and he had a right to be, Ellie thought. Apart from the nasty scar on his chest, he was perfect.

'How did you get that scar?' Ellie asked.

Jack lifted his hand up to his chest and immediately turned away. 'Operation.'

Ellie rubbed the ends of her hair between the folds of the towel. 'What operation?'

Jack walked past her and swatted her backside. 'The one I had in hospital.'

He stepped into the *en-suite* bathroom and Ellie heard water hitting the shower door. Well, that had gone well. *Not.* Obviously his scar-causing operation was not up for discussion. Ellie wondered why not. It couldn't be that big a deal, surely?

Jack raised his voice. 'This is such a waste of water...you should've let me shower with you.'

Ellie smiled at herself in the dressing table mirror. 'I couldn't trust you not to have your wicked way with me again.'

She'd thought about yanking him into the shower with her but she didn't think she could stand another bout of that sweet, sweet torture. Or maybe she could—in an hour or two, when all her nerve-endings had subsided slightly.

'You like my wicked ways.' Jack's voice was chock-full of self-satisfaction.

'I do? How can you tell?'

'Well, I think your begging was a huge hint,' Jack said dryly, before she heard the shower door open and close.

Ellie pulled fresh underwear out of her dresser drawer and quickly slipped into a matching aqua-green set. White shorts and a pretty floral top were perfect for a day to be spent at home…she had to stock up on cleaning products and dog food, spend some time on the internet paying personal bills, and she needed to finalise the arrangements for Jess's bachelorette party.

Maybe after that she could persuade Jack back into bed…

Jess! Jess and Luke! Oh, *man*! She'd forgotten that she was having lunch with them. She picked up her watch from the dresser and cursed again. She had barely ten minutes before they were due to pick her up. This was Jack's fault and his ability to make her forget everything when his clever hands were anywhere near her body.

Ellie stomped over to the bathroom and looked into the steam to the stunning body beyond. Tight buns, broad chest, a nice package…. A very nice package that knew exactly what it was doing…. *Concentrate, Ellie!*

'Jack?'

Jack, his head full of shampoo, turned around and lifted one eyebrow. 'Changed your mind? C'mon in. I'll wash your back.'

Ellie gestured to her clothes and tipped her head. 'No—no time. Listen, I just suddenly remembered that I made plans for today.'

She saw the disappointment on Jack's face before he re-arranged his features into a blank mask. 'Okay. Have fun.'

Ellie tried not to roll her eyes and failed. 'I'm having lunch with Luke and Jess—I forgot. Want to join us?'

Pleasure, hot and quick, flashed in his eyes. 'Sure.'

Ellie thought she'd push her luck and try to satisfy her curiosity. 'So why won't you tell me about your scar?'

Jack tipped his head back under the stream of water. 'Because it's not important.'

'If it wasn't important then you'd talk about it,' Ellie told him, and sighed when she saw the shutters come down in his eyes. She was beginning to recognise that look. It meant that the subject was no longer up for discussion. Ellie blew out her breath. She'd made sweet love to him all night but that didn't mean she could go crawling around in his head. 'Okay, then, be all mysterious. But hurry up, because they'll be here any moment.'

Jack rinsed out the last of the shampoo, switched off the water and grabbed a towel that hung on the railing. He wrapped the towel around his waist and shoved his hair back from his face. Catching Ellie watching him, he placed his hand on her shoulder and leaned forward to drop a kiss on the corner of her mouth.

'You okay?'

'Fine.'

'Not too sore?' Jack placed his forehead against hers and his hands on her waist.

She was a little *burny* in places that shouldn't burn. 'A little.'

'Sorry.' Jack kissed her forehead and stepped back. 'I'm going to find something to wear. Jeans and open-collar shirt?'

'No, shorts and a T-shirt,' Ellie said, following him out of the bathroom. 'We'll probably end up on the rickety deck of some about-to-fall-down shack…'

Jack pulled a face. 'And that's where we'll eat?' he said, doubt lacing his voice.

'That's where you'll eat the most amazing seafood in the world. Luke knows all the best places to eat up and down the coast,' Ellie replied, and sighed when she heard the insistent pealing of her gate bell. 'That's them—early as usual. I'll see you downstairs.'

'Ellie?'

Ellie turned at Jack's serious voice. Oh, God, what was he going to say?

Jack's smile was slow and powerful. 'Thank you for an amazing night.'

Ellie floated down the steps. Ellie Evans, she mused, sex goddess. Yeah, she could get behind that title.

In the late afternoon Jess and Luke, seeing the old lighthouse a kilometre down the beach, decided that they should take a closer look at the old iron structure. Ellie and Jack, who were operating on a lot less sleep, shook their heads at their departing backs, took a bottle of wine and glasses to the beach, found an old log for a backrest and sat in the sand.

'How are you doing?' Jack asked, pouring wine into a glass and then handing it to her.

Ellie squinted at him. 'I'm utterly exhausted. I think we got about two hours' sleep.'

Jack covered his mouth as he yawned. 'I'm tired too. So, did you have fun?'

Ellie blushed. 'Yes, thanks. You?'

Jack laughed. 'I think the fact that I couldn't get enough of you answers that question better than I could with words.' He watched her face flush again and internally shook his head. Her confidence had really taken a battering at some point and never quite recovered.

'Tell me about your ex.'

Ellie looked as if he'd asked her to swallow a spider. 'Good grief—why?'

'Because I think that he messed up your head—badly. Dented your confidence.' Jack dug his toes into the sand as he looked at her. 'Did he?'

Ellie picked up a handful of sand and let it drift through her fingers. 'S'pose so. Not that I had much to start with.'

'And why would that be?'

Ellie tipped her head at him. 'Jack, you saw me. I was plump and very shy, and standing firmly in the shadow of my famous father—who was everything I wasn't. Good-looking, charming, erudite, confident. Then I went to art school.'

He loved that secret smile—the one that lit her up from the inside out. 'And…?'

'And I flourished. I found something I loved and excelled in. I was happy and the weight fell off me. Boys were asking me out on dates, and although I never went I *was* being asked.'

'Why didn't you go?'

'As I said, I was shy. They asked and I said no and I got the reputation of being hard to get. And, boys being boys, they thought that was cool, so I became more popular, which made me more confident and I finally started dating.'

'Where does the grim gallery owner fit in?' Jack asked, draping a possessive leg over hers.

'He was a friend of one of our final-year lecturers and he came to give a talk to the graduating class. On a whim he said that he'd look at our work in progress. He asked to see my portfolio, said that I had talent and told me look him up if I ever got to London, saying that he might offer me an exhibition.' Ellie watched a crab crawl out of a hole and scuttle towards the waves. 'A couple of months later I did meet up with him in London. We started a relationship and he slowly eroded every bit of confidence I'd worked so hard to acquire.'

'How?'

'My art wasn't up to standard.' Ellie shrugged as thunderclouds built in her eyes.

'Why did you stay with him?'

Ellie bit her bottom lip. 'Because he told me he loved me and said that he'd never leave. The two sentences I'd waited to hear all my life.'

Jack rubbed his eyes. 'Oh, sweetheart.'

'Then, during the little time he spent with me, he started on everything else. Clothes and hair. Weight. My cooking, my friends, my skill in the bedroom.'

Jack felt his mouth drop open with surprise, which was closely followed by the burn of fury. 'He said you were a bad lover?'

'No, he said that I was a damned awful lover and a blow-up doll would be more fun.'

If that…Jack swallowed the names he wanted to call Ellie's waste-of-skin ex. No wonder she'd frozen the other night. No wonder she seemed constantly to second-guess herself.

Ellie dug her bare feet into the sand. 'Merri thinks that he and my father scarred me emotionally.'

Well, yeah. 'What do you think?'

Ellie sipped her wine and dropped back so that her elbows were in the sand. 'Of course they did. I'm scared to get close to people because I don't want to run the risk of getting hurt and I know that they'll leave me. I tend to keep myself emotionally isolated. It's safer that way.'

'Safer isn't necessarily better,' Jack pointed out.

Ellie slanted him a look. 'You do the same thing, Jack Chapman, and don't think you don't.'

'What do you mean?' Jack asked, bewildered by her suddenly turning the tables on him.

'You observe, watch, report and walk away. You don't get involved, so you're as much as an emotional coward as me.'

Jack sighed as her well-made point hit him dead centre. He took a minute to allow his surprise to settle before placing his hand on her knee. 'Maybe I am, El.'

Jeez, he wished he could get the words out. It was a perfect time to tell her that they had no future, that she shouldn't expect anything from him, that he couldn't consider settling down with her—with anyone. That he couldn't afford to take this any deeper, to allow her to creep behind the doors and walls of his self-sufficiency.

Ellie's teasing voice snapped him out of his reverie. 'You awake behind those shades, Chapman?'

'Yep.' Jack hooked his arm around her neck, pulled her to him and dropped a hard kiss on her mouth. 'Just thinking.'

'Careful, you might hurt yourself,' Ellie teased, and yelped when his fingers connected with her ribcage. Her wine glass wobbled in her hand and she dropped it when his other hand tickled her under her arms.

'Jack! You wretch! Stop...please, Jack!' Ellie whimpered, and then her breath hitched.

He realised he was lying on her, her mouth just below his. Tickling turned to passion and laughter turned to need as he plundered her mouth.

Jack felt his heart sink into his stomach as he placed his head in the crook of her neck.

Dammit, Ellie, how am I ever going to find the strength to walk away from you?

'I hate hangovers,' Jack thought he heard Ellie mutter.

She was showered, teeth brushed and dressed, but she still looked headachey and miserable, huddled into the corner of the couch, tousle-haired and exceptionally grumpy. But, amazingly, still so sexy.

'Why did I drink so much last night?' she wailed.

Jack crouched down in front of her and smiled as he handed her a couple of aspirin and some water. 'Hey, in reply to every drunken text you sent at various times throughout the evening I suggested that you stop. You told me that you could handle it.'

'Well, I can't,' Ellie sulked.

'Tough it out, sunshine.'

It had been Jess's hen's party last night and Ellie had hosted the pre-clubbing ritual of cupcakes and champagne. When he'd run down the stairs at eight Ellie had been sitting on the edge of the couch and his eyes had rolled back in his head when he'd seen what she was—almost—wearing: a piece of sparkly scrap material covering her breasts, held in place by strings criss-crossing her back, tight jeans and screw-me heels. She'd pulled back her hair into a severe tail, and with dramatic make-up she'd looked dangerous and sexy.

She'd had 'trouble' written all over her face. He'd decided to leave the house before he carried her upstairs, made her change and lectured her on exactly what the men in the club would think, seeing her in that outfit.

When he'd heard her stumble in—with Jess, Clem Copeland and Maddie—it had been after two. The dogs had wandered upstairs at three, and at three-thirty he'd heard the shouted suggestion of skinny-dipping in the pool. He really deserved credit for not looking.

He'd known he must be getting old when he'd chosen to roll over and go back to sleep rather than spy on hot naked women cavorting in the moonlight.

He grinned as he placed his cup on the coffee table in front of them. Oh, he was enjoying this, he thought as he took the opposite corner of the couch and settled in, his laptop between his crossed knees.

Ellie held her head. 'What's with the computer?' she demanded. 'Oooh, I think there are a hundred ADD gnomes tap-dancing in my head.'

'You and I are going to talk about Mitchell,' Jack said pleasantly.

Ellie groaned. 'No, we're not.'

'Mmm, yes, we are.' Jack looked from his screen to her.

His eyes were alert with intelligence, his fingers steady

on the keyboard. He was after a story and she was part of it. 'Jack, please...'

'It's just a couple of questions about your father.'

'Questions I don't want to answer,' Ellie said stubbornly.

'Why not?'

'Because it doesn't change anything!' Ellie shouted, and watched as her head fell off her shoulders and rolled across the room. 'He wasn't there for me, *ever*! He was a drop-in dad, and I loved him far more than he loved me.'

Jack shook his head. 'How old were you when your parents got divorced?'

'Fifteen,' Ellie snapped.

'And how did your mother take it?'

'How do you think? She was devastated.' Ellie leaned forward to make her point, groaned and sank back. 'Do you know she never fell in love again after him? He was her one love. And he brushed us both off like we were nothing...'

Ellie felt a sob rise and ruthlessly forced it down. She'd shed enough tears over her father, her ex, men in general. Hangover or no, she wasn't going to shed any more. But she wanted to. She wanted to tell Jack how much it hurt, how much she wanted to be loved, cherished, protected. She didn't *need* to be—not as she had when she was a little girl—but she still had a faint wish to be able to step into a strong pair of arms and rest awhile.

Like now, when her head felt separated from her body and her stomach was staging its own hostile rebellion.

'So you ran from an emotionally and physically absent father to an emotionally and physically absent fiancé. Why?'

'That's not a question about Mitchell,' Ellie retorted.

'Why, El?'

'Because it's what I deserved! Because my love was never enough to keep someone with me! Because I choose badly!'

Jack sighed. 'Oh, El, that is off-the-charts crap. You had

a father who was useless and you had a bad relationship. It doesn't mean that *you* are useless!'

'Feels like it,' Ellie muttered. 'And might I point out that you dig around in my head, throwing questions at me, but you won't answer any of mine?' It wasn't fair that he wanted to delve into her life and emotions and he wouldn't allow her into his.

Jack's hands stilled on the keyboard and he sent her a shuttered look. His sigh covered his obvious irritation. 'What do you want to know?'

'You *know* what,' Ellie muttered. She gestured to his chest. 'Tell me about that scar. How did you get it?'

'Heart transplant,' Jack said, his voice devoid of inflection.

'Excuse me?'

'You heard what I said.'

Ellie sat up, her headache all but forgotten under this enormous news. 'But you look fine.'

'That's because I *am* fine! I've been fine for seventeen years!'

Ooooh, touchy subject. Even more touchy than her father issues. 'Hey, I'm still processing this—just give me a second, okay? How would you like me to react?'

'Well, for starters, I'd like you to take that look of pity off your face!' Jack picked his computer up and banged it down onto the coffee table. 'That's why I don't tell people—because they instantly go all sympathetic and gooey!'

Oh, wait… His sharp, snappy voice was pulling her headache right back.

'Stop putting words into my mouth! I never said that.' Ellie pulled her legs up and rested her chin on her knees, her eyes on his suddenly miserable face. His expression practically begged her to leave the subject alone, but he'd opened the door and she was going to walk on in. 'Why did you need a heart transplant?'

'I caught viral pneumonia when I was thirteen. It damaged my heart.'

'And how old were you when you had the transplant?'

'Seventeen.'

'Geez, Jack.' Ellie wanted to crawl into his lap to comfort him, but knew that any affection right now would be misconstrued, deeply unwelcome.

'Nobody outside of my family knows,' Jack warned her. 'It's not something that I want to become public knowledge.'

'Why not?'

'Because it doesn't define me!' Jack's eyes flashed with irritation.

'If it didn't define you to a certain point then you wouldn't keep it so secret,' Ellie pointed out. 'What's the big deal? So you were sick when you were a kid, and you got a new heart—?' Ellie sat up, curiosity on her face. 'Do you know whose heart you got?'

'Yes. It was another teenager. Killed in a car crash,' Jack said curtly. He nodded to his computer and glared at Ellie. 'Can we get back to the subject on hand?'

'No.' Ellie shook her head. 'I'm still trying to wrap my head around this. So you got viral pneumonia, which damaged your heart, and you were sick for a long time. Then you got a new heart and now you're fine?'

'I take anti-rejection pills every day and make a point of keeping myself healthy. Apart from that, and the scar, I'm as normal as anyone else.'

Physically, maybe, but Ellie suspected that there was a whole bunch of psychological stuff still whirling around in his head. She needed to understand how it had moulded the man in front of her. Because she had no doubt that it had. How could it not have? It was too big, too life-changing—in every sense of the word. 'Tell me about those years between falling sick and having the operation.'

'You're not going to let this go, are you?'

Jack rested his forearms on his knees in a pose she was coming to realise was characteristic of him and linked his hands.

'I became housebound, lacking energy, lacking breath. I got sick frequently. Sport, school, partying, girls were all out of the question…it was an effort just to stay alive. At the end stages just before the op, my heart was so damaged that I could hardly walk. I…*existed*.'

She could hardly imagine it—this vibrant, energetic, amazing man, who should have been an active, lively teen, restricted by his failing heart and deteriorating health. 'Frustration' and 'resentment' were words far too weak to describe some of the emotions he must have experienced at the time.

'And that time defined the rest of your life?'

'Yes.'

'How?'

'I hate being told what I can or can't do, that I have to stay in one place, that I can't pick up and leave. I lived a life of very few choices. I vowed to never limit myself again. For the best part of my teenage life I was so…*confined* that I promised myself I would never be again. And I promised Brent—'

'Who?'

'My donor. I promised him, and myself, that I would *live* life, not exist. Not try to protect myself. That I'd do everything he never had the chance to.'

Phew. Well, she'd asked.

Jack stood up abruptly. 'I need more coffee. Do you want another cup?'

The door slammed shut. Ellie shook her head and wished she hadn't. *Ow, my head!* How was she supposed to take in and think about Jack's monumental disclosure when her head was splitting apart?

No fair.

CHAPTER NINE

JACK LEFT THE room and Ellie stared at the spot he'd vacated and forced herself to concentrate. A heart transplant? Was he being serious? Of course he was, she'd seen his scar, but... *holy mackerel*. She'd expected to hear about a big operation, but a heart transplant was a very big deal. How could it not be?

Ellie heard Jack's footsteps behind her and sent him a wary look as he sat down beside her, another cup of coffee in his hand.

'You still want to talk about it, don't you?' Jack asked, his expression stating that he'd rather have his legs waxed.

Ellie leaned back and put her feet up on the coffee table. 'It's just another part of your history—like stitches or breaking a leg...though on a much mightier scale.'

'You laughed when you heard about those incidents. I can handle humour. I can't stand pity.' Jack glared at her.

'Sorry, I'm a bit short on heart transplant jokes,' Ellie shot back. 'And stop glaring at me! I didn't torture you to tell me.'

'You'd be surprised,' Jack retorted, looking miserable. 'I look into your eyes and I want to tell you...*stuff*.'

Ellie batted her lashes and Jack laughed. Reluctantly, but he laughed. 'You appear to be sweet but you are actually a brat, do you know that?'

'Sweet? *Ugh*.' Ellie wrinkled her nose. 'What a description. I prefer "amazing sex goddess".'

Jack's laugh was a lot easier this time. 'You are that too. But you'll have to keep proving it to retain the title.'

Ellie slapped his groping hands away and captured the hand closest to hers. 'I will, but I need to say something to you first.' His expression became guarded at her serious tone, but she decided to carry on anyway. She took a deep breath and spoke. 'I'm sorry for what you lived through but, although you probably won't believe me, I don't feel pity. If anything I'm in awe of what you've achieved, how you've refused to allow your past to limit you.'

Jack shoved a hand into his hair, squirmed, but Ellie ploughed on.

'You could've chosen to protect yourself, to hide out, to nurture yourself, and everyone would've understood. But because you're you you probably said to your heart, *Right, dude, we've both got a second chance. Hang on—we're going for a ride.* Am I right?'

'Yeah…I suppose.'

'I respect the hell out of you. You're also…well…not ugly… which doesn't hurt.'

Jack's laugh whizzed over her head as he reached for her and pulled her across his lap. Ellie looked up at him and swallowed. When she teamed her respect for him with his sharp intellect, his dry sense of humour and the fact that he was a very decent guy, her heart started doing somersaults in her ribcage.

Add their physical chemistry to the mix and she had a soupy mess that could blow up in her face.

Since they'd started sleeping together she'd refused to think of him as anything other than a brief affair. Whenever she found herself thinking about him in terms of more, she reminded herself that she only had tomorrow or the next day or the next and closed the door on those fantasies. She wouldn't think of him in any other context other than that of a short-term, big-fun, no-strings affair, because it would be so easy to allow him to slip inside her heart and her head and that way madness lay. He would leave—he'd told her he would—and she would be left holding her bruised and battered heart.

Jack's thumb brushed over her lips and he just looked down at her with a soft, vulnerable expression on his face that she'd never seen before. It was encounters like this that dragged her deeper into an emotional quagmire. He was so enticing, on both an emotional and physical level, that it was difficult to not slip over the edge into deeper involvement. She was teetering on the edge. But she had to step back...because thinking of anything else was, frankly, stupid.

There were a couple of things she was sure of: she could love him, really love him, but he didn't want or need her love. And he'd never need her, love her, as she needed him to.

Life was tough enough without having to compete with his job for his attention and his time. History had taught her that she'd end up either disappointing him or being disappointed. Both sucked equally, so why risk either? No, falling all the way in love with him was *not* an option, she thought as his mouth drifted across hers.

But it might be easier said than done.

It was the start of a new week and Jack, after spending hours at his computer, chipping away at Mitch's story, felt as if he needed a break. It was the middle of the afternoon so he walked down to the bakery and ducked behind the counter. Sliding behind Samantha, he shoved a mug under the spout and shot a double espresso into a cup. Yanking a twenty out of his pocket, he dropped it in the pocket of her apron and snagged a chocolate muffin before walking through the stable door into the bakery.

As was his habit, he spent a moment admiring Ellie's legs beneath the scarlet chef's jacket before walking over to her table and pulling at the ponytail that fell out of her baseball cap.

Ellie lifted her fondant-full hands, smiled at him and eyed his muffin. 'I'm starving—can I have some?'

Jack held the muffin to her mouth and sighed when Ellie took an enormous bite. 'Piglet.'

'I didn't have lunch,' Ellie explained. 'I got involved in this cake.'

Jack ran his hand down Ellie's back and popped the rest of the muffin into his mouth.

'You have people who slap together sandwiches for your customers not twelve feet from you—order something,' Jack suggested.

'Crazy day,' Ellie told him, and resumed working on a delicate cream rosebud that looked almost real.

He peered over her shoulder at the sugar-rose-scattered wedding cake. 'That's really pretty.'

'Thanks,' Ellie responded, her brow furrowed in concentration as she resumed work rolling a tiny petal.

Jack sat on a stool next to her table and watched her work. Her laptop stood open on the table in front of her and he gestured to it with his coffee cup. 'What's with the laptop?'

Ellie spared it a brief glance. 'I've been trying to talk to my mother about the having-to-move-the-bakery situation and she promised to find a place she could Skype from. I'm waiting for her call.'

Progress of a type, Jack thought, but he doubted that Ellie would share the full responsibility of Pari's with her mother. He could see the tension in the cords of her neck, in her raised shoulders. She didn't want to burden her mum and would find any excuse not to. And if he knew her—and he thought he did—she would downplay the situation she was in.

Sometimes Jack wanted to shake her. She had about five months to purchase the property, do the renovations and move the bakery if she didn't want to lose any trade. She was wasting daylight in so many ways…trying to charm the owner of the building into selling when she should be threatening to walk away...chatting to her mum via Skype when she should have demanded that she return home weeks ago... Jack sighed. He tried to negotiate, rather than confront people, but he could kick ass when he needed to. Ellie's confrontation style was that she didn't essentially *have* one.

Although she *did* have a way of making him emotionally vomit all over his shoes, Jack thought, thinking about their discussion yesterday. He couldn't believe that he'd told her about his operation, his life before he'd started living again. He'd never told anybody—never discussed his past. God, if it wasn't for his mother nagging him about his check-ups he wouldn't discuss it at all.

That would be the perfect scenario. How he wished he could erase the scar, the memories, the feeling that someone had him by the throat every time he thought about it. Ellie didn't understand how difficult talking about it had been for him. He'd felt as if he'd been giving birth while he was sitting on that couch, forcing the words through his constricted throat. He'd been catapulted back seventeen years to a place he'd never wanted to revisit. He'd always been reticent, selfcontained, and being so sick had isolated him from his peers and made him more so. He didn't allow people into his mind or his heart easily.

Yet Ellie kept creeping in. Did that mean that they'd moved from being a casual relationship to something that mattered? If so, he sure hadn't planned on that happening...how had that happened? And when?

A day ago...a week ago...the first time he saw her in the bakery?

He'd thought that he'd be able to live with Ellie, sleep with Ellie and remain unaffected...*hah!* And some said he was a smart guy! He shoved his hands into his hair and tugged. Being in Cape Town was becoming a bit too complicated. He felt far too at home here in Ellie's house, among her things. He'd never meant it to be a place where he could see himself living…

Yet a part of him could. Maybe it was Ellie…okay, most of it *was* Ellie, but it didn't help that she lived in possibly one of the most beautiful places he'd ever seen. Mountains and sea, sunny days, aqua and cobalt water, a pretty town. She had nice friends, people he could see himself spending time with, an interesting job, a relaxed, comfortable house.

It was miles—geographically and mentally—away from his soulless, stuffy flat in London, with its beige walls and furniture…although he *did* miss his kick-ass plasma TV. If he ever moved here that would be the only household appliance he'd pay to ship out here…

Jack gripped the edge of the stool. He was allowing the romance of the setting, his sexual attraction to Ellie and the prettiness of this area cloud his practicality. He was going soft—and possibly crazy.

He needed to go back to work. Needed a distraction from his increasingly sentimental and syrupy thoughts. There was nothing quite like a conflict, a war or a disaster, to slap your feet back to the ground.

Jack's reflections were interrupted by a Skype call coming in on Ellie's computer. At her request, Jack hit the 'answer' button with his non-sticky finger and Ellie's brown-eyed mother appeared on screen. They could be sisters, Jack thought. A couple less laughter lines, long hair instead of short, blue eyes, not deep brown.

'*Namaste*, angel face,' said Ashnee, blowing her a kiss before wrapping her bare arms around her knees and grinning into the camera.

Ellie leaned on her elbows and stared at the screen. 'Mum, I miss you so much. You look fabulous!'

Ashnee fluffed her short hair. 'I feel fabulous. I see that I'm in the bakery. Busy?'

'Hugely,' Ellie said. 'And that's what I need to talk to you about.'

Jack listened as Ellie explained the situation to her mum, and from beside the computer watched the emotions cross Ashnee's face. There was sadness, regret and then resignation.

'And we definitely can't afford the new rent?'

Ellie shook her head. 'Nope.'

Ashnee looked down at her hands, beautifully decorated with henna designs. 'So we have to move? To the old Hutchinson place?'

'Mmm, if only I can get Mrs H to sell.'

Ellie looked up as the stable door opened and lifted her hand to greet Merri who, as per usual, had Molly Blue on her slim hip. She indicated that she was on a call and Merri nodded and wandered over to the table where she usually worked, where two less experienced bakers were making macaroons.

Ellie listened with half an ear as her mum repeated her words back to her. She knew it was Ashnee's way of thinking the problem through, so she half listened and watched the conversation between Merri and the other bakers. Merri looked cross and the bakers frustrated, and when Merri picked up a batch of baked macaroons and tossed them into the dustbin behind them Ellie felt her temper heat.

Merri had no right to do quality control when she wasn't even working on the premises. Right—she needed to sort this out before she ended up with no macaroons and no bakers.

'Mum…' Ellie reached out her hand, grabbed Jack's hard arm and pulled him into the camera's view '…meet Jack. Jack—Ashnee. Jack and I are kind of seeing each other… have a chat while I sort something out.'

'Uh…'

Jack looked from her to the screen but Ellie ignored his panicked face. Good grief, anyone would think she'd asked him to meet the Queen! Ellie rolled her eyes and walked across the bakery. One pair of annoyed and two pairs of mutinous eyes looked back at her.

'What are you doing, Merri?' she asked, keeping her voice low and even.

'The macaroons were lumpy,' Merri stated, allowing Mama Thandi to take Molly from her. Merri placed her hands on her hips. 'That means the mixture was under-mixed.'

Ellie walked over to the dustbin, opened it and grabbed one of the discarded macaroons. It wasn't Merri-perfect but they could have sold the product. And, dammit, Merri had wasted time and energy, electricity and ingredients, when she wasn't even supposed to be at work.

Ellie dropped the pastry back into the bin, closed her eyes and hauled in a deep breath. She felt like an old dishrag, with every bit of energy and enthusiasm wrung out of her. And the two people who'd always been her backstop, her support structure—the other two pillars of the bakery—were wafting in and out or, in her mum's case, wafting around the Indian sub-continent, while she buckled under the responsibility of keeping the bakery afloat.

It was her fault. She'd allowed them their freedom. But enough was enough. She was done, and if they didn't step up she'd collapse under the weight and Pari's would come crashing down.

She would *not* let that happen.

Ellie opened her eyes and as she did so took a step towards Merri, grabbed her wrist and pulled her across the bakery to her table.

'What is *wrong* with you?' Merri demanded when they reached Jack, rubbing at her wrist in irritation.

'You! *You* are what is wrong with me!' Ellie snapped back,

and then she pointed her finger to her mum, on the other side of the world. 'And you! Both of you are going to listen to me!'

Jack cocked his head and stepped back. *Clever man*, Ellie thought. Get out of the area about to be firebombed.

'You first.' Ellie looked at Merri. 'You either work here or you don't. You aren't allowed to walk into my bakery if you don't and do quality control.'

'I was just…' Merri's words trailed off.

Huh…Ellie thought. *My scary face is actually scary!* She steeled herself to say what she needed to. 'I love you, Merri, and I desperately want you to come back to work. Next week is the beginning of a new month. Either get your ass back to work on that day or get fired. Have I made myself clear?'

'Ellie, let's talk about this,' Merri replied, in her most persuasive voice.

'We're not talking about anything! That's the way it is. Be here or don't bother coming back.' Ellie held her stare until Merri turned away and flounced off.

Round Two, Ellie thought, and looked down at her mum. This next conversation would be just as hard, if not harder. She bit her lip and looked for the words. 'Mum, I know that I told you to take this time to travel, to live your dream, but I'm yanking you back. I need you here. I cannot do this alone.'

Ashnee looked at her for a long time and Ellie held her breath. What if she said no? Refused to give up her travelling? What would she do then? Ellie felt panic rise up in her throat at her mum's long silence. Just when she didn't think she could stand it any more Ashnee's huge smile filled the screen.

'Oh, thank God!'

Ellie blinked once, shook her head and blinked again. What was she so excited about?

'I didn't think I could stand another minute!' Ashnee cried. 'I've been desperate to come home! I'm sick of the heat and the crowds.'

'But… But…' Ellie looked at Jack, who was quietly laughing, obviously enjoying every minute of this drama. 'I don't understand.'

'Me neither!' Ashnee said cheerfully, dropping her bare feet to the floor. 'All I know is that I'm catching the first plane I can. Which might take a couple of days, since I'm somewhere near nowhere.'

Ellie sat down on her chair and looked bemused. 'Okay. Good. This is a bit overwhelming.'

'Love you, baby girl!' Ashnee blew her a kiss. 'I'll e-mail you as soon as I have some flight deets.'

And with a wink and a grin her mum was gone.

Ellie stared at the screen for a moment longer before looking up and around. Her mum was gone and Merri was nowhere to be seen. She rubbed her hands over her face, feeling slightly sick at her actions and her words. The impulse to go after Merri was overwhelming…what if she didn't come back? Ellie half stood and felt Jack's strong hand pushing her back into the chair.

'Don't you *dare* go running after her.'

Ellie looked up into Jack's laughing eyes and hauled in a deep breath. 'What have I done?' she whispered.

'Something you should've done ages ago,' Jack replied. He hooked a friendly arm around her neck and chuckled. 'And I have to say…when you finally decide to kick ass you don't take any prisoners.'

A few evenings later Jack wandered into the kitchen as Ellie took a plastic container from the fridge and placed it on the counter. After kissing her hello and getting a lukewarm response he sent her a keen look, trying to work out what was wrong—or more wrong than usual. He knew that she was super-stressed at work, and he suspected that their undefined relationship added another layer of tension to her.

They were reaching a tipping point, he realised. Soon one of them would have to fish or cut bait.

Leaning his forearms on the counter, he peered through the clear lid at tuna steaks covered in a sticky-looking marinade. In the past couple of weeks he'd had more home-cooked meals than he'd eaten since he left home, and fresh fish, properly done, was a treat he never tired of.

Ellie rolled her head and he knew that the knots in her neck were super-tight. 'Spit it out, El. What's wrong?'

'Apart from the normal?' Ellie tipped her head back and looked at the ceiling. 'Horrible day.'

'What happened?'

Ellie placed a strange vegetable on the wooden board and removed a sharp knife from the block of knives close by. He didn't recognise the vegetable and wrinkled his nose.

'Bok choy cabbage. It's good for you,' Ellie stated.

'If you say so. Your day?'

Ellie tossed the cabbage into a frying pan. 'Psycho bride, late deliveries, flood in the upstairs toilet. Samantha wrenched her ankle. Elias is sick.' Ellie took a huge sip of the wine he handed her and sighed with pleasure. 'I need this.'

Ellie pushed a tendril of hair back from her face as she heated another pan for the tuna. Working quickly and competently, she took the tuna steaks to the stove and tossed them into the hot pan. 'Will you get some spring onions out of the fridge, please?'

The steaks sizzled and the room was filled with the fragrant aromas of soy sauce, ginger and garlic. Grabbing his own knife, Jack sliced up the spring onions and asked her where she wanted them.

'In the pan with the bok choy,' Ellie replied. 'Can you get plates?'

Jack handed her the plates as directed. 'Did you manage to get to chat to your mum about the new premises at all?'

Ellie rubbed her eye with her wrist. 'I took her to see the place and showed her the plans that James the architect drew up. She likes it—likes the building, the plans. I'm not quite sure if it's the travelling or the jet lag or her spiritual journey, but she shrugged off the issue of me not having enough money in my trust fund to buy the building at Mrs H's price and do the renovations, insisting that it'll all work out.'

Ashnee had smiled, hugged her and told her that she just had to have faith—a commodity Ellie had run out of a long time ago.

She was also on the brink of losing her mind, and her life was a pie chart of confusion. The segment labelled 'Jack' was particularly large. Ellie looked at him, sitting at the kitchen table, savouring his wine, his long legs stretched out and his bare foot tickling a dog's neck. She knew that she had only days, maybe hours left with him, and every time she tried to envisage life without Jack in it, her breath hitched in her throat.

She'd never felt fear like this before… What she felt for him terrified her… This was true fear, being confronted with a life without Jack in it. He was only ever supposed to be a fling… when had he turned into someone so damn important? Someone she thought she was in love with?

Thought? Bah! Someone she was horribly, unconditionally, categorically in love with. Dammit…he had her heart in his hands and she knew that when he left he'd drop-kick it over a cliff. It was going to hurt like hell.

Ellie shoved her fist into her sternum and hoped like hell that she was confusing what she was feeling with indigestion. Well, she could always hope…

Ellie quickly plated the tuna steaks and sprinkled sesame seeds over the bok choy before putting them onto the plates.

She gestured to his plate. 'Eat. It's getting cold.'

Jack, looking thoroughly healthy and relaxed, eagerly took her advice and concentrated on his supper, which he ploughed through. He caught her look of amazement at his empty plate. She was barely halfway through hers.

'Hungry?'

'For food like that? Always.' Jack stood up and helped himself to the last piece of tuna steak and the other half of the bok choy cabbage.

'By the way, your mum phoned the bakery today, looking for you.'

Jack lifted his head and frowned. 'What? Why?' He picked up his mobile and shook his head. 'My mobile has a signal. What did she want?'

Ellie smiled. 'That's the odd thing…nothing, really. We had a perfectly pleasant chat about the bakery and what I do and…'

'And she was sussing you out. I told her I was staying with you.' Jack leaned back in his chair and sighed, frustrated. 'Sorry—only child, doubly over-protective mother because I was so sick for so long. She nursed me through it all and can't quite cut the apron strings.'

'I enjoyed chatting to her. Luckily I can talk and ice at the same time, because it was a long call. She said to remind you about Brent's memorial service. He's the donor of your heart, isn't he?'

'Mmm. He died when he was seventeen. It's been seventeen years…'

'Your mum said to let his family know if you can go. She said that they'd understand if you were on assignment.'

'That's code for *we'd rather not have you there*,' Jack sighed. 'It's a gracious invite, but I suspect that seeing me would be incredibly difficult for them. I imagine they'd feel guilty for wishing he was alive and not me. *I* feel guilty for being alive…'

'Oh, Jack.' Ellie rested her chin on her fist. 'Survivor's guilt?'

'Yeah. Are you going to say something pithy about me not needing to feel that?'

'I wouldn't dare. How could I, not having walked in your shoes?' Ellie toyed with her fork. 'So, are you going to go?'

Jack's eyes flickered with pain. 'I really don't know. But I do know that I have to be back at work some time next week.'

'Ah.' Ellie felt a knife-point deep in her heart. So he'd be gone within the week? Her heart stuttered and faltered and felt as if it would crumble. She had only days more with him. Days to make enough memories to last her a lifetime.

'El, don't look at me like that.'

'Like what?'

'Like you wouldn't say no if I took you right now,' Jack replied.

Ellie cocked her head, pretending to think as heat spread into her womb. She had such limited time to make memories that would have to last her a lifetime so she figured she might as well start immediately. 'I wouldn't say no.'

Jack's eyes widened and Ellie laughed at his shocked face.

'You're joking,' he said, his voice laced with disappointment.

Ellie fiddled with the edge of her top and sent him a slow smile. 'What if I'm not?'

Jack's fork clattered to his plate. 'I think my heart just stopped.'

He lifted his hand, leaned across the table and, as per usual, pushed back a strand of hair behind her ear. Ellie shivered as his finger rubbed the sensitive spot there and trailed down her neck.

'No going back, Ellie. Right here, right now,' Jack muttered, his eyes on her mouth.

Ellie leaned back in her chair and grinned at him as she pulled her tank top over her head to reveal a white, semi-transparent lacy bra.

Jack clutched his chest. 'Heart attack imminent.'

She stood up and walked around the table, standing in front of him while she undid the button that held her soft wrap-around skirt together.

'Well, I will slap you later for joking about that—right after I've had my way with you.'

Jack's eyes dropped as the skirt fell to a frothy puddle on the floor, showing her amazing long legs and the smallest scrap of white lace. Placing his hands on her hips, he turned her around. His finger traced the line of her underwear.

'Good God, I'm a goner,' he muttered, placing his mouth on the sensitive dip where her spine met her bottom.

'No, but you will be,' Ellie promised as she turned back. She gave him an impish look. 'Are you game to see how much this table can actually take?'

'Next week' was here. Despite her not wanting it to, it had crept stealthily and inexorably closer and had finally arrived. Despite her every effort Ellie had not been able to hold back time, and Jack was booked on a flight to London later that morning.

It was time to face reality, pay the piper, face the music, bite the bullet…to stop using stupid idioms.

Jack's clothes were on her bed, his toiletries were in a bag and not on her bathroom shelves, and he was preparing to walk out of her life. Ellie sat on the edge of her bed, sipping a cup of coffee she couldn't taste and wondering what to say, how to act.

It was D-day and she knew that she would have to break through the uneasy silence or else choke on the words that she needed to verbalise. Because if she didn't she was certain she'd regret her silence for ever.

He was too important, too crucial to her happiness for her to let him waltz away without discussing what he meant to her, what she thought they had. Courage, she reminded herself, was not an absence of fear but acting despite that fear.

She had to do this—no matter how scary it was, how confrontational it could become, he was worth it. She was worth it. *They* were worth it.

Too bad that her knees were knocking together and her teeth were chattering. She'd practised this, she reminded herself—had spent the past few nights lying awake, holding him, while the words she wanted to say ran through her head.

All she could remember of those carefully practised phrases was: *I'm in love with you* and *Please don't leave me.*

Ellie put her coffee cup down on the floor next to her feet and crossed her legs. She sat on her hands so that he wouldn't see how much she was shaking.

'Jack…'

Jack looked at her and she sighed at his guarded expression. 'Mmm?'

'Where to from here?' Ellie asked. She winced, hearing the way that the words ran into each other as she launched them out of her mouth.

She saw him tense, caught his jaw hardening. He picked up a pile of shirts and shoved them into his rucksack. 'Between you and I? Ellie, I'm coming back. I mean, I'd like to come back between assignments. To you.'

Well, that was better than him saying goodbye for ever, but it wasn't quite enough. Ellie sucked in her bottom lip. 'Why?'

Jack's eyes flashed in irritation. She could see that he'd been hoping to avoid this conversation. *Tough luck, Chapman.*

'What kind of question is that?'

'A very reasonable one,' Ellie replied. 'Why do you want to come back?'

'Because there's something cooking between us!'

Ellie stood up and walked over to the window, staring out at the sunlight-drenched garden. '"Something cooking between us"? Is that *all* you can say?' Ellie demanded.

'I don't know what you want me to say!' Jack was quiet for a long time before he spoke again. 'Okay…I've never felt as much for anyone as I do for you.'

Ellie shook her head and her ponytail bounced. Seriously? That was all he could come up with? Where had her erudite reporter gone—the one who relied on words for his living? Where had he run away to?

Well, if he wasn't going to open up she would have to. *Courage, Ellie.*

'Jack, this has been one of the best times of my life. I've loved having you here, with me. I don't want it to end but I am also not prepared to put my life on hold, waiting for you to drop back in.' She pulled in a breath and looked for words, hoping to make him understand her point of view. 'I can't spend my life wondering if you're alive or dead, worrying about you constantly. I don't want to deal with crappy signals and brief telephone calls and even briefer visits home. Living a half-life with you, missing birthdays and anniversaries and special days!' Ellie stated. 'I've lived that life. I hated that life.'

'That was your father, not me! Stop judging me by what he did and said. We are nothing alike!' His expression was pure frustration. 'I am not your father and I don't make promises I can't keep! When I say I'll do something, I'll *do* it. And might I point out that technology has made it a lot easier to stay connected.'

Ellie sent him an enquiring look.

'We have mobiles with great coverage, and when I can't get a signal on my mobile I'll have a satellite phone. I could be on Mars and still be able to call you. There is internet access everywhere, and we could talk every day—hell, every hour, if that's what you needed. And I couldn't survive only seeing you every six weeks. A week, two at the most, and I'd be home.'

'But you can't *guarantee* that!' Ellie shouted.

'Nobody can, Ellie! But I'll do my damnedest!'

Ellie swallowed. She wanted to believe him. She really did. And she believed that he believed it—right now. But without a solid commitment, a declaration of love and trust, it couldn't last. Long-distance relationships, especially those tinged with danger, had a finite lifespan. If he couldn't make a commitment then she had to let him go now, while she could. Now— before she completely succumbed to the temptation of heaven and hell that loving him would be.

Heaven when he came back; hell when he was away.

No, that grey space in between the two, purgatory, was the safest place for her to be. It was the only place where she could function as a semi-normal person.

Ellie shook her head. 'I'm sorry, a mostly long-distance relationship is not an option. I…can't.'

Jack threw up his hands. 'I don't understand why not.'

'Because all you've told me so far is that I am somewhat important and that you'll come back when you can. How can you ask me to wait for you when that's all you can give me?'

Jack pushed both his hands into his hair and linked his hands around the back of his head, his eyes devastated.

'Ellie, I'm doing the best I can. There's never been anyone who has come as close to capturing my heart as you. Ever. But I won't tell you something you want to hear just because you want to hear it. I'm giving you as much as I am able to. Can't you understand that?'

Oh, God, how was she supposed to resist such a naked, emotion-saturated statement? But she had to. There was too much at stake.

'It's not enough for me, Jack. It really isn't.'

'Ellie—'

Ellie held up her hand. 'Wait, let me get this out.' When she spoke again her voice was rich with emotion. 'Over the past couple of weeks I've come to realise—*you* taught me!—that I'm worth making sacrifices for. I think *you* are worth making sacrifices for. But the reality is that you're the one who would always be leaving. I can't force you to change that, I can't force you to need me, and I certainly can't force you to love me. All I can be is a person who can be loved, and I am. I know that now. I want it all, Jack. Dammit, I *deserve* it all!'

'You're asking me to give up my career—'

'I've never asked you to do that. I'm asking you to look at your life, to adjust it so that there is space for me in it. I'm asking you to make me a priority. I'm asking for some sort of commitment.'

Jack's voice was low and sad when he spoke again. 'I need to be able to move, Ellie, breathe. I can't live a humdrum life. I can't be confined—even by you.'

'It's not good enough, Jack. Not any more.' Ellie felt her heart rip out of her chest. 'I can't be with someone who thinks life with me would be humdrum, tedious, boring.'

'I didn't mean—'

'Yes, you did!' Ellie shouted, suddenly pushed beyond her limits. 'You want to think that a life with me would be unexciting and dull because anything else would mean that you would have to get emotionally involved, take a stand, make a choice that could lead to pain. Don't you think you're taking this protecting-your-heart thing a bit too far? You've stopped *living*, Jack.'

'Of course I'm living! What the hell do you think I've been doing for the past seventeen years?' Jack roared, his eyes light with fury.

'That's not living—it's reporting! Living is taking emotional chances, laughing, loving.' Ellie shoved her hands into her hair. 'I'm in love with you and I'm pretty sure that you're the man I can see myself living the rest of my life with. Would you consider loving me, living with me, creating a family with me?'

He stared at his feet, his arms tightly crossed. His body language didn't inspire confidence.

'This is emotional blackmail,' Jack muttered eventually, and Ellie closed her eyes as his words kicked her in the heart. And here came the pain, roaring towards her with the force of a Sherman tank.

'I'm sorry that you consider someone telling you that they adore you blackmail. Goodbye, Jack.' Ellie turned away and folded her arms across her torso, gripping hard. 'Lock the front door behind you, will you?'

'Ellie—'

Ellie whirled around, fury, misery and anger emanating from every pore. 'What? What else is there to say, Jack? I love you, but you're so damn scared of feeling anything that you won't step out of that self-protecting cocoon you've wedged yourself into! Of the two of us, *you* are the bigger pansy-assed coward and I am done with this conversation. Just leave, Jack. Please. You've played basketball with my heart for long enough.'

She heard him pick up his pack, jog down the stairs. From behind the curtain of the bay window Ellie watched him storm to his car, his broad shoulders tight and halfway up to his ears, his arms ending in clenched fists.

I love you, she wanted to say. *I love you so much it scares me. I wish you knew how to take a real chance, how to risk your very precious heart.*

But two sentences kept tumbling over and over in her head. *Please don't leave me. Please come back.*

But he didn't stop, didn't turn around. When she saw his car back down her driveway and watched the tail-lights disappear down the road and out of sight, Ellie sank to the floor and buried her face in her hands.

It was over and she was alone. Again.

CHAPTER TEN

FIVE DAYS AFTER he'd left Cape Town Jack and his cameraman were standing next to a pile of rubble that had once been a primary school on the outskirts of Concepción, Chile. What had originally been a black car was buried under a pile of rocks. A massive earthquake had hit the region and Jack had been asked if he'd like to report on it. He hadn't even left transit at Heathrow. He'd just caught the first flight he could to Chile.

Behind them were mounds of bricks and twisted iron and the half-walls of the decimated school. Since the quake had struck early in the morning most of the children hadn't arrived yet for lessons, but Jack knew from talking to the family members who stalked the site that there had been an early-morning staff meeting and there were still a few teachers unaccounted for. Their relatives were still digging through the rubble, slowly moving piles of bricks to find the bodies of their loved ones. Few held out any hope for their survival. The devastation was too widespread, too intense, for hope to survive for long.

Jack rubbed his hands over his face as he prepared to link live to New York. He didn't want to be here, he thought. He wanted to go home to that bright house with its eclectic art and two rambunctious dogs. He wanted to run with the dogs on the beach, stretch out on the leather couch, listen to the sea at night and the wind in the morning.

He wanted Ellie.

But Ellie would mean giving this up, Jack reminded himself. He couldn't…this was what he did, what he was. He needed to work.… Jack blew out his breath. But was that just years of habit talking? He couldn't avoid the truth…he *needed* her. As much as his work. More.

Jack leaned back against a dusty car and lifted his head to the sunlight. He'd been seventy degrees of dim that last night in St James. He'd thought he was so strong, so in control. While she'd launched those emotional arrows at his soul he'd kept telling himself that it wouldn't hurt, that he'd be fine. Now, five days and too much horror later, he felt as if he'd taken a series of punches to his stomach and heart. He was doubled over in pain.

He was generally level-headed and unemotional, and in truth he'd never been a crier. He could count on one hand the amount of times he'd wept since he was a child. Even the bleakest times of his illness, the fear he'd felt when he'd had the transplant and the relief of being normal again had never reduced him to tears, but the fact that he'd lost Ellie had had him choking down grief more than once or twice. The early hours of the morning were the worst; that was when he felt as if his heart was being physically yanked from his chest.

What was he going to do? Sacrifice his job for her? Sacrifice her for the job? Be bored with a normal life with Ellie in it or miserable with an action-packed existence without her?

He didn't know—couldn't make a decision. All he was certain of was that he missed her, that his world had gone from bright colours to monochrome, that he was plodding through each day feeling adrift without his connection to her. He was fine physically. Mentally and emotionally he was a train wreck. He felt as if he'd been stripped of all his internal organs—heart included—that he was just a shell of a man, marking time.

Ted, his cameraman, told him he was about to go live so Jack stood up straight and waited for the signal. He greeted the anchorwoman and launched into his report. Death, destruction, the cost of rebuilding people's lives...

Jack was midway through when a commotion from the decimated building behind him caught his attention. He knew that noise—it was an indication that someone had been found. Still live to New York, he bounded with Ted over the rubble to where a lone man, his face ravaged with grief, was furiously tossing bricks and stones off a pile. Jack recognised his look of terrible excitement, of despair-ravaged hope. He'd found someone he loved...

Jack, forgetting that he was live on international TV, picked up his pace and scuttled across the rubble to where the man was sinking into a hole he'd dug. Jack saw a strand of long black hair flowing around a half-sheared brick and his heart stopped. He swallowed. It was exactly the shade of Ellie's hair...

The young man was sobbing as he yanked debris away from her. *'Mi esposa, mi esposa,'* he muttered frantically, tears streaming down his face.

His wife. All he could see was his wife's hair...

Jack swallowed and jumped into the small hole with him, started to throw bricks, planks and stones away from where he imagined her head and body was. The problem was that her hair was so long—she could be lying in any direction.

Minutes felt like hours and his back muscles and biceps were screaming in pain. His shirt was soaked onto his body but Jack refused to quit. There was no sound coming from the victim but Jack knew that didn't mean she was dead. He refused to believe she was dead...

What if this was Ellie? How would he be feeling? The thought kept hurtling through his brain. Desperate, out of control, terrified. He wouldn't be able to live without her...

Jack lifted a board up and away and there she lay, her beautiful face unmarked by the falling building. Her eyes were open, glassy, but Jack didn't need to check her pulse to see that she was still alive. The hand lifting up towards the young man was a solid enough hint.

Jack yelled at Ted to call for the medics and was surprised to see that Ted was still filming. Why wasn't he helping them? Surely the woman was more important than the story? He felt sickened by Ted's callousness, the fact that he could just observe and not participate, to report but not become involved.

Then again, he couldn't blame him either. Wasn't that what *he* did, story after story, situation after situation?

Jack caught the bottle of water someone threw down, cracked the seal and gently poured a tiny bit of water into the woman's mouth. He didn't want to lift her neck, he had no idea what injuries she had, and her legs were still pinned beneath the debris. Her husband had his face buried in his hands, sobbing uncontrollably.

Jack gently dripped water from the bottle into her mouth and they waited. The young man was now talking to his wife, and Jack felt the lump in his throat grow as he watched them interact, listened to their conversation. It was blindingly obvious that they loved each other so much, that they were ecstatic to be given a second chance.

All his life he'd avoided love, thinking that it equalled confinement. That he'd lose his freedom. That a love affair would hamper his individuality and compromise his independence. He now realised that, compared to losing Ellie, none of it meant a damn thing. His feelings for her scared him, but he knew he was a better man for loving her and that she was worth any emotional risk. He'd been so careful to control every aspect of his life and it was a revelation to discover that being out of control was the best feeling in the world. Being in love felt marvellous. He loved the way it made him feel...

With her he'd found the place he most wanted to be—the home he'd thought he didn't need. She was the one person, the one place, where he could be truly intimate and feel safe. Secure. Looked after. Loved. She had given him the gift of balance and stability and his throat swelled with emotion. He needed to get back to her...

Jack wet the corner of his T-shirt and wiped the victim's face. He saw relief and gratitude in her eyes.

'Muchas gracias,' she whispered between dry and swollen lips.

Jack swallowed, nodded and ran his hand over his head as he heard the rescue workers and medics approaching. He sent her a quick smile and backed away, lifting himself out of the small area to allow for medical assistance.

It was only as he walked away from them and Ted that he realised that his face and cheeks were wet with tears.

Across the world Ellie worked in her bakery, waiting for her staff to come in to work. Her heart was haemorrhaging, she decided, as a lone tear dripped off her chin and landed on the pale pink wedding cake beneath her. It had been nearly a week since Jack had left and she missed him with an intensity that astonished her. The memory of the night he'd left was on constant replay in her head, and she relived the moment of her heart ripping apart on a daily, hourly basis, causing pain to shoot through her system. There was no relief from the memories. Every room in the house made her think of Jack, and she hadn't been able to eat at her kitchen table since he'd left.

She wasn't eating, wasn't sleeping, wasn't thinking. Her hands shook. She felt constantly cold. Ellie looked at the tiny tearstain on the cake and felt grateful she could cover it with a sugar rose. Idly she wondered if she should be making wedding cakes with a scorched heart. Wedding cakes should be made with love and hope, not with sadness and regret.

Ellie looked up to see Merri in front of her, dressed in a bright pink apron. 'Reporting for duty, ma'am.'

Ellie just managed to smile. She'd totally forgotten her threat to fire her if she didn't arrive for work, and now a part of her wished Merri *hadn't* come back, so that she would be so busy she'd never have to think, feel, again.

'It's about time,' Ellie muttered, and held out her arms for a hug.

She stepped into her friend's arms and hung on. After a while she stepped back, felt Merri's hand between her shoulderblades and turned her head to look into her deeply concerned face.

'You okay?' Merri asked.

'Jack left.' Ellie shook her head and wiped her eyes with the corner of her apron. 'I can't seem to stop hurting. I think I'm okay, then it sneaks up on me and *wham*! Dammit—I'm dripping again.'

'God, El, how long have you been like this? Why didn't you call me?'

Ellie winced, feeling the headache pounding between her eyes. 'I couldn't—can't—talk about him.' She bit her lip. 'I feel like I've been eviscerated with a butter knife.'

'Oh, sweetie. You're fathoms deep in love with him.'

Ellie nodded.

Merri sat down on the chair next to Ellie's table and sent her a sympathetic look. 'I'm sorry you couldn't make it work, but sometimes love just isn't enough.'

'It's supposed to be,' Ellie whispered.

Merri's voice was laced with regret and loss. 'In books and movies. In real life...? Not so much.'

Ellie stared past Merri's head. 'I'm worried about him. My imagination is in overdrive.'

'Jack knows how to look after himself.' Merri put her arms

on the table. Her face was uncharacteristically serious. 'Ellie, I've never seen you so unhinged. I'm worried about *you*.'

'So is my mum.' Ellie stared at her flour-dusted shoes. 'She keeps telling me that I can't live like this, that I have to do something about him…but what can I do? Nothing! He's gone and he isn't coming back.'

'You need to try and relax. Get a decent night's sleep and find a way to work through this.'

'I'm trying—'

'Try harder. If you carry on like this you'll be on anti-depressants in a month, in a loony bin in three months.'

'I know that I'm a mess.' Ellie gripped the bridge of her nose with her thumb and forefinger. 'I feel like I am marinating in pain.' She flipped Merri a tiny smile. 'Does that sound desperately melodramatic?'

'Yes, but you're entitled.'

Merri draped an arm across her shoulder and they both looked down at the wedding cake. Merri tipped her head so that it touched Ellie's. 'Sweetie, I'll be here to hold your hand every step of the way, to talk to you and to cry with you. But this cake…?'

'What's wrong with it?'

Merri picked up a swatch of fabric off the table and held it against the cake. 'Wrong shade of pink, honey.'

Jack shoved his hands into his coat pockets as he left the church where Brent's memorial service had just ended. It was over, and yet he didn't feel the relief he'd expected to. He'd delayed his return to Cape Town to be here but he wondered if he'd ever manage not to feel guilty for being alive. He needed to get to Ellie. She'd understand, help him work through this.

Now he needed to avoid the Sandersons if he could. What could he say to them? He was sorry? He was…but it sounded stupid, seeing that he lived because Brent had died. There they all were—Mrs Sanderson hugging his mother by the gate, Mr Sanderson, his eyes pink from cold and tears, talking to his dad.

He should say something. Anything... But he really just wanted to walk away. They couldn't—wouldn't—want to talk to him.

Jack had made it halfway to his car when he heard his name being called.

'Jack!'

He felt the hand on his arm, turned and looked down into Brent's mother's elegant face. He winced internally.

'Where are you rushing off to?' she asked.

Jack, guilt holding his heart in a vice grip, looked around for a means of escape. 'Uh...'

'I'm so glad you came. *We're* so glad you came.'

Oh, Lord, now Mr Sanderson had joined them. Any moment his parents would join the party and he'd be toast. Jack forced himself to put his hand out and shake Mr Sanderson's hand. 'Sir. It was a nice service.'

'We're very happy you made it, Jack. And call me David.'

'I'm June.'

Oh, this was getting to be fun. *Not.* Jack jammed his freezing hands back into his coat pockets and reluctantly nodded when David asked him if he'd take a short walk with them through the cemetery. Jack sent his mother a miserable look over his shoulder and followed Brent's parents to Brent's headstone. June dusted some snow off the face of the stone and rested her gloved hand on top.

'We've wanted to talk to you for a while. We've been following your career,' David said. 'You've made quite a name for yourself.'

'Thank you.'

'You didn't want to come today,' June said. 'You didn't want to see us. Why not?'

Jack looked at a point beyond her face. 'I thought it would hurt you too much.'

'And? Come on—spit it out,' June coaxed.

Her eyes encouraged him to be honest, and for a moment he felt as if he was seventeen again and terrified.

'And it kills me to know that Brent had to lose his life so that I could have mine,' Jack said in a rush, scared that if he didn't get the words out he never would.

June's eyes filled with tears and her face softened. 'Sweetheart, his death had nothing to do with you. It was his time to go...'

'But—'

'But nothing. I'm just grateful that you had a second chance at life. Grateful that you haven't wasted his gift...' June took his hand between hers. 'Yet your mother tells us you have no home, no family, no partner. It worries her. It worries *us*. Why not?'

'Uh—'

'When we gave you our son's heart we expected you not to waste your second chance. We also expected you to make the most of your second chance,' David stated, his voice firm but gentle. 'But we never wanted you to feel guilty—only thankful.'

His mother must have had more than a few discussions with them about him for them to be having this conversation, Jack realised. He wasn't sure whether to be grateful or to wring her neck for interfering. He smiled inside. He'd go for grateful.

'So you think it would be okay if I fell in love? Had a family? Even knowing that Brent never had that chance and I do, with *his* heart?' he asked, holding his breath.

David placed his hand on his shoulder and squeezed. 'Not only do we think it's okay, we think it's important. It's another chance—another opportunity for you to be fulfilled—and that's all we ever wanted. For you to make the most of his gift, to wring out as much happiness as you can from life. Brent had a generous spirit and that would be his wish.'

'And it's ours…' June added.

Jack swallowed the tears he felt at the back of his throat as their words picked up the last of his guilt and flew away with it. He managed what he suspected was a watery grin. 'Well, there is this girl, and she's been giving our heart a run for its money…'

June grinned and put her hand into the crook of his elbow. 'Ooh, a feisty one. I like her already.'

Three days later Ellie sat cross-legged in the middle of the driveway and gazed at what she was privately calling Ellie's Folly. Fascinated, she rested her elbow on her knee and her chin in her hand and just looked. The house preened in the spotty sunlight that appeared now and again from between low black clouds, like an elderly showgirl remembering her former life.

Rolled up and sticking out of the back pocket of her shorts was the agreement of sale that Mrs H had finally signed an hour before.

'Enough is enough,' she'd told Mrs H, after carefully explaining what she intended doing with the property. 'Either accept my offer or I'm walking away.'

'But—'

'Permanently. Pari's will close down, jobs will be lost and St James will lose a landmark institution. I'm tired of your vacillations and games. I'm dealing with enough drama as it is and I don't need any more. The ball is in your court.'

Getting tough had paid dividends and the old lady had signed at a price that allowed her enough cash to do the renovations. She was now the owner of a gorgeous old building that needed lots of love and attention. Thank goodness—because she seriously needed the distraction of hard work.

It had been a good day. If she ignored the fact that she was still miserable and heartbroken and so, so sad.

Ellie felt something cold nudge her shoulder and looked sideways to see a large frappe in one of Pari's takeaway glasses. She'd told her mum that she'd be here and wasn't surprised by her presence.

'Isn't she stunning?' Ellie breathed, unable to take her eyes off the building.

'She is—but you are even more so.'

Ellie scrambled to her feet as that deep voice caressed her. She looked at him, wide-eyed with astonishment.

Jack was back and he was standing in front of her, looking fit and fantastic.

Ellie took a step back, feeling totally disorientated and more than a little scared. Why was he back? Oh, her battered heart had lifted at the sight of his wonderful face, but how it would hurt when he left again. How would she survive this? Would she ever get used to him dropping in and out of her life?

Yet…she didn't care. After the past days of hell on earth it didn't matter. None of it mattered. Because, as sobering and shocking as the concept was, there was nothing she wouldn't do for him. The reality was that she'd never loved anyone or anything as much as she loved Jack…she would give up Pari's for him, move to the ends of the earth for him…she'd even live through having her insides scraped out with a teaspoon every time he went on a dangerous assignment if it meant having him smile at her, laugh with her, hold her after making love to her.

He was back, she loved him and she'd do anything to be with him.

Ellie dropped her iced coffee to the driveway and only just stopped herself from flinging herself against his chest and weeping like a fool. Instead she put the heels of her hands to her temples and shrugged her shoulders. 'Okay, I surrender.'

'You surrender what?' Jack asked conversationally, his finger tapping his still full cup of coffee.

'Do you want me to leave Pari's? I can make cakes in London. I'll take Rescue Remedy and yoga and meditation classes every time you go on assignments to hellholes. I'll get through it.' Ellie stumbled to the low wall that ran parallel to the driveway, sat down and dropped her head into her hands. 'What do you need me to do?'

'Now, *why* would you do all that, El?' Jack asked.

She felt him sit down next to her. 'Because I love you and I can't live without you,' Ellie muttered to the concrete. She felt his big hand on the back of her neck as tears dripped onto the paving below.

Jack pulled her head to his shoulder and held it there as he continued to sip his coffee. 'That's a hell of an offer, El.'

Ellie looped her arms around his waist, still staring at their shoes. She sniffed, the reality of what she'd offered slowly sinking in. She'd miss Merri and her staff, her customers and this new building that she'd never have the chance to turn into something special. And her house—she really loved her house—but she'd take her pets. That wasn't negotiable.

She'd miss the beach and the city but she'd have Jack... Her racing heart settled. She'd have Jack sometimes and it would be all right. Anything was better than nothing.

She felt Jack's kiss in her hair before he let her go. Ellie wiped her eyes with the back of her wrist and sniffed.

'I have a counter-offer,' Jack said, his voice vibrating with emotion.

'You do?'

'As it happens, I love you too.' The corners of his mouth kicked up when her mouth fell open. He put his finger under her chin and pushed it up so that her teeth clicked together. 'I can't—won't—ask you to uproot your wonderful life. But I *can* ask you if I can share it.'

There went her jaw again. 'Sorry?'

Jack pulled his feet up, bent his legs and rested his arms on his knees. His cup was on the wall next to his feet. The late-summer breeze blew his hair off his forehead. 'I want to stay here, live in your house with you. On an on-going and permanent basis.'

'Uh—'

Jack managed to grin. 'Work with me here, darling. I'm trying, very badly, to propose.'

'Propose what?' Ellie said blankly, still stuck three sentences behind, on the 'I love you too' comment.

'I can't imagine my life in any form without you in it so... will you marry me?' Jack asked.

'Uh—what?'

'You? Me? Married?'

'You want to *marry* me?' Ellie squawked.

'That's what I keep saying. But the question is, do you want to marry *me*?'

Jack bit his lip, anxiety written all over his face. Ellie couldn't believe that her tough warrior—a man who'd faced untold danger, who'd lived through and overcome so much in his life—was scared of rejection, scared that her answer might be no.

Gathering her last two wits together, she leaned forward and placed her hands on his knees.

'Yes. Absolutely.'

Jack dropped his forehead to his chest in relief and Ellie rubbed her thumbs over the bare skin on the inside of his knees. He was warm and strong and vital and her world suddenly made sense again.

'I *do* love you, El,' Jack muttered, his voice hoarse as he looked at her with blazing eyes.

Her heart constricted and fluttered and, lifting her hands, she gently held his face. 'I love you too. Welcome home.'

* * *

Ellie sat sideways between Jack's legs, his arms loosely around her waist and his chin on her head. They'd been quiet for a while after his proposal, both happy to savour the moment.

She didn't want to break the spell, but Ellie knew that they still had a couple of issues to work through. 'What about kids, Jack? Do you want any?'

He looked down at her and half shrugged. 'Sure. When?'

Ellie blinked. 'Excuse me?'

Jack squeezed her waist. 'I don't think you really heard me before, or took in what I said, but I want it all. But it starts with you. If you want kids now, later, whenever... I just want to make you happy.'

Ellie blinked, swallowing as emotion—love—grabbed her heart. 'Oh, you slay me.' She pushed her hair back. 'I'd like your baby, Jack—hell, I'd *love* your baby. But not right now. I'd like us to take a little time for ourselves. Just to *be*, to get used to our new life together, before we throw another person into the mix.'

'We can do that.' Jack pulled up her T-shirt and put his warm hand on her bare skin.

Ellie shivered at his touch and hoped that she never stopped responding like this.

She tipped her head back and sideways to look up at him. 'You said that you just want me to be happy but I want *you* to be happy—how are we both going to be happy?'

Jack let out a joyful laugh. 'You really didn't hear me earlier, did you?'

Ellie blushed. 'I kind of tuned out after you told me you loved me. Tuned back in when you proposed. In between it's a bit blurry.'

Jack scooted backwards so that he could look down into her face. He was hers—a warrior soldier with a scarred body, warm smile and vulnerability in his eyes.

'Okay, are you concentrating?'

Ellie laughed. 'Jack!'

'El, I love it here—love your dogs, your city, your friends. I'm happier here than anywhere else.' He ran the edge of his thumb over her trembling bottom lip. 'I've been a fighter all my life but I'll fight hard for you—fight to share your sunshine-filled life.'

'But your career—'

Jack shrugged. 'I still want to do parts of it—with your support. But I can pick and choose my stories a bit better. I don't always need to go into hot areas, chase the conflicts. I can do human drama stories, crime, special reports. I might have to go away now and again, but I meant what I said. There are ways for us to communicate every day and I wouldn't want to be away from you for long.'

Ellie swallowed. How long was long? 'A month? Two?'

Jack laughed. 'Are you mad? I couldn't survive that long without you! A week—maybe ten days at the most. And that would be pushing it.'

Ellie grinned. Jack was not going to be an absent husband, a forgetful lover. He was right. He was nothing like her father.

She tapped his knee in warning. 'Do *not* get hurt again.'

She felt his lips smile against hers. 'Deal.'

Ellie toyed with his fingers. 'But, Jack, if you need to go into a situation that's dangerous, I meant what I said. I'll find a way to deal with it. I don't want you to miss it or feel cheated.' She needed him to understand. 'You were right. You are nothing like my dad or my ex. And I am nothing like that shy, plump insecure little girl. I can cope with you being away for short periods as long as we keep communicating...'

'Don't think this is only from your side. I need to connect with you as well, sweetheart. I missed you so much when I was in Chile. I felt...*bereft*.'

Ellie draped her thighs over his and scooted closer, so that she could link her hands at the back of his neck. 'Was it bad?'

'Yeah. It was.' Jack nodded.

'I saw the footage of you rescuing that woman,' Ellie said quietly. 'Merri caught it on the news and I downloaded the clip from the internet.'

'I guess they aren't calling me unemotional any more, since I was caught crying on camera.' Jack rubbed his forehead with the tips of his fingers. 'She looked like you. Long black hair, creamy skin. Gorgeous. Her husband was a train wreck and I kept thinking: how would I feel if this was you? Gutted, shell-shocked, scared witless.' Jack frowned. 'I've been scared in my life, El, but nothing compares to how terrified I was when I considered what it would feel like to lose you permanently.' Jack shuddered before he spoke again. 'I went to Brent's service—spoke to his parents.'

'That must have been hard. How was it?'

Jack smiled. 'It was...healing. For all of us. Me especially.'

'I'm so glad.' Ellie's breath hitched. 'I know that you're not into these mushy moments, but I just want to keep telling you how much I love you...'

'I don't mind hearing that.' Jack's mouth kicked up as his hand cradled the side of her head. 'And ditto for me. There's so much I still want to say...'

'Like?'

'Like my world has colour again now that you are back in it.' His eyes turned serious. 'El, I love my work, but I love you more. I'll never cheat on you. I promise to be faithful. And I promise, as far as I'm humanly able, to be here when you need me. I promise to be with you on the important dates, and if and when we have kids I'll look at my career and see what I can change to be an active, involved dad.'

Ellie opened her mouth to speak but Jack shook his head.

'You're my life. You're what makes me happy. I want to

wake up next to you, wander down to the bakery for breakfast, be with you at night. Unfortunately I have to earn money, and I do enjoy what I do. But if I have to choose between the two I'll choose you.'

'You don't have to choose.' Ellie gulped as Jack lifted his thumbs to wipe away her tears. His mouth lifted at the corners and his eyes darkened with emotion, and Ellie caught a glimpse of his soul, overflowing with love for her.

He took her hand and placed it on the left side of his chest. 'I've protected my heart in every way I can. Physically, emotionally, spiritually. It's on loan to me and now I'm giving it to you…this heart that saved my life—it's yours.'

Ellie gulped a sob and the stream of tears that she'd been holding back slid down her face. Leaning into him, she placed her cheek against his, and when she thought she could talk sensibly again she took his hand and echoed his action by putting it on her chest. 'Then take mine. Keep it safe.'

'I promise I will.'

And they both knew, in a way only lovers could understand, that their hearts were joined—married—on that low stone wall outside a decrepit house in the late-afternoon summer sun.

EPILOGUE

Six months later

ELLIE FELT HER mum's arm around her waist as she stood at the edge of the crowd, waiting to be called by the Master of Ceremonies to make her speech. Merri stood on her other side, with Molly Blue in her pushchair, sucking a doughnut.

It was the day of Pari's grand re-opening and the new building was restored to its formal splendour. The gardens might need a year or two to mature, but spring was almost upon them and she could see tiny shoots of new growth on the rescued rose bushes, on the trees and bushes.

The bakery had been operating for a week and there had been problems—but nothing insurmountable. Business was booming in the bakery, in the new restaurant, in the tiny art studio/gift shop she'd set up to display her artwork and some works by other artists from the area.

She only had one little issue… Her fiancé—the man she was due to marry in a month—was not yet home. He was nowhere to be seen. She had no idea why he was delayed because every time she called him his mobile went straight to voicemail, and he'd left his satellite phone at home. She could feel her mum and Merri's rising annoyance—this was her big day and he wasn't here. Ellie knew that her mum was trying to keep back all the 'I told you so' and 'war reporters—consistently unreliable' phrases that she desperately wanted to utter.

Ellie resisted looking at her watch. Jack would get here, and if he didn't he would have a damn good excuse for not being able to make it. Over the past six months he'd done everything he'd said he would and he loved her absolutely, intensely, ferociously. He'd never deliberately hurt her and sometimes things happened. *Life* happened.

'Relax, guys,' Ellie told them, sending them both a great big smile. 'I am.'

'Has he forgotten how to use a phone?' Ashnee demanded. 'I'm really quite annoyed with him—'

'You can read me the Riot Act later, Ash,' Jack said from behind them, and Ellie squealed in delight as she whipped around. 'Right now, I'd like to kiss my girl.'

Then his big hands were cradling her face, his lips were on hers and the tectonic plates deep in the earth shifted and settled. When he finally lifted his head he smiled down at her. 'Sorry—battery on my mobile died. And I got a speeding fine on the way here.'

'I *knew* you would get here on time.' Ellie smiled. 'Missed you.'

'Missed you too,' Jack replied.

Ellie pulled her bottom lip between her teeth. 'How did it go with the cardiologist?'

His heart transplant wasn't a secret any more. It wasn't something he discussed, but it was out in the open. 'Fine—situation normal. He says that you're looking after my heart beautifully.'

Her lips twitched. 'Good.'

'I'm sorry that I had to delay my return. I really wanted to be home sooner. But I decided to wait for your present.'

Ellie held his hand between both of hers. 'My present? What is it?'

Jack's eyes flashed with mischief. 'It's a few things, actually. Two of them are my parents, who insisted on being here for Pari's re-opening.'

Ellie and Ashnee, who'd instantly bonded with Jack's mother Rae, danced on the spot. 'That's fabulous news. I'm so happy they're here. Where are they?' Ellie demanded, looking around at the sizeable crowd.

'Over there. With your other present—Mitch. He flew back from New York with me.'

Jack gestured to the crowd to the right of them and Ellie's heart hitched when Mitchell raised his hand and waved it in her direction. Her dad was here...finally...at one of the most important occasions of her life. Ellie felt her heart stumble. This was Jack's doing, she knew. She *so* appreciated the fact that he'd gone to the effort of getting him here, that he thought that Mitch being here would make her happy. And it did— sort of. She'd invited Mitch but never expected him to come. It was such a relief to know that she didn't need her dad's approval any more; she'd finally accepted that her father wasn't father material and his lack in that department had nothing to do with her.

He was—had been—a shocking father, but she could forgive him anything since he'd sent Jack into her life.

'Thank you.' Ellie rose up on her toes to kiss Jack's mouth.

'Pleasure.' Jack ran a hand over her hair as the Master of Ceremonies began his speech. Jack bent his head to whisper in her ear. 'I love you. I'm proud of what you've done, and it's fabulous. But...'

'But?'

'But keep the speeches short, sweetheart, so that I can pull you into a pantry and kiss the hell out of you.'

'That's all you want to do?' Ellie looked at him and shook her head, eyes dancing. 'Damn, I must be getting boring! Got to watch that...'

Ellie grinned as Jack's shout of laughter followed her all the way to the podium.

True happiness, she decided, really was laughing and living and loving well. She tossed Jack a grin as she launched into her very, very, *very* short speech.

After all, she had her man to kiss…

* * * * *

FOUR BRAND NEW STORIES FROM
MILLS & BOON MODERN

The same great stories you love,
a stylish new look!

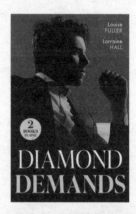

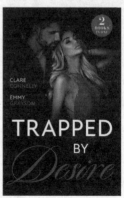

OUT NOW

MILLS & BOON

Afterglow Books is a trend-led, trope-filled list of books with diverse, authentic and relatable characters, a wide array of voices and representations, plus real world trials and tribulations. Featuring all the tropes you could possibly want (think small-town settings, fake relationships, grumpy vs sunshine, enemies to lovers) and all with a generous dose of spice in every story.

♪ @millsandboonuk

@millsandboonuk

afterglowbooks.co.uk

#AfterglowBooks

For all the latest book news, exclusive content and giveaways scan the QR code below to sign up to the Afterglow newsletter:

afterglow BOOKS

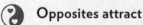 Opposites attract

 Fake dating

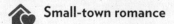 Small-town romance

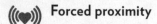 Forced proximity

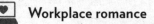 Workplace romance

 Spicy

OUT NOW

Two stories published every month. Discover more at:
Afterglowbooks.co.uk

OUT NOW!

Available at
millsandboon.co.uk

MILLS & BOON

OUT NOW!

Available at
millsandboon.co.uk

MILLS & BOON

LET'S TALK
Romance

For exclusive extracts, competitions and special offers, find us online:

- **f** MillsandBoon
- **X** @MillsandBoon
- **○** @MillsandBoonUK
- **♪** @MillsandBoonUK

Get in touch on 01413 063 232

For all the latest titles coming soon, visit
millsandboon.co.uk/nextmonth

MILLS & BOON

THE HEART OF ROMANCE

A ROMANCE FOR EVERY READER

MODERN   Prepare to be swept off your feet by sophisticated, sexy and seductive heroes, in some of the world's most glamourous and romantic locations, where power and passion collide.

HISTORICAL   Escape with historical heroes from time gone by. Whether your passion is for wicked Regency Rakes, muscled Vikings or rugged Highlanders, awaken the romance of the past.

MEDICAL   Set your pulse racing with dedicated, delectable doctors in the high-pressure world of medicine, where emotions run high and passion, comfort and love are the best medicine.

True Love   Celebrate true love with tender stories of heartfelt romance, from the rush of falling in love to the joy a new baby can bring, and a focus on the emotional heart of a relationship.

HEROES   The excitement of a gripping thriller, with intense romance at its heart. Resourceful, true-to-life women and strong, fearless men face danger and desire - a killer combination!

   From showing up to glowing up, these characters are on the path to leading their best lives and finding romance along the way – with plenty of sizzling spice!

To see which titles are coming soon, please visit

millsandboon.co.uk/nextmonth

MILLS & BOON
A ROMANCE FOR EVERY READER

- **FREE** delivery direct to your door
- **EXCLUSIVE** offers every month
- **SAVE** up to 30% on pre-paid subscriptions

SUBSCRIBE AND SAVE

millsandboon.co.uk/Subscribe

GET YOUR ROMANCE FIX!

Get the latest romance news,
exclusive author interviews, story
extracts and much more!

blog.millsandboon.co.uk